Intercepting

ARAGON

Other books by this author

Genesis Makers
Evolution
Evolution 2 - Induction
Emissary
Emissary 2 The Sixth Extinction

Intercepting Aragon

by

Scott K Bywater

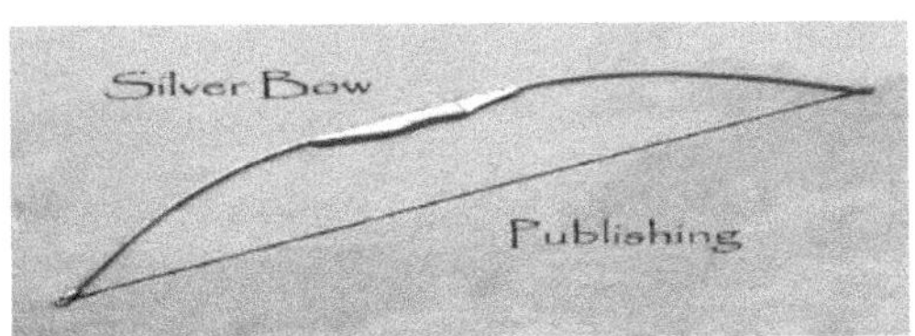

720 Sixth Street, Unit # 5
New Westminster, BC V3L 3C5
CANADA

Title: Intercepting Aragon
Author: Scott K. Bywater
Cover Art: by Joshua Nicholas Bywater
Layout and Design: Candice James
Editing: Candice James

ISBN 9781774033142 (softcover)
ISBN 9781774033159 (e-book)
© 2024 Silver Bow Publishing

Library and Archives Canada Cataloguing in Publication

Title: Intercepting Aragon / by Scott K Bywater.
Names: Bywater, Scott K., 1962- author
Identifiers: Canadiana (print) 20240439554 | Canadiana (ebook) 20240439619 | ISBN 9781774033142
   (softcover) | ISBN 9781774033159 (Kindle)
Subjects: LCGFT: Science fiction.
Classification: LCC PR9619.4.B99 I58 2024 | DDC 823/.92—dc23

To Mary, Josh and Alysha –
thank you for helping me
through a trying period of life.

And to Ian from BHS –
thanks for helping me get through.

Chapters

Prologue

Come
"Remember to look up at the stars and not down at your feet."
~ Stephen Hawking

Sooner or later, it was bound to happen. Oumuamua proved that Earth does not live in a vacuum, segregated from the rest of the Universe. It is open to a visitor or two from the next suburb down, or anywhere really. Our solar system is in a cosmic shooting gallery – and Earth should expect to be shot from time to time. But by this object, probably not. This thing was genuinely one for the books.

The asteroid was pinky-red in colour, and like Oumuamua, was on an unending journey through space. And the solar system, four hundred metres in length and half that across and maybe thirty metres in depth. It tumbled through space along its long dimension, with a light curve that was highly variable.

Travelling at seventy kilometres per second, it was moving unusually fast. It was supposed, by many on Earth, to be a piece of a planet destroyed by a supernova. In this case, of its own yellow star in the Ursa Major constellation, in the Messier 82 galaxy, a few million years ago.

Starting as a fast-moving light in space, and getting more detailed, was a light-blue and triangular craft that hit the asteroid like a gnat hitting a sticky trap. It adhered to the stony, rotating object. Once it was down, it remained there, held on all sides by a sticky glue. To leave the asteroid, those onboard would break the adhesive by spraying it with an acidic solution by automation.

Out of the circular airlock of the craft came two lanky, tall beings, dressed in full pressure-gear. Their helmets were large and deep, presumably to accommodate large and deep heads. All their limbs appeared lithe and thin, hidden by a light blue vacuum suit, two legs and two arms, each with three long fingers and a short thumb within dark bluish vacuum gloves that protected them.

The creatures were at either end of a black object, with sparkling silver bars carried under their arms. The black thing was a large almost-cube that had small handles built into it. Even though they appeared experienced, doing *anything* was tricky on this loosely aggregated asteroid which had very little gravity. They walked slower than slow, waiting for their spurs to enter, then exit the fine-grained surface.

Their boots dug deeply into the stony surface, courtesy of long and sharp cleats that they attached to their boots before they departed the vessel. The surface of the asteroid had been bare for billions of years and was loose and powdery and in places, a gooey mess, from millennia of cosmic ray exposure.

A fold-up spade was removed from a waist pocket and folded out into a small digging device by both of them. Soon enough, they had excavated a hole and buried the black thing. The taller being tamped the surface down with the back of his spade until the hole was barely noticeable. For a time, a small torus of dust formed behind the asteroid like a tail, as it continued to motor through space, tumbling as it went.

Both creatures made their way slowly back to their vessel, waiting for their cleats to push into the loose rock and exit before taking their next step. Their job was complete. Once they were back inside the vessel, they sprayed each corner of the craft remotely. To remove the adhesive, and its hold on the vessel. It glided free of the asteroid, and on into unrestricted space. The species that buried this on the asteroid knew exactly where this rock was headed.

A nearby world sent the craft to the asteroid with the plan to bury the object, making sure it operated correctly, and then letting the asteroid go on its way. Without altering the asteroid's trajectory. The world was hopeful that it would attract attention from a race that they knew was insatiably curious.

They wanted to meet humans – they presented as an intriguing race. The technology to do so was now in hand, so they decided to go "fishing" for them. They wanted contact with another intelligence that was far enough away from their own world to be an example of "different life". They knew about other life in their own system, but they were pretty sure it was seeded by their own planet or maybe vice versa.

Their goal was lofty indeed. Finding a brand-new life event that had experienced self-replication. And evolution on a different planet in a different solar system. Reaching the stage of technical intelligence. They believed Earth had ticked all those boxes.

1.

Asteroid

"Many people find the universe confusing - it's not."
~ Stephen Hawking

The asteroid was named after an ancient region of Spain. "Aragon" meant "spiritual enlightenment" and was originally found by the Spanish telescope in the Canary Islands, *Gran Telescopio Canarias*. The nickel-iron-silicate core asteroid entered the solar system from near the Vega star and the Lyra constellation *again* – same as Oumuamua.

It entered our solar system just after Uranus, and NASA said it was likely to exit after being pulled around Venus, under the Sun's and Venus' gravitation. It would pop out beyond Venus and continue its interstellar voyage toward the Sulafat star. Initially, NASA's interest was mediocre at best.

James Webb peered at the fast-moving object and almost imaged the asteroid, returning some intriguing data to Baltimore in Maryland. It imaged a roughly ovular, thinnish, pinky object about thirty metres in depth. The asteroid rotated, long end over long end, every ten minutes and yawed in space about 30% giving quite a chaotic and muddled light curve. A pancake shape – wide and thin –

satisfied the light-curve and was supported by JWST images. It was small, and still very blurry. NASA wanted more. It had learned a lesson with Oumuamua. The science community across the world, the space industry and NASA itself, demanded crisp images.

Most intriguing was the infrared spectroscopy of Webb which was stunning and captivating. It showed iron, nickel, magnesium and clay minerals – no surprise there, but there was a surprise in the trace elements it found. A spectacular shock. It showed, of all things - terbium, holmium, cerium, yttrium and scandium. And *stable moscovium,* as well as gold and platinum, and a tiny bit of lithium, beryllium, tungsten and copper. Elements whose presence was really hard to explain. There were a few theories, some of them wild, but none that satisfied the science community, the space-industry or NASA. The only course of action to solve the issue could not be taken remotely, most realised that. The entirety of the space-industry conceded that too, after viewing the results. This thing deserved further, *closer* attention. Standing on its surface, was out of the question, but not so, doing closeup analysis. It'd been done before. And it needed to be done here. With better instrumentation.

Maybe Aragon was something to do with a supernova, but Earth had never seen anything like Aragon before. Nothing close to it. Hence, it had the attention of NASA and its planet. The asteroid was suddenly making headlines in the legacy media, in social media and even appearing on morning TV, and was the subject of numerous Youtube videos. It made it onto several afternoon News Services. Aragon was the astronomical flavour of the month.

The presence of strange metals where they shouldn't be, had the world panting for more. Every continent wanted more. Many were theorising about *how* the metals managed to get there. NASA and other space agencies, the science community generally, and Universities were having conniptions. Aragon and its nature were brand-new to science. There was the suggestion that this time, it really might be it.

So, space agencies went hammer and tong. NASA and the world knew what had to be done. Just looking at it just wouldn't do the job. Joe public, physicists, and everyone else, wanted not only eyes-on, but proper close-up analysis and imaging. Like Osiris-Rex did with Bennu, but better. Earth didn't want much. They wanted it all. This thing promised so much, now Earth had to take advantage of it and deliver results.

Oumuamua whet our appetite and promised much more than it ultimately delivered. It was a disappointment to most, because humans didn't get close enough to it. It just cracked the door far enough open to allow wild theories to roost. Oumuamua left the inner solar system and all we had were questions and theories, some of them crazy and ill-founded. There was far too much guessing and shooting in the dark, because humans didn't get a good look at it.

This one seemed to be the real thing. It had components that were brand new to humanity. What the elements indicated were anyone's guess. Many on Earth wanted someone to get up close and personal with it to characterise its identity. Incredibly, NASA was listening, and wanted the same thing.

The unique componentry of the asteroid justified its own mission, many said. All eyes were squarely pointed at NASA. They were the US and world experts on anything *space*, so, it was up to them to tell the rest of the world what it was. NASA felt the same, but a single mission would be too expensive. Its budget was already committed to Artemis.

If it can send a craft to asteroid Bennu and analyse the hell out of it, then, it can do the same with Aragon, which showed extraordinary promise.

Most believed this asteroid was very different to the one's that came before it. Oumuamua was the first – but this one appeared to be much more than that one. Its components said it was *very* different. It needed eyes-on to answer the questions that were on the lips of billions. Otherwise, we'd only be left with wild theories *again*.

NASA knew SpaceX was eyeing the asteroid closely, which made NASA move quicker than it ordinarily would. NASA was determined that this rock wouldn't be their's. This thing had global appeal, and as such, it should be NASA that would deliver results.

*   *   *

Harry Watkins and Abby Mansfield were both astronauts with NASA, and had done their training in Florida back in 2007. Each had done two stints on the ISS, having attained the ranks, respectively, of Pilot and Mission Specialist. Abby especially, was very proud to have gone so far with NASA.

Her goal had been fulfilled just by joining NASA which made her parents incredibly proud. Harry himself saw it only as a stepping-stone to greater things. For him, the sky was the limit, but he liked NASA's reputation and wanted to climb the ranks there. He didn't have an overall goal, but to make Pilot so young, put him well ahead of schedule. Having a desk job didn't thrill him, but he realised he was probably headed that way. Still, if he was bringing home the big-bucks, he was sure he'd get used to it.

Both of them spent fifteen hours a month flying t-38's around Ellington to maintain their mental acuity and general sharpness. They were both considered NASA "up and comers", with especially bright futures. Harry was mentored weekly by the Administrator himself, who not only knew of him but expected him to be lauded by the public one day. Not bad if the boss is saying that, he thought proudly.

They were both part of the Artemis Program and due to spend time on the Gateway platform, orbiting the Moon, very soon. They would be only the second crew to permanently stay on the platform, and both felt quite chuffed to be doing it. Many astronauts had applied – *they* had been chosen.

That had to say something, Harry reckoned. NASA thought they were doing okay and held them in high esteem. Their written assessments and practicals based on work in the NBL – the Neutral Buoyancy lab swimming pool - and in the ISS had been noticed by those that matter. They were both well regarded by their peers and by the government agency responsible for the US civil space program itself...called NASA.

*   *   *

Their current abode was the Bay area, near Clear Lake in Houston, Texas. Both of them lived there and worked each day at the Johnson Space Centre. Every day saw them get a little more edgy about entering the SLS rocket and blasting through the atmosphere.

Despite the dangers, both wanted to be in space like an addiction, exploding test-rockets or not, and wanted to go as far as they could with NASA to get there. Harry's want was a compulsion. There was also SpaceX as a backup – if the whole NASA thing went belly-up. A private venturer into space offered a lot of opportunities, that NASA as a government agency didn't. Anyway, at this stage, Harry was all over NASA and treasured what he did and what NASA stood for. He was pretty sure they thought he was going okay – his last checkpoint was 9.5/10 – so someone liked him within the ranks.

Harry loved anything to do with Virtual Reality and had done almost everything it offered, from touring the ISS to docking a spacecraft with the great structure. It was easy to do something when you didn't have the risk of killing yourself and your partner, as well as creating a catastrophe in space. He knew it was a double-edged sword. His and Abby's true abilities would only be tested in space where every move was a risk.

He'd then moved onto Artemis and Gateway and recently, he'd driven a rover on the Moon, and used VR for SLS rockets. Harry had spent many hours, even in his downtime, learning how to pilot the new Orion spacecraft. He'd become obsessed by the damn thing.

Harry had even hovered next to an asteroid to let the crew gather some samples from it. VR was big with astronauts at JSC, and also at the Ames Centre in California...in fact everywhere at NASA. It allowed astronauts to do something and learn without taking risks. In fact, you could do it from your lounge-chair, and Harry frequently did.

Abby preferred more grounded and less ambitious pursuits, and wasn't overly keen on VR. She'd done all she could within the Neutral-Buoyancy Pool, where they had a complete mock-up of the ISS. Gateway was coming soon. Abby had done everything on the submerged ISS, and seen everything, down to the external Japanese "gardens". Abby did a lot and got a lot of exercise in the outside world, and she told Harry that frequently, while digging him in the ribs with an arm. Harry wasn't a big exercise for exercise-sake guy.

She'd also done numerous "space-walks" in the pool. Now, her main occupation, apart from flying a t-38 occasionally, was reading romance novels – *anything* by Nora Roberts. She was a huge fan. Abby also counted down on the fridge calendar, waiting for her role in Artemis to become a reality.

Abby read books to while away her time until Artemis actually started. She'd read, play-acted, and observed a lot about the programme, and was impatient for the bloody thing to start. Abby had seen Harry quite regularly and knew he was scheduled to join Artemis at the Gateway Platform like she was.

She also knew, as a team, they'd be working closely together on numerous tasks and research projects. It was incumbent on them firstly to get to know each other and to "get on". Knowing your stuff, was only the first requirement of working with NASA. Being a team player and getting-on with your peers was critical to your survival, figuratively and literally. They both realised that and knew NASA was huge on teamwork.

That excited her a little, because she liked what she saw in Harry. He seemed nice enough and certainly looked okay. She was looking forward to working with him. When asked by a friend if she was satisfied with him as her Artemis-partner she beamed back, 'he'll do.' She smiled widely and had a twinkle in her eye and felt a twinge in her loins.

The future was unwritten, but it looked pretty good. It was very early days, but she was hopeful. She didn't want to be single all her life, but the way it was going, Abby reckoned she might end up that way. So, if Harry measured up and he was interested, well, you never know, she thought. Of course, her job came first, second and third, but the downtimes might provide a meagre opportunity for romance. At the moment, she reckoned, it was a big fat unknown. Abby had read too many books centred around romance. She loved the very idea, but had to admit, she was lousy at it. The one relationship she'd had, was short and frightful. He was very good looking, but he had numerous ex's that were always sniffing around. She ended it abruptly. Abby knew Harry too was single and inexperienced with relationships...she'd done her research on him a while ago.

Harry was part way through VR/lunar surface and Argos training which provided a mock-up of the lunar south pole and the Orion landing area. Harry loved the simulation-based drills. It was useful for things like EVAs and exploring the Moon. But it was a truly immersive experience in really visualising Artemis 2 and 3. And the south pole Moon-base called Artemis 1, which included mock ups of the local lunar geomorphology. He did it over and over again, until he was very familiar with it Harry loved anything to do with space, not just Artemis. He watched Youtube incessantly if it was space-related.

Harry had even tested the SLS-Orion spacecraft's three screen set-up and emergency evac system to determine to what extent it was an improvement on the shuttle's thousands of buttons. He had to overcome an Apollo-13 style power failure – using its ADS – an automated means of diagnosing problems with its onboard software. He reckoned the Orion craft was pretty damn good. Compared to the shuttle, it was a Japanese supertrain versus a
steam locomotive.

So far he and the craft using VR were doing really well. Abby preferred lecture-style sessions. One-on-ones with experienced techs and astronauts to learn the ins and outs of the systems she'd be confronted with. She, unlike Harry, only used VR when she had no other choice. It was too contrived and unnatural for her liking. Two astronauts – two different methods of learning. *Cie la vie.*

Artemis 1 had previously lifted off and circled the Earth and the Moon. It was totally unmanned, testing the viability of SLS and Orion mainly, and the NASA techs were happy. Well, *satisfied* anyway – they were a listless lot, although very good at what they did.

All NASA had to do was have SLS deploy Orion into space a few hundred kilometres before the Karman line. SLS would transfer power to Orion, then the probe would enter the atmosphere, heat to red hot, and splash down in the Pacific Ocean, all was straightforward apparently. Hopefully, Orion would function to expectation.

The SLS rocket would deliver the power and propulsion element. That, along with the habitation module (HALO) would form the first Gateway Platform. The whole lot orbited the Moon and would be permanently inhabited with astronauts from NASA. Gateway would orbit the Moon in a weird polar ambit – a near rectilinear "HALO" orbit. Orion and also the SpaceX Dragon could then dock with the Platform and deliver and pick up astronauts, survival gear, and whatever else was required.

*   *   *

Harry was watching as Orion made preparations for its first break into the atmosphere.

'How's it going Hank,' Harry said, smoothing out his tee as he spoke, having watched him tracking the craft, high in the sky, waiting for Orion to appear from the clouds and arrow downward.

Hank had one eye plastered on a binocular lens, looking at the spot in the sky he thought Orion would emerge from. 'Er...yeah, good, I think.' His phone rang, and in trying to retrieve it, Hank dropped the lot, binoculars and phone. Then his glasses joined them on the ground, dropping like a stone from his shirt pocket...they clattered on the ground.

'Oh...*shit*,' Hank spat, annoyed by his clumsiness and general awkwardness. He picked them all up with two sweeps of an arm, re-hung his glasses and gawked at his phone. It was an alarm, as he thought – he could tell by the irritating tune it played.

Hank had the binoculars firmly in both hands now, focussed on a flaming ball of light, Orion, as it entered the atmosphere like a bus. Then he lost it, and panned out a bit, picking it up when he adjusted the focus. A huge parachute slowed its spiral to subsonic until he saw that one vanish and the pod drop in freefall until three red, white and blue chutes inflated to gently introduce the pod to the Pacific Ocean.

Hank covered his mouth with a hand, dropping it to his side when Orion gently hit the ocean. A slow smile covered his face.

'Thank *fuck* for that,' he blurted, still smiling. He was happy that the centrepiece of new NASA hardware had returned from space and settled safely in the ocean. Artemis could now start in earnest. All hardware had been tested and astronauts were on standby. Artemis was a GO.

*   *   *

The black NASA taxi would arrive at 8AM sharp for Abby and 8.10AM for Harry. It would ferry them both from their Houston homes to the Florida spaceport, Cape Canaveral. They would briefly join two others and allow them to return to Earth from the Gateway station that orbited the Moon in a recti-linear polar orbit. Harry and Abby would then be alone on Gateway – their plan for research into heliophysics, the "science of the Sun", would then swing into full action.

Jack and Pete's time on Gateway had expired. All had gone to plan for them - they would return to Earth and from their perspective, they couldn't wait to get here.

Artemis and the occupation of Gateway beckoned for Harry and Abby. And from their perspective, they couldn't wait to get there. They'd counted down the days – and it had finally come. *Artemis*.

*   *   *

Harry and Abby were now past Orlando and heading for the east coast of Florida, toward Indian River and the KSC John F Kennedy Airfield. From where they were, they could see the SLS rocket, bigger than a Saturn 5, and far more powerful, towering over everything else. The rocket looked enormous and terrifying, which was fair enough - it was essentially a bomb ready to explode upward with them aboard. Abby especially, was terrified. She looked wide eyed at the rocket and thought, you must be kidding.

It was in the nose cone that Abby and Harry would sit, inside the Orion spacecraft, which was carefully placed by the techs, just below the Launch Abort System which would pull them to safety in an emergency. They were both anxious to get the show started. And a show it'd be. *Fuel, fire, vibration, earsplitting noise and inertia.*

Abby was doing her best to be brave, but she knew this was the riskiest, scariest and most audacious thing she'd ever done. Abby had gone to the ISS with SpaceX and that was one thing. But this was a newer, bigger rocket and a completely different capsule...and it felt very strange. She was going to space with the Artemis Program, which would probably start a new life for her. Everything felt new and untested. Which wasn't the way she wanted it to be.

Abby wasn't sure if she should be ecstatic, nervous or terrified, so she went with all three. She could feel her heart pounding like a drum on her soft palate. Seeing and now hearing the fuming, smoking rocket, which looked like something out of Beelzebub, she questioned her career choice. She admitted it wasn't a great time to do it.

*   *   *

Harry and Abby got into the astro-van which drove them close to the launch-pad. The rocket was huge and smoking in front of them – a gleaming white phantasm, maybe twenty stories high. It was making an ungodly noise, the fuel pumps and the "cracking", the extreme cold, and the metal of the rocket reacting to it, apparently. This was one humungous and scary rocket. Abby was a trained astronaut with NASA, but she felt like running. This thing in front of them was ridiculous.

Harry reckoned it looked like a mythical beast, snorting and snarling at them. White clouds were billowing from the base of the rocket like angry spits and gasps. Now that he really considered what they were about to do – he felt an uneasiness in his bowels. Are NASA insane? He thought. Don't they see, we're about to strap ourselves to a bomb that's going to blow us hundreds of miles into the sky?

Incredibly, Abby looked happy and content about the journey, staring at the rocket with a huge smile on her face – making Harry feel slightly better. Ignorance was probably better, he thought anxiously. Little did he know – Abby was deeply appalled, ready to panic and had resigned herself to dying in an almighty explosion. With it came an internal peace.

There was no Customs or even showing ID here. Abby guessed if you were stupid enough to turn up – you went. Two uniformed NASA employees accompanied them to the launch tower amid the noise and clatter, and the clouds of steam. They took them both to the elevator and the doors closed behind them with a loud bang. The elevator started with a lurch and shudder and Harry had visions of them dieing in an elevator accident, even before entering Orion. Harry shook his head to rid himself of the ridiculous images.

Expectation had to be erased from his brain. Just be present and react to whatever happens, he thought. In other words, do what he was told - don't *expect*, just let the take-off unfold.

Both Abby and Harry were taken to the summit – to the launch platform – where at 300 feet above the ground, they stood with two men from NASA. The view from there was amazing and scary. She felt super-exposed. One at a time, they were ferried over to a small white room that was virtually empty, apart from several metal chairs and a picture of a rocket taking off, which was fixed crookedly on the wall.

Abby and Harry waited for ten minutes in total silence before a rotund little man helped both of them attach a parachute harness which was needed in case of emergency. That was a great show of faith in the tech, Harry thought. But it was necessary given the explosive nature of what they were using for takeoff. And overcoming the horrendously deep gravity-well of the planet.

Then they were each escorted to Orion and assisted to strap-in to a seat, army-style. The seat looked like it was made of Meccano parts but was strangely comfortable with its high headrest. Dressed in an orange pressure-suit and helmet, he supposed this was as good as it got for astronauts. Glancing at Abby, she looked like an orange Wiggle with a helmet on. Both were strapped in and ready to go.

Now they waited and waited and *waited* some more in utter silence. It was just them and their thoughts. Despite all the NASA mental-training Harry's first thought was the '86 Challenger disaster. STS-51 and the crew were oblivious to the problem until it happened. The craft exploded mid-way through the atmosphere and none of the crew were any the wiser. He felt like crying for them. *What was fucking wrong with him?* He questioned the value of the psych training NASA offered as he struggled to put the disaster out of his mind. The Safety-harness didn't save them in '86, Harry noted.

Harry and Abby both saw their watches slowly count down and they both wondered when the SLS-show would actually start. Abby thought her watch was actually going backwards - it was taking *SO* long. Everything around them was brand-new and sparkling clean which Abby would normally regard as a good look. But here, she wasn't so sure. Brand-new normally meant untested or under-tested, although she knew the SLS was well established. It recently flew on a mission which was a great success. Strapped into it and ready to go, might be a little late to worry about its bona fides as an exit to space – but it was also natural to be concerned about its performance.

Harry mentally rehearsed his responsibilities when he and Abby were alone on Gateway. It was a bit difficult to see through her visor but he could see enough. By Abby's look of concentration, and worry-lines on her forehead, she was thinking vigorously. Lift-off was now twenty minutes late.

After three hours which was broken frequently by the Launch Team confirming status and parameters, it finally got *serious*. The noises made by their rocket were increasing in volume and urgency. It was finally readying itself for takeoff.

It started with the earsplitting auxiliary power units turning on – the beast was waking up fully. Soon enough it'd be completely alive and fuming. Welcome back to the chilling cracking sound he hadn't heard since being on the ground.

Abby gawked at the countdown clock on the wall and Harry did the same, watching it go past thirty seconds. The rocket was belching, cracking and rumbling at deafening volumes, enough to scare the beating-heart out of Abby. Her eyes widened to the point where Harry thought they might snap. He patted her hand, more for him than her. Harry needed human contact right now. His fear level was at eleven, as the noise enveloped him.

They couldn't hear the external countdown but they could feel the rumbling and hear the rocket reading itself. Abby thought she'd ridded her brain of the '86 Challenger disaster, but apparently not. Like Harry, and probably all astronauts, it was burnt into her retinas. Every time her eyes were closed – there it was. *KA-BANG*. The image of the shuttle blowing up was front and centre in her mind. Her sleep for the past weeks had been filled with nightmares and fears, and now, here she was, doing the exact thing that caused it all.

She and Harry hoped that NASA had learned a thing or two. And added some safeguards, because she didn't want the '86 disaster to repeat. Not now, not ever. Abby crossed herself, and Harry saw it out of the corner of his eye. He shook his head, closed his eyes and hummed an inane tune. He knew Abby wasn't a religious person and even if she was, they didn't need guidance or help from a spiritual being. Fear and anxiety were fine, but anything with overt religious overtones was a bridge too far for Harry. They made him feel uncomfortable and achieved the opposite. So, Harry looked away and continued humming. His faith was squarely with NASA.

Abby knew the SLS rocket was brand new tech from the ground up so it should be safe. Although worrying about the outcome was a pretty natural reaction, she thought - astronaut or not. She looked at Harry who, like her, was strapped tightly into Orion, wondering if he was a mental mess like her. Apart from some mumbling and grunting, Harry hadn't uttered a word for an hour. He was sweating and red in the face and no doubt was doing his own brand of thinking, worrying and waiting.

When the huge RS-25 engines ignited six seconds before lift-off, the entire rocket rattled and shuddered like the launch complex was suddenly beset with a massive earthquake. A deep, profound rumble shook the cabin as the main engines came up to full thrust. At T-minus-zero, the solid rocket boosters ignited, giving both astronauts a massive kick in the back as NASA blasted the whole thing off the pad, using nearly nine million pounds of thrust.

The pounding, throbbing exhaust from the twin boosters shook the Orion craft like a rag doll as acceleration caused 2.5 Gs, driving Harry and Abby deep into their seats. SLS ripped through the lower atmosphere with seven million pounds of thrust. Pitch-over was executed on-par and its trajectory was precisely on point.

A few minutes after lift-off the three empty boosters peeled off with a gigantic bang, bathing Orion in a momentary flash. The three main engines still ran at more than a million pounds of thrust—but with almost no vibration now — pushing both of them upward with a comfortable 1G acceleration. The rocket was now above most of the atmosphere, so the massive noise of whistling and screeching air was behind them. Abby relaxed slightly in her chair. Rigid and tense muscles became marginally looser.

At main engine cut-off, Mach twenty-five, thrust dropped to zero in just a half-second, the pressure on everything vanished, and they were both afloat under the straps, in free fall at last. Abby could feel her eyelids and knew she was weightless, and no longer captive to Earth's gravity. Weightlessness caused her eyes to feel like they were popping out on her cheeks. It was a silent white-knuckle sense of happiness and relief at the passing of that perilous phase of lift-off, pitch-over and climb through the thick atmosphere to orbit.

Harry noticed it was now dead quiet – they were in *space*, incredibly doing 17,500 kilometres an hour but not registering any sound or sense of movement at all.

After jettisoning the boosters, service module panels, and launch abort systems, Orion had its bolts and pins explosively release, and the craft with Harry as pilot and Abby as co-pilot, was set free into orbit around Earth. It was goodbye to the SLS rocket and hello to Harry and Abby's scheduled arrival at Gateway in six hours.

They had now survived the hard part, blasting through the atmosphere. Orion had been successfully released into space and they were ready for the next part of the Artemis mission. It involved flying through the lunar corridor to Gateway which was currently orbiting the Moon.

*   *   *

Gateway was a staging outpost near the Moon and was designed to act like a basecamp when you're climbing a mountain like Everest or K2. It was essentially, a waystation, on the way to the Moon or on the long haul to Mars. Gateway itself, was an orbital platform come space station, like the ISS, orbiting the Moon. It was composed of a service module for spacecraft, a communications module, a connection module with an airlock and a place for astronauts to live. The heliophysical experiments called HERMES were mounted outside the Habitation Module and designed to exist in the exact lunar-Sun environment.

Jack Warden and Peter Jennings had been aboard the station since it came into service forty-two days ago and were well overdue to leave Gateway. They would do so, once Harry and Abby arrived to take over their duties. Their contract to manage Gateway had ended, but the way the contract was structured, it gave NASA extra 'wiggle' room by stating they would be relieved "as soon as practicable" after the contract had expired. They had flexibility written into the contract. In other words, NASA had a license to be slack with its astronauts.

Both astronauts had had enough of what had turned out to be the banal, trite activities on Gateway. If they never watered or tended another plant in their career, it would be too soon. The plants could all die as far as Pete was concerned. Now when he'd water the plants and seeds in this place, his loud cursing and general profanity directed at the seedlings, was the only thing in this place Jack found hilarious. Pete lookec at the plants sideways, like they might have the temerity to talk back.

Pete even found the Planetary Science and the entire Heliophysics experiments boring after a while. They were good for a time, but repetitive and annoying after a few weeks of doing the same thing. He felt like spacing the damn incubators and centrifuge. The sameness of the noise they made, really pressed his buttons. Just turning them on was almost too much. He'd literally had enough of this entire place, and space itself. Every time he gazed at Earth, he was reminced of his wife and the hostile reception he'd get when he finally walkec through the front door.

'Where the hell are they?' Pete irked, resentfully, 'they should be here by now, or at least in sight, shouldn't they?' He boomed, looking daggers through the nadir window.

He couldn't wait to leave and get home to his wife, who was ill. She had Stage two breast-cancer and wasn't coping well with Chemo. He knew about her negative reaction before he left, but there was no excuse for tardiness like this. NASA were too tied up with the rest of Artemis to be concerned with a contract run-over. Pete wondered where the love was for him.

"Do you think they give a crap out my wife's situation and how she needs me by her side right now?" he complained.

'Dunno,' Jack replied impatiently, '...maybe there was a lot of traffic,' he added rubbing his chin and grinning wearily, 'everything went fine at 39 so they shouldn't be long,' he said, more sedately, taking his eye from the Celestron telescope near the window.

'*Wait...here they come now,*' Jack said excitedly, putting his eye back on the scope.

'*Thank Christ,*' Pete boomed. 'I am so ready to get off this bag of bolts.' He was being very unkind to NASA's Gateway which was in high demand among astronauts. He watched the Orion craft emerge into sunlight and make its way toward Gateway...he was ecstatic and felt warm because the appearance of Orion meant going *home*.

Executing a long burn and then a number of smaller RCS bursts, Harry lined up Orion with the Gateway's I-Hab docking port. He tapped the left-hand front touch-screen a few times to move the cross-hairs and then the flight computer took over. The capsule's docking mechanism woke up its counterpart on Gateway. Soft dock was quickly followed by the craft being pulled in for hard dock. Harry had executed a perfect docking.

Within a minute, the Orion capsule was dragged in and locked in place by twelve motorised latches. There was now a fully pressurised means of entering the Gateway from Orion which was no different from entering the ISS.

'Harry Watkins and Abby Mansfield from Orion coming aboard,' Harry piped, using Orion's S-band. There was no response from Gateway, but the hatch was unlocked with a thump, so he guessed that was their welcome inside. Harry's heartbeat increased slightly. He knew how long Pete and Jack had been aboard, realising they were keen to get home, and expected the worst.

Harry had gotten to know Pete during his training and even met his wife Shellie. She had terminal breast cancer and that in itself was a travesty. He knew Pete would be keen to get home to her. The fact that NASA had "extended" his stay was bad news for everyone.

Harry and Abby both attached magnetic plates to their boots and pushed open the Gateway hatch, both of them floating up and then into the NASA station. Unlike the ISS, where weightlessness was a way of life, here on Gateway, it was done a little differently. The magnetic metal plates they all wore, kept them attached to the floor, as long as they were touching or close to the floor of Gateway.

It was an art to walk - skill and strength were required to remain upright and move forward. Strong stomach muscles and an ability to always keep one foot grounded were essential. Walking inside Gateway looked a lot like ice skating. Both Harry and Abby had practised as much as they could in full gravity conditions. Abby did it mainly in the NBP and Harry, predictably, used VR.

'*Hello*?' Harry boomed, and the echo came back. 'Anyone home?' Harry said louder. His voice echoed slightly. Jack stepped through and behind him was Pete. They both looked pale and tired.

'About friggin' time you arrived,' Jack said to Harry wryly, running his hand through his hair.' His peaked cap was folded up in his pocket. 'We've been looking forward to you arriving...especially Pete here - he's been climbing the walls of this place...counting down, desperate, to get the hell out of here...and get home.' Jack looked at Pete and smiled in amusement. Pete growled at Jack like a dog.

Pete was only partly kidding. He'd genuinely had enough of this place. Pete now despised space, weightlessness and generally, everything he did as an astronaut. For him, being late home was soul-crushing. He became more sarcastic but he kept telling himself he'd soon be home, although he knew what horrors *home* would bring.

Pete was amused in the background, and was gawking at the back of Jack's head, pointing his finger toward him repeatedly, damn sure it wasn't just him who wanted to go home. Jack continued talking, despite Pete's protestations.

'Poor guy,' Jack said, turning his head around. 'He's truly had enough experimenting with space...he wants *out* and home.' Pete was holding his middle finger up.

'So, er...welcome to Gateway guys. As soon as we've handed over, we're both out of here, hope you don't mind.' Jack looked drolly at both of them, hoping they'd understand, but not really caring if they didn't. Their only priority was getting back to Earth, and out of here. The opposite of Harry and Abby.

Jack and Pete counted the days till they joined Artemis, but that was long ago. Now they couldn't wait to leave it. The paradox of space-flight, Harry thought grimly. It didn't take much to get sick of it.

Abby looked sideways at Harry and muttered, 'got it.' She stared at Jack and said, 'no problem at all, Jack, good to see you enjoyed your stay.' Abby tried to keep sarcasm out of her voice.

With that, Pete "skated" to the comms hab to let NASA know that Orion had arrived at Gateway. He was supposed to have already done it but had forgotten. Then he suddenly remembered. Being up here for so long, his memory wasn't like it used to be. Pete put it down to weightlessness, and fully expected it to recover once he returned to Earth.

'Something I said?' Abby joked, seeing a T-shirt clad Pete disappear into the next module, clearly eager to get ready to leave Gateway and get home.

'This is Gateway, Houston, do you read?' Pete said to HQ, pinpricks of moisture dotting his forehead. He wondered what muppet would answer, hoping for Pat but knowing it was unlikely.

'This is Paul from Houston Pete, go ahead.' The guy who answered the phone sounded harried and short on patience.

'Orion is here. A2534 is confirmed – all well...them and the capsule.'

'Okay, good, noted, comms confirmed. Out.' With that, the NASA line went dead. NASA had disconnected the line rather abruptly.

'Righto...good talk.' Pete said, still holding the inactive phone, then putting the receiver back on its charging cradle. 'Could NASA be any colder and shorter?' Pete's eyes stared at the phone morosely. 'They're supposed to give us encouragement and inspiration up here. Wonder when that starts?'

Abby's forehead wrinkled with the effort of suppressing a giggle. She needn't have bothered as Harry tossed his head back and laughed uproariously, and stared at Pete who was clearly over this place. 'Um...is that what we've got in store?'

Jack nodded at Harry with a serious face. 'Oh yeah,' he said morbidly, with distended eyes. Jack then grabbed Harry and marched him into the open airlock, leaving Abby by herself in the Utilization Module. Jack gazed at Harry skeptically. He pursed his lips and shook his head, suggesting something negative was brewing. He cleared his throat and said, 'I've seen the way you look at her Harry,' Jack said, shaking his head. 'Trouble lies in that direction, for you, Abby and for NASA. Focus on work Harry, all that romance-stuff can happen back on Earth. I've seen too many astronauts' careers ruined by getting involved with the opposite sex...or the same sex I suppose. So, all I would say is, be very careful Harry.' Jack spoke in a soothing tone.

Harry nodded his head. There was no point denying it, Jack had read it in his eyes. 'I will Jack.' Harry was still nodding. Jack looked at him full in the eye to reinforce its importance. Harry smiled at Jack amiably, knowing in his heart that he needed to tread carefully with Abby. The last thing he wanted to do, was harm her career. He liked Abby, but his intentions were clearly self-evident. Harry needed to do something about it.

Pete returned to the Habitation module and grabbed Harry by the shoulder and took him to the same spot to talk about the exact same thing. *Fuck me*, Harry thought. This guy was obsessed with getting home and still noticed my infatuation with Abby. Jack agreed with Pete. Then he and Pete returned to the Habitation Module. Abby leered at Harry and smiled bleakly - she knew something was up.

'It's definitely time to go,' Pete said gruffly, not impressed by HQ or any of their attempts at support for him and Jack back on Earth. 'But before we go, you need to be introduced to HERMES, ERSA and IDA.' Pete smiled knowingly at Abby who understood what he was talking about. Pete smiled, 'they're not girlfriends, they're our heliophysics experiments that aren't possible on the ISS or on Earth.' Pete said. 'We need proximity to the Moon and Sun to do them properly. As the names suggests, they are formulated to study the effects of radiation on astronauts and devise ways to mitigate it and make them capable of long-distance journeys, like going to Mars. That's why NASA and by extension, us, do these things.'

Harry and Abby already knew a lot about the experiments from reading NASA online and working documents supplied by NASA. All of these experiments would attempt to add to the understanding of space weather. And the Sun's influence on human beings, once outside the magnetosphere of Earth and on their way to other places. Astronauts would be exposed for long periods on their way to their destinations. Hopefully, these Gateway experiments would help.

Harry then told Abby about his conversation with a friend of his at a local bar. In response to a question, he spoke about his duties on Gateway and the experiments he'd be doing regarding space-weather. 'The guy asked me, *for real?*' Harry said, with bloated eyes, "oh, does it rain in space". 'That's what we're up against, complete fucking ignorance about what we do. Of course, at the time, I found it hilarious, but it really proves that the general public have no idea about space. Even though most don't think it rains in space, my statement remains. There's a lot of fuck-wits out there who pay none or cursory only, attention, to what's above their heads.'

Pete knew home was close and he almost sounded normal, flashing a sudden grin and saying, 'once you've changed your clothes and have recharged from your journey here, please meet us back here at 11:30 UTC.' With that, he turned and "skated" gracefully, disappearing into the Habitation node called HALO, to check the accommodation schedules. He left both of them on their own with the image of the beautiful shining Moon in the rearward window.

Harry was worried that they'd be lodged in the same room, not that he'd mind – but Abby probably would. She seemed happy enough with what was happening though, so he was probably making a mountain out of a molehill. Abby probably knew the answer anyway – having had intercourse with NASA. Harry had been told enough times by peers and managers, that he thought too much. So, he closed his mouth and put his brain in neutral.

Jack came back a couple of minutes later and showed the new arrivals to their individual rooms. He watched Harry's eyes dilate, while he tried to scratch his ring-finger beneath his gloves in zero-g, and knew what his problem was. Harry was blinking rapidly and had eyes set like a cornered animal. The poor guy was nervous about the sleeping arrangements.

Jack was shocked that someone like Harry didn't know already, Abby certainly did. The same sexes like Pete and Jack were in bunk beds in the same room, but Harry and Abby got separate, though smaller, rooms which overlooked the brilliance of the Moon. Not a bad view, she thought. The Moon was huge and dazzling, the craters so close and detailed. Abby felt like she could reach out and touch the damn thing. Apart from the Apollo astronauts, no human had ever had such a close and intimate view of the Moon. She also knew that at its closest point, they would only be one thousand five hundred kilometres above its craters.

Currently, her room was staring at the mountains in the north of Mare Cognitum, directly ahead of her Gateway perspective, huge and beautifully in focus. The Apollo 12 descent stage was there somewhere but she couldn't see it. But the line of footprints made by its pilot, Pete Conrad, went around Surveyor Crater, and were observable from here. It was nothing short of amazing in the light from the Sun. This "astronaut" stuff was occasionally hairy, but pretty damn good most of the time.

Abby knocked on Harry's door and entered on hearing an "okay". She found him lying on his bed in his Gateway sleeping-bag that was tied at four corners, to a regulation bed. He was looking sheepishly at the Moon. 'It must be dull up here, er...*boring*, if Pete is any guide.' Abby said glumly, 'Jack seems little better.' The delight of making it through the atmosphere had well and truly worn off for Harry and Abby. The grim attitude of Pete and Jack brought them back to reality quicker than they would have liked.

'*Fuck me*,' he spat from his bag, 'it can't be that bad, surely. There's plenty to do and see,' Harry implored, '*interesting* stuff. I know Pete's wife is ill, but they make this place out as tedious monotony.' Harry said, stunned by Pete's negative reaction to their enthusiasm. Like NASA, he should also know better. He groaned and bitched about NASA, but his own demeanour was no better.

'They've been here more than a month Abby...so, it's way longer than their contract and the recommended time. It's probably fair enough to be annoyed, *pissed-off* with NASA even,' Harry responded bitterly, 'they've both had enough...clearly. I mean, despite their best initial intentions, everything probably crept up - the food, the isolation, the sameness of the work, the lack of different people.' Harry was breathing in tight, angry gasps, hoping the same didn't happen to them, but fearing the worst. 'It's probably a repetitive nightmare Abby. It starts off great, but after a while, it grates. *And* Pete's wife is sick. God, what a horror for him. I know he oohed and aahed about even coming...and then *this*. Stuck a quarter of a million miles from home.

'Yes, he knew about all this prior to leaving, and yes, he is an astronaut...but he's not a stone, nor is Jack. NASA best remember that. He has a life beyond space.' Abby's mouth was gaping, hoping they weren't treated like that.

'Hopefully, you and I will get on,' Harry piped, 'or this will be a *long* month, Abby.'

Both of them smiled happily at each other and nodded, both knowing it would get way more challenging than this. Jack and Pete probably thought the same thing when they first arrived. They were probably just like them. Enthusiasm and spirit were probably higher than high – the view, the structure itself, Pete, NASA, the accolades of being first...amazing how time and sameness, can wear things down. Pete and Jack now despised Gateway and reviled each other. Great result NASA...*not*.

Harry knew he was way more attracted to Abby than he should be as his partner in space. His father, not to mention Jack and Pete, had warned him about it. He had a habit of not listening to family, but Jack and Pete gave him pause. She looked good, but he knew there was way more to it than that. Whether or not there was something meaningful between them was yet to be seen, but it was looking hopeful. Harry had no idea what she thought of him. Abby was probably a slow-burn, he reckoned.

Harry could hear Jack talking loudly to Houston in the background. They'd rung back on the KA band – and now Jack was hollering with an angry tone. He was saying something loudly about a "damned asteroid". Harry knew he'd have to wait for Jack to finish on the phone to get the full story, but, so far, it didn't sound good. His whole demeanour and tone was off. He sounded annoyed and frustrated. A call from Houston was supposed to be full of encouragement and praise – NASA said so. This one was the very antithesis of that. Harry looked at Jack and shook his head. He knew something was really wrong and wondered what they'd walked into.

Jack listened mostly, but did say a few things to NASA – *angrily* and *heatedly*. Whatever was being said by NASA – Jack wasn't happy with. He was red in the face and sweating profusely, with eyes like granite. He said, *"how long?"* and *"fuck...you are joking"*, more than once and he sounded livid. It sounded like Pete and Jack needed to spend more time on Gateway. Which he obviously pushed back on. It sounded more like an exchange with an enemy than a conversation between someone and their employer.

If Jack and Pete had to spend more time on Gateway, what happens to them? Harry wondered. Had something gone wrong? Had something happened to funding of Artemis? Fearful and anxious, Harry, Abby and Pete watched on as the argument escalated, interspersed with some bits that simply made no sense at all.

They all watched Jack as he continued to speak angrily to NASA HQ in the Johnston Space Centre, Houston. Jack just held a palm up to ask for continued silence as he beseeched NASA on a call that continued to frustrate him but was not yet finished. Jack made *"ooh"* and *"aah"* sounds while listening to whatever was said by JSC, suggesting it wasn't all bad. Just, *most of it*. Jack's angry words and his frustrated expressions interspersed with total fascination, suggested there was more to the call that they didn't understand.

Gazing at Jack and seeing his pained expression, Abby wondered if she wanted to know at all. Abby had sweaty palms, and an upset stomach, hoping against hope that it wouldn't affect Harry or her negatively, but pretty sure it would. Otherwise, NASA wouldn't have made unscheduled contact.

Because Jack had such a reaction, it clearly impacted Jack and Pete negatively. Which would flow on to Harry and Abby. *Fuck*, she thought to herself. It was only day one. She'd been here for less than an hour, and it was already falling apart.

Jack replaced the HQ receiver with a bang, terminated the line with Houston and snapped his head around. Pete, Harry and Abby were in a line, waiting for a download. Jack looked blood-red, baking-hot and wet-through with sweat, and he was shaking his head. *'If that don't fucking beat all,'* he boomed, loudly and aggressively. *'Fuck...fuck...damn,'* he yelled with feeling. 'They want you two on a new mission straight away.' He looked at Abby and Harry. 'To...'

'Hang on,' Harry boomed. *'We JUST arrived on Gateway.'* He was deadly serious and his eyes were lit by anger. Jack returned Harry's glare with interest.

'Just listen Harry...it'll all make sense,' Jack yelled back. He was pissed...severely, and he showed it with several deep lines on his forehead and several annoyed gasps. NASA had been inflexible, demanding and stubborn, and worse, had treated him like he didn't

matter a dram. His and Pete's feelings were totally ignored...treated as immaterial to the bigger picture NASA had now chiselled in stone.

'Another interstellar asteroid has decided to pay our solar system a visit,' Jack said, 'and they, as in NASA, want you two to have a look, because, this time they know what it's made of – and they've found some *really* unusual and interesting stuff...you won't believe it.'

Jack was red in the face and wiped sweat away with a two-finger swipe. 'JWST has been deeply involved. They found rare earth's, Holmium, Yttrium and the like. Cerium, dysprosium and would you believe, moscovium as a stable element. NASA are baffled, which says something. Przybylski's star has really odd elements, but it's not a piece of that...definitely not.' Jack grabbed a chair and sat down. He was puffing from exertion, and exuding profanity between puffs.

'The really good news is,' he said sarcastically, 'is me and Pete stay put until you get back. *L-Lucky fucking us*,' Jack gawked sorrowfully at Pete who turned around and issued a low moan.

They were already late to leave. Jack was outraged, Pete was super-annoyed too. Both had pinched expressions and narrow eyes and stared straight at Harry, then at the floor. Jack couldn't believe NASA could be so tunnel-visioned. Him and Pete mattered too.

NASA were too focussed on Artemis - their astronauts had to be looked after as well. They weren't stones. Pete's wife suffered a turn for the worse, while he was here on Gateway. He could quite easily have opted out of his contract, which he didn't...and now this.
NASA had shot themselves in the foot.

'That was a short stay then,' Abby said. 'So, when do they want us to leave?' She asked, ready to move at a moment's notice. Gateway didn't sound like a fulfilling place to work anyway, thanks to statements by Jack and Pete. What they'd read, and what they'd found were two diametrically opposed pictures, thanks mostly to the occupants who were negative and gloomy.

Jack gazed impatiently at Harry. 'You are expected to leave as soon as NASA can send me a dump of data on Aragon and you've fed it into Mapcam on the Orion. This will firstly, allow you to find the damn thing.' It was a statement, directive and order by the way it was delivered. He'd obviously been instructed by NASA and JSC that this was an absolute, not a preference.

'Er...okay, no problem,' Harry replied, I'm all over Mapcam and already have NASA JPL small bodies database loaded. So, good to go.' Harry could feel the nerves, making his whole-body tingle.

'Okay...good Harry. Good for you, bad for us. *Whatever*, NASA is the boss. And I must say,' Jack said, 'this object has certainly got them all intrigued. In fact, sorry Abby, but it's got them by the balls, NASA I mean. The last one was "Oumuamua", and some believed, erroneously I'm sure, that it was an extra-terrestrial craft. With this one, NASA really wants to know. Stop the bullshit speculation.

'With Oumuamua, we got no visual of it, only an anomalous light in space – it was too dim, too far away and too small. That led to a lot of guessing.' Jack coughed and grimaced at Pete as if to say, "all bullshit". 'Actually, we as humanity let it slide by,' Jack said, 'without making a decent attempt to characterise it. NASA is determined that it won't happen again.'

'This rock comes from an area of the sky similar to the last one,' Jack continued. 'Apparently, because of its odd composition, it is likely not related to the first one, but with the curious readings, NASA's appetite is well and truly whet. They are super-stunned by its components.' Jack took a gusty sigh and smiled stiffly. He wasn't looking forward to more time on Gateway, especially with Pete. Jack had already said goodbye to this place, now he was forced to spend more time here. He saw it as a massive travesty and felt exploited. So much for a contract, Jack thought.

'They are adamant,' Jack said, 'they want you two to run it down and visualise it with the onboard cameras, Mapcam, Polycam and Samcam, which should allow you to firstly find it and then image it in all light – if you can. And then do as much analysis as possible.'

Jack stopped talking and stared at Pete vacantly. He wanted out and back home - for him, for Pete and for Pete's wife. Both of them were fed up. The view was spectacular, but lost its appeal on day two. Life intervened.

Jack was intrigued by this asteroid, which by all reports, was truly remarkable. Never before had Earth been confronted with these elements in anything that was space-related. NASA told the world that this one was a *first*. Even POTUS, the Five Eyes, and the G7 leaders were now following Aragon with focussed eyes.

Jack had paced while he spoke and now he stood still by the wall, but every muscle was rigid, tendons visible in his neck. Despite how he was feeling, he was captivated by what this asteroid offered. Jack had a feeling about this rock but he kept it to himself. He scrutinized Harry closely. His energy was low, and he had a cracking headache, but he needed to pass this on. NASA said he had to.

'Harry, you will be mission commander and pilot. Abby, you'll be co-pilot and mission specialist,' Jack said, 'ranks that may be made permanent by NASA, after this mission. In other words, it all depends on how this mission goes,' he said, popping out his eyes. 'NASA tells me that would be a promotion for both of you. So at least someone will get something from this [cough] little adventure.' Jack scowled at Harry and crossed his arms, then relaxed a bit and smiled wryly at him.

'We have been asked to stay until you return. Both me and Pete just have to suck it up – like good astronauts do.' His voice was strained and his eyes were darting from Harry to Pete and then to Abby, but he grinned ironically when he finished, breaking the tension he'd created. 'We don't mind staying...*really.*' He looked at Pete and they both smiled wanly.

Jack had genuinely had enough of everything and everyone. But for Harry and Abby, he tried to keep it on the down-low with sarcasm. Jack reckoned he was doing a piss-poor job of it.

Both Jack and Pete were staying on Gateway because they had no choice in the matter. NASA wanted eyes-on this asteroid and they considered Harry and Abby the best fit. In NASA's words there was a "higher calling" that demanded Pete and Jack be patient.

In a few short years there would have been a craft sitting and waiting for Aragon. *Comet Interceptor* was currently being designed and built by ESA and JAXA. It would sit and wait at the position of L2, close to the position of the JWST telescope.

When an interstellar interloper came along, it would pounce on it and analyze the shit out of it. The craft was scheduled to be launched in eight years. Until then, NASA would have to improvise. That's what Orion and Harry and Abby were – *an improvisation.*
NASA hoped against hope that they were doing the right thing. They were desperate to see this thing up close, for themselves, and because so many on Earth were intrigued by it. Aragon had the science community generally salivating for more.

It was NASAs duty to deliver them results and definitives. If they didn't succeed fast enough - SpaceX or Blue Origin would do it for them. Which would put NASA's funding at risk, *and they wouldn't allow that.* Their funding from the American Federal Government was very precious indeed.

*   *   *

With everything uploaded and synchronised to the Orion mainframe, it was time to leave Gateway. The Orion computer was a thousand times faster than the old analogue Shuttle, so they knew it would be a huge asset to have what was basically a flying digital computer. Jack had taken the Orion to the Esprit node of Gateway, and filled it completely with fuel, and ensured it knew what was ahead of it, by updating the computer. So, all was in order to leave. AI was ready to go, and so too were the humans.

Their destination was Aragon which was currently passing Jupiter and heading rapidly toward Venus. At that point it was expected to go around Venus and then exit the solar system. They would intercept Aragon, Earthside of Mars, about two percent of an AU distant, or about 4.5 million kilometres away.

Aragon was really moving too, sixty-nine kilometres per second, only slightly slower than Oumuamua, and it similarly wouldn't be captured by the Sun's gravity - the asteroid was hyperbolic, it exceeded the solar system's escape velocity. In other words, it was soon goodbye forever, and NASA knew it. Characterising it before it left the solar system was super-critical.

Harry glanced at Abby again, double-take style, and liked what he saw. She was no supermodel - Abby was slimish and shortish but very pretty in her own feminine way. Harry knew it went far deeper than that anyway. Looks weren't that important to him - Abby was smart, strong, witty, quick and wasn't overly loquacious. She was a mainly facts first and last girl which he liked.

He didn't want to start anything like a relationship here, his partner in astronautics had just started with NASA, so his experience with her was short, and her experience with NASA was the same. He had been warned by Jack and Pete, so he had to treat her with kid-gloves and don't stare at her hungrily - like he wanted to eat her. In short, they only knew each other on a shallow work level so far. More personal stuff would hopefully come later. But he reckoned the future looked pretty good, although so far, she'd shown no interest in him whatsoever. Harry thought staring at her longingly might encourage her a bit, but so far it had been an abject flop. Even when she did look at him, there was only curiosity in her eyes, nothing else. Abby was trying to work him out. *WTF*? Her disinterest in anything but work was palpable, but understandable. They were at work, afterall. Harry was disappointed so far, but hoped the personal situation between them would improve and perhaps deepen in the future.

Harry already had the overwhelming desire to look after her, He had to be careful though, and he knew it. A stern warning was already his. He might have been smitten, but he worked for NASA and so did she, and they had an important job to do, that just got more important, and hopefully lucrative. Anything else had to be left until later – right now they needed to focus intently on work. They both desperately wanted to be employed by NASA, and now that they had achieved it, they both didn't want to let them down. So, a steep focus on mission parameters was key. But he struggled to drag his eyes off her. From now on, he needed to look elsewhere. Harry knew his brain and other bodily parts had a different priority.

NASA had invested a lot of time and money training him and her – and he didn't want to ruin the relationship. He reckoned Abby felt the same. Any thoughts of a romantic relationship had to wait until he got home, post-mission. Having said that, he knew his desires had tiny little minds of their own, that wouldn't be diverted by anything as trivial as "thinking".

The seats in Orion looked a bit like dentist's chairs but ironically, were quite comfortable, but the degree to which the straps had to be tight made it tough for anyone to be truly relaxed. Maybe that's how it was supposed to be, Abby thought. Astronauts were meant to be resilient and staunch...apparently.

So, there were four seats but only *two* were needed – which meant two were always empty which looked like they were waiting for someone. Abby reckoned that two seats should be removed because sure as hell they weren't needed by herself or Harry. They reminded her of something she didn't want to be reminded of, so if they were to be removed, she wouldn't object.

Abby's sister's husband was killed in the 2021 American Airlines crash in Tokyo, and the chair that he always sat in at home was *retired* to the dark reaches of their shed. It was too depressing to look at because it was *his* chair. The two empty chairs on Orion, had a similar effect on Abby. Someone wasn't coming back. But until they truly got in the way, they stayed.

Harry gave separation instructions to Orion and to Gateway, which released hooks and latches from the airlock. Once released into free space, a short burn was followed by a larger burn to get them on their way. The onboard computer was the heart of the ship, but the drives were hidden underneath their seats. They did most of the work but weren't allowed to be seen. The other paradox of modern spaceflight.The Polycam, an eight-inch telescope supported by driver software that was linked to Orion would assist in self-automating the craft to find the target with Right Ascension and Declination, a bit like GPS in three dimensions.

Aragon, an asteroid that came from the Lyra constellation, entered the solar system a million kilometres Earth-side of Uranus and would leave after it passed Venus, under the gravitation of both the Sun and Venus. It had the intelligent people of planet Earth baffled. The components it boasted had never been seen before, apart from on Earth. The complexity made many wonder. What on Earth did the elements point to? It was Harry and Abby's job to get more details. On behalf of eight billion other residents of the planet. *No pressure.*

Orion's mapping OLA and ranging LIDAR devices, would act cooperatively and measure distance to Aragon, once they got closer. The instruments were more advanced, than the instruments aboard NASA's Osiris-Rex asteroid lander that analysed asteroid Bennu. It was a huge step forward for NASA. The Orion had similar instruments to Osiris-Rex, but they were even more sensitive.

Aragon was a truly interstellar rock, because it would continue its journey beyond the Sun and beyond the solar system and would never return. It was unfazed by the gravitation of planetary or solar masses. The asteroid would not be gripped by the pull of the Sun – it was going too fast and would burst through it and go beyond.

Their craft would intercept Aragon after it flew past Mars. The world was gripped. The guesses from the science establishment on Earth ranged from an interstellar craft to a supernova remnant, to a nitrogen or hydrogen iceberg. Like Oumuamua, none were correct.

The truth with Aragon was more bizarre than any of the guesses on Earth. Humans thought the Universities, the space, and aerospace industries, defence partners of the US, and the science-community generally, were full of very smart people indeed. When compared to others in the Universe though, they weren't smart or intuitive at all. Intelligence was highly relative, not only within a species, but outside it too.

Harry was in the pilot's seat and Abby was right next to him. He had the three screens right in front of his face – they were in front of Abby too. They were huge and the definition was amazing. They beat the hell out of the shuttle which was plagued with problems.

Harry found it hard not to look at Abby and her long brown hair, even with so much happening around him. He wondered if other astronauts found it this hard to concentrate. Given his state-of-mind, and lack of focus, Harry wondered if he was up to it. He shook his head, and continued, hoping he was.

Around each screen on Orion were buttons, exponders and digital switches. Harry could fly the craft by tapping on the screen to select, and using his translational hand controller, he could tell the craft "How much" he wanted. He also had a mouse and cursor. Anything you used on your home computer, could be used here. It just did a hell of a lot more. Orion was essentially a computer, put into space. It was digital and gorgeous. Everything before it was analogue and clunky and resigned to history.

Harry and Abby would locomote in space using the translational hand controller, and there was one for the pilot and one for Abby, that she wouldn't touch unless asked to. Being in control of a craft scared her to death, but she knew she had to eventually do it – or die a slow death at NASA. Harry made flying a multi-billion-dollar craft look like shelling peas – his hands were so precise, she hoped she'd be like that, one day. She gawked at Harry in wonder.

Abby had the knowledge, all she needed, was the confidence and the experience, Harry reckoned. Both came hand-in-hand. It was easier said than done, she knew. Harry glanced at Abby and was certain she would eventually get a gig as a pilot with NASA. And hopefully a more personal gig with him.

Harry couldn't get his mind off the target - *Aragon*. It was probably a moderately interesting asteroid – a nickel/iron core surrounded by metres of unconsolidated rock that were quite loose. A few people, some very educated and intelligent, thought that maybe the last one was an extra-terrestrial craft. Perhaps hosting a light sail, similar to the ones being proposed by Breakthrough Starshot. Both of them believed that such an assumption was spurious and ridiculous – and way short on empirical evidence.

Abby eyes were wide and staring, and her hands might have been covered with gloves, but they didn't hide the occasional tremor. The exotic elements in Aragon had them all wired, including NASA and the entire planet. Everyone on Earth wanted to know the whys and hows of this strange, alluring object. The science community realised the results of this mission, meaning the photos – if the mission was successful - weren't far away.

The entire globe was waiting breathlessly for the object to be intercepted and dealt an analyst's once-over. Most believed the elements weren't there for no reason. Earth wanted that reason resolved empirically. Abby and Harry were aware of the huge weight they carried. Harry looked at Abby, hoping like hell they were up to the job. Because this could make-or break both of them with Earth's space industries. Harry looked at the screen in front of him and braced himself. He looked at Abby and realised he needed to give everything to this mission. She would have to wait.

Earth generally, was as amped as those making the trip. The general feeling was that this asteroid was something totally out-of-the-box. NASA themselves were cock-a-hoop about the object – hence their dramatic change in plans - which they never did lightly. The normal way was to concede that the asteroid would soon be gone, "but we'll be on our toes for the next one". They would normally just continue with the Artemis Program and throw well-worn motherhood statements at the people on Earth. That was the NASA way.

This change in direction at mid-ships, showed the massive interest NASA and the public held for the object. They were truly hooked on Aragon and were determined to find out what the odd componentry meant before the asteroid left the solar system.

This time, NASA would be all over it. They also wanted to keep the private venturers to space out of it. So, NASA acted quickly and were unusually fleet of foot. Maintaining their funding from the US federal reserve was very important to NASA. That meant beating everyone else to the punch.

Orion, with Harry and Abby, was now a thousand kilometres from Gateway which was behind the Moon and invisible. In contrast, the Moon itself was huge and resplendent in the light from the Sun in their rearward vision. Harry glanced and smiled generously at Abby, looking away from the tri-screens, now the auto-pilot was engaged. She too, took in the gorgeous visage of the shining Moon, glancing at Harry and smiling at the two alluring objects. To Harry's masculine ignorance, Abby actually noticed him in a vague romantic sense.

Abby hoped *she* was up to the mission - it was nice to know NASA thought so, but still she had twinges of insecurity. She folded her arms with a thump and looked straight ahead at the tri-screens. *She belonged*, Abby repeated over and over to herself. Problem was, surrounded by all this expensive tech, she was overwhelmed with feelings of self-doubt and questions swirling around incumbency.

They, as in Harry and her, were both in charge of a multibillion-dollar spacecraft with its cameras and software, which hopefully would ensure they obtained the required data. Together, they would employ the Ocams and Otes devices. If they got visual photos of it with Polycam and the SAW cameras, and the infra-red thermal spectrometer analyses with Otes, the mission to Aragon would be a success. Anything less than that would be mission failure. If the mission failed, they would both return to Gateway with their tails between their legs. The pressure was well and truly *on* and Abby especially, could feel it crushing down on her like a lead weight. Harry was focussing hard on Aragon and trying to ignore the other alluring object sitting near him.

Abby felt the cold sweat on her back and under her eyes. The tightness in her face told her all she needed to know. NASA had helped by promoting her, but she needed to up her confidence. Abby took solace from the fact that she was with Harry, who was all over Orion and the instruments it carried. She looked at him and felt her confidence grow.

Harry exuded capability, not only with NASA itself, but with the Orion vessel, that would execute the mission under their guidance. All they had to do, was deliver Orion to Aragon and have its instruments look at it. That's all that stood between them and mission success. Jack had said over and over; he was right. Harry agreed, and Abby needed to focus on that. The rest was just debilitating white-noise.

Abby tried to forget it but couldn't get *Oumuamua* out of her mind. It was like horrific visions of 9/11...they never left her mind. She'd read a lot of articles about the asteroid, watched a few videos on Youtube; there was no doubt, Aragon was similar -an unbound, hyperbolic rock of strange shape, rotation and componentry.

So many people thought Oumuamua might be an alien spacecraft, that is *light-sail*, it wasn't funny. *Thankyou Professor Loeb*. But the light curve was all wrong to explain the peak-to-peak brightness of such a 1000:1 structure. So, in her and Harry's opinion, it was just a rock, although an interesting one. A prosaic explanation, both Harry and Abby agreed.

It probably wasn't fair to send someone so green on such a mission...but it was what it was. She and Harry were work-arounds - a convenient improvisation. Without doubt they, he and Abby, were in the right place at the right time. Green they might have been, but they were the only ones familiar with Orion's specialised systems. They knew a lot about the Orion craft generally, and were specialists in its added tech, which was supposed to be for the Moon, but would be invaluable for Aragon too. So, they were right for the mission, and so too was Orion. The craft and them got a huge tick from NASA.

Harry tapped the MPS on the screen and pushed the translational controller down and they increased velocity to 230,000 MPH. Aragon would eventually come into view on its trajectory through the inner solar system toward the Sun and then beyond. Abby knew it wouldn't slow down to let them catch up. Everything they achieved out here, had to be *earned*. So, Orion had to go faster than its manufacturers recommended.

Before interception was possible, Orion needed a *lot* of speed, it would travel around Jupiter to obtain the requisite gravity-assist, to catch up with the fast-moving body after it went past the red planet. It would acquire some of Jupiter's momentum and travel faster than Lockheed Martin ever thought possible.

*   *   *

Harry and Abby performed the required orbit of Jupiter and arced upward and outward, and away from the huge banded planet, still accelerating. They were now on the tail of Aragon, which flashed Sunward. It was destined to leave the solar system entirely, and continue its endless voyage toward the Hydrus constellation. Then it would garner a brand-new destination. They'd seen the beautiful ice-clouds of the banded planet, the enormous red spot, as well as its multiple dusty rings that were backlit by the Sun.

Now, after seemingly endless blackness, they were coming up on red Mars, not far from seeing Aragon, for the first time. They were travelling very quickly indeed, thanks largely to the fly-by of the giant planet and the acquisition of some of its momentum. Abby thought about the host of questions Oumuamua left them with. And to think we were about get answers to all of them. No mysteries with Aragon, she thought, smiling nervously. Everything, down to the finest detail, would be answered.

They saw Aragon slowly crystallize from the blackness ahead, tumbling as it went. It came from the darkness and they saw it fairly clearly – a flattish, lenticular body resembling a pancake, but there was something quite clear and shining on its surface in the weak light from the Sun. Then it went dark and then shone again, as it rotated in and out of the Sun's light. The asteroid itself was pinky-grey and very fine grained at the surface. Harry needed to see more. He felt his skin tingle...and fire bolts of energy down his spine.

To Harry, it looked like a fairly typical asteroid so far. It blinked – one second it was bright, then black. Abby saw it too and wiggled in her restraints to get a better view of this rock that had Earth so captivated. The entire asteroid was rotating quickly and wobbling. It did everything you'd expect from a chaotic rock that was efforted into existence by a random event in another galaxy.

Abby was craning her neck and head, bending forward as far as she could, fighting with the straps to get a better look at Aragon. But Harry was best positioned to see it through the cabin window. It looked like a pancake, but the silver handles he spied were unexplainable. Inexplicable, anomalous, baffling.

His heart started beating like a drum in his throat as the sight of the objects downloaded. The handles were clearly *artificial*. He felt sweat run down his back in lines, and he immediately thought it must be a mirage.

Harry racked his brain for an answer, but incredibly, there was only one, *if* it was real. He gasped and hacked in the artificial atmosphere of Orion. Harry closed his eyes, then re-opened them, and it was still there. Metal posts on Aragon.

They were now starboard to the asteroid and it looked like...*no it couldn't be*. His brain refused to believe it. Harry shook his head and stared unblinkingly forward, keeping his head as still as possible. It wasn't a trick of the light. It was *real*. Aragon looked like it had swimming pool guide rails set into it.

Harry felt like shaking his head again. He must be seeing it wrong, *surely*. But Abby said she was seeing the same thing, in a voice that was more a cry of anguish. She knew, too. Incredible as it seemed, the object was *really* there. *Artificial objects on Aragon.*

Harry gazed through bloated eyes – it appeared undeniable. Abby was stiff in her chair, despite the firm restraints, and her eyes bulged out of her skull as she held on rigidly to the sides of her chair and stared forward. Abby had seen them too - and also had no explanation. She panted and gasped and called them metal posts.

The posts had to be artificial. That was a given. There was no way they could be natural. Harry gawked in disbelief at the photos taken by Polycam – and it showed the same story. *Pictures don't lie.* Harry froze and so did Abby, both of them speechless. *These things couldn't be natural – no way.* They both turned to gawk at each other wide-eyed and incredulous, silently sharing the unimaginable.

Abby looked back at Aragon and gasped, and her mouth dropped open like a sinkhole. Harry just stared at Abby wide-eyed and empty, without words or sound. He knew the meaning of the Polycam image in the first second. So did Abby.

They were both gazing at *metal posts on an asteroid*, both on the photograph and "live" as well. It was truly incredible. Everything about Aragon was dazzling. He expected something unusual...but not like this. Not as obvious as this. The asteroid had some incredible components – but they didn't point to *this*.

Harry felt tilted, his whole world was upside down and he knew Abby felt the same. Her mouth was still wide open and her eyes were enormous, like something from an amusement park. She blinked at him and smiled hugely, hitting her thigh with a half-closed fist. Both of them realised it couldn't be natural...*no fucking way.*

Harry felt like his head was going to explode, thoughts were being asked by his brain at the speed of light. It left him weak and unable to move. He had seen something in space that he didn't think was possible. Harry continued his pregnant stare at Abby and yelled, '*Fermi paradox*,' and smiled hugely. What started as a humdrum assignment had just become the most meaningful mission in human history. Harry was turning the photo through 360 degrees and making nondescript howling noises. He really couldn't believe it. He expected something, but not like this. *Here, NOW.* It was nothing less than staggeringly spectacular, and completely ridiculous, and *so unexpected*. NASA was interested in this intriguing body, but no way they expected anything like this either.

They probably thought it was an interesting rock, with odd elements that would keep scientists busy for years. Something like this would never have been expected. They'd die with a leg in the air, if they saw photos like this. Scratch that, *WHEN*, they see photos like this. Harry reckoned their futures had suddenly been dipped in gold.

Shocked, surprised, elated didn't come close to describing their emotions. Both of them were floored. The entire planet would be the same. NASA and they, had spoken about the likelihood that "others" existed, just by sheer numbers...sheer planetary plenitude.

There were even people, *scientists*, who believed we might be *alone*. Can you believe that, Harry thought in disbelief. 'What a crock of shit,' he reckoned, looking straight at the silver posts. The true story of the Universe was very different. And now we knew, he thought deliriously. *And now we knew...*

Harry's mind kept flashing back to Arthur C Clarke and his statement that "extraordinary claims require extraordinary evidence". Was their evidence "extraordinary"? He reckoned it was, and with a nod and a smile, he recalled they had data and photos from Polycam and Samcam, and the photos and videos from the SAW cameras on the solar array. No doubt, this was *extraordinary*. It was undeniable, Harry reckoned.

'Well, now we know for sure,' Harry said, gazing at the dazzling photographs. 'Now we know unambiguously. *They exist.*'

And both of them realised that they, Harry and Abby, were the tip of the spear, to be revered by all of Mankind forever. They had found concrete evidence of *them* and they were looking at it. Taking it all in. In real-time. The view from here was awesome, Abby reckoned, as every hair on her body stood erect. She was electrified and wired.

2.

Aragon

"God is the name people give to the reason we are here."
~ Stephen Hawking

Harry wouldn't bother with Gateway. They were supposed to be the "go-to" for advice and reports for this mission, but he would go straight to Earth, direct to JSC at Houston. They were the only ones who could provide advice on big things, and missions themselves; everywhere else, like Gateway, was only a substation.

So, he'd forget Gateway for the moment. This deserved to go straight to HQ. Straight to the top. All big issues should go direct to the leader. And this was as big as it got.

He knew the big wig at mission control, Pat Datsun – he used to be an astronaut – a very good one. The rest of them at Houston, he had no idea about. But knowing the boss at the Johnston Space Centre, and calling him friend - was pretty decent, Harry thought. Even if the relationship was brokered by his father.

At least he'd listen to Harry, at first...probably call him all sorts of names, but he'd at least stop what he was doing and listen to what he had to say. Pat had a direct line to the Administrator of NASA, so it was critical to get him 'on-side'. Harry set up his KA-band communicator with a click.

'Mission...this is Harry Watkins of Orion, out of Gateway, in-transit for Aragon. Harry waited impatiently for his comms to be responded to by Houston. Harry hoped for some degree of priority. He tapped his left finger on the headset while he waited. Harry was talking to thin air so far, no-one picked up his cry for help. And that's what it was – they needed urgent help and advice.

Harry and Abby were beside themselves - their hair was literally standing on end. Both of them had laid their peepers on the *incredible* in space. They were shaking all over. Harry's eyes were closed, Abby was staring at the bulkhead with glassy eyes. He hoped against hope that someone would hear their call to HQ...eventually. They needed support in the most traditional of senses.

Suddenly, the line was picked up. It wasn't anyone Harry knew, he could tell that, and his heart sank immediately. It was someone he'd never heard of.

'This is Mission Control Harry, my name is Paul Dunn, not really expecting your call but that's fine – are you, uh...okay? We're not your agent on this job.'

'Yeah, I know Paul...but you're gonna want to hear what I've got to say. Ahead of us is the interstellar asteroid Aragon, and on it is something clearly artificial – we want to know how we should proceed?'

There was just silence and static on the other end of the line, '*HELLO?*' Harry eventually yelled. Still more silence. He looked at Abby, and shook his head. '*Fuck*, what is wrong with this guy?' Harry whispered angrily to Abby. 'We need to speak to Pat. Over.' The guy was clearly a greenhorn and didn't know how to respond or even if he should respond.

'By, er...*unnatural*...what do you mean? Over.'

Harry looked at Abby and rolled his eyes and rubbed his arm. Was this guy on the level? He *had* to realise what it meant. 'We have metal posts set about fifteen feet apart on this asteroid. It ain't human. OTES analyser says it's a source of Holmium, Terbium, Scandium and Rare-Earth's that was picked up by JWST earlier. I've looked at it live and on close-up photos using our Polycam. *It has to be non-human.*' Surely, that had to get him, Harry reckoned. There was a long silence before the penny finally dropped like a metal ball.

'Fuck...sorry. Holy shit, Christ...I'll get Pat...don't hang up.'

There was more silence and static after he dropped the phone, which made a loud *clunk* in Harry's ear, but the line still hummed green and remained connected.

While he waited for Pat to come on-line, he wondered how in God's name it had happened - to *him*, no less. The Fermi paradox ... *gone*. It was truly ridiculous. But then, he thought more about it. The science community believed it would eventually happen, which meant it had to happen to *someone*, and he was an astronaut, so it was him. He was the lucky "someone". Or *unlucky* – he wasn't sure how the game was played from here.

The likely downside was Pat himself. No way he'd believe him. He was a known sceptic for anyone or anything suggesting aliens. Pat reviled Avi Loeb. He was a Professor at Harvard University and he believed the asteroid called Oumuamua was an alien spaceship. *Look at the fucking light curve,* Pat would yell. He could still picture him saying it, in an avalanche of forehead lines. So, he didn't hold out a lot of hope for his assertions that they had a non-human structure before them. Pat would call him a dickhead, or likely much worse.

Harry heard someone pick up the call from the JSC.

'Er...this is Pat Dallas from Mission, Harry. Um...aliens should be a *last* resort – you know that. It's never aliens until it simply has to be, *remember*.' He delivered the last word emphatically. Pat was tough, tenacious and had a rock-hard stance against this sort of thing. Moving him in any direction was nigh on impossible. If you could move Uluru, you had a chance.

'Yeah, yeah – I know, I know all that, and I agree.' Harry implored. 'I know you need to be careful and vigilant. But there is literally no other option Pat. I've seen the posts, photos taken close-up by Polycam, and no way they're natural.' Harry held his breath. There was nothing, so he continued. 'Some of the elements were detected behind the bars, inside the asteroid. Trust me, Aragon carries non-human assets.'

'Sure...sure, Harry. There's always another option. Tell me what you've got. *Describe* it for me in detail and I'll give you a few.' Pat was very calm and a tad sarcastic and condescending, expecting a heap of qualitative data to come down the phone. He doubted Pat had listened to a word he'd said so far. So, he was determined to speak slowly and deliberately, be detailed and be heard, so Pat really knew what he was saying. Because in Harry's mind, it was empirical. It was undeniable. Harry knew the evidence he had was impossible to refute, as long as his words were absorbed and digested. With the statements he made, speaking slowly and deliberately, and repeating himself, it sounded like he was talking to a simpleton. He knew he wasn't – this was Pat Dallas. The genius who saved the ISS and now ran the place known as JSC. Problem was, he was so smart, that sometimes he didn't hear you. He heard the last word first, and ended with a jumbled mess, that meant nothing. So, he hoped, speaking slowly and repeating himself, would obviate all that.

Harry breathed deeply; the first thing he did was make sure Pat was truly listening to him, and then he kept it simple, to hopefully mitigate the avalanche of questions he'd have.

'It's pretty simple Pat. We've got metallic bars on an asteroid and these bars or posts have a high concentration of Scandium and like metals. There are some metallic readings behind and under them too, but most of the metal readings are in the posts themselves. OTES told us so, and it's quantitative.' *Take that'*, he thought. If he still didn't believe him, he supposed he could send the photos to him. Orion had taken pictures of Aragon with Polycam and its sixteen SAW cameras that sat on the solar array of the Orion. Any one of those could be sent. And the story would be empirical – *close-up and focussed pictures don't lie.* Unless humans had been there, which they definitely hadn't, the pictures spoke for themselves. A non-human intelligence had done it. *Period. Case closed.* Harry heard hacking and gasping on the other end of the line.

Pat was wheezing like a dog and his heart started pounding in his neck like a bongo. The realisation of encountering an immediate techno-signature had descended on him like a hard kick to the solar-plexus. Harry hoped he hadn't killed Pat, because sure as hell, it didn't sound good.

Pat thought Harry was going to talk about a radio signal or FRB that they'd managed to pick up – which he could quickly put to bed. He wasn't expecting *this*. This was *fucking* huge and crazily unexpected, and there were photos to back it up...and to prove it unconditionally. *Fuck*, Pat thought. *They'd done it*...somehow, it had been unfurled hook, line and sinker in front of them.

Pat felt lop-sided and dizzy. He didn't think it would ever happen. *It couldn't be...could it?* Yet it was right in front of NASA's astronauts, all backed up by photos and spectroscopy. He knew what tech their Orion carried and the story left no room for argument. Not even from him. They'd discovered a *ridgy-didge* arm's-length techno-signature from a probable non-human civilisation. When he rolled out of bed in Houston this morning, this is the last thing he expected.

'*Fuck, fuck, holy shit Harry*...okay okay...you two need to document this, which you've already done...photos, thermal imaging. Okay. Okay. Send the results to me and I'll forward it all on...*right*? What is your next step per your mission with NASA?' Pat was in Houston and wiped his forehead with a two-finger swipe. He had to calm down, slow his heartbeat somehow. Pat looked at the clouded sky through the window of the lab at JSC, and knew that this day was one for the fucking books. Pat kept gawking at the clouds, while his heart-beat slowed.

'Continue to analyse it I suppose,' Harry said. 'Our Mission brief was to use our suite of imaging on Aragon, which we've done. The mission, per the specs, has just about finished. Then, we return to Gateway and presumably stay there. But the nature of this asteroid has sort of changed everything right? We'll report further when we have, er...more data. Over.'

Harry disconnected and knew he needed to contact the Administrator of NASA right away, although he was sure Pat would do that anyway. This was massive news. Harry could feel his undergarments, wet-through with sweat. He saw Abby's red face, wide-eyes and visibly sweating, the moisture dotting her forehead. She was the same as him. This whole episode was well above her pay grade, but she was ecstatic to be here, despite feeling anxious and terrified about what they'd found.

Abby knew how historic and big this was, but still felt a huge pang of personal doubt. Thank God for Harry, she thought, watching him gawk curiously at Aragon. She tried to take everything in, garner every detail, knowing what an extraordinary moment it was for Earth, for Mankind. This was the '*first*' time. God knows what it meant for us. Abby rubbed her eyes with the back of her knuckles, trying to clear her vision, looking squarely at Aragon and saving the extraordinary picture in her mind. She'd remember this moment the rest of her life.

Abby watched Harry closely who was a picture of concentration as he pawed over Orion's consoles. This was a man, Abby thought, who was almost lost to the space industry. He almost became an NFL player with the Jets and gave up any aspirations to work for NASA. When he was cut from his New York team, rather than go back in the draft, and end up who knows where, he got out of the system completely, and became what he was today. From NFL hack to the most uniquely important man in the world.

Quite the transformation, Abby thought proudly, and she was right behind him. She too, wondered what the future held for them as a couple. Harry had no idea she was even interested. Abby was. But Aragon deserved her full attention at the moment.

'*I want to get closer*,' Harry said feverishly, and Orion did, sliding toward the stony block, which looked so much like a pink pancake tumbling through space. They were flying within a hundred metres of it, and the silver bars were very noticeable – lit up by light from the Sun and sparkling and then vanishing when Aragon tumbled. Abby wondered what in God's name they were there for? Who or what had installed them? What was their purpose? Abby's mind did somersaults, trying to draw answers from nothing but the stony aggregate in front of her. She grabbed Harry's arm and made sure he knew she was there. Looking at Harry's face, she could tell how terrified and wired he was. He was blinking rapidly, with incredulous wide eyes. All his features spoke emphatically...*WTF*.

Harry knew how historic this was and didn't want to let it out of his sight, for even a moment. Incredibly, he was worried Aragon or the bars might vanish forever, and they'd be left with nothing. Harry's mind did back-flips and for the first time, he noticed how tired and fatigued he was. The writing and the apps on the Tri-Screens were becoming fuzzy. Maybe he was more overwhelmed and drained than he thought.

Both Harry and Abby lost consciousness in their chairs, still tightly strapped in. One second, they were awake and aware, the next, they were in deep slumber in their chairs. Both were comatose and totally unaware of future happenings. Orion continued its inevitable movement toward Aragon.

Harry should've taken Orion further away, rather than moving closer, but it was too late for any of that. The craft was caught by some space-time curvature that was pulling the craft toward Aragon, and wouldn't let go. Both he and Abby were asleep and contributed nought to their movement.

Orion was pulled toward the metal bars, irrevocably, like a deeply hooked fish being hauled toward a jetty. Their movement was irreversible. Even MPS at full burn would have no effect. Aragon had become an inescapable destination.

Behind the bars, something extraordinary was buried. The tech was unknown to humanity – it was something Mankind could barely dream of. It detected approaching objects and grabbed those that met its prime directives, dragging them in with billow lasers. No amount of Orion power could sidestep it.

Orion was first pulled onto the asteroid's surface and then wrenched between the metal posts and over the buried machine. The Orion spacecraft vanished entirely as it went between the posts. Now their craft was gone from Earth's Galaxy and the Universe entirely. Something entirely unexpected had afflicted the NASA astronauts and craft – something so bizarre that no one on Earth would believe it. Because it represented technology that was totally unknown, involving particles and theories that hadn't yet been discovered or formulated on Earth. This was what Arthur C Clarke was talking about when he said, *"any sufficiently advanced race is indistinguishable from magic"*. Never was a quote more relevant to Aragon.

From a distance it was an extraordinary visage. A small capsule hitting the asteroid head-on, followed immediately by a blinding flash of pure white light. Then, no capsule. Aragon continued tumbling, unaffected, toward the Sulafat star ... the buried machine unaware that its prime directive and reason for being there had been achieved.

3.

Werinn

"I like physics, but I love cartoons".
~ Stephen Hawking

Harry abruptly woke and looked around the cabin groggily, seeing their speed was zero, and seeing a black sheath covering the nadir window. He looked at Abby in panic, but her eyes were closed, and she was clearly fast asleep. Harry rubbed his eyes with the back of his knuckles and shook his head, and the sheath remained. He was half-asleep but could see brightness near the window edge. He mumbled and choked out some sounds as he woke fully.

Where the hell was Aragon, he wondered? Where the hell am I? *'Fuck me,'* he screamed and looked around the cabin in dread.

More awake now, he wondered if this was all a dream or a hallucination? Harry looked at the screen closest to him, it showed the correct numbers – so a dream hadn't likely kicked in...so whatever it was, it wasn't a dream or a hallucination and was probably *real*. He gasped loudly and shook his head and wiped sweat from his forehead. The last memory he had was watching Aragon and the metal posts.

And then he woke up here and it was bright outside...which made no sense at all. Harry wondered what he was missing because a fair chunk of time was just gone. He felt like screaming at the top of his lungs, but knew panic lay in that direction.

Orion was now in thick atmosphere, and inside a huge pliable net that tightened around the craft and brought it slowly to a complete stop in the air. Harry thought about it, and was fairly sure the net was controlled by something that wouldn't let them be harmed by anything as prosaic as inertia. Because, sure as hell, he knew that stopping too fast could easily turn them into soup.

The change in environments happened in a snap. Abby was still unconscious and was held tight in her seat by the restraints but was coming around slowly. Grunting and groaning became spastic movements beneath the restraints. Harry knew she had a massive shock coming after she woke up. He knew, Abby had to be treated with kid-gloves.

Harry looked timidly at the screen again and could see the craft was powered to zero and caught in netting or mesh covering the nadir window with narrow strips. He played it all back, realising that somehow, it was all real. From space, Aragon, to here, incredibly, it seemed to have actually happened.

'*Holy fuuuck,*' Harry shrilled and Abby moaned something louder but still incomprehensibly. He could feel movement. '*Wha-,*' he half-shouted again as the craft came in right-way up to sit on the ground, free of the net which had now been retracted above them. Abby craned her head around the interior of the cabin for the first time and resisted taking anything in. '*Holy-,*' she yelped.

Her eyes were slitted open and she brought a shaky hand to her forehead, panting in terror at the bright light that hit her eyes. 'This is not... happening,' she puffed slowly, struggling to believe any of this was real. The last location she remembered was deep space, and seeing Aragon. Now they were...*here*. To her, it didn't seem possible, so she closed her eyes tight and folded her arms over her chest and pushed herself sideways.

The change in location and illumination was immediate and bewildering. When she reopened her eyes, Abby started playing the whole sorry event forward in her mind. Aragon and then...*here*. '*Fuck,*' she screamed to herself – where were they, and *why* were they here?

She grabbed Harry's hand, but he looked as stunned and dumbfounded as she was, there was no strength in his limb at all. It was like grabbing a dead fish. Harry's eyebrows were arched into triangles as he looked beyond the main window, trying desperately to work it all out...and failing. He knew he was missing something very important, but he couldn't figure out what? His mind was cornbread. Nothing computed. One second...space, then *here.* When he described it, it sounded like the delusion of someone in desperate need of medication. For Abby it was way too much to take in. She felt light-headed and faint

Everywhere Harry looked was a blur. Light streamed in from the front and the sides, creating a reactor of bright white light they were powerless to penetrate in any direction. NASA used acrylic plastic in Orion windows rather than glass, and they conveyed light and heat even better than glass. Harry and Abby were surrounded by light and plastered by it. Everywhere in the cabin, it was blinding.

What they underwent had an overwhelming sense of unreality to it. Abby felt like she'd knocked her head on concrete, which left her dazed and concussed - having no idea about much at all. Thoughts and questions were just impulses. Abby closed her eyes and loosened her restraints, hit by nausea in sour waves that competed with an ache in her stomach and a loud ringing in her ears.

Abby tried to right herself, pulled her toes tight, to breaking point, and opened her eyes wide, knowing she was somewhere she probably shouldn't be. Her first sight was Harry trying to awkwardly extract himself from his own chair. Abby grabbed his hand firmly and he returned the grip this time. She was terrified of being left alone and hung onto Harry tightly and looked deeply into his eyes. Harry could see the panic in her teary eyes.

Wherever he was going, she wanted to go too. The thought of being alone, wherever she was, terrified her. Despite her attempts to hang on, Harry loosened her grip and made his way toward the main hatch of Orion. He was determined to find out where they were. He knew any answers lay in that direction. Abby's preferred direction of movement was opposite to Harry. She felt like hiding.

Outside, was something she had no words for. It wasn't Earth. The plants she could see were loosely Earth-like in morphology but almost *black* in colour. Ever since she was a little girl, she wondered about non-humans, was terrified by dreams of their black eyes, had seen innumerable TV shows about them...now it was totally fucking real. She was an astronaut and she was somehow on another fucking world. Because of non-human tech that she had no idea about.

There was a line of beings coming toward Orion and not only did they look odder than odd, they appeared to be firm in their direction of travel. They were clearly coming to inspect their little sailing ship. These creatures were clearly part of the group who brought them here.

Abby's heart was banging like a bass-drum against her larynx. *'Fuck',* she thought, watching them come closer. She could hear the noise of their approach, like a herd of Wildebeest. Unconsciously, she looked around the cabin for a weapon to defend herself.

'Jesus' shit, Harry...they're, er...not human,' Abby yelled as she ran behind her chair and hid. She continued to utter curse words as she dug herself in deeper but could still see out of the main window. *'Shit,* they're coming straight for us,' she said, double-taking and ready to cry. Abby saw death closing in.

Harry saw Abby move quickly and hide but hiding or panicking wasn't the answer. 'I think they know we're here Abby,' Harry said calmly to her, trying to keep sarcasm out of his voice.

What she did was understandable. He felt like hiding too, but knew it'd do no good. Orion was small. Harry knew they and the Orion weren't here because of an accident. They were brought here for a good reason – Harry just hoped the "good reason" was benevolent.

Harry wondered about a lot of things, but front and centre was the air and pressure out there. By the movement of the beings he'd seen, gravity was similar, but was there an oxygen atmosphere out there? He assumed so, they appeared to respire like humans, but he really didn't know.

There was a loud banging on the Orion hatch. Eventually, after a lot of it, Harry tentatively cracked the hatch open and moved back. He expected almost anything from the welcoming party who might be hostile. But, he had the unwavering belief that they wouldn't bring us here just to watch us flinch and spasm and die in an oxygen poor or poisonous ether. He hoped to God he was right.

Harry was assuming their thinking was similar to humans. Xeno-psychology was a big fat unknown, he conceded that, so their reasons for bringing us here was totally unknown. Equating them with humans was just plain wrong. Potentially, they may have brought us here to *watch* us die. Humans had to acknowledge that possibility. The mind-set of these non-humans was a total unknown. The slightly open door, caused no decompression, so that was a good start, Harry thought. The rest would be just guess-work.

Harry knew he wasn't on Earth. He also knew he needed to answer the knocking properly, or it would likely get worse. The hatch was partly open, so they might just come in. It was up to him, but it was pre-supposing that his traumatised legs would work, which he doubted. They'd both been to hell and back.

What he saw out there nearly made him collapse in morbid slobbering terror. With bulging eyes, he took a step or two back, so he was hard up against the superstructure of Orion. At just arms-length, were a line of creatures that were all looking closely at him and his craft. They had black eyes and bobbing heads, huge wide eyes and they seemed to be displaying what looked like extreme curiosity.

Some of them appeared fearful and crouched silently in the background, not keen to engage. Others seemed emboldened and stood very close to Harry. They assessed and prodded him with wide-open eyes and six pendulous fingers, hooting and chattering while they did it. All of them hailed from a different solar system.

Thankfully, the air was okay to breathe. Harry was inhaling it and he felt physically fine, although psychologically he wasn't sure. Close to him was less of a line of beings and more of a general approach. Several of the creatures were at arms-length and inching closer, looking directly at him, like they were inspecting a test-tube growth. Their eyes were huge and their pupils small and focussed. Some were so close he could smell them – an unpleasant farmyard odour.

Soon, he was scared, they'd be all over him. Harry needed support. He didn't want Abby to come outside because he was sure she wouldn't cope, but he didn't want to do this by himself. They were inspecting him like a pathogen.Harry needed someone else for them to gawk at. He felt alone. If this was first contact, he needed help. The bobbing heads continued to inspect and poke him. Some of them had a brilliant yellow crest, that seemed to come from the back of their necks and extend over their heads.

They were all standing upright, and were humanoid and very similar...of the same species and genus no doubt. All of them were wearing green trousers, very similar to cargo pants and loose collarless tops of various colours, but mainly red. That's where the similarity to humans stopped. *Their clothing.*

Harry was stunned and a little sickened by their appearance, but tried desperately not to show it. That was the least he could do. He looked back at Abby, who was still inside the craft and looked mortified.

He could just see her face, peering from behind her seat. She was in no hurry to join the horror-show outside. She was happy to remain crouched and safe behind her chair. Abby would leave it to Harry to do the initial introductions. He was the mission-commander and pilot afterall. That said, she was terrified for him. He was much more than a Mission-Commander to her. Abby knew that Harry had no idea, but she had feelings for him. She would never say anything, in a work environment. Not even in downtime. Reciprocation was one worrying item - she didn't want to make a fool of herself.

Abby combed the back of her hair with her fingers and gazed at poor Harry, squashed hard-up against Orion, and surrounded by a pack of horrific non-human things. They were pushing at him and prodding with long, slender fingers. No doubt they were the reps of a civilisation that lived on this planet, that wanted to meet us. Abby realised she was one of the two lucky ones. Strange thing was, she didn't feel lucky at all. The exact opposite, really.

Harry tried desperately to lead by example, but it was so hard just to look at them without wincing. He realised this was first contact, so not appearing terrified was critical. Most of them didn't seem scared of him, so that was a good start, he thought. They might have been humanoid, but they looked nothing like your average human. Harry wouldn't choose to meet them at any time of the day. Mr Hyde or Frankenstein had little on this lot, Harry reckoned.

These creatures had huge and intricate ears...multi-panelled lobes of flesh with near-surface, bloated blood vessels which followed the line of the head and didn't protrude far outward. Neanderthal-like thick brows had two eyes that were set deeply within, giving them an aggressive look from the get-go. Heads were fairly flat on top and hairless but extended backward a long way, providing a "big-headed" look, and most had a narrow depression or a divot right on top.

Their bodies were sort of like ours except they had standout ropy muscles, which probably extended beneath the clothing as well. Hands were overly "busy" with six thin and long fingers and a thumb, and feet were hidden by large, high boots so anything was possible with their feet.   Overall, they didn't present as a handsome race to the human eye...both Harry and Abby found them repulsive to look at. hey were humanoid but Harry supposed Frankenstein was humanoid too.

Harry realised Abby hadn't emerged from the craft yet. It was time, he thought but she didn't seem to want to move – she was nauseous, fatigued, and couldn't keep her eyes open. Outside was a terrifying version of the Twilight Zone. This wasn't why she joined NASA. Abby wasn't fascinated by "other" life, like many at NASA.

She wanted in with NASA because of their hugely respected name and the fact that they paid rather well, especially if you went into space. She also enjoyed the work-life of an astronaut. And it kept her parents quiet. The lectures by her employer about "other life" were treated as highly rhetorical by Abby. She never thought they would apply to her. Yet, somehow, they ended up being pertinent. Non-humans incredibly, ringed the entire craft, seemingly waiting for her to exit the craft. Then, she knew, they'd be like bugs to a light.

She'd seen what was going on out there and the nightmare Harry had to contend with, and wanted none of it. Harry saw her peering through the starboard window with huge and terrified eyes, hidden by the co-pilot's chair. The poor girl looked mortified and teary. She knew what was out there waiting for her, so she desperately wanted something solid between her and the outside world.

If this was first contact, she wanted nothing to do with it. She was happy to leave it to Harry. Abby was certain that her revulsion and dread would just make effective contact more difficult.

'Abby...you might wanna come out here,' Harry shrilled, to be certain she'd hear him. Harry knew they meant no harm - she couldn't put it off forever. These creatures knew she was in there. They'd come looking for her eventually, and that could end in abject disaster.

After more coaxing and encouragement, and knowing she couldn't avoid it forever, Abby cautiously emerged from her hiding place. She tentatively stood up, exited Orion, and inched along the spacecraft to nervously stand next to Harry, knowing what terrors were in store for her. She opened her eyes and saw the creatures, bobbing their heads near Harry, and looking at her hungrily.

Abby stared at Harry and saw the heart-rending tenderness of his gaze. He was clearly concerned about her, when he should be worried about himself. The realisation that Harry really liked her, hit Abby in the chest with the force of a kick. Harry licked his lips and gave her a yearning look. Now, she knew.

The creatures were closing in on both of them. What started as a fairly straight line was now a broken, free-for-all. Abby saw many of the bobbing-heads were angling toward her. She was horrified by them all. They were looking at her, bobbing their heads, seemingly knowing she was female, waiting for what, she wasn't sure. Abby had shifted her gaze solely to their nodding heads, and was gasping for breath, and covering her face with her hands, in a visual display that didn't augur well for open-minded first contact.

Mind you, Harry thought, they didn't make it easy by being so in your face. Surrounded by non-humans was one thing. But the crowd of them was verging on the ridiculous. Probably the last thing she expected to happen, when she embarked on this mission. They were sent to analyse a friggin' asteroid. This was far throw from that.

Harry reckoned it was fair enough to be curious, but this was way over the top. Harry didn't know who was wrong or who was right, so he just went with it. Poor Abby, he thought, she was trying to be brave, but the lead being kept poking her, which made the her cringe and moan. She was calling his name, as if he could do anything about it. The touching and feeling, which tended to centre on Abby, was thankfully slowing - seemingly, they'd had their fill. Harry felt like sweeping in and helping Abby, but knew it was the wrong thing to do.

The tallest being came forward and looked directly at Harry, and tilted his head in his face and wiggled the flesh where a human nose would ordinarily be. *This'll be good*, Harry reckoned, trying to comprehend their movements and language. He was sure none of it would be any better than utter gobbledegook. Language was just so much qualitative and personal diatribe, he thought. So, he expected everything to follow to mean nothing.

Harry automatically squeezed himself further back on Orion...waiting for the noise and the creatures to envelop him. Harry gazed at the creature and waited for him to "speak". Hopefully, he'd use his paws to "tell" him something. He knew basic body language was all he could rely on as long as it was obvious. Harry exhaled and conceded their body language might be very different indeed.

'Please follow me,' he or she or it said, in perfect slightly high-pitched English. Harry glanced at Abby with huge sparkling eyes, '*huh?*' He shouted, totally bemused. '*English*? You must be *fucking joking.*' Harry whispered to Abby, looking at the ground, which was rough like bitumen...but bright red. He whipped his head up and gawked incredulously at the creature. His eyes were so wide, they threatened to rupture. His eyebrows almost went under his fringe. *WTF*, he thought, gaping at Abby.

'*H-How could you p-possibly speak English?*' Harry yelled. It was impossible, wasn't it? That was a *human* language...and, um...totally arbitrary, he thought. What was going on? How could an alien race be fluent in it? Harry stared at the creature, and felt like he was wobbling on the edge of a deep chasm. If it wasn't for Orion behind him, he would have fallen to the ground in deep shock, and probably passed out.

The alien told Harry he was part of the Werinn people and this was their planet. The creature spoke perfect English. *What the hell was going on here?* Harry felt like screaming. They'd obviously intercepted our TV EMAR but that didn't explain perspective.

The Creature's wide cleft mouth caused a slurring of S-sounds, but he was eminently understandable. Harry again wondered how they did it. It wasn't like our language was based on mathematics - it was totally arbitrary. So, the basis of their linguistic abilities was unknown.

The creature pointed, so Harry and Abby, without a reason to say no, walked behind him, until they came to a green pyramidal structure. That was their destination apparently. They were left by themselves in a plain room, with a floor that was a deep blue color and soft, but not made of carpet as you'd expect on Earth. Looking more closely, by tipping his chair, Harry decided it was more like something you'd grow not engineer. *'Whatever'*, he thought, focus on the beings, details about their environment could come later.

No effort had been made to make them feel comfortable. It was just the humans, and three triangular walls, covered by a very fine-grained colour. There was no furniture or pictures or chairs or *anything*. Abby wondered if pictures, and table and chairs, ornaments and curios, were a human thing only. It didn't make human sense for it to be so empty.

Four of the Werinn came back in, each carrying two chairs and a short device, resembling a weapon of some kind. The chairs were made of glass or maybe acrylic. There was ornate patterning around their sides. The humans were glad there was something to sit on, and something to break-up the emptiness of the room.

Why were these beings bearing arms so visibly, if they were weapons, which they appeared to be, Harry and Abby wondered grimly. The weapon-things had a short muzzle, no front sight, a short grip, no hammer or cylinder and clearly didn't shoot anything as prosaic as a bullet.

The people of this planet seemed to be expecting trouble of some sort, which was strange at such a generous first meeting. Both of them were more on guard than they had been. What did they think we were going to do? And why?

For whatever reason – the Werinn didn't trust humans. Abby deduced as she reached and loosened her top. The Werinn visibly stiffened, becoming ready for action. Harry could see they were extremely wary of humans. There seemed to be almost no good-faith in the way humans were treated, which was odd.

Every move made by a human was carefully assessed and caused the Werinn to become rigid in their chairs and ready for action. The Werinn were waiting for something combative to happen – hence, the weapons. This was supposed to be first contact. The initial get-together and benevolent meeting. To say hello. Not a *fucking* showdown. It was very odd behaviour indeed.

The weapons they brought in looked like laser or plasma devices - Harry reckoned. They were transparent and certainly didn't shoot bullets. Harry could see what he thought were beam optics inside the breech. *Why* they brought them here was another question entirely. Were they really expecting trouble? At the initial get-together? They were clearly missing something important.

If this was their first encounter with humans, it made it even more bewildering. What did they know about other civilizations, that humans didn't? Trepidation and doubts were growing in Harry that had no place in a meeting like this.

Despite himself, his own wariness grew and he could tell, Abby was already on guard. These creatures had managed to get both sides uneasy and suspicious. So much for good-will and altruism, Harry thought.

Both races sat down next to each other. Abby still had huge trouble looking at them without shuddering and was unconsciously looking at the floor. Harry was doing better but he had his own problems. He was drawn to their ears and the way they encircled the large, flat head that had no hair – not even stubble. He had to force himself to make eye contact.

The Werinn sitting next to him, suddenly sat taller and stiffer in their seat. Somehow, they knew what was coming. Their leader was about to speak.

'My name is Oshn,' the tall-being said in English, 'with me is Rsha, Padna and Hunsa, we speak English, Mandarin, Russian and Spanish from your world.'

Abby was squirming in her seat, and generally looking uncomfortable while Oshn was talking.

'*B-But how?*' Abby asked, the pain of absurdity smeared all over her face. 'How could you do that? She said agog, sounding more like a groan

'We've spoken long about having to use body language to describe very basic concepts...and now *this*', Harry gasped. 'You speak our languages.' Harry jerked his head back and took a gusty sigh, as if their cogency with English was unbelievable.

Oshn sat very still and silent for almost a minute before breaking into incredibly clear English. 'If there is any *offence*, I apologise in advance.' Oshn said, emphasising "offence" by fairly yelling it and gazing at all the humans in turn. His ability to speak English was way more than either expected in their most colour-soaked dream. Both Harry and Abby thought it'd be a two-way fest of body language - facial expressions and finger-use to make the simplest of points. Abby was worried and confused by his use of the word "offence". It didn't sound hopeful.

Abby looked at Oshn, and noticed that his ears had dropped, so that the ends of his ears were below his neck. Normally, they were erect, and in line with the head. The change was dramatic, and came with stony eyes. Abby reckoned he was angry. It definitely appeared to be an *uh-oh* moment, especially when it was combined with his warning. How bad could it be though Abby thought - we'd just met them. They didn't even know us...yet.

Any problems or issues should come way later, surely? Harry thought about it and reckoned it had to be minor, or a generalisation, perhaps.

He addressed Harry and Abby more formally and gave a small cough like a human. Oshn inhaled deeply and gave the impression of determination. 'Welcome to Werinn.' He said graciously. 'Our world is eleven light years from your planet and we have known about you for some time. Your television and radio, unlike ours, is not shielded, so we know a lot about your world. Mankind and your planet have been known to us for a long time.' Oshn coughed again and yawned straight after, a very unusual look indeed. Werinn body language was unknown to humans. So, drawing conclusions from it was dangerous, because it'd probably be wrong.

Oshn gazed at Harry bitterly and made him jump with fright when he continued talking abruptly. 'We were coming to Earth several of your decades ago,' Oshn said. 'Using our space shortening vessel. We stopped at Mars in your solar system to get some data about humans from your Mars Telecommunications Satellite. We did so with our lasers. Our craft sensed the data and identified that it might be of some value to us. So, we exited the forward corridor, and retrieved it.' Oshn stopped and took a rib-stretching breath.

'We encountered your human internet for the first time and got a lot of information about you, that we didn't expect to get. By the time we almost arrived at Earth, we turned around and returned to Werinn. We were troubled by what we read, and decided we shouldn't make contact with humans. We considered that at this time in your history, humans were a very dangerous race. Based on the behaviour we read about. *Too dangerous* to get close to.' Oshn stopped talking and rubbed an eye by dragging a large knuckle over it.

Oshn stared at the humans one by one with eyes that were huge and bloodshot...Abby looked away, at the floor. Harry didn't blame her. Oshn had taken on the form of a demonic teacher, soaring above them, not ten feet away. He had clearly riled himself up - a white membrane briefly covered his eyes and a hidden brilliant yellow crest appeared from his lower cranial area.

It was all over in a few seconds. Oshn returned to his normal appearance, which was *anything* but normal, for a human.

Harry was stunned and speechless – he didn't think the story of humans was bad at all. In fact, he reckoned it was pretty bloody good. What were the Werinn talking about – it didn't make any sense. The medical achievements, art, space industries, Declaration of Human Rights, the Olympics, United Nations, works of William Shakespeare, Da Vinci, cultural masterpieces, tech generally, Eistein, civilisation itself. What the *fuck* were the Werinn talking about?

Harry sat in his chair and gasped in utter astonishment at what he'd just heard. Stunned at the ridiculousness of Oshn's contention, and dazzled just to be here at all, and be witness to this extraordinary and at times, bizarre display. Both Harry and Abby struggled to believe they were really here, *actually* doing this. Not long ago, they were in Florida on Earth, doing very Earthly things like shopping, flying and exercising.

Even though NASA told them repeatedly, that any of their journeys into space could lead to them being "the chosen one" who was involved in "first contact" no-one who worked for NASA believed they'd be going far enough for that to be a remote possibility. They were certain NASA was just going through the motions, and keeping them motivated.

The sterile observations made by Earth, together with the absence of repeat narrow-band radio signals, suggested that non-human intelligence was either absent entirely, or at best, exceptionally rare. Turns out that the latter was probably right.

The Fermi paradox was no more, thanks to Aragon, and was replaced by a more frustrating and cryptic paradox, if that was possible. We'd found them, but they didn't want to know us. Our history was not to their liking. It was baffling and ridiculous. They claimed we were *dangerous*. We could argue with them, but if the "eye of the beholder" says we are dangerous, then it is true.

Oshn hadn't finished yet. He looked suddenly very serious. His eyes came together and his brow and ears moved down again, giving him a very grave air. His eyes shone yellow like a black Jaguar. Abby gulped, she supposed this was where the "offence" bit came in.

Oshn started out severely with nuggety, hostile eyes that narrowed alarmingly. '*The brutality and enslavement of African people*,' Oshn said vehemently, critically, and loudly, glaring at Harry, 'the genocide of native people in America and Australia, murder, genocide and ethnic cleansing during the Inquisition and the Crusades, and the 1940's. The killing fields of Cambodia, the world wars, Vietnam, Korea, the Middle-East. Burning people alive, murdering children and babies. Killing animals en-masse for food, shooting them, maiming, even of endangered species. Neanderthal Man was only made extinct because they battled with humans over food and territory.' Oshn stood tall and glared at Harry angrily, then Abby. All Abby could think about was "offence". Pretty hard to take offence when it was all true. It was part of history. But it was old news...ancient stuff that they taught at Schools and colleges now.

'*THEN*,' Oshn said with great emphasis. Harry gulped and wondered who in God's name he thought we were? We weren't responsible for these abominations. Then the penny dropped like a lead weight. We were human, so we were part of it. *Responsible*. Oshn loomed over them and angrily continued.

'There are the current newspapers which are full of violence and stories of crime and killing across your planet. Your world is savage and brutal, and your species makes it so. Only the strong, rich or powerful prevail. The rest just make up the numbers.

'And there is no reason for any of it,' Oshn spat accusingly. 'Millions starve in Africa for *no* reason – there is enough food and room for everybody on Earth to thrive. It is the fault of government and world systems which allow avaricious, rich persons to take too much, leaving nothing or insufficient for everyone else. Your world is full of horror stories to the point where it steeply outweighs all the virtuous things that humans have created. Nearly nine thousand wars speaks for the human race itself really.

Harry felt like arguing, there's no way we've had that many, but he wasn't totally sure. No doubt, we've had a lot. Harry was worried – if he argued the point, it could escalate out of control. Oshn didn't strike him as someone who would back down, or change his mind. So, Harry sucked it up. Because Oshn *could* be right.

'There were wars occurring now, that are probably still on-going.' Oshn said furiously, grimacing and frowning darkly at Harry and Abby. The inference was that humanity was aggressive and barbaric, and without basic morals. Pretty hard to argue, Harry reckoned, it was all on the record. For an interstellar species to read it, and shove it all in our face and make the claims it was making. And humans couldn't argue – it was part of our history...detailed on our own internet. *Fuck*, Harry thought, we'd shot ourselves in the foot big time. We'd detailed it...and the Werinn had read it.

Harry's head was in his hands and he felt mentally numb. He glanced at Oshn, 'Well...yeah there's that,' he said. It was hard to argue with truth, when it's staring you in the face. It's not as if we could do anything about history. Harry was confused and shook his head – what did Oshn expect Mankind or him to do about it? Maybe he was just pointing it out – but that seemed odd too.

This was *first contact* - hardly the time to talk about foibles. Pointing out weaknesses in our history. Harry remembered we were still doing it – still declaring war. So that probably made it worse. Both Harry and Abby had a bad feeling – they or he wouldn't point out these issues to pump humanity up. Clearly, the Werinn were highlighting it for a good reason. And the good reason was likely bad for humanity.

Oshn said, 'I'm sure you, yourself are not like that – but your species as a whole is; it is written in your history. Even though your space industries are peaceful now, it won't last long. Your species seemingly only advances by using warfare and killing as a tool. We counted five thousand wars, humanity had inflicted on itself, before we made the difficult decision not to contact Earth. We started the process to turn the spaceship around.' There was little doubt that Oshn was disappointed with the nature of their first interstellar visitor. He wanted us to be different, to have a benevolent history like the Werinn had.

That pointed toward a peaceful future. That the Werinn could get close to, as a friend.

Oshn looked down at the floor. He was opening and closing his mouth without making any noise. He cleared his throat and then continued speaking. 'There are many more conflicts...we stopped looking during the 1400's.'

Harry stared at Oshn and met his accusing eyes without flinching. He didn't agree with the Werinn. Harry knew he couldn't argue with history, but humanity's endeavours in space were exploratory only. Of course, we couldn't guarantee that it would last, but right now, it was purely pacifist exploration for exploration's sake. In his view, it was unfair to extend their warring on Earth into space.

To say it would eventually become aggressive and hostile was too much. The Werinn couldn't know that definitively. History would suggest that though. That was the problem, Harry supposed - they *might* be right. He looked back at Oshn's bobbing head and large eyes and felt like throwing his arms in the air, giving up and agreeing, *but he couldn't*. As far as he was concerned and he knew Abby agreed, *history was history*. The Werinn disagreed, vehemently. For them, history was everything. It pointed to behaviour in the future.

Oshn said, 'We'd read more than enough to make a decision about your world. Mankind reverts to war...invasive imperialism to advance and to "get ahead". Our history is nothing like yours, yet we are in front of you in tech and understanding of the Universe after comparable amounts of time. You make frequent claim in your internet, that warfare was "good" for humanity generally. The Werinn civilisation themselves are evidence that it is not. If we made contact with humanity and set up a cooperative alliance, there is little doubt that you would eventually treat us the same way.' Oshn glared at Abby and then Harry, eyeballing Padna, then continued in the same vein, bitter, exasperated and furious. Harry gazed at Abby and was disconcerted to see her chin trembling and her eyes full of tears. He grabbed her hand, nodded and smiled disarmingly at her. She was taking the assault very personally indeed.

He knew the Werinn were holding Abby and him responsible only because we were human and there were no other people here. Harry nodded crisply at Abby, to let her know that he was with her, to support her, and looked back at Oshn, who continued to criticize. Harry knew there was nothing he could do for her, until the big Werinn had finished speaking.

'There would eventually be war between our species in space.' Oshn said. 'You currently have no vacuum weapons, but it is our belief that you would soon weaponise your technology and produce them. It is what you do. And we would likely be the losers as we are not schooled in warfare and do not wish to be. Humans are craven and barbaric, and would run over us in any confrontation. The Werinn do not have the mind-set for war. Humans clearly do. We readily concede that.' Oshn stopped talking and drew in a quick breath and continued rapidly.

'So, we spoke seriously about withdrawing the shift on the asteroid you called 'Aragon'. Ultimately, we didn't because we considered the work to run the asteroid down wasn't justified. We believed that meeting a few of you on our own planet was acceptable. We didn't consider it an uncontrolled risk. We made the call, and it was accepted by our Union.'

Harry was certain he was red in the face, same as Abby, who was the colour of blood. He felt swelteringly hot and covered by sweat, wiping it away with his hand the moisture on his shining forehead. Harry was a little embarrassed, taken aback, and felt like his ears were on fire. He thought how unfair and biased it all was. Instead of being hailed for a stable and highly creative civilisation, we were decried because of the way it evolved. Warfare was a way of life for humans. Abby gazed at Harry and sighed deeply. She swallowed heavily and shook her head, dismayed that it had come to this unexpectedly horrible ending.

When talking and negotiation break down, the next step for humans is aggression and war. For the Werinn, they never get to that stage. Negotiation breakdowns are referred to a global Court, whose decision binds all parties. Clearly, the Werinn were a completely different species and psychology, because that would never work on Earth. Humans were far too aggressive, stubborn, and yes, violent.

What Oshn said was right though, there was no excuse for so much warfare. Harry had never thought of it before. Probably because his family and friends were shielded from current wars and really had no idea about wars and battles of yesteryear. But it was real...and true. What the Werinn said was true. Anyone who knew our history in detail would balk at becoming friends with us. We were the "toughie", known for starting fights and generally being super-aggressive. Few wanted a bully for a friend. Certainly, the Werinn didn't.

Once your reputation is tainted, like humanity's - it's almost impossible to rectify or redeem it. History was history. *It's written.* Quite simply, we'd engaged in too much war and too many battles. Billions of humans had been killed, marking Mankind forever. Just read the Earthly internet, the Werinn said.

Harry mulled it over and came to the only realistic conclusion, and he didn't like it. *Mankind wasn't like that.* Surely, it couldn't be true, could it? Harry had never considered it – but it could actually be truthful, after what Oshn had said. It all made sense – and Harry didn't like it one bit.

Harry was mortified, for anyone who knew our history, we could be well and truly on the Galactic outer. Everyone else would talk about us, even too us, but no-one would truly make friends. We weren't to be trusted. Warfare and killing was only an argument away...*'just look at their history'*.

Most on Earth thought that our history was irrelevant to whomever we managed to locate in the Great Wide Open. Our biggest challenge would be communication, which most were certain would be non-verbal. That was totally and utterly wrong, from beginning to end. History was very relevant – which was fair enough. We, as humans, just didn't understand it. You didn't want to embark on a new relationship that might seriously backfire, to the point where your entire population was at risk. And communication wasn't a challenge at all – thanks to the internet.

In any event, it was what it was...it crafted what we were today – the medical advances, Art, the Olympics and the advances in technology and computing. It wasn't all warfare and killing and the Werinn should see that. It was innovation, discovery and creation as well. But the Werinn saw humanity's penchant for warfare and destruction in capital letters, overwhelming everything else.

Changing the human mindset was nigh on impossible and attempts to do so would be useless. Humans were what they were. Warfare was permanently imprinted on our history and was endemic to our thinking. If some didn't like it – there wasn't a whole lot we could do about it. Keep it hidden, Harry reckoned, which meant no internet for anyone. Harry knew how impossible that was.

Oshn looked at Abby with an expression approaching empathy, because he could see her pain. His eyes relaxed and his features softened. 'Some of our race believe we are looking in too much detail.' Oshn said gently. 'They say if you just look at the highlights, it remains an impressive rise to technology. The discovery of fire about a million years ago, led to your Neolithic revolution, and then irrigation, the production of iron, discovery of gunpowder, building, and use of windmills, the magnetic compass et. Cetera and so on, up to the internet and the space industry.' Oshn's features hardened into animosity.

'*But*...you can't paper over the very real problems,' Oshn said heatedly. 'Yes, the rise to technology and quantum understanding, at a high level, was impressive, but the number of humans and animals killed was totally unreasonable and entirely out of proportion to your gains. I'm sorry, but your species is viewed as *uncivilised* by our world. Mankind is too aggressive and vicious, compared to the Werinn.

Oshn pulled his ears down, and spoke, trying his best to keep his head still. 'For your own safety,' he said, 'you will need to leave this world. We have made contact, which is important to both species, but now we will need you to go.'

Harry started to protest but could see that Oshn was under strict direction from the Ruling body of this planet. Oshn continued to talk over Harry, and was very resolute. He made it clear with his stiff left hand that any rebuttals from Harry weren't going to be accepted. The Werinn had decided that Mankind weren't for them.

Earth and humanity had been heavily tarnished. Harry wasn't sure who was right and who was wrong. For the second time, *doubt* entered Harry's mind – could humanity be the rabid barbarians that the Werinn thought we were? Did blood, death and brutality dominate the growth and evolution of our people? Was Earth's history going to come back and bite humanity on the arse once it was known beyond our planet? Harry felt sick and could hear a loud ringing in his ears. It wasn't just making contact that was important, it was what off-world species thought of us as a civilisation. Mere contact with the Werinn was just the beginning. It was way more complicated than we could have expected. Our own internet had detailed our history too well.

Abby was considering just that. Before there was an internet, an interstellar species wouldn't know anything about us, only how we presented ourselves. Our history would be hidden. But they would know eventually. It was inevitable. Our computers, phones and the internet itself, would give it all away and put a cherry on top. Could it all rise up against us? All our technology? The answer had to be an overwhelming YES.

But would it really happen, especially in space? Humans bore absolutely no weapons in space, and never had. Maybe the Werinn weren't worried about now, but were concerned about the far future.

They'd said as much. Once an imperialist...*always* an imperialist. That was what the Werinn were concerned with. The psyche of humans.

Abby knew that humans had an innate desire to have what the next-door-neighbour has, be it material or not. Sometimes war is declared simply because you think you're better than they are or want to get back at them, *revenge*, or don't like them, or want their assets...*want what they have.* For humans – the motive for war can be very trivial indeed.

Harry's own country was complicit in many wars, he knew that. Some were ill-advised. But the military and NASA were very different and very separate entities even though the space-force was now a thing. Weaponising space had never been spoken of. The space-force was created for administrative purposes, but it didn't bode well for the future. No doubt the Werinn would see it as a prelude to arming it. And they could well be right. No other "Force" in America was unarmed, and existed for altruism only. Food for thought for all humans.

Abby tilted her head and considered it - it wasn't as if the Werinn were wrong – their contention that there were wars and killing and destruction going on today was entirely correct. So, what was the answer to their argument? There wasn't one. Earth and humans had to admit to it, and state honestly, that we didn't take that mind-set into space. But we are what we are. Our history is written. We couldn't argue with the Werinn and against our history.

Harry couldn't deny sometimes humans acted aggressively without justification. In fact, he reckoned, history...the internet, was full of examples. It was either like-us or lump-us, Harry thought. There was nothing we could do about it. It seemed that the Werinn expected an explanation of our passed behaviour – but there wasn't one. It was what it was. Humans did what their psyche dictated - next step – war.

Oshn gazed at Harry curiously, and glanced at Abby. Both the humans could see the issue and their ears were ringing. They both felt like they'd been scolded, which in a strong sense they had been. They were part of the population in question. Oshn didn't yell, but what he said, hit them hard...and it hurt. Oshn was chewing-out Mankind and they took it all personally, as they should. It was meant to be personal.

Abby looked at Oshn's face and shuddered, closing her eyes and admitting that he hadn't lost any of his monstrosity. He appeared to be hopping almost on the spot - like someone's nightmarish vision. Oshn had large black eyes and a bobbing head, like an ostrich, giving the most obdurate human pause, and probably painting Mankind as the juvenile species it was.

Oshn was standing to his full height near Abby, and he bent his upper body to look directly into the eyes of the two humans, like a large and intimidating teacher. He clearly had something to say, and wanted to make sure humans didn't miss it or get it wrong.

'Humans must leave this planet,' Oshn boomed, pointing at them with two of his six fingers. 'I'm sorry, but that is the planet's decision. We brought you here to make contact at our own risk. We have done that. Your craft has been filled with liquid hydrogen and lies just short of our Quantum Cryptograph that will fold space and shift your craft and you back to the asteroid you call Aragon.'

'The asteroid is currently past Venus in your own system, so your planet and your Gateway is within reach of your craft.' Oshn stared at Harry with huge, vacant eyes and shrugged his shoulders, and continued talking. Surprisingly, his shoulder-move seemed a natural one for Oshn – similar to a human movement of indifference.

Oshn glared at Harry, bobbing his head as he spoke. 'We will need a formal consent from your United Nations,' Oshn said loudly, 'stating that there should be no further attempt to contact the Werinn and that humans will require an invitation to the planet, if any human comes within four light-years. This agreement is to be unending.'

Oshn shrugged again, 'Sorry, but this is required by our Union for our world's peace of mind, given your, er...rather turbulent history. The Union demands it. We will pick it up from your Gateway, if you agree.

Harry frowned, bit his lip and looked uncertainly at Oshn. He felt like saying, *you fucking what?* Harry knew he couldn't *disagree*. 'Er...yeah, fine, if that's what you require, won't be a problem, I don't think.' Abby nodded rapidly in agreement. Turned out that the Werinn could read human minds, so everything the humans knew, the Werinn did too.

Abby staggered a couple of steps backward and her eyes were wide, a bit shocked and saddened by the proximity request. She was a little uncomfortable with the whole saga. That the history of humans was laid out naked and viewed as "unacceptable" to the extent that the Werinn rejected humans as friends. And demanded a formal juxtaposition agreement was very troubling. It was something Earth didn't expect or even remotely foresee.

Abby's eyes were downcast as she heard Oshn's rather harsh words. To think, she thought - w*hat COULD have been?* The Werinn could have been a great friend and advocate, being the first, and being so advanced, but all their knowledge and technology, and there was a lot, that they probably would have shared with humanity, was reduced to a pipe-dream by our *history*. Humanity would now get *nothing.* It was a dreadful outcome.

With that, a group of four large and tall Werinn came to escort them to their craft. The voice behind them was loud and clear. 'Show them a house first – mine.' Oshn finished speaking and threw a load of very thin cards to the leading guy, who caught and pocketed them, with his left hand, like a sportsman.

Harry wouldn't have been surprised if he was just that – he had broad shoulders, arm muscles and a square jaw, like a QB. But that's where the resemblance to a human stopped. If he stepped foot on the grid, a packed stadium in LA would empty in five minutes. Such was the nature of Earth. Physical form was everything.

'Okay then...please follow me,' he said, flourishing an arm to walk along with him. Harry didn't know his name because he didn't introduce himself. Still, he and Abby fell into step behind him because the request seemed reasonable. They followed and walked through the wall like it wasn't there, and across a red path and along a verge covered with a bluey grass-like substance. Then they entered through the wall of a house, again, like it wasn't there, that was presumably Oshn's residence. By "unlocking" the house, it seemingly freed up the walls as well. Every part of the dwelling was an open door.

Harry gazed at Abby and smiled mercurially at her, cutting his face in half. Abby wasn't nearly as ebullient, looking at Harry with a glassy stare, stunned at what they'd just done, and expecting anything to happen. Her anxiety was maxxing, because front and centre was a *non-human* house. The sky was the limit. They'd witnessed their tech, so *anything* might follow. Abby's skin was tingling and she sucked in a quick breath as she waited for something mind-boggling to materialise before her.

Why they were taken to Oshn's house in particular was anybody's guess. They were told that his house could be unlocked remotely, otherwise, *any* entry would not be possible, they said. Abby took that to mean any entry at all, wall or door, was impossible. Abby glanced at Harry to see what state he was in. Harry was blowing out a series of short breaths and was smiling indiscriminately at everyone. He too, was beset with anticipation.

Oshn's house was disappointingly empty – just four prosaic white walls, a blue carpet-like floor, and no furniture or tech in the first room and there were only two rooms, that they could see. Hopefully it got way better from here, although the line of beings seemed to have come to a stop in this room. They were waiting for something, or someone perhaps.

Abby looked around the room and thought it was unusually dreary, which surprised her. She expected to be amazed and dumbfounded – but it seemed to be the exact opposite. She was annoyed, sighing heavily. Why bother bringing us here if there is nothing to see? She expected something mind-blowing, that would really show us what wonders we were foregoing by being shunned. Instead, we seemingly got very little. Oshn was determined that we see his house – he threw his key-cards with a high degree of excitement, and then *this*. What did we get in the first room – three blank triangular walls. '*Wow*'.

The large Werinn held something small in his hand and pressed a button quite deliberately. One entire wall, side to side, became a high-definition television screen and out of the wall behind them was pulled a kitchen, replete with cooking utensils, devices, white-goods, table and chairs. Before that, the wall was entirely blank. He then put it back in the wall again with a flicking motion using his hand. *Wallah*...the house was empty again.

On Earth, we used the motion to flick from scene to scene on a phone...here it was used to arrange houses and keep them tidy and secure. Harry and Abby were both frozen to the spot and watched the goings-on with eyebrows that almost reached their hairline. This was more like it, she reckoned, with popping eyes, waiting, excited for more, watching with unbridled fascination. *Dimensions*, Abby thought.

'We can do the same thing with bedrooms and the rest of the house,' the leading guy said, who seemed keen to talk with Harry. 'Laundry, toilet and living rooms. When you leave a house, everything folds back into the wall. This is new technology and came as a spin-off of biological teleporting and folding space.' The large Werinn continued to make the flicking motion with his paw, showing the humans how he did it. '*Amaaaaaazing*,' Abby piped.

'Everything is cleaned by automation,' the Werinn said, 'including clothes...we use AI which is provided free of cost to our people. The days of cleaning and washing have been over on our world for some time. You have forgone a lot of technology – by fighting,' he said. 'Wars and battles have held you back significantly. Putting the aggression aside, and the loss of life, building assets of war takes a lot of time and uses a lot of resources - and so does war itself. Time and resources that can be far better used on other pursuits. Recovering from war causes a long hangover too.'

'Overall, war and aggression have held you back. Judging from your internet, you seem to believe that war aids economic growth and stability of economies. You are wrong.' The large creature shook his head in dismay, just like a human.

'*We* are your comparison, our world...the Werinn have never had a single war. And we are noticeably in front of you. Humans are yet to formulate a GUT – until you do this, the gap between us will continue to widen. Like you, we are two hundred thousand years old, yet we have made advances well beyond humans. Remember, we have your internet, and we can read you, so what you know, we know. So, we know all we need to.' The large creature continued to gaze at Abby long after he stopped speaking, looking like he was trying to work her out.

They were moved across what looked like a red street. Abby and him both saw the house they'd just come from and those that were lined up along the "street". Every one of them was pyramidal in shape. They all had polygonal faces of various heights. Harry's interest was piqued, *why the hell were they all that shape?* He asked himself silently. There had to be a reason. He really wanted to see a "city" building, to see if the profile carried over. Climate, geology, defense, or economy weren't the likely reason for this shape. Looking down the crimson "street" and seeing the uniformity of house shapes, Harry was intrigued. Everything in sight was three-sided.

The one thing Abby had to know was how the house she'd just left worked. Was it compressed by dimensions? Did the Werinn have a comprehension of string theory that actually related to the real Universe? Is that how the house worked? The questions were burning hot in her brain. If she dared to ask, she feared the response. And what then, she wondered? She settled on the GUT as the backbone of the technology, and the main reason humanity didn't have it.

Harry was feeling the same crush of questions and simply *had* to ask about the red stuff on the ground. It was everywhere, and it looked as though something drove and certainly walked on it. There were tracks and dusty Werinn footprints on it. The redness was coarse like bitumen but clearly not that, because it was dark red and a finer texture. Harry looked deliberately at the large Werinn and tilted his head to the side.

'What, er…is this stuff?' Harry kicked at it and his boot stuck to its surface.' It had amazing adhesive properties. He stood there and pointed to it, questioning the huge creature.

The Werinn wondered if he should reply, eyeing his buddy, who shrugged, deciding that he might as well. Abby was shocked to see another Werinn make such an Earthly gesture as shrugging, and gaped at him, to which he smiled broadly. The movement must be pretty common on Werinn. Was it *their* body language, or ours, learned from the internet, or TV? Abby averted her eyes and looked at the ground. Eye-contact with these creatures was still a challenge.

Oshn appeared and walked over saying, 'It is mainly melted and micro-processed plastic which binds the stone aggregate and gives it a distinctive red color, and it doesn't decay. It sucks up a lot of atmospheric carbon, when it dries.'

Harry reckoned they could use it on Earth as long as it had good tensile strength. In the building industry maybe, on roads perhaps. Abby's eyes were drawn to the edge of the redness. She went totally silent and her eyes widened more. Abby knew what they were, but they were very different from those on Earth. What was growing there sort of resembled trees, but were more complex and composite.

The tree-things consisted of fibrous material that was growing parallel to the ground. On Earth trees grew straight up, but here, they grew in oblate circles, one trunk upon the other. These things looked deformed and were around twelve feet high and had grown to that height by one circle of trunk growing on top of another and so on, only reaching that height by the trunk first growing as circles. Looking with an Earth-eye, they looked buckled, or like Bonzai trees. To Abby, they look forced to grow like that, but that's how they grew naturally. Similar, but unmistakeably different to Earth.

Looking at the nearby "forest", which was way darker than on Earth, it seemed that all the trees grew like this. The "trees" in front of Abby were almost black and very dense in their mid-sections, a function of how they grew, and the most efficient colour to extract the most energy from the EMAR of its small red Sun.

The "trees" had black or dark grey chlorophyl - and branches, leaves, fruit and flowers emanated from the bark of these things. They grew from all sides of the strangely shaped trunk, like they did on Earth.

The Werinn then escorted them back to their Orion craft, Harry eventually saying loudly that it was not an atmospheric craft. After being ignored, Harry ended up yelling at one of them, *'it's not a fucking plane,'* to which he received the soft reply that it was "all taken care of". Whatever that meant, he reckoned. Harry was beside himself and ready to throw his hands in the air. No one would listen to him, or bother to give him a decent audience on the vessel's incapability to fly like a plane. *'They should know that,'* he spat to Abby. 'Advanced race indeed,' Harry whispered.

They continued to ignore him and had great confidence that the vehicle would be "fine". This seemed to be another attempt by the Werinn to show their superiority when Orion fizzled in the atmosphere like a skyrocket. Harry explained the problem in detail, and went to pains to describe the capsule's role in Earth's space-industry. He was again waved away and told that "everything had been taken care of". Glaring at the Werinn with flaring nostrils, he gave up, having some inkling of what might be going on. Why don't they just tell us, he wondered angrily? Why the stupid game?

Harry and Abby entered Orion through the side hatch and could smell the fluid that covered their vessel – a potent antiseptic smell. Was Orion de-loused, he wondered? Surely not – bit late for that? They both sat down as if they were getting mission-prepared. Harry had some clue as to what was going down, so did Abby, but both questioned whether it could possibly work.

They had heard it discussed, but positive-lift, was a cartoon-concept back on Earth. Looking out the nadir window at mid-ships, Harry saw a clear cocoon surrounding his Orion. His confidence grew, that this was what they were referring to when they said, "it was all taken care of". He hoped that this was how it was supposed to be. Inside the bubble, they were insulated from the gravity of the planet. He sure as hell hoped so. If that *wasn't* how it worked, they were in serious trouble because their capsule did not boast positive lift.

Harry pressed the RCS icon with his cursor. The "mouse" or CCD transponder was on the left of each seat and near his and Abby's knees. It fitted in your palm nicely and made spaceflight so easy. But they were in the gravity-well of a large planet. We'd do what they said.We had no choice.

After the burn began, the ship behaved like it was in space even though it clearly wasn't. It was still atmospheric, and gravity from the planet incredibly, which was very counter-intuitive, had no effect on

NASA's baby *at all*. Whatever the grainy fluid was and whatever that clear sphere was, it stopped gravity in its tracks. Inside the envelope, they were effectively flying in free "weightless" space. Harry wondered if spacetime was wrapped around them?

Harry was navigating as though he were plying interstellar space. He was stunned and felt his skin tingle and prickle. Orion was weightless and unaffected by the planet's gravity-well. If NASA could see them now – it'd be comical. Pat would flat-out not believe it.

Anti-gravity was only to be dreamt about for homo sapiens. The US government were striving for it, by reverse engineering the tech of non-human craft they'd come to acquire. Their Defence partners had gotten nowhere, because the tech that drove these ships required undiscovered particles. On Werinn, they clearly enjoyed their benefit. Harry dreamed about a world where gargantuan rockets weren't needed to pierce a planet's gravity well, which is exactly the tech that the Werinn already had.

He imagined using positive-lift to boost to orbit and the same to land again. Forget airplanes, *anything* could fly, without wings or other aero-dynamic surfaces. It was a good argument against war. Look at *them* and look at *us*.

The Werinn clearly had a much rounder understanding of physics than humanity. Harry glanced at his co-pilot with an arm clutching his stomach as he gazed around the cabin and witnessed what he considered as the impossible and downright ridiculous.

Abby smiled back at Harry and shook her head, wondering, "what could have been" with the Werinn. We were the ones who lost out, because we had a history littered with violence and aggression. Mankind, with the Werinn's help, could have touched the sky. But now it was just a glimpse of grandeur, followed by a long standing shift in the naughty corner.

After a few minutes they were ready to go, and by the words of the Werinn, they were keen to see human backsides. All the Werinn stood taller with their arms crossed and surveyed the humans closely, taking a step forward *en masse*. It was time-to-leave for the humans and we weren't, as a species, allowed to darken their doorstep again.

Their orders were clearly to get rid of us as soon as they could. The Werinn's Union had decided. It decreed that Homo Sapiens were to be excluded from their world for its own safety.

From their words, the inference was that they were scared of what humans might do. Harry reckoned the Werinn were wrong, because humans were nothing but passive in space. It was just exploration and adventure for science.

But given our history, you couldn't blame them for having concern over our aggression. If you perused human history ou were left with the overall impression of aggression and war. Forget artistic endeavour – overall, it was hostility.

The circuitry to shift to the asteroid was to their left now, it looked like the LHC in cross-section, with metal pipes, rotating parts, wires, tubes, cables, cords and narrow pipes everywhere in a bunch of electronic complexity. Presumably, if they moved past this machine, they would be shifted to the site of the other machine which was buried on the asteroid. Space was folded between here and there apparently...did that invoke a wormhole, Abby wondered?

The machine itself had lit up, and was generating ear-splitting noise, and was clearly "on" and waiting for something to pass it. Abby had images of gene-spliced monsters or inside-out horrors. But maybe true teleportation was not how this thing worked.

Abby stared at the machine like an owl, she was afraid of this thundering device, that now had her total attention. Would it kill them instantly or shift them, she wondered fearfully? Abby knew it shifted them here in the first place so, she guessed, it should be trusted this time. She was deeply unsure and felt panic close.

As long as they get back, she thought. Looking at the machine and its blinking lights made her feel ill, just looking at it. This thing had such potential for horror, she reckoned, and focussed on the whiteness of the floor. Abby waited for it to do its job. She wanted it over with.

Orion was slightly off the ground as it waited to confront the spatial tech of the Werinn. 'Okay,' Harry grunted to himself. They were ready. There was no pull or drag to help them this time, it was all up to Harry, and Orion. RCS was displayed on the screen. Harry hopped onto it and gave Orion a short burn using the CCD. In a few seconds they were back in space and over the dusty pancake that was Aragon. They weren't aware of the shift at all – it just happened. Last time they were unconscious, but this time, not.

They saw everything, which was nothing. The change in view was immediate but this time she saw a flash of a mouth that swallowed them, suggesting that folding space was indeed the method of transmission. Semi-bright became darkness in a flash. Abby expected it but wasn't ready for the almighty change in environments. She went from light to dark, quicker than the internal lights of Orion could respond. The technology dumbfounded her.

Thrusting away from Aragon, Harry ignited MPS and ensured that the onboard tech knew where they were going. Destination was lunar Gateway where they would download to Houston and tell the United Nations what they needed.

Harry wondered if he could even get what the Werinn sought. He'd said "yes" they could get the document, and he still believed he could, because it was logical – but doubts were growing in his mind. On Werinn, he felt positive about it all, but closer to Earth, everything became way more problematic.

As he piloted Orion toward Gateway, Abby was staring and silent, but he had qualms about something else...something much more fundamental. Would *they* be believed? *That* problem again. Harry imagined spinning the story to Jack and getting his over-the-top reaction. Teleportation...*oh shit*, he thought. He didn't know one person on Earth who'd believe that one.

Harry's doubts grew to Statue of Liberty size. He imagined telling Pat from NASA and he threw his arms in the air. He and Abby would be treated as crackpots. He could kiss his future with NASA goodbye...and Abby too. *Teleporting...dimensions* - free up the neoprene room, he reckoned.

Finding non-humans was one thing, but claiming everything else. He could see Pat's face in his mind, dominated by lines of hate and hardness, red questioning eyes. Filling his mind were images that he could've done without. '*Fuck,*' he said to himself, not looking forward to what he knew was coming. Telling NASA about non-humans was one thing, but this was completely different and way harder. Harry knew they had right on their side, but he wasn't sure that was even an advantage. Playing it forward, all he could see was a mountain with slopes that were vertical and a peak that was permanently covered by acidic clouds.

4.

Gateway

"Life would be tragic if it weren't funny."
~ Stephen Hawking

Executing a number of small RCS bursts, Harry lined up Orion with Gateway's docking port. He tapped the front touch-screen a few times then the flight computer took over. The capsule's docking mechanism woke up its counterpart on Gateway. Soft dock was quickly followed by hard dock. Within a minute, the Orion was pulled in and locked in place by twelve motorised latches. There was now a fully pressurised means of safely to enter the Gateway Platform.

Harry and Abby had no idea how they were going to broach it. Harry had decided on an approach, but realised it probably didn't matter how much he practised, and how well he did it. It'd still end in a hostile feud. And by 'feud', he meant being called a liar, a story-teller and worse. Abby and Harry had plenty of time to talk about it and mull it over. But they were no closer to deciding how to do it, because they knew how it'd end, no matter what they did. The concepts, the ideas, the notions, they had already seen in active operation, were simply too much for NASA and Earth to accept. Whichever way they said it, it would sound like fabricated crap. They ultimately decided just to tell them both what happened – step by step. And whatever happened...*happened. Que sera sera.*

It was a simple plan that would probably end with NASA terminating their services, replacing them, and permanently marking their employment records. It'd be goodbye to space for both of them. Again, non-humans were one thing, but...

If Abby heard about it, she wondered if *she* would believe it...or call bullshit and liar. She honestly didn't know. It was a *lot* to believe. What she did know was that believing the whole story was a stretch. I mean non-humans...a teleporter, and a room that hid other dimensions...*yeah right*. It sounded like concocted fantasy. They may as well have read a paragraph from Asimov.

Whatever, they both reckoned, it was what it was. At least *they* knew what was real and what wasn't. They exited Orion and once again entered an untidy Gateway, typical of two guys living there unsupervised for more than fifty days. There were glasses, laptops and papers, dirty plates *everywhere*. Jack and Pete had left Gateway, but with Pete's wife doing better on chemo, were now back. And guess what? NASA was late in replacing them. *Again. C'est la vie.*

'So, um...how did it all go?' Jack said abruptly, Abby could tell, he still held them responsible for him having to be here. He still wanted home with a fierce determination. There was no "how are you" and nothing personal at all. He was straight down to business.

'Er...yeah, fine...*fine*.' Harry glanced at Abby, and she admonished him with smouldering eyes and then showed a flicker of surprise. After all we'd said and what he agreed to, he says we went "fine". That really didn't compute with Abby. She turned her head and frowned at Harry, and Jack picked it up. Abby turned away and muttered something inaudible.

'Okaaaay, what are you *not* saying. You, um...said it was mission success, b-but what else?' Jack was staring at Harry with a questioning gaze, hands on hips, knowing something was being hidden. He knew something was up by Harry's negative body language. Abby too had given it away with her displeasure and stuttering.

Oh, fuck it, Harry thought. He knew they'd been found out...it was time to come clean and he knew it. Harry's heart started pounding fiercely in his chest and throat, and he darted his eyes to Abby. He knew it was time to lay it out naked, come what may. Jack could cut them to pieces, he really didn't care.

'*We...um, made contact Jack.*' Harry said loudly then went quiet to let him chew on that little pearl for a bit. He knew they didn't know a thing about it – JSC were keeping it quiet. Harry knew Pat like the back of his hand.

'Yeah, right Harry...you went to a fucking asteroid.' Pete came in and stood next to Jack who had his hands on his hips. He could tell how red in the face and flustered Harry and Abby both were. They'd clearly been busy doing something.

'Okay...so what'd I miss? Pete said, seeing the harried state of Harry and Abby and an exasperated Jack who still had hands on hips. Jack ignored Pete and continued to grapple with what he assumed was a couple's concerted grab at fame and fortune. He'd been there before and seen it all. Jack expected more from these two though. He shot Harry a scornful smirk and shook his head as if to say, *not you?*

Harry and Abby had discussed it, thrown it around, and thought that the time was nigh. This was the result. A fucking travesty. Blurting it out and getting rebuked. Jack eyed Harry condescendingly this time, hands back on hips. His body language said, *yeah right.*
'Please continue Harry,' Jack said, gesturing with a slow-motion hand, thinking, *I got you.*

Harry gave him a detailed account of exactly what happened to them, from the beginning to the end. 'We were taken to their planet by a shift the Werinn had buried in the asteroid to fold space. That's where JWST found those stunning elements. The Werinn knew about us from the *Mars Telecommunication Satellite*. They downloaded our internet, or at least what it had, which was plenty.' Jack still had his hands on his hips, but he had less of a grip, and his eyes were now glassy as he listened carefully.

Jack turned his head and smiled, then narrowed his eyes to a squint and looked at Harry like a parent, who couldn't believe their child was responsible for such a mess. 'Okaaaay...fine Harry. But how on Earth did they read our language...you said yourself, they were non-human. Our languages are arbitrary, so speaking them is a human only thing surely?'

Jack and Pete were expecting an apology, or at worst, some rabid back-tracking. They got neither. Instead, Harry played it forward. He took a step forward and smiled at Jack. *I got you,* he thought.

'The Werinn have a great capacity to learn. That is the first thing you ought to know. The internet contains many "how to" documents on speaking English, Mandarin, or any language you choose really. They also receive our TV EMAR. They are experts in speaking several Earth languages. They, um, want a document from the United Nations,' Harry said indignantly, 'stating that we won't come within four light-years of the Werinn planet without a specific invite.' Harry paused and sucked in a quick breath that caused the lines on his forehead to grow longer. 'The Werinn will pick up the document from Gateway which will prove our case to you.' Harry gave Jack a curt nod and with a set jaw, looked directly at him, tightening his fists.

Jack's eyes widened to the point of splitting. '*Fuck me'*, he breathed hoarsely. Jack's skin tingled and his thoughts were fuzzy as the reality of finding NHI started to sink in. Harry was nothing but credible and authentic. And his evidence would be eventually indisputable. According to Jack, Harry wouldn't lie barefaced about something that was so eminently verifiable. Apparently, the Werinn *were* coming to Gateway.

Jack was at a loss for words, and mentally numb from what he'd heard. His voice simply refused to work. He moved his mouth but there was no noise. *No voice.* Jack was struggling to believe what he'd just heard, because if it was true, and it appeared to be, it would be the greatest day in his and Earth's life.

Harry was totally believable...but there was no immediate evidence. He had nothing, although he claimed to have photos and analytics on-board Orion. He also said the Werinn were coming to Gateway to pick up the document. *Pretty hard to fake that,* he reckoned.

Jack's demeanour had gone from disinterest and resistance to amazement, from stony-eyed to being focussed like an owl and doing a fist pump and a skip. Harry believed what he was saying – no doubt about it, and Jack could see that. Harry had passed the first test with flying colours.

'Okay,' Jack said hoarsely – 'how the hell are you going to sell it to Houston – just by telling them...*I don't think so.*' Jack drew his eyes together and cleared his throat. He'd watched Harry and Abby carefully, and listened to Harry, and was sold. As far as he was concerned, Harry spoke the truth. They had made contact.

The incredible and the ridiculous were a fact. Jack was a master in body language, and he could tell by their eyes and expressions. Harry was telling the truth...but the next bit was much harder...NASA and Pat were remote.

Their man was Patrick Datsun and he was akin to a bulldog when it came to this subject. If you could convince the Pope that his denomination was Buddhism, you might stand a chance. He'd brought several long termers to tears. Pat was granite, through and through. If what you said was even slightly askew, he would pick you to pieces. And what Harry and Abby intended to say was preposterous and contentious to the max. Abby and he had to tell Pat that they not only detected a non-human intelligence, but also met them, after teleporting to their world. *Holy fuck,* Jack reckoned.

Harry relaxed a bit, 'I-I don't think you fully understand Jack. To get hold of the UN document, they intend to come personally to Gateway, and pick it up. Craft and all.' Harry looked at Jack and offered a thumb. 'So, selling it to Houston will be easy...you'll have CCD video you can send them.'

'*Holy shit...yes,* that'll do it,' Jack boomed, turning around to Pete who was smiling and nodding like a lunatic. Pete nodded back manically. '*They were coming here.*' Jack realised that contact was coming to him...to his doorstep. 'Holy...*yeah,* right, we'd better prepare... Jack was suddenly like a teenager, not knowing where to look or what to do first.

If it wasn't so serious, it'd be hilarious. Jack was normally so serious. He'd lost the plot because the Werinn were coming to Gateway. First contact for him would be here, right in front of him, and he couldn't be happier about it. Nerves could attack him later.

'We have to get Pat to contact the UN,' Jack said excitedly, 'and provide the formal declaration and undertaking they seek. It won't be as easy as it sounds you know. First, we need to convince Pat, which won't be easy in itself.'

Jack was breathing in gusty sighs. He knew how much work he had in front of him. The fact that they had already spoken and gotten his belief, wouldn't help him with the rest of it. Questions from Pat would be relentless. He would be the proverbial stubborn mule.

Jack was struggling and deeply stressed by the thought of non-humans coming to *Gateway.* It sounded preposterous, ridiculous and hugely improbable. His heart was pounding like a drum and he felt faint. NASA didn't construct Gateway for that purpose, but like it or not, it was apparently going to happen, on his watch.

Jack felt like running and hiding, but knew he had to meet this thing head-on. He looked at space with a glassy stare and couldn't believe this was really happening. Humanity had waited so long for this and it ends up occurring on a platform that orbits the Moon.

They had all been to NASA meetings where they were told that contact with "others" could happen at any time, and at any place, and to be ready, respectful and open. They all thought it was just random lip service. Not one astronaut who ever attended those sessions truly believed what they said, but NASA was dead right, as usual.

What started as a regulation space mission turned into a historical event, probably as important as any in human history. It was a travesty that humanity was being shunned on their first meeting with an extra-terrestrial species. It had never been forecast as even a remote possibility, yet, it happened. Space was like that; it was so vast the unexpected should be expected. Unfortunately, humanity wasn't smart enough to see that as even a remote possibility.

Astronauts the world over didn't think they'd ever be going deep enough into space to encounter multi-cellular *anythings*.

Now...they were confronted by this. Most believed the Fermi paradox would eventually be broken, but not like this. *No way.* Most assumed it would be achieved by intercepting EMAR produced by another civilization or sighting a techno- or bio-signature, proving unambiguously that non-humans existed. Not by direct contact such as this. This stunned eight billion residents of the human planet.

On Gateway, Jack picked up the NIKA phone, which looked like a thick Apple Iphone, and rang JSC on the KA band, to speak with Pat Datsun, President of JSC. About something "rather" important. He was the only individual with enough clout within NASA to make contact with. As far as Jack was concerned, the Band-Aid needed to be ripped off in one motion. That involved Pat – and no-one else.

Pat had a set against using aliens as a reason for anything, made worse by Professor Avi Loeb who really stuck his foot in it, and claimed Oumuamua was an alien spaceship. Pat reckoned Avi was a raving lunatic for claiming aliens based on such spurious evidence.

Now, all bets were off. Jack thought about texting Pat first, to let him absorb it, before ringing. But then he thought, *oh fuck it*, he knew about it anyway, so he just rang him. And let the cards fall where they would. Might as well get it over with, he thought, thinking of the Band-Aid.

He knew what Pat would say when he rang. But he had no choice. The fact that truth was on his side made no difference. Pat would tell him to go *fuck himself* and to think about it properly. He could almost hear his words, being volleyed back harshly. The words were ringing in his ears.

But Pat was the only one with enough reach and prestige within NASA – so, he firstly needed to find him, then needed to convince him. It was the last part that gave him a sour stomach and heartburn. He knew what sort of shit and defiance he was in for. Pat wasn't known for his understanding and patience. Discussing topics like teleporting and extra dimensions was a recipe for utter disaster.

Jack eventually got onto Pat and told him all about it, and as he thought, he flatly refused to believe any of it. He knew about *them*, as builders of the metal posts, but not what was to follow. Not only that, he refused to discuss it initially. He just said STOP and repeated it several times, talking over Jack's attempts to speak.

Then, Pat reckoned, Harry and Abby were straight-out lying, for fame and money. It was a topic of discussion with NASA and they all worried about it. But to date, no-one had done anything formal about it. Pat reckoned this sounded like a prime example. He accepted the techno-signature as proof, but the rest, he said, "was fabricated crap". He said it on several occasions, while laughing humourlessly, which didn't fill Jack with a lot of hope. In fact, he was outraged that he could be so blinkered.

Even the people who were clearly spouting bullshit about non-humans, would be picked up by the media, in all its guises. There were ratings and money in it. Astronauts were perfectly positioned to make a fortune, if they had a bit of imagination and creativity.

It didn't matter what Jack said or how he said it, Pat was a totally closed book. Eventually, after hearing his fill, he disconnected the line without offering a morsel of hope.

'Pat is a no-go.' Jack said flatly, grimacing and shaking his head like a dog. 'He simply will not believe it. The story, apart from the metal posts, is a lie apparently...for monetary gain. He wouldn't even let me talk, he shut me down on every point I tried to make.' Jack rubbed the back of his neck and looked sorrowfully at Harry who was clearly angry.' Harry felt like throwing something and glared at Abby and pointed angrily at the phone. *'Fuck it,'* he screamed loudly and tortuously. Jack walked closer to Harry, stopping short of hugging him, but could see the pain written in his tired, red eyes.

Both had had enough of battering their heads against an iron block, and knew it shouldn't be like this, but had worked in space-services long enough to realise there was no other way. Extraordinary claims demanded extraordinary evidence. Which they were sure they had. Pat disagreed and reckoned our claim that the Werinn were coming to Gateway was bullshit.

Jack smiled at Harry and relaxed his face, understanding what he'd been through. 'We'll give Pat time to digest it and then you and Harry will need to call him again.' Jack said. 'Without Pat onboard, we're dead in the water. We can do nothing.'

Jack smiled at Harry again and looked him right in the eye. 'He's a goddamned bulldozer, I know...good luck shifting him. But if we can get it through his thick head, NASA themselves will listen and accept it.' Jack shook his head and ran his hand through his hair. He knew they were in the right. And on this occasion, Pat was in the wrong. Harry was glaring at Abby and pointing angrily at the phone.

He could feel his body tensing as he thought about it. Harry sighed heavily. This was bigger than big, and he wanted desperately for the whole story to be believed. Harry was worried about the impact on Abby, she'd given all of herself to this, and now couldn't even be believed. Harry knew she made every effort, despite herself most times, to properly represent humanity, and now...*this*. It was way less than she deserved. Harry stared longingly at Abby and took large, deep, savouring breaths.

'*For monetary gain*...is he fucking serious?' Harry's lip curled up. 'Bullshit is what it is. What is wrong with him? Skeptical, I can understand, but he's accusing us of straight-out lying? Come on. *JESUS*.' Harry looked around the hab. 'I need to ring him.' Harry bared his teeth and glared at Jack, shaking his head.

'*Do it...now.*' Jack boomed. 'No time like the *fucking* present. And, good luck.' The man is an iron block. He didn't expect success – but they had to try. Right was on their side. For once, Pat was on the wrong side. As hard as it was, Pat had to understand that he and Abby had come into contact with the extraordinary. Humanity had never seen that kind of tech before.

Harry picked up the phone and let it dial on the KA-band automatically. After half an hour he was still onto Pat. He was a stubborn, dogged, skeptical son-of-a-bitch. Harry had gone through their experiences in granular detail for the last ten minutes - it had been an unproductive, unfriendly, openly hostile Q&A session.

Pat was looking for holes in his story and inconsistencies. He was searching for discrepancies that would reveal a lie. His reaction so far was *really?* Pat wasn't taking them seriously, which came from debunking hundreds of apparent signals. Cynical or distrustful, years of non-human repudiation, had given Pat a skin that was harder than Kevlar. As far as he was concerned, the idea of teleporting living biology and extra dimensions was fake news, manufactured by the creativity of the human brain. Pat was having none of it. He called straight-out *'liar'*!.

Pat wanted to speak to Abby, to compare their stories...see how well schooled they were. Harry, red in the face, hot, sweating and balling his fists, gave the phone over to Abby, who tentatively said 'h-hello,' to Pat. Harry dropped into a seat and held his head in his hands. 'This isn't right,' he boomed angrily. Jack nodded and kept listening to Abby, whose verbal convolutions and difficulties with Pat had just started.

She swung through the same thing Harry did. Pat was very stern with Abby, and displayed no sense of belief at all, again saying *'really?'* It was clear to Abby that Pat thought her responses and recollections were all hoax driven. Abby was hunched over the phone, and by the end of the conversation, felt like hurling the lot into the air. Biting her cheek, and bowing her head, she knew NASA shouldn't be that way. But deeper down she knew how big this thing was. Due diligence was fair enough – but surely this went way beyond that. NASA had to get it completely right though. Abby was claiming non-humans, and other stuff, probably the height of any news flash on Earth...*ever*. So, Pat and NASA got a pass, despite their negative, dogged and contrary behaviour.

She thought, maybe NASA, as part of the US government, would want the whole story concealed. Maybe they'd want this treated like the thousands of non-human UAP's sighted each year. That somehow get to Earth to assess Mankind's technology. All of them have such ridiculously high security classifications that meant the only people who could view them is in the government. *For the people of Earth,* Murphy's law.

Abby was certain that nothing could keep this quiet – there were too many moving parts. Too many people like Harry and her, knew of it. There was too much evidence, too many *photos*. In the next breath, she was sure they'd find a way to keep it under wraps if they wanted to.

Abby was sure that Pat thought we made it all up to fit the story of the metal posts we saw. He didn't have any faith at all in our claims that non-humans were coming to Gateway. He thought that was badly concocted drivel.

Abby couldn't wait for that meeting to occur, and to then send the SAW and Gateway CCT video to Pat. Who would be floored then? She was super-pissed at Pat for giving Harry such a hard time about it. He'd know how far away their planet was. His mind would do the math instantaneously. *Floored* wouldn't come close to it.

After twenty minutes, word-beaten and totally over it, a gasping, sweating, frustrated and lip-chewing Abby gave the phone back to Harry with a tired, wry smile. 'H-Hello Pat,' he said tentatively, waiting for more irritation to follow.

Pat's tone was different...softer, more accepting. He sounded like a normal person. 'Either you've rehearsed very well, or you are conveying the truth. I am still a massive sceptic,' Pat said, to which Harry felt like saying *'really'* himself, but didn't. 'But also, I am, uh...er, prepared to believe your account...that you encountered non-humans. Teleported to their world...it's difficult to believe that *anyone* has worked that tech out. *Holy Jesus shit,* I can't believe I'm saying it.' Harry heard Pat gasping like a cement-mixer on the other end.

'*Harry*...we've...*you've, done it. Finally.* And it wasn't just a signal, or observing a distant techno-signature...it was direct. *Fucking direct...who would have thought*?' Pat was yelling and gasping at the NASA phone in pure disbelief. He put the chances at almost 0%, yet, incredibly, it had happened.

The line was eventually disconnected. Houston and Gateway were left to ponder an arduous, historic phone call, where intelligent life from a race that inhabited a stellar system headed by the star Ross128 was directly encountered by humans. And their tech was front and centre. There would be no government cover-up on this one. It would be announced to the world. From the East Wing of the Whitehouse, POTUS would make the announcement "live" on TV to the US. Then it would hit every country in the world and head every media type - legacy and social. It was news the entire planet needed to know, news that Pat and NASA knew would come eventually to Earth. There were too many planets in the cosmos for it *not* to happen. But no-one on Earth expected this.

Mankind doubted it would be direct contact. Encountering and characterising EMAR was much more likely. So was a bio or techno-signature. Pat and NASA knew that there would be vision of the Werinn's visit to Gateway from the CCTV cameras mounted in the space-station. There was also the vision of Aragon from Orion's SAW cameras mounted on its solar array. There would be enough vision to persuade the most ardent sceptic of the claim's substance. NASA and the world would have images of *them*.

Only problem with visitation and first contact was – the Werinn didn't trust humanity. Earth and humans were to be avoided at all costs. Because of Mankind's long history of warfare, they considered humans way too aggressive to create an alliance with. They were certain that Earth would weaponise their space technology in future years, and eventually wage war on the Werinn. They were taking pre-emptive action to formally distance themselves and their world from humanity and Earth, to protect the lives of the people on their planet.

5.

UN

"People who boast about their IQ are losers."
~ Stephen Hawking

Mankind had declared or engaged in warfare 8,713 times since it split off from the apes two hundred and forty thousand years ago. That's a number so high, it is at first sight, *unbelievable*. Yet it is true. Higher economic activity and more sophisticated technological development has apparently been the result of each war, and many say it shaped human evolution.

If it advanced our technology, then humans should be ahead of a similarly aged society that *didn't* engage in warfare. That was not the case. In fact, it was the exact opposite. The Werinn were our control example. So, the people on Earth who said it, were wrong. *Period.*

War may have shaped Mankind and even helped them economically, but it made the human civilisation look barbaric and highly aggressive to a third party. It would give non-humans pause, if they wished to set up a cooperative alliance.

Because if they were to set up such a cooperative, it may come back to bite them squarely on the arse. Better to be alone in the Great Wide Open, than shackled to someone who might be a serial murderer.

Because, by the time you find out, it may be too late for the entire planet.

War may or may not have pushed us on, but it had a terrible downside. Almost a billion people killed, a huge number of souls with long term physical or psychological injuries, awful environmental damage and general material waste. Furthermore, they are a horrible waste of time - dirty, muddy or dusty and disgusting – a bad look for Earth and humanity, whatever way it was looked at.

Because of our long history of aggression, we were shunned by our first interstellar contact. And who knows how many were to follow. It was a travesty for a world that thought what we'd built and developed was incredible, and something to be very proud of.

According to the Werinn, Earth was a violent world, home to a vicious society of intelligent beings to be avoided at all costs. Your average mum and dad on Earth, didn't feel that way and would feel indignant and outraged if they knew of the Werinn's opinions and statements. Because, they didn't feel like they were violent at all.

Get enough humans together though, with the right leader, and the human 'hive mind' takes over, and attack and general aggression is the outcome. God help anyone on the other end of it. The Werinn knew what Mankind was capable of. Just look at the internet, was their proof.

We'd been blackballed by a species who was only eleven light years from Earth, because they knew what we were. They were cognizant of how we got to our current position. Evolution on Earth was a nasty and violent process. As a species, the Werinn had never had a war at any point in the history of their planet. The Werinn knew that humans killed off the Neanderthal, and we were now being held to account for the killing of billions of Earthly souls.

There was a large difference in technical status between the two species that created a fascinating dilemma. The question that remained – was war good or bad for the technical and general status of a species?

Earth said wars moulded Mankind by promoting increased economic activity, into what it ultimately became. Yet, warless Werinn was the clear leader in tech and general physical understanding, after comparable amounts of time. So, what is the real answer? Forget the internet, and nonsense-hypotheticals.

The Werinn had a fuller understanding of the Universe and physics, and their technology had significantly benefitted from *not* having wars and violence. And they were happy to share everything with friends. But they would *not* share anything with a race that might rise up against them. Mankind was firmly in that category.

Would humans be forced to hide their history, or worse, lie about it? Make up a story to negate or mitigate? Our aggression was too much for some. That was proven. But for the rest of the species in the Universe, how would they feel about us? Once Mankind's reputation was ruined or tainted...would it be too late? The thought was exactly the scenario being thrown around by NASA, ESA and nearly every space industry on Earth. Guesses were easy, but none of them were sure of the answer. People from Earth who knew, feared the worst.

POTUS, the G7, and Five Eyes leaders were considering it. Did we need to ensure that the internet was kept for human eyes only? Did it need to be removed from space? And send Elon Musk spiralling out of control? Most people knew, starting a relationship and hiding something that was potentially damaging was a bad idea. Even POTUS knew that.

*   *   *

Pat knew what he had to do. The Werinn wanted Earth's agreement that they would not approach their planet. And they should have it. Luckily, Pat had a good family friend on the Security Council of the UN who could help them through the vagaries of the United Nations. Pat briefed him on the situation along with George Stewart from SETI's Carl Sagan Centre, who understood the details of the situation well.

John McNee worked for the UN and to say he was stunned and overwhelmed by the revelation was a gross understatement. The poor fellow was floored. He was upset that it had escalated to such unfriendliness. The attitude of the Werinn was understandable, but regrettable, all the same.

And yes, John believed the UN could help procure such an undertaking, even though he believed it was massive and unnecessary over-kill. This planet was close in Galactic terms, but still a long, *long* way away in absolute terms. The Werinn had nothing to worry about. With current tech, even John knew, it'd take thousands of years for Earth to get there.

The fact that the Werinn had FTL and space-folding, amongst a horde of other stuff, didn't help Earth at all. They made it clear that they wouldn't provide the intel to Earth. But at least we, as Mankind, now knew the tech was possible. Aerospace companies, the American Department of Energy, and Universities around the world would continue their research into anti-gravity and Zero Point energy with renewed vigour.

Harry guessed that the Werinn assumed we'd eventually get a lot smarter, and faster – pose more of a risk to them. The document that was requested, was in Earth's interest as well, because the Werinn had tech that was FTL. They could appear on our doorstep very quickly and without prior notification.

All they needed were the weapons, they already had the technical understanding to produce them. And the fact that they were pacifist now, didn't mean they'd always be that way. Maybe one day in the future, they would become aggressive, marauding pirates, and the only thing that could save us was a piece of paper that *they* demanded. Unlikely scenario, but it argued *for* an agreement between the races.

As far as John was concerned, it was all boxes checked for the UN. The Werinn definitely wanted it, and it was in Mankind's interest too. So, the document acquisition should be straightforward. Emphasis on "should", because nothing slated for the UN should ever be taken for granted. The wheels wobbled sometimes. John was confident that generally, the right outcome came to pass. And he suspected, that the same would apply here.

Currently, the Security Council were in the mighty General Assembly, weighing the situation in the Middle-East and East Africa, specifically in Somalia and Libya. They were looking to maintain the peace and security. And the tenuous cooperation between those countries and the departments of the United Nations. Very home-spun issues that ignored the rest of the Galaxy entirely.

All the members required for this off-planet decision, that had been prioritised by the UN, were present in the chamber, but a short outline of the agenda would be necessary, which would be forwarded to Pat in the first instance. They could read the topic from the agenda, but the words would reverberate in their ears for years afterward.

The issue heard by the UN was strange and unexpected but also appropriate for the hallowed halls. No-one would argue against the order - it was a travesty of the highest order, but it was already agreed to by the planet, and it was in everyone's interest. The UN was only a rubber-stamp. It did show how powerful the topic of warfare was, they supposed. The Werinn were rightly scared of it...and scared of us.

The Werinn boasted FTL and possibly wouldn't always be pacifists, so it was in Earth's interest too.

The members in the chamber were those needed to finalise this matter - the USA, China, Japan, Canada, Russia and seven other countries who would vote on a rather unusual resolution, named S/PV 127211.

After John became involved, the special resolution was passed by all members – he believed they comprehended the situation quite well, even though it was very dissimilar to regular UN issues. The great halls had never witnessed anything like it. The great halls in New York had never been witness to non-Earth issues.

Hearing about the vagaries of an interstellar relationship was a first for the planet too. The Fermi paradox was testament to that. Paula Jenkins was the member for Canada and she'd had some exposure to the CSA – the Canadian space agency. She wrote about Julie Payette, the fist Canadian woman on the ISS, for a local newspaper in 1999 - so achievements in space held a special affinity for her.

But when John took the mic and started talking about the Werinn and Earthly astronauts from Gateway making contact for the first time, she was thrown for six. She felt numb and grew tunnel vision that gradually narrowed on John who was the only one visible in the hall. Everything else including the hall became an inconsequential blur. She was glued to his presentation until he finished.

Then Paula put her head in her hands and cried, saying over and over, "what a tragedy" it was. She struggled with the idea that Mankind had been shunned because of the contents of the internet. Paula was familiar with the Fermi paradox and familiar with tragedy. Her first husband had died suddenly a decade before, and the feeling of loss was very familiar to her.

It was a travesty but humans had done what the Werinn requested...without resorting to violence, he thought, with a wry smile. What they wanted, they got. It'd take thousands of years to get to their planet in any event. So, it mattered not to Earth...at the moment.

*   *   *

The problem for those on Gateway was – no one knew when the Werinn were arriving. All they could do was be ready...at any time. Easier said than done, Harry reckoned. This wasn't the sort of thing you

97

turned off and on. When they arrived, we might not be prepared. We might be tired, exhausted, sick, or busy, or even not here.

Harry came close to panic at the thought of someone else being here when they arrived. *Christ*, he thought, were they expected to brief the next few astronauts on Gateway? *"By the way, a civilization might come knocking, trying to get their paws on a document we have".* *Hopefully not*, Harry thought dismally.

Gateway had received the signed document from the UN, sent via the KA-band, printed on Gateway's Canon and signed by Jack as trustee for NASA. The Werinn said they'd pick it up – but when?

Distance didn't seem to be an inconvenience to the Werinn. What was an impenetrable barrier to humanity, the vastness of space and the incredible distances to interesting objects, was no bother to the Werinn.

Why have such a bar to interstellar travel...as the speed of light? It made things impossible. Werinn knew that and were smart enough to find a way around it. Because, if you tried to go straight through it, you were doomed to sub-light speed and possible dilation forever.

The speed of light itself was fast, but *not* quick enough. Many objects that need visiting are too far away, if light speed is the maximum. No species can realistically meet...and the Werinn recognised that. Humanity too. Folding space and anti-gravity is the only way a space-industry can work effectively.

The Werinn were smart enough to know that, and crucially, to overcome it, with what effectively, was warp drive. They used gravity as a propellant as well, that was unlimited and virtually silent. The Werinn's understanding of physics was way beyond humans. Not having wars did them a great service.

Those on Gateway didn't have to wonder for long. They worried that it might be a long time, maybe a very long time, but they needn't have stressed – the Werinn were front and centre. A huge white rounded tube without markings slowly approached Gateway, like a huge toothpaste tube bereft of anything to ruin its tubiform shape. Harry was reminded of the tic-tac UAP that had been spotted on Earth near an aircraft-carrier early in the century. But this thing was much longer.

The bizarre occupants of the craft were visible through the front end of the tube. It was transparent, as though there were nothing there, but something must have kept the pressure in – be it, glass, plastic, acrylic, quartz, or an invisible field of particles. The Werinn were showing humans the technology they had forgone, Harry reckoned.

Jack shielded his eyes from the glare with his hand and saw gnarly arms, legs and several strange heads and torsos near the front of the tube. *Great*, he thought, and felt his body stiffen. The craft docked with Gateway by extending a shining, translucent silver cocoon to form an airtight seal over the entry hatch, and it touched the pins and latches in just the right way. Sensing pressure within, the hatch opened automatically. It allowed the occupants of the ship free access to Gateway. Abby felt like being sick.

Harry wondered if the alien air should be allowed access to Gateway, realising it was far too late to worry about it. They themselves would soon be onboard anyway. *C'est La Vie*, he supposed. He'd always thought that anything genetically distinct wouldn't represent a major problem to Mankind. Xeno-bacteria and viruses simply wouldn't know how to infect humans. Neil DeGrasse Tyson had told him that. He hoped he was right.

The four humans were standing in the HALO module where they lived and slept. They glanced at each other and realised how far in the deep-end they really were. Outside was a ship-full of non-humans and it was up to a chosen few to greet them and try and make some sense.

Holy shit, Harry thought. Abby felt like running, but realised the futility. She made no attempt to stop tears coursing down her face and dropping onto the floor. They probably should have greeted the Werinn at the airlock – but they could hear walk-thumping, coming closer and closer. So it probably didn't matter much. They were almost here. The sound of errant walking was getting louder as the Werinn approached. Harry's heartbeat hammered in his ears and also got louder as their footsteps got louder. At the entrance to HALO, the "walk-thumping" stopped abruptly and everything went space quiet. The Werinn had stopped, just out of sight. For some reason, *contact* was on hold.

'Fuck,' Jack whispered under his breath to Abby, knowing what was coming, but oddly, had stopped. His eyes were as wide as anyone had seen *'This isn't happening,'* Harry whispered to Jack, who looked stunned that they'd stopped. Abby and Harry were both the same, wondering *WTF*. All of them were gaping in astonishment, waiting for the Werinn to keep walking and come around the corner.

Gateway was lit up like a Christmas tree but was space silent. With a huge and unfamiliar craft docked to it. Jack looked at Harry and shrugged. It'd be what It'd be, he thought. Actually, he was mortified, gasping air though burning lungs, wondering why in hell they'd stopped? Abby's eyes were like an owl, looking at the floor, then nervously glancing at Harry, waiting for it to happen. It was so quiet – they all wondered, what the hell were the Werinn doing?

Why had they stopped? What game were they playing? There was no noise at all. Just the Moon shining brightly through a window. And four confused and bewildered humans, waiting for the Werinn to continue their journey a little further. Abby glanced at Harry and Jack, and for a long moment they stared at each other, wondering, trying to guess why in God's name the Werinn had stopped moving. Harry wondered how long they should wait, before going looking for them?

Harry winked at Abby broadly to tell her to hang in there. It was still silent, but they all expected that to change. Harry whispered, 'strength,' to her, and held himself tall and tightened all his muscles. Abby smiled and did the same.

The group of four Werinn walked heavily and casually into HALO, having "docked" with the International Habitation Module which was right in the humans' line of sight. The Werinn stopped again to look at the Moon which was beautiful and shining in the Sun's light, observable through the zenith window.

All the Werinn had huge heads, and were dressed identically, in loose T-shirts and brown pants, long like Chinos. They didn't look anything like astronauts. Their heads were exceptionally long. They had huge, intricately layered ears that followed the head closely, with a bony ridge that led to two prominent, large eyes and a small downturned mouth. Their non-humanness was loud and clear. And so too was their similarity to the mythical Frankenstein. And they were here – in Gateway, the name taking on a brand-new meaning, for all the humans that were present.

The first sight of them by the humans prompted an emphatic '*oh hell*,' whisper, which said it all. Abby tried to display the strength that Harry had instilled her with, but it failed, in the face of them. She felt like a rubber caricature, and pulled all her muscles tight, like Harry had told her, desperately trying to stay upright and still, but her legs kept shaking. The beings from Werinn loomed over her.

A lot of the Werinn bodies were hidden by clothing. They had light bluish skin, six fingers and a rather small oppositional thumb - the feet were covered by shoes, so, the nature and number of toes was anybody's guess. From what they could see there was not a hair on them...anywhere they could see.

Overall, they appeared very different from humans, even though they were overtly humanoid, and seemed to respire the same way that humans did. Harry watched them all pull in air, then exhale. There was no expression on their faces that he could read. The Werinn just stood there like trees and looked blankly down at the humans and did nothing, and made no noise at all.

If anything, they looked confused. But that was probably their regulation expression, because of the bony ridge that underscored the eyes. More than anything, they looked at the humans vacantly, glancing at all of them, wondering what the hell we were, presumably.

Oshn, the tallest of the group, suddenly held his arm straight out like a sword and Jack grabbed it and shook it and felt the hard and cold flesh.

Knowing he was cognizant with English, Harry felt more confident, but he was still seriously spooked. This wasn't his role, he thought. A diplomat he wasn't, but then he remembered what NASA had told him. *Anyone at any time.*

'W-Welcome to our G-Gateway station,' Harry said, stammering and choking out the words. He felt sweat on his forehead and running down the small of his back. Sweat continued to drip down his back, making him more off-balance than he already was. He looked at Oshn and was struck by complete confusion, to the point he had no idea how he got here.

'Thank you,' Oshn said in reply.

'Internet,' Harry piped to the group, suggesting that's where the gesture and the language came from. The internet carried a lot of language lessons, from beginners to advanced. And the Werinn were very proficient learners. 'They also received our TV signals,' Harry said, 'for perspective and the like.'

Pete gawked at the group and immediately wondered how anything so ugly could possibly be that intelligent. Dark Matter, Dark Energy, FTL, GUT...and teleporting living biology. He knew superficial thoughts on appearance betrayed humanity's immaturity...but the thought was front and centre in his mind. He tried hard to put it aside, but looking at them he couldn't. The Werinn looked primeval. They looked like they'd crawled out of the primordial sludge.

Yet, this species in front of him was proficient in quantum physics...and physics itself. The capability of these creatures was in his face, by the sheer fact that they were here at all. Eleven light years in a few days, he contemplated. The same distance would take humans centuries...probably more.

Their Standard Model of Particles included the dark particles and other things that humans simply didn't know about. Mankind knew 5% of everything – the Werinn knew 100%. They could teleport live biology for God's sakes, probably the pinnacle of all things. But Harry knew there was a big problem – they objected to humanity.

We desperately craved their intel, but they wanted nothing to do with humans. It was a huge conundrum, seemingly without an immediate answer. Humans couldn't change their history any more than a leopard could change its spots. But the Werinn's intel was critical to the human race. Without them, it might be *five to ten centuries* before Mankind was in a similar position to the Werinn.

This whole issue only became a problem because of NASA and SpaceX desires to put an orbiter around Mars to, amongst other things, provide internet services to the first settlers on the red planet. The internet it contained ended up "alerting" the Werinn to the history of humanity which no-one expected would ever be a problem. If not for this, the Werinn would only have seen the Mankind of today, as we did of them.

We weren't in possession of the Werinn internet, so we can only know the current model Werinn. There were probably parts of their history that they'd want hidden too. The Werinn said that they didn't have wars – but should they be believed? Maybe we should ask for their internet too, so we can check on them?

Harry admitted that it sounded a bit like tit for tat...immature stuff. But Abby wasn't so sure. She was convinced that the Werinn weren't perfect. What drove them on? She wondered. Surely, they too, were competitive? She was sure they were hiding something.

Gateway was supposed to be a way-station and research facility. Harry had looked at the Werinn and all he could see was *Fermi paradox,* written in their eyes and all over their faces. Where had they been for God's sakes? They were exactly what Enrico Fermi was talking about. The Werinn mentioned "shielding" of EMAR, but weren't pressed on the point. Maybe that's why SETI didn't find them.

The Werinn were relatively close to Earth, which probably meant intelligence was widespread in the Universe. To think, some of the science-community believed that humanity was *alone*. Mankind had tested a bath-tub volume of space – and because it lacked evidence of non-humans, that was it. *There was none, anywhere.* What an unscientific, backward, seat-of-the-pants approach, Harry thought.

The fact they didn't want to be friends with Mankind was immaterial to the paradox. It was broken, shattered, call it what you like. But the real issue, Fermi paradox aside, was that they rebuffed us, because of our behaviour over the past few thousand years.

That's not how it was supposed to go. But you can understand their decision. It was logical and common-sense. It was also harsh and punitive, but kudos to them, they were decisive. They knew what they wanted and it wasn't humans. It was a shame, because the Werinn knew so much. So much intel that humans couldn't work out...despite trying at such great personal cost. In a different Universe, humans would benefit from having the Werinn as friends.

So, you don't like our history, is that right?' Jack asked indignantly, staring wide-eyed at Oshn. The Werinn were afraid of what humans might do and might become. Jack was thunder-struck.

'That is correct,' came his clipped reply in English. After a lot of hand movement, mainly above his head, Oshn continued. He hadn't learnt how to skirt around insults yet, which was fair enough. Oshn was straight to the point.

'Too much warfare... too much aggression. We are not happy with the nature of your humanity, which is exposed in these actions and described in detail by your internet. War even occurs today and it extends as far back as you can go. *Anyway,* we are not here to justify our decision.' He gazed around the group and looked content with the verdict. The decision was already made by their Union – he was just passing it on.

'The decision has been made and it stands.' He said brusquely. All the humans raised their eyebrows, shook their heads, and looked down. They disagreed with Oshn's decision to reject humans. From an Earthly perspective, history was just that – the humans felt that judging a species as a whole for what happened, mainly in the past, was deeply discriminating. But, like he said, the judgement was made, and it was *final*.

Jack took a deep breath and looked him in the eyes and handed Oshn the document. He read it slowly, then folded it up and put it in a rear pocket. 'Thank you,' he said, tilting his head up and making eye contact with Harry and nodding. The note was passed to each of the creatures, then it came back to Oshn. He gave a crisp nod to Harry, to confirm that they'd satisfied the request.

And with that, the four from Werinn turned on a dime and walk-thumped back to their ship, and withdrew the high-density plasma airlock. The humans saw them disappear around the corner, followed soon after by a slurping noise that was made by the airlock between the two craft withdrawing.

'*H-Holy s-shit,*' Jack yelled in a quaking voice to everyone. 'Did t-that *h-happen?*' He flexed his neck, and brought a shaky hand to his forehead, and turned his head to Harry. With one bulging eye on the window, he gawked at the now empty dock. He was gobsmacked that the Werinn had come and gone.

Harry scratched his jaw and was at a total loss for words. Jack whispered hoarsely, 't-they actually c-came here *themselves* to pick up the letter.' Jack spoke very slowly, while staggering a couple of steps backward to the wall of Gateway. He was stunned to meet them in person and his eyebrows were still at the top of his head. '*Holy fucking shit,*' he dribbled.

Jack was quietly trying to process the fact that they'd come and gone. Harry was ecstatic that they had CCT video of the whole event to prove that it actually happened. All the humans stood rigid like statues, and struggled to move, but Harry was smiling like a Chesire cat, knowing what had just transpired in front of him and the cameras. *Incredible, amazing, unlikely* – but it was a fact.

Jack was blood-red in the face and seemingly ready to burst. He was grunting and groaning, and crying real tears in a display of emotion that was confused at best. Jack was punch-drunk and unglued by the face-to-face with non-humans. Harry looked at him anxiously. He thought he was suffering a real medical emergency, but instead of collapsing to the ground in a heap, he vomited words. And seemingly couldn't stop himself. '*Seriously...on Gateway? The Fermi paradox broken on Gateway?*' Jack shouted incredulously. 'No one would have anticipated it...*NO ONE.*' Jack screamed. It was crazy. His legs were rubber as he collapsed into a chair and gazed at the Moon with swollen, half-closed eyes. He could feel his heart hammering in his chest. The lines on his forehead were now deep and furrowed.

The huge white tube slid past Gateway and on into deeper space, illuminated brilliantly by the Sun, and reflection from the Moon. Why it wasn't branded at all, they didn't know. It seemed they took introversion to a new level. For some reason they didn't want anyone to know it was them. Compare that to a human, NASA craft, which was covered head to toe with emblems and flags.

The craft from Earth were clearly emblazoned, without a hint of humility. Such was xeno-sociology, he supposed. Nothing should be taken for granted. One thing is certain, proven by the Werinn, other intelligences think differently and have different values to humans.

6.

Help

"Quiet people have the loudest minds."
~ Stephen Hawking

The rotating asymmetric triangle set down in a suburb of Werinn ten days after Harry and Abby left the planet. The Werinn weren't expecting anything or anyone. The object from space just came. The craft from Biapene, a planet in their own solar system, arrived completely out-of-the-blue. It floated to the ground like a shot, and had no propulsion, as humans would identify it. It was clear that this craft boasted gravity-tech very similar to the Werinn.

Large masses like planets had no effect on the vehicle. These craft could avoid curvature in spacetime and the mutual attraction of all things that have mass. Gravity-sponging was technology that, to Mankind and Earth, was priceless, because they didn't have it.

The Werinn were stunned to see the alien craft breach their Karman line, and then proceed to float to landing on their planet, surrounded by Werinn craft, that met it high in the atmosphere and followed it down.

The Werinn knew that their own solar system was populated; they had telescopes, both visual and radio. Their ground-based and orbital telescopes had picked up a living planet and imaged it. EMAR from the next planet down had been received for a long time. The Werinn had travelled to its sister planet and plans to create a formal alliance were in progress.

The only thing both worlds didn't know was how life on each planet came to be. The Werinn believed that a single life event was probably shared by the two planets, leading to the Werinn on their world and the Biapene on the next planet down. Two very different species had evolved differently indeed, from the same spark of life.

The Werinn lived in a four-planet solar system, the inner world too hot and the outer-world too icy for their kind of life. That left two planets that were habitable and indeed, two civilisations had developed on these worlds.

The Werinn detected the Biapene vessel when it approached the Werinn Karman line. What they didn't know was why it was there and what it wanted. The Werinn had visited Biapene, and the latter had been here already. Both wanted much more though.

Emerging from the main hatch of the triangular craft were six Biapene soldiers and one individual dressed very differently – far more casually. There were twenty more soldiers inside, weaponised to the hilt, just in case ... apparently.

Enough was known about the Werinn to take the planet as their own – it was well established that the Werinn hadn't weaponised their technology, even to address a simple home-town fight. The Biapene wanted the Werinn planet as their own.

The Werinn would offer little significant resistance to the Biapene who not only occupied a planet but wanted the Werinn planet too. Their own world was rapidly changing for the worse. To the point where the Biapene world was losing its habitability. But the Werinn world was a paradise and had precious infrastructure.

The Biapene were from a world slightly larger than Werinn. They wanted the Werinn planet because their own planet was dying. Biapene's magnetosphere was no more. Their planet had slowed its rotation and had now had completely halted, including its core. It arrowed through the cosmos, totally at the mercy now, of its red dwarf Sun – which had no mercy on its inner planets. Huge flares spewed from the middle of the star. It struck Biapene direct, hitting the planet at mid-ships, without any interception by protecting particles.

The ozone layer was now just a memory. A huge percentage of the Biapene population had died from rapid and horrible genetic diseases. A majority of those left had cancer. The "pure" needed a new planet – and that planet was Werinn. It was perfect for their type of life as long as the infrastructure of the planet remained intact.

But there remained an agonising and aching problem – that planet had its own indigenous population. The Biapene knew it had a massive problem that had no reasonable solution – it wanted a planet that was already populated by an intelligent civilisation. It was an age-old problem - what they wanted, was already taken.

The Biapene knew that Werinn was easy pickings. The planet next door was unlocked and open...*waiting*. They had no munitions or weapons or anything related to a military - or weaponization.

Consequently, the Biapene issued an ultimatum to the leaders of that world, giving the entire population thirty days to leave the planet. Or they would all be killed to make way for a new population. And worse, they demonstrated how they'd do it with their acoustic weapons on a *brunnit* (local animal) that unfortunately went waddling past in the forest. Its timing was terrible.

It ended up as a few particles that blew away on the wind. There wasn't even any blood. This was what was on offer to the entire population of Werinn – instant cremation with audio waves. The Werinn knew instantly that they had a massive problem. Statements, refusals, imploring, appealing or pleading did no good whatsoever. The Biapene were deadly serious. They wanted the planet...*period*, to replace theirs, which was no longer viable.

The Biapene knew it was wrong to take the Werinn planet for their own. And kill an entire population of intelligent beings. Reduce them all to dust. But the planet of Biapene had voted to do it. The population's leaders were left with an agonizing choice. Watch their entire population, including children and babies, dissolve in a disease-ridden Armageddon, or seek a new planet, as they were doing. With heavy-hearts, the beings of Biapene chose Werinn.

They could no longer watch their young ones die. It had to be done. It was a horrible choice, tainted by the visuals of their population's own horrid deaths, in pools of blood and torturous pain.

The obvious question for the Werinn was – where the hell would they go? It wasn't possible. They had to move...*planets*. But it wasn't possible. Especially in thirty short days. Maybe in a year, but even then, it was deeply steeped in the unknown. Still, the question was *where*? The Werinn ruling family knew it was hopeless, but still they tried to effort solutions that were not drop-dead hopeless.

The Werinn knew of a few exo-planets, but they had investigated none in detail. A new FTL engine was available, but deeper space remained a mystery to them. They simply hadn't investigated enough. With their space telescopes, they'd observed a lot of potentially hopeful planets, but hadn't been beyond their solar system. They had the potential to go far...but where? They reviled their lack of foresight

The Biapene left the Werinn world and said they would return in thirty days to take care of business. Any Werinn left on the planet would be annihilated. *Period*. The threat was short, but very serious indeed. The Biapene required vacant possession of their planet.

The Werinn took them for their word – they were terrified and desperately needed help. Because sure as hell, they couldn't defend their planet against the weapons of the Biapene. Without help, the Werinn had no hope.

Oshn realised the Werinn needed help, but help from *who*? They only knew of one race beyond the solar system and the Werinn had them on a short lead indeed. Humans were formally barred from approaching their planet. They needed the human mind-set though. He freely conceded that. To fight the Biapene, the Werinn needed aggression. They needed the capacity to bite back. Currently, they had no military capability at all. The Werinn were ripe for the picking.

The answer to their predicament was obvious. As part of the tech for teleportation and space-shortening, the Werinn had a strong grip on entanglement and slipspace. They could now engage in FTL communication. Which meant they could contact a planet "NOW", irrespective of how far away their planet of choice was. Space-time was reduced to just space.

In other words, the speed of light no longer provided a restriction to their comms. Instead of 'looking *back* in spacetime' when they dealt with distances, they were simply 'looking' at space. Time played no role.

Using slipspace, quantum non-locality, tunnelling and entanglement, the Werinn believed they were provided with some avenue of aid to the Biapene threat. They hoped recent dealings with the humans hadn't totally ruined their relationship. It should have, but they literally had no other avenue to explore.

It was either contact them, or rely on the mercy of the Biapene. And from recent conversations, it was known with conviction, that the Biapene had no mercy. Not toward the Werinn, anyway. They wanted possession of their world. The entire population of Werinn were no more than an inconvenience to the Biapene. They'd threatened and would kill them all.

*   *   *

Using FTL comms, the Werinn issued Earth with a distress message, sent in a narrow-band pulse, encoded in binary and sent on two frequencies, with a pulse in one frequency standing for "1" and the other for "0".

They included a count from one to five - mathematical operations like addition and multiplication, simple trigonometry and a description of electromagnetic waves, pretty sure that Earth would be capable of reading it. It was written in Earth's own language, but encrypted, to ensure that no-one else could intercept it and read it.

In fact, they knew humans themselves could read it. ASCII was part of the Earthly internet. They could have sent the message in an Earthly language if they wanted, but that was not the Werinn way. Someone else may intercept the message which just wouldn't do. This way they could be more certain that it would be received and decoded to real meaning by Earth-only.

The Werinn were a very careful, discriminating race. They knew no other way, even in these chaotic times where the greater population was threatened with death.

The message was encrypted for humans to both receive and decrypt, and they hoped and prayed for a semi-positive reply. Humans were their only hope. They were the only other race they knew of, and they were all that stood between the Biapene and oblivion.

The Werinn weren't idiots – they realised they had made their job a lot harder, but Mankind were the *only* ones they'd so far identified. It was the Werinn's consideration that Mankind was well suited to helping. They hoped against hope that their recent "contact" wasn't an assistance-killer, but they feared the worst. They expected the worst. Humanity's attitude according to their internet - suggested antipathy was a common emotion that permeated the planet.

The Werinn saw the irony of asking humanity for help. They had just shunned them and effectively told them *NO*. A document was extracted that formalised a non-visit agreement. But the Werinn realised they possessed something Mankind had sought for a long, *long* time. Mankind were tired of throwing good money after bad at it.

The other issue which was front and centre was *how* the humans would get to them? The Werinn agreed that it didn't sound hopeful. If Oshn were them, the answer to the Werinn would be *no*. But he, and their Union, knew a thing or two about the humans. They would do nearly anything to extract intel and tech that they didn't have. He and their Union were confident it would form part of the human decision-making process.

Without folding space, it would take humans centuries to get to Werinn. Perhaps they could use the shift on Aragon? But that limited the number of them that could come. And the size of the craft. Both races knew it wasn't meant for high volume traffic nor large-size craft - it was designed for use by a single craft to visit their world. That's what Oshn had told them.

Anyway, the Werinn knew where Earth sat with regard to space weaponry. It couldn't defend them, even if they did get here. So, that part of the request was probably moot. Advanced space weapons weren't the human thing.

What the Werinn really wanted was humanity's aggressive mind-set and attitude. They realised they had erred in not weaponizing their technology for whatever might come at the planet from space.

Werimm might be a serene world, but the Universe itself was perilous and unsafe. It was filled with species who wanted more, or somewhere else, or something better. Imperialistic, Nationalistic species demanded and threatened. Unfortunately, the Werinn realised it too late.

7.

Message

"Aggression, humanity's greatest vice, will destroy civilization."
~ Stephen Hawking

'*Gateway, Houston*...pick up my *fucking call*,' Pat demanded loudly and curtly, after six rings. Swearing on an open line was forbidden by NASA, but Pat didn't give a shit. This was as *urgent and momentous as it got*. Pat from home-base at KSC needed Gateway to pick-up the phone stat. Jack finally answered, partly curious and partly annoyed that Pat had dared to ring them again.

Jack held the NIKA "Apple-like" device to his ear, and wondered why Houston was calling, so soon after the last lengthy call Pat made to them. Soon enough, he found out, and he was bemused and a little amused.

Jack looked sideways at the phone, shook his head and listened to Pat who sounded breathless and dumbfounded. 'NASA has received a message,' he said, 'that every radio telescope and even a few two-way radios were picking up. It was super strong and emanated from the Ross system like an FRB. SETI and Breakthrough and Keck were fairly much blinded by the damn thing, even though the source was distant. The message came from eleven light years away and its source was lit up like a fucking Christmas tree. NASA is swinging JWST onto it, but we already know with certainty where it's coming from.

'The legacy media already knows all about it Jack. It'll be splashed over the front pages of newspapers and in the Social's tomorrow.' Pat stopped talking and caught his breath. 'It's proximal to Ross 128b Jack, the star is a red dwarf and the planet is rocky, Earth-like and inside the habitable-zone of its star.'

Pat stopped talking again, because of the unpleasant heat behind his eyes and the tingling in his stomach from what he was about to say and the spice he'd eaten for lunch. He took a deep breath and went on, first making sure Jack was still there. Even though coms were improved, they were still notoriously unstable.

'The most interesting thing is how this message looks through the 'scope. It is actually *visible* to JWST,' Pat said vigorously, 'which is nothing short of astounding. Normally, these discharges are only visible to *radio* telescopes. In this case, the message was lit up by light blue Cherenkov radiation, emanating from Ross 128b. Yes … that's right, *Cherenkov* radiation…and you know what that means.' The FTL nature of the message could be seen by all.

'No doubt though,' Pat continued, 'the most interesting part of the message was the actual meaning. It was sent in narrow-band at 1420 Mhz and the EMAR was ultra-strong, directed, more or less, toward Earth. It consisted of binary numerals, divisible in English, using ASCII. The Werinn knew more about human capabilities from the internet than Earth could've hoped for.' Once Pat realised how it was sent, he saluted the heaven's and swore an ancient Greek allegiance to Zeus. To say he was overwhelmed with excitement was a severe understatement. The man was totally floored that a civilisation would go to this trouble to reach our planet. It was close to impossible to amaze Pat, but the Werinn had achieved it.

The Werinn realised that messaging Earth was a last resort. High in their minds was the fact that the Werinn rebuffed human attempts to build closer ties – and they obviously regretted it…now. The blue pearl was the only other planet, and only other intelligence they knew of. The rest wrote itself.

So, it was Earth that got the message to help. It was literally, a shot in the dark. But they had to do something. The Werinn didn't want to die alone, in the dark, without having exercised every option, as hopeless and forlorn as it was.

'The Werinn understood the futility of doing it.' Jack said. 'They had just made it clear that humanity wasn't a friend of the Werinn, and then followed up with this message. They needed our help. To send a threatening race packing.'

Jack grimaced, smiled wryly and shook his head. You must be fucking joking, he thought. He immediately thought of Earth and Mankind, and conceded that it would be a nightmare if it happened to us. No-one would go to work, economies would grind to a halt, stock-markets would crash and law and order would be a memory. Medical care – *forget it*. Civilisation would rapidly depart. He concluded that humans would literally throttle every option to avoid annihilation.

'What's the message actually say?' Jack boomed impatiently. He'd had about enough of them and their coded bullshit.

'It says that the Werinn have been threatened by another race in their own solar system, whose planet's bio-zone is perishing from its loss of a protective magnetosphere. The Biapene race occupies a planet in the same solar system as the Werinn, and are dying from the effects of radiation from the same flare star as confronts the Werinn. Almost the entire population of Biapene is suffering from radiation sickness, cancer - genetic problems are everywhere, the death-rate is horrendous apparently. And they can take no more, can watch no more of their own, perish.' Pat swallowed hard and wrinkled his nose. The mental image of people dead and dying on the streets was awful. But enough to threaten an entire world – *NO*.

'The Biapene decided,' Pat went on, 'that they needed a new planet. But their space industry remained in its infancy. For the Biapene, the closest world that was known to be habitable was Werinn, which was very near and in fact, in the same solar system. It was the only planet they could reasonably get to. And it had housing that would suit the Biapene, so keeping the infra-structure of the planet intact was critical.

'They want to shift three billion Biapene to the Werinn planet but there was a problem, and it wasn't because the Werinn world was populated. This was a problem that stemmed from their own psyche.' Pat smiled wryly. 'They wanted Werinn for their own but they, as a population, reviled space itself. The vacuum of space spooked the Biapene. To cross it, was torture personified, and few wanted to do it...even if it meant salvation from death.'

Pat made a snorting sound and shook his head as though he didn't understand their strange behaviour. He thought about it - the

Biapene don't like space...so they'd rather die than grapple with it. He snorted again and reckoned that was a hell of a disorder...and *had* to favour the Werinn. The Biapene didn't have many astronauts for that very reason.few of their population wanted to go into space.'

'Wow...a whole 30 days to vacate...very nice,' Jack piped on the phone. 'And where are they supposed to go?' The DoD would say an unweaponized technology is just inviting trouble, because soon enough, it will be known, and guess what?'

'The unfortunate situation,' Pat said wistfully, 'is that the Werinn have no capability to move en masse. A few of them, *fine*, but all of them, no way. Hence, the distress call to us. The Werinn have made the obvious decision to stay put. They've been graciously granted thirty days by the Biapene, but they've chosen not to use them.' Pat stopped talking and shook his head dismally. That meant only one thing would happen. Death of a civilisation. Pat made a hissing breath. It was a travesty of the highest order.

'No doubt, the thirty days are meant as a token only.' Pat continued. 'The Biapene know they won't use them. It's not enough time to vacate an entire planet. Moving a planet full of beings takes a *lot* of time. Do it quickly and panic will be the result - and likely death to millions.' Pat's eyes never left his phone.

'Also important in all this,' Pat continued, 'is the Werinn's complete lack of weaponry, a fact known to the Biapene, who don't expect much resistance, probably *none* in space. So, the Werinn are strong in technology but weak in defensive or offensive capability and ripe for a militaristic race like the Biapene.' Pat's granite eyes were still on the phone. He knew he was right.

'Hence, they have sent humans a distress call in sheer hope, because we are the only off-planet civilization they know of.' Pat was audibly panting from frustration and irritation. 'What are we expected to do?' Pat stared at the phone blankly and felt sorry for the Werinn. Alone and vulnerable, threatened by a weapon-laden race, it was no wonder they were trying every option.

Pat put Earth in their position, and he knew we'd do exactly the same thing. We'd try *everything*. 'A civilisation is at stake for Christ sakes.' Pat's top lip curled up and he shook his head. The Biapene attitude was criminal, he reckoned, although who knows what state the decision-makers are in. It was quite possible that they or their families were terminally ill from the widespread radiation that hit the planet.

The Biapene probably deserved a break. But threatening another civilisation, was no answer, whichever way you cut it.

'I wonder why they even bothered to send us a message?' Jack said sourly, sneering at Harry while he spoke on the phone. 'It's not like we could get there – and have anything useful to provide them. We can offer nothing for ex-atmosphere battles. We are as powerless as they are in space and they should know it. They've got our fucking internet,' he snapped.

Harry thought about it, screwed his face up and demanded the phone from Jack, with an outstretched hand. He wanted Pat's ear to offer something that just came to mind. The Werinn held invaluable wisdom, so *fuck* it, why not? Harry reckoned it could help someone like the Werinn, who had nothing offensive at all. He was unsure about its viability in space.

'What about the laser developed by the US Airforce and Navy?' He said to Pat uncertainly and cautiously. 'T-They've been, er...w-working on that for almost f-forty years and recently mounted an iodine-oxygen version in a 7-747. NASA could install it in an Orion, couldn't they? It's been through the shift once - it could do it again, right?'

Harry knew the Biapene didn't like space, so the scare-factor to succeed would be pegged pretty low. Harry had a playful grin on his face, he liked what he ended up saying, and glanced at Abby who was smiling back at him. They forgot Pat was part of the audience.

'One craft versus God knows how many of theirs...yeah, great idea...*brilliant Harry*. Tell me there's a little more to your idea?' Pat gave a gusty sigh when he'd finished talking to Harry that was loud on the speaker- phone. *No way*, Pat thought, *you're tripping*. His cynical reaction angered Harry who thought they'd impressed.

'*Yes Pat*,' Harry said into the phone. '*Indeed,* there is more.' He looked stony-eyed and very serious as he addressed the phone. 'They do not expect any resistance in space from the Werinn. They do not expect any of their craft to even turn up. Any resistance would only come in the atmosphere, and that would be minimal. They would have done their homework on the Werinn and would know they haven't weaponized their technology, either for space or within the bio-zone of their planet. And it's too late to start doing it now. So, they will not be ready for any significant resistance.' He swallowed, nodded crisply and narrowed his eyes.

Harry continued. 'It's not like we can send them a heap of Super-Hornets for atmospheric defence. We could never get them there, or tanks and missile launchers, ordinance etc. *Same fucking problem*.' Harry swore and pointed his fingers harshly toward the window. 'So, we have the surprise element Pat. Remember the biggest attacks on the US – Pearl Harbour and 9/11. Admittedly, both had more firepower, but the first, unexpected shot can have huge *fear* ramifications. And they don't like space, in fact they revile it, astronauts are hard to source on Biapene...so, I say, there is some chance,' Harry said, grinning and chuffed with his ability to read NASA. 'I say there is a chance', he repeated.

Abby looked at the phone with wide, beckoning eyes and he held it out toward her, guessing that she wanted to add something. She didn't want to speak on the phone, but she did want it relayed to Pat, to tell him that she used a version of the oxygen-iodine laser at Johnston. So, she relayed it to via speaker phone.

'It was an indoor trial of the technology and they wanted four astronauts who weren't familiar with it – to try it. One of them was her', she said. 'It worked really well and was extremely potent and quite destructive. What the tech was for, and what happened to it, I have no idea. All I know is what happened. It was something to do with the Military. But the what or where, I have no idea. The main point is, I was told it'd work well in space.' she took a deep breath and sat back waiting for their reaction.

'Okay, so forget the bona fides of the mission for a minute.' Harry said. 'Who would take this and run with it, if approved and, um...use it in anger? Astronauts, obviously...but who?' Harry had no idea how this would work. NASA couldn't endanger their astronauts ...could they?

'It's for NASA to decide, the craft belong to them. An aerospace company like Lockheed's would make the changes to Orion, but NASA'd pay for it...so, it's for them to give a go/don't go. And see who is agreeable to do it and who ultimately is rostered onto the mission. We're talking about the genocide of an entire global population. We'd like to think that someone would help if humans were being forcibly evicted from our planet.' Harry thought about the horror of being threatened like the Werinn were.

They's have to vacate the planet or be killed where they stood. Harry could think of few things worse. And there were issues which indicated that the Biapene wouldn't make good soldiers in space. It sounded like it wouldn't be difficult to scare them off. But it might just sound and look that way. They knew nothing empirical about the

Biapene, only what the Werinn had told them, and God knows how accurate that was.

Pat tried to step out the next few challenges he had. 'I need to update NASA, but the world will soon know what is going on with the Werinn,' he said. 'We can't and don't wanna keep this quiet. It's too big. I'll revert to you once I know more about our response to the message. Houston out.' Pat had done enough talking on the phone. Now came the really hard bit. Getting a decision from the Administrator of NASA. He knew that the only way to make an inclusive decision was to get all the stakeholders together in one room and get their specific buy-in – and only then, get a decision democratically - by voting. This would be done the American way – if the decision wasn't obtained from stakeholders, it wasn't worth jack.

Pat knew that the only way to make a global decision was to talk it through with the stakeholders who really mattered. NASA agreed and had organised a meeting. The Five-Eyes Intelligence Network agreed and so did the G7 leaders. It would bring all the stakeholders together in one room to hopefully hammer out a way forward.

The space-industry and a few others would soon vote on the planet's response to the Werinn request - after a debrief and Q and A, including government parties and a few from the private sector.

*   *   *

Senior scholars, diplomats and heads from the space industry nations were waiting anxiously to ferry details back to their respective Governments. As were numerous Heads from NASA's network facilities at Langley in Virginia, JPL, Ames in California's Silicon Valley, the John Glen and Armstrong Centres, Goddard Space Flight Centre and the Stennis Space Flight Centre in Mississippi. Also, there was the President of the US, ex-Presidents, Director Generals or Secretary-Generals of ESA, CSA, JAXA, the UN and even Roscosmos who was permitted to attend, even though their government was involved in fighting a very unpopular war. The US had a very strong presence. SETI arrived, with four members from the Carl Sagan Centre in California who were front and centre.

The director of the Astrophysical Council was there as were four members from the SSEC and Heads or seniors from the US Army, Navy, Airforce and Spaceforce. The heads and Number twos from NASA, DoD, and heads or Ministers from China, India, Australia, the US, Europe and

Africa were there. The US Department of Energy, the State Department, Department of the Interior, Department of Commerce and Labor and US Homeland Security were also there. From a government perspective, everyone was in attendance that would play any role in the proposed events.

Harry, Abby and Pat sat near the head of the mighty table in the East-Wing of The Whitehouse. POTUS was eventually ushered into the room and was told the large camera was there only to record important shots. Every time he saw a camera, he wanted to use it as an opportunity to make a re-election speech, especially with the Primaries so near and his recent GOP nomination.

With this audience, he could barely hold himself back. Eventually, he was coaxed away from the podium and took a seat, after talking the ear off a couple of dignitaries. He was told by the Secretary of State that these people weren't here to listen to him. POTUS huffed and sighed heavily, but knew Congress had been suspended, allowing certain people to attend this meeting – so the urgency and importance was obvious even to him.

They occupied the East Wing Boardroom, to consider assisting the Werinn. The men in the room would consider whether HELIOS-style lasers would be integrated with Orion technology, manned by our astronauts, and offered to the Werinn. NASA would accept the verdict of the entire governmental space industry, conditional on stand-alone decisions made by individual astronauts. No-one would be forced or even encouraged to be involved. It needed to be a fully self-compelled process.

The decision needed to be shared among all interested parties. Everyone present knew what hung on the end of it. But the mission had to be viable on its own. Harry knew that separating the latter from the former, was near on impossible. Like trying to separate the Statue of Liberty from its meaning.

Harry knew what his role in this meeting was. Pat had told each participant what was expected. Harry's heart pounded and he prayed that he didn't make a complete fool of himself in front of these people. They were the highest-level humans on Earth. Directors, Generals and CEOs were everywhere around the table.

He and Pat stood and walked stiff-legged over to the podium. It was nearly time for kick-off and he felt like running and hiding.

Harry twisted the ring on his finger and bit his lip, wondering how he got roped into this. A few days ago, he'd never heard of the

Werinn or the Biapene, *but now,* they were mega-important in many people's minds, including NASA, him and Pat. He'd always thought Earth deserved contact with non-humans, now he wasn't so sure.

Harry watched Pat grab the mic. None of the dignitaries looked happy or attentive – in fact quite the opposite. The meeting was organised quickly, and that was reflected in their disinterested faces. They were all compelled to be here, faster than a bullet, leaving most indignant and thinking about other things. Hardly the right frame of mind for something of this magnitude. Harry felt like going home. He felt like he was about to address a roomful of hungry lions who had not the slightest interest in him whatsoever. What they didn't know was the red meat he had for all of them.

All of them looked angry, downcast or bored...not ready for any sort of significant dialogue, certainly not one that carried such global consequences. He had little choice though. Harry stared painfully at Pat and waited patiently for his turn to speak. The longer it took, the better. He definitely didn't want to affront them. He hoped Pat's intro kept going and going...but it didn't. Soon enough, it was his turn.

His heart was jackhammering in his throat, so he loosened his tie and unbuttoned the top button of his shirt. Because it was nearly *time*. It was difficult to breathe, but easy to sweat. He gazed around the table and wished he hadn't. General Robson from the NSA was flicking a pen between two fingers and looked impatient and annoyed. With flaring nostrils and protruding eyes, he looked like a dragon, ready to decimate anyone who said a wrong word. The General looked him full in the eye and Harry felt his stomach tighten. This wasn't going to plan at all. He hadn't even spoken yet, and already, he was petrified.

'Gentlemen...we will start with an overview,' Pat glanced at Harry calmly while he spoke, '...and then we'll have a Q and A to deal with specific queries.' Pat looked around the table and tried unsuccessfully to make eye contact with anyone.

Everyone was looking down at their phones or at Pat's pre-prepared spiel about the meeting. Pat had a look of concentration and awareness, and with a raised eyebrow and furrowing forehead, he continued. 'And then each of the space industries will vote on the proposal. There are five of you, so a tie is out of the question.'

'Harry Watkins,' Pat said, with a small smile and flourished hand proudly pointing toward Harry, 'was part of the team that first intercepted the Werinn. He made first contact for NASA and Earth and will give you a first-hand debrief.'

Pat handed the mic to Harry who promptly dropped it on the floor. Picking it up he said, *'oh fuck,'* to himself he thought, which was amplified to the entire room. There was muffled laughter around the table. Colonel Winton from Homeland said loudly, 'I like him already.'

'S-Sorry about t-that,' Harry started. 'M-My brief is to give you all a feel of what happened with the Werinn.' He said nervously. Denis from Roscosmos was gawking at his phone and paying no attention whatsoever, which was typical of him. You would expect that he'd be on his best behaviour, given recent events. There was huge debate whether to include Russia in this, because of their atrocious treatment of Ukraine.

Ultimately, they were included because of the separation between the Kremlin and space. And now *this*. Harry reckoned they should have just been banned...*period*. Send them a message. But greater powers than he, invited them here along with everyone else.

Harry coughed and proceeded with his talk, trying to push down the nerves. 'I, uh...went to lunar-Gateway with Abby Mansfield as part of the foundation phase for Artemis. We were immediately asked to chase down an asteroid by NASA, which they said was similar to Oumuamua and came from the same area of space. NASA found that it was composed of some very unusual metals. They'd never been encountered in an asteroid, like, *not ever*. So, obviously they wanted to know more. NASA didn't want it to leave our system without it being characterised.'

Harry took a quick look around the room. 'Aragon entered the solar system just after Uranus and we intercepted it after it left the neighbourhood of Mars, using our fully-loaded Orion craft.' Harry coughed and drank some water from a glass that sat on the podium, courtesy of sweet Abby. All the suits seemed to be looking at their part of the table. Some were typing away on phones and those that were looking toward him, seemed angry or impatient. They either didn't want to be here or had somewhere else they needed to be. Probably both.

POTUS was still in his chair, so that was a good result. He had a reputation for departing meetings soon after they started. Currently, he had his head turned a little to one side, listening to Pat, but in a position to take the entire table in.

Harry wondered if the unrest and unfriendly faces was normal, or was it just him? They probably wondered who in God's name I was? A nobody from NASA, who was now a somebody, courtesy of the Werinn. All he was here to do, was give them a brief, he understood that the rest would take care of itself. Ultimately, they'd decide the future of the Werinn. Do we throw them a bone or don't we?

From his own perspective, it was the briefer the better, he reckoned, looking at the hostile faces that surrounded him. He felt like throwing the door open and getting the hell out of the room. Running for his life, but he had to finish his brief. So, he powered on.

'On the asteroid, our detectors aboard Orion read Gold, Titanium, Scandium, Holmium, Yttrium and other rare-Earth's. We, that is, me and Abby and our Orion vehicle, were pulled into the asteroid,' Harry coughed again and took a longer sip of water, 'we were then...*transported* to their planet. Harry tried to talk over the noise in the room, but couldn't talk loud enough to be heard, so he stopped. It was like a football crowd, but instead of Adrenaline and excitement, it was boorish noise and ugliness.

It wasn't his brief to convince anybody about anything, so he didn't try. He just waited for the yelled questions and accusations to die a natural death. The room was full of noise like gunfire. No one believed his "transport" thesis but again he was only here to tell them what happened. They could do and say what they liked. Words like *crazy, bonkers, loony* and phrases such as *lock him up* and *waste of time* filled every corner of the room. *Fuck 'em,* Harry thought. He crossed his arms and felt like hitting someone.

Eventually, the room became quiet enough to speak. Harry did his best to ignore it all, and not fire a curse-laden assault straight back. 'It, um...was a rocky planet like Earth with a very similar atmosphere, although appearance, *colours* were very different. That is where and when we met the Werinn. Their tech and understanding of the Universe was way in front of humans. Their Standard Model of Particles included dark matter and dark energy.' Harry raised two disbelieving eyebrows and gazed straight ahead.

'The Werinn were on their way to Earth a few years ago,' the background noise level went up in the room again, and everyone stared at Harry who again stopped his oration. The whole table looked up from their phones and laptops, piercing him with bright, feverish eyes. Harry had the strong feeling that several were simply waiting for him to reveal an inconsistency, that could be pounced on to catch him out. And be done with this unnecessary waste-of-time. Others scrutinized him closely, their intrigue level through the roof.

Even Denis from Russia was staring right at him. Harry felt it. What was disinterest ten minutes ago became razor-sharp attention.

All eyes from thirty-eight people gawked directly at Harry, waiting for more. *Wanting more.* He did his best to ignore them all and continued at his own pace. *Fuck*, he thought to himself. Harry was finally the centre of attention at the head of the room. He preferred the atmosphere before.

'T-They were c-coming to Earth from a planet near the red dwarf star Ross128 using space shortening to get here. Which means they travelled FTL to get here, but they stopped at Mars to learn a bit more about us before arriving. The Werinn detected the Mars Telecommunication Satellite and stopped to analyse it, realising it was unnatural and understanding it may help them, which it did, apparently.

'They downloaded the Earth internet from the Satellite and consequently learned how to speak our languages. The Werinn also learned a lot about humanity itself, some of which they found offensive and simply unacceptable.'

He spat the last words at everyone in the room, like bringing up spittle. Background noise went up like it did the first time, but even louder. General Hoyd from the NSA, who was never short of a word was chuckling, and said, '*offensive* indeed...what the Mona Lisa or David?' He snorted, grunted and then sat back down, still chuckling, handing the floor back to Harry.

The General took his seat, still chuckling on the way down. Everyone in the room, felt that the allegation was preposterous. They knew, *they believed*, that the history of Mankind was first-rate. Relative to what? Harry didn't know. The Werinn disagreed vehemently.

'It turns out,' Harry said, 'that humans declared war over eight thousand times, which according to the Werinn, cedes us as a vicious and violent race. More than a billion humans have been killed by war. And God knows how many injured physically or psychologically. They made the decision we were dangerous and aggressive to meet in person and turned their vessel around, too afraid to visit. *Too afraid to visit Mankind*,' Harry emphasised. This was a calamity of the highest order.

There was huge consternation in the room. Not one of the dignitaries realised the human penchant for warfare was *that* bad. They were aware of a few in our recent history, but that's about it. Most of them scratched their chins and oohed and aahed, surprised the figure was so incredibly high. *Vicious and violent...*well if the shoe fits, they all supposed but none of them had ever looked at it like that. It was hard to deny though. Over eight thousand wars, with Russia currently fire-bombing its neighbour, Ukraine – it *was* how it seemed. Denying it was simply a retort of regret. We'd been called out for it. The table generally thought the decision by the Werinn was harsh and punitive, but correct. No-one conceded that. *God no.*

The Werinn's decision to exclude humanity wasn't expected by anyone on Earth. General Hoyd mumbled and grumbled, not saying anything that was audible as words. He wasn't happy though. This time, it was the crusty Secretary of Defence for the US who spoke up. '*What is wrong with them?*' He yelled. 'Warfare is part of who we are.'

'Er...yeah, that's the problem,' Harry answered, not sure if he should have used "sir" and also not sure if he should have answered at all. He paused and was quiet, and so was Pat, so Harry took that as an "okay" to keep talking about his experiences.

'So, uh...they, as in the Werinn, decided they would continue to "fish" for humans, believing they could manage the risk of a few humans coming to Werinn. But they decided that Werinn as a whole, would not friend Earth, and it led them to asking for a document to formalise that agreement. Our UN was informed of the Werinn, and they ultimately provided that agreement.'

Harry reached for the glass of water again and took a sip from it. The room remained fairly quiet, although there were some groups that had split off and were grumbling to each other. The Secretary of Defence shook his head and looked especially unhappy as he griped and grumbled to the poor sod next to him, showing him something he'd written or drawn on a sheet of paper.

'The next part is probably the most interesting,' a more confident Harry said, standing up straighter at the podium. 'The Werinn received a visit from the Biapene, a race of creatures that are essentially highly evolved bipedal lizards, from a super-Earth in the same solar system.' Harry exchanged a quick glance with General Hoyd, who had zeroed in on him with narrowed eyes. Harry gulped hard and continued.

'The Biapene magnetosphere and ozone layer are no more, and a huge proportion of their population has developed galloping genetic diseases like cancer. Their planet is terminal, gentlemen.' Harry had a tinge of sadness in his eyes as he glanced at the General, who was still observing him with beady eyes.

'The Biapene have given the Werinn thirty days to vacate their own planet,' Harry said, 'so it could be made into the Biapene's new home, because theirs was no longer viable. The decision to threaten the Werinn was very unfortunate and obviously one we disagree with.

The Secretary of Defense stood up loudly and Harry knew why, so he hurried onto the next section, that would hopefully answer his question.

'The Werinn haven't weaponised their technology at all, because they haven't had the need, so the planet is essentially open to threats from space. Their homeland has never known war. Terrorism is not known and crime is rare and dealt with by other means. So, the Biapene's job would be fairly easy. They have told the Werinn that any of their population that remains after thirty days will be destroyed. Gentlemen...we have been asked to help.' Harry gazed around the mighty table with narrowed eyes, grateful that his talk had finished. He'd leave it to the feds to mull it over, and eventually vote on a decision. They all looked disinterested at best.

'...*Ar fuck 'em*,' General Hoyd yelled, they rejected *us*, so we do the same back to them.

Kiyoshi from JAXA repeated the same thing. Several suits nodded their heads angrily, and many more clearly agreed with the sentiment. By the yelling and the anger in the room, many thought what was good for the goose, was good for the gander too. Hence, Hoyd's reaction of *'fuck 'em'*, and the manic agreement with it.

This meeting was getting rapidly out of control and chaotic, Pat thought. Harry handed the mic back to Pat who took it with a firm nod. Both could see this going the wrong way fast. It needed firm action to hopefully get it back on the rails. These people were exhibiting the same behaviour that saw us blackballed by the Werinn. Pat watched them and nodded. *Christ*, he thought, scanning the table despondently.

Pat kept casting his critical eye over everyone in the room. He could see this turning into a yell-fest which is not what he or any of those present wanted. They came into this meeting chasing agreement, but so far, it was the exact opposite. The NASA No. 1 Boardroom had never been subject to this disagreeable bullshit...*ever*.

'*It's not as simple as that,*' Pat said loudly and clearly. 'They're our first contact and we have to take their request for help seriously.' Pat was deadly serious. His eyes were now flinty and sharp. He knew well what might be on the line. Tech and knowledge such as that held by the Werinn was indescribably precious. So, if we help them, and the outcome is to their satisfaction, the sky is the limit. The mob around the table had to realise it, *surely*.

Pat, Harry and Abby were all banned from explicitly linking their intel to the decision, but it was as obvious as the nose on your face, look at the shift they had on Aragon. Humans had nothing like it. The Werinn had a lot of tech that humans didn't - *period*. You'd have to be severely challenged not to recognize that.

'I am taking it seriously,' General Hoyd shouted. The answer is still *NO.'*

With that, everyone in the room laughed and the tension was broken. The General high-fived some of those nearest him. By the reaction, it was clear that most people present felt jilted by the Werinn. Unfortunately, all that was on show was the shallowness and mixed-up nature of the human condition. No-one on Earth had a remote understanding of the Werinn. They were very different, and so was their psychology, and no-one on Earth had a clue about them. The Werinn were expected to behave like humans and expected to be affected by different stimuli, in the same way as humanity. Harry knew the belief was a load of bollocks.

The fact that they were able to speak English confused everybody, and made them seem more like humanity than they really were. The fact was – they were *nothing* like humanity.

The Werinn were the *only* example of non-human life that we knew of. And they were asking for our help. Pat knew what had to happen. It's just that these *fuckers* in this room were so myopic that appreciating anything off-planet was next to impossible. Everything, everyone, every issue they were involved with, was here, on Earth.

Deep-down, he knew everyone in this room *got it*, but on the surface, they all took the statement by the Werinn very personally. It wasn't his role to massage their thinking and bring the bigger picture into crisper focus. It was up to the individuals in the room to do the right thing. The Administrator of NASA made all that clear. Pat knew what his and Harry's role had to be. Pat took it a step further. He did and had done all he could to ensure the Werinn received the help they sought. Any more and he would be breaking the agreed rules.

Pat smiled at the room and said, '*Okay*...this is now the Q and A part of the meeting, now that you understand the circumstances involved. Thanks Harry,' who sat next to Abby and watched Pat closely. Harry nodded at Abby and looked at her with soft eyes and a warm smile, happy that his formal part in this infernal process was over and done with.

Pietr Henry from ESA stood and directed himself toward Pat. 'This is a really tough one.' Pat nodded and said, *'indeed.'* 'On one hand they declined our friendship, claiming we were too vicious and violent, but on the other, they are our first and only contact. It's a vast Universe out there – and most of it is desert. So, every civilisation is precious. They may be our only contact...ever.' Pietr nodded at Pat and smiled generously, looked down, then continued.

'The Werinn's entire population is at stake including God knows how many of their children, who definitely don't deserve this. If it was Earth, we'd hope and pray that someone would help us – *think about it.*' He boomed to the room. 'They must feel alone and helpless. No weapons, no friends, no hope. They haven't helped themselves, but who are we to *judge*?'

'Well said, Pietr...well said, indeed,' Pat responded, with his thumb raised. 'We should never judge another species, even if we are judged.' Pat glared straight at General Hoyd who was flushed in the face and coughed several times.

Akio from JAXA suddenly piped up. 'Please tell me more about, er...this HELIOS laser we've been hearing about.'

Pat flourished with his hand to sit back down, 'take a seat Akio. It is not our intention to discuss this in detail here. Just know that it will work if we get the mandate to do it. The Biapene are expecting little resistance on or near Werinn.

'Lockheed Martin will install the laser defence system, HELIOS in the Orion craft, and we will transfer to their planet using their shift.' Easier said than done, Pat immediately thought. He stopped talking and gazed at the table of suits, waiting for the next question which he could tell wasn't far away. A lot of them were talking amongst themselves, some elbowing others to stand up and ask a question.

Overall, there was a lot of activity and chatter around the table. Pat could tell how unusual this issue was for them. Everyone was giving it their best shot, but Pat doubted anyone really got it.

Guy Janssen from NASA-Ames stood up, noisily pushing his chair backward along the floor, clearly having something to say. 'Maybe they're right.' He claimed. 'War occurs now and has occurred all through human history. We even believe it has had a positive effect on economies and it has even shaped human history.' He shook his head as if to say, "bullshit".

'It is quite hilarious that we are called out for it by a non-human race. We should have seen it ourselves. I, for one, agree with them –

we are a violent and super-aggressive race. There is no getting around it. History is history – there's no changing it. We are what we seem to be. I know that's not a question, more of a statement, but I agree with what they say about us.' With that, Guy sat down with a thump and a grind as he pulled his chair in. It seemed that most agreed with him. Humans were an example of a warring civilisation. History proved it empirically. There was simply too much evidence that proved who and what humans were.

The PM of India stood uncertainly and directed himself toward Pat and Harry. 'Y-You say the Biapene are u-uncomfortable being in t-the vacuum of space. Can you tell me more?

Pat looked at Narendra and scratched his jaw, wanting to be as upfront as possible. 'I don't think we know any more...Harry? He handed Harry the mic. Harry looked again at the Indian PM and saw a terrified, nervous little man who blinked rapidly, and was taking quick breaths, and had very tired, red eyes. He was obviously well out of his comfort zone, and was anxious for his hundreds of millions of citizens who were all deeply spiritual.

'The general population of Biapene has a problem with heights, we are told,' Harry said. 'Acrophobia afflicts virtually the entire population, which as we know here on Earth, causes a major issue for astronauts.' Harry flourished his hands to show how massive it was. 'The Biapene have few astronauts and those they do have, need to push hard through their fear. So, Mr Sharma, it is *always* a problem for them. We would play upon that fear.'

George Lezar from the Canadian Space Agency was next. He stood unsteadily and gazed at Pat, needing his help. 'What do *you* think we should do?' He was lost. This decision was too much – they needed direction. *Pat's* direction.

'That's not the question we meant, George.' Pat was annoyed, staring at George with a pinched expression and narrowed eyes. 'It needs to be your *own* opinion...but I would say, if I was asked, that because this is our first contact and they are talking about losing their planet to a species who are essentially scared of space, we should look favourably at it. I realise they have shunned us, and that complicates the issue, but they have asked for our help. *Human help.* And it's within our scope to help them. Mankind can assist the Werinn to defeat the Biapene. Help them retain the residency of their planet.' Pat stopped talking and put his fist gently on his chin and looked like he was suddenly praying.

Fuck it, he thought. They might as well know the reason for NASA's strangely affirmative state-of-mind. Probably cost him dearly, but at least they'd all know what was at the root of it all.

'The Werinn have intel and tech that humans spend billions of dollars each year to find, and to date we have been unsuccessful.' A mission NASA would normally walk away from was given oxygen. *Surely,* most knew that there was something else on the line here. Otherwise, this mission wouldn't have been given the time of day.

Harry was floored when he heard it. Pat warned him not to mention it at least six times, and he told Abby the same, even though she wasn't talking formally. And now he goes and says it himself. Both of them looked at each other in consternation. *WTF?* He warned us not to do it, then blurts it out himself. '*Go figure*,' Harry said forcefully to himself.

'NASA's contention is that the Werinn would share everything with whomever successfully helps them. They are a very advanced technology – and in one fell swoop – humans could effectively become *them.*' Pat scrubbed a hand down his face and was visibly sweating. 'That's more than I meant to say George, but there you go.' Pat's knees were weak and he felt like the room was closing in, but he knew he had to stay strong for this mob. They might have been very senior with the government and hold TS/SCI clearance, but this stuff was way ahead of that.

'So, (cough) y-you believe we should, er...help t-them?' George asked, pressing his lips together. He stood with his hands locked together, swallowing rapidly, still having no idea what to do.

'That's your decision George, we are here to assist you only, not control your thinking. NASA wants your choice to be untarnished by us. Our opinion on these matters is irrelevant. That goes for all the agencies.' Pat said, looking at them all, individually. George took his seat and Pat waved at them all, suggesting the same from them. An untarnished opinion, based solely on their thinking, after hearing the spiel from Pat and Harry.

Pat reiterated, 'the debrief provided by Harry Watkins, gives you all the details from his interactions with the Werinn, and the Biapene, and from that you decide whether we help the Werinn. There may be casualties, you need to go into this with your eyes wide open. But one thing is certain, humanity only gets one crack at helping the first interstellar species that comes its way. I don't care what bullshit is thrown at that statement – it is true.'

'*Be certain*, that this cause is the right one.' Pat took a seat, and let them suck on his words for a while. He'd done all he could. Any more specific direction and he ran the risk of breaking the rules and being open to indictment by the American DoD. They spoke to him and warned him, just prior to this meeting.

Jim Hall from NASA HQ stood up and couldn't hold himself back. He spoke quickly, with a voice full of enthusiasm. 'What did you see on their planet Harry?' Jim's eyes were like full moons. He found the whole issue of completely different life fascinating and massively intriguing.

This was out-of-scope for this meeting, and Jim knew it, but Pat played along, he empathised with Jim's curiosity. The fact that he was good friends with Jim had a bit to do with it. So, he let him go without intervening. Instead of reprimanding Jim, and telling him to sit down, Pat handed the mic to Harry. 'That's a bit off-topic Jim, but we'll let you go.' Pat smiled wryly, pointed at Jim, then nodded at Harry, to give him the okay.

'The Werinn kept us on a tight leash, probably because we were destined *not* to be friends. Remember though, they have found and characterised dark matter and dark energy, so their tech is well ahead of ours.' Harry held a shaky hand firmly on the podium, Jim was floored they'd found and quantified the characteristics of dark matter. The Werinn knew 100% of the state of the Universe versus Mankind 5%.

Harry gazed at the table of officialdom and saw several of them lean forward, keen to hear what he said next. *Finally, some real interest*, he said to himself, smiling drolly at the suits around the table.

'I can tell you Jim that they have red colored roads that are composed of micro-processed plastic, and contain plant steriles, which act as cement. It binds stone aggregate and importantly, *absorbs carbon dioxide from the atmosphere when it cures*. It has more tensile strength than asphalt or regular concrete they say.' Jim started smiling widely...and his eyebrows disappeared under his fringe. He urged Harry on with his eyes and a nod of the head. So far, he was stupefied by what he was saying.

'Also, we saw their cities from a distance, and all the buildings were pink or red. They were tetragonal or isosceles triangles from what we could see. The three-pointed buildings and homes are made that way by law. Legislation demands that any building occupied by a Werinn needs to comply with the three-point plan and be polygonal in nature. I am told that the Werinn themselves are only sustainable if this law is enforced.'

No-one in the room cared for the three-point law, mainly being interested in "what's in it for me", which in this case was removing carbon from Earth's atmosphere. Global warming haunted everyone around the table. The next question was predictable.

'How much, um...*carbon* can the new concrete remove Harry?' Jim asked.

'All of it. The sky's the limit. If we had it, the problem with excess carbon in the atmosphere would just go away. It'd all be fixed in the concrete forever.'

'*Fuck a goddamn duck,*' Jim blurted. Er...s-sorry about that,' he said, looking around the table, bright red like a traffic light. Many around the table were chuckling and sniggering, and shared Jim's enthusiasm. Many were mouthing "all". Others were cheering loudly, still others were holding their arms in the air and some were just fixed silently on Harry, stunned and enchanted by what he was telling them. The red roads could remedy the problems with climate-change on Earth, and it had them all firmly by the coat-tails.

It seemed so simple. All they had to do was save the Werinn's arse, and scare the Biapene off...and climate change would be a bad memory. Everyone in the room made the connection. The Werinn were Mankind's ticket to survival and growth.

And the dark particles, FTL, GUT...they seemed like impossible fantasies. Everyone around the room was cheering. Even the crusty old Secretary of Defence for the US looked happy. What started as a ho-hum meeting, had turned into *this*. Everyone sitting around the table now realised what Earth would gain if they helped this species succeed. It *wasn't* just about the mission. It was a means to an end.

The Werinn hadn't specifically used it as bait to encourage the humans, but Earth was reading between the lines. They knew it was there - at least they were pretty sure it was. If the mission happened, and if it proved a success, the intel and the tech from the Werinn would be theirs.

General Hoyd squinted triumphantly at Harry. For the first time, he thought the Werinn were worth saving. He didn't give a shit about dark matter or dark energy, but climate change? Yes he did. General Hoyd knew that Earth's weather and the GOPs constituents, needed saving. Hurricanes, floods, tornadoes, wildfires and droughts were all snow-balling. Governments around the world only had a few short years left to sort it out and he realised it was moving too slowly – green hydrogen, wind turbines, solar and nuclear were good, but an energy hungry world like Earth needed more.

Fusion was too far off to be a solution. The red stuff, it seemed, was what the planet needed. To get it, we needed to do one thing. General Hoyd, Colonel Roberts and several others rubbed their hands together and held their thumbs up. They were all-in. The Werinn were definitely, without question, worth saving, even if it cost a few astronauts.

Harry continued, chatting about what he'd observed on the planet. 'Houses and buildings were all triangular in shape, to take advantage of the golden ratio. It keeps the Werinn population balanced and energised. The most amazing thing is their ability to secure tables, chairs, tv's, white-goods inside walls that are entirely invisible to the human eye once they're locked off. The Werinn's use of extra dimensions has provided them a technology Mankind could only dream of. With Werinn help on physics and extending the Standard Model, liaising with players like CERN, and the aero-space industry, like Lockwood Martin, the tech can be ours,' Harry said, with glowing eyes. 'It would be a fantasy come true.' He finished on.

Background noise increased in volume again. The overall reaction in the room to the wall thing was *"huh"* – a rush of bewilderment came through loud and clear. No-one understood what the hell was up with that one, but knew generally, if humans were able to take advantage of it, amazing things would likely follow.

They all realised, that with the understanding of the Werinn, transferred to humans, amazing things would happen on our planet. New industries would rise, new products would come to dominate, and brand-new technologies would wend their way across Earth.

Being the saviour of the Werinn made good economic and technical sense to the entire room. The actual mission...not so much. Providing assets of war to Werinn needed to make sense. The mission itself, should stand on its own two legs. Harry knew it didn't. Not enough was known about the Biapene.

Harry continued to amaze. 'The whole lot folds back into the wall, and could be pulled out at will, using just your fingers. Similar, is a formerly blank wall becoming a TV in its entirety. When you leave a house, everything is put back in the wall with a flick and it is locked off. 'So, you see,' Harry said, knowing Pat had green-lighted it. 'There is a *lot* to learn from the Werinn, starting with the physics of the Universe itself.'

After noise levels reduced, Jock from US Homeland stood tall, and asked Pat and Harry, 'you mentioned dark matter...did the Werinn say exactly what it was?' Jock's eyes glowed, and were wide open like billiard balls, waiting for the answer which he knew would likely blow his mind. The search for dark matter had gone from space itself to the LHC to the deepest mine shafts on the planet and cost hundreds of billions of dollars. He had sweaty palms and trembling hands as he stood there and hoped Harry had the answer that so many astrophysicists on Earth sought.

'All they said Jock, was that it was a special type of Higgs, that was invisible inside their collider, before it was shut down.' They wouldn't be more specific, although they did say that it was found through missing mass. Adding up the mass of the shattered Higgs, they realised that some of it was missing and had transformed into something else.'

'Er...okay,thanks.' *Holy fuck*...that's a step forward, he reckoned. They'd narrowed the field substantially. At least they knew it was a real particle. Some had given up and thought Einstein and Newton were wrong. And some modification to their theories needed to occur when they analysed gravity at a distance. Now they knew for sure. The old timers were correct. The dark articles were real.

'Er...right...' Jock said, blinking and trying to refocus his eyes and doing his best to right himself, but felt dizzy at the abrupt realisation 'What happened to the Biapene magnetosphere...do we know?' His mind was still spinning with the sudden info on dark matter.

Harry cleared his throat 'They believe, rightly or wrongly, that it was their collider that impacted the core's rotation. It was this that created their magnetic shield in the first place. Everything about the planet stopped rotating. All the magnetics died. The ozone layer soon went.'

Jock answered Harry's oratory with a questioning look, 'So, the entire planet was wide open to its rather unstable and close star as well as the wind from the Galactic centre. There was nothing left, apart from the atmosphere, to deflect or absorb ionising particles, which proved to be very bad news for Biapene. The population got the lot. Which wasn't good for anyone. It was like being arms-length from the broken reactor at Chernobyl. Remember how close their star was.'

Jim Hall grimaced. Like most, he thanked God that humanity had theirs intact. Or Earth would be in the exact same boat.

Jock sat back down and Ben Portman from the Csa bobbed up. He was an absolutely brilliant mathematician and provided a lot of help, not only to others in the Csa, but to space agencies generally. He stared at Harry seriously. 'So, they continued to "fish" for humans and then tell us they don't approve of us. Odd behaviour is all.'

'*Here here,*' came from around the table with enough force to part the hair of those at the front of the room. A lot of the suits started clapping.

'*Okay...okay,*' Pat said, waiting for the noise and the anger to subside. 'They know no one else. *We're it*, and they reckon our mind-set might be useful. We should take that as a compliment...I think.' Pat returned to his seat. Maybe it's *not* a compliment, he thought. They wanted our input because we were used to killing. *Shit*. Perhaps he needed to change his thinking. The Werinn thought we were an asset because we were murderous. Great compliment. *Not*.

'Who the hell do they think we are? Barbaric philistines...the whole lot of us?' Joules from JAXA said, with his tight Japanese accent. His hands were clenching and unclenching by his sides. He reckoned they had us pegged all wrong but admitted our history read badly. Even our recent history looked bad – Palestine, Ukraine, Afghanistan, the routing of Iraq. Humans were very aggressive – there was no denying it. On paper, it looked dreadful.

'Basically...yes.' Pat said. 'They think our mind-set and weapons can send the Biapene packing. The Werinn's view is that it won't take much. Any offense that is organised by the Werinn will be a massive surprise...if the Biapene have a fear of being sucked into the vacuum, we've won I believe.' He glanced at Harry who looked mortified. 'That's not designed as encouragement,' Pat said caustically, 'that is my personal opinion only.' Pat sat back down and handed the mic to Harry, then looked at the clock and realised that the time for Q and A was over. Much like his career, he reckoned. He'd said way too much. He'd been warned not to do it, but he blurted it out anyway.

Pat put his hand out for the mic, and Harry handed it happily back. 'Time to vote gentleman,' Pat said. 'Each of the five space agencies, JAXA, ESA, CSA, NASA and Roscosmos will provide me their vote within the next ten minutes. The sound of his own voice was loud in his ears. The subject is, "Should NASA provide assistance to the

Werinn." Individual votes will remain anonymous...my business only,' Pat said, trailing off.

Pat returned to his seat again, smiled and shrugged. It was now a waiting game, while the groups got closer together and, in some cases, split, to discuss the fate of the Werinn world. Which so affected Earth.

Apart from saying too much, Pat felt good about the meeting. He cast his eye over the huge table and thought they all had an understanding of what was at stake. If they didn't, they had no business being here.

On the one hand there was the security of the Werinn, on the other, was what Mankind could gain from a successfully assisted Werinn intervention. Their tech and intel was all up for grabs. Humanity had obtained little of it and probably wouldn't for hundreds of years. Pat hoped the decision came back the way he wanted. But he knew the Werinn mission had to stand up too. NASA decried risk, but he felt a slender acceptance of it from the Administrator, at their final briefing. He too, desperately wanted what the Werinn were pedalling.

NASA wanted what the Werinn possessed, even if it meant engaging in a rather risky mission, a rather different mission to the norm. NASAs missions so far had been scientific and investigative only. But the Ark of the Covenant was at stake with this one. And NASA wanted it more than anything in its history. With it, leaps could be made like never before.

8.

Surprise

"While there's life, there's hope."
~Stephen Hawking

The space agencies, through Pat, indeed said *yes*. They couldn't turn their backs on a planet full of beings that were faced with planetary eviction, when asked directly. Also playing a large role was the intel that the Werinn civilization could add to human culture on Earth. The decision demanded that the mission stand on its own two legs, but it was always a combination of the two. Especially since Pat blurted it out, and effectively made it formal.

Everyone who voted knew the mission had to stand by itself. The decision they made, though, included a bit from the first and a bit from the second. The space agencies had failed to make a decision on just the mission itself, simply because they were homo sapiens. *"What's in it for me"*, could never be fully eliminated.

Harry was sure that the statement by NASA was a complete load of bollocks. They couldn't turn down the first interstellar species Earth met. I mean, *come on. Let's get real*. The fact was, no-one on Earth could work them out or find them – humans weren't smart enough and chasing them was costing a fortune. What the mission stood on was a wealth of intellectual property that no-one on Earth could find, or do the math for. *Period.*

Mankind, or at least those in the driving seats, saw it as a chance to advance themselves overnight, by putting together a rescue package for the Werinn. And hopefully benefitting from it. If they played their cards right - should the Werinn triumph, with humanities help, they would likely be lavished with secrets that have permanently eluded Mankind. There would be no standing on shoulders here – they would be outright gifts from the Werinn. That was the hope from Earth anyway.

The risk of losing astronauts and craft had to be high, most thought. Yet, so far, there was little official mention of it. It was simply a statement of risk. Earth generally, suspected that *quid pro quo* was involved. Because, on its own, most realised, it didn't make a lot of sense. Humans *must* expect something for putting lives at risk. Giving anyone a free-ride wasn't something humans were known for.

NASA gave the impression to the world that it was a conservative, risk-averse group. *Okay, then...what happened?* NASA claimed that it was a democratic answer to a very difficult question, and that everyone on Earth knew as much. Then they leant back on their favourite phrase. That Earth would never say *no* to its first interstellar contact.

*   *   *

Lockheed Martin in New Orleans were the engineers of the original Orion capsule and were now working on the installation of laser systems into their docking tunnel. Then the modified craft would be shipped to the Kennedy Space Station in Florida. NASA would send seven modified Orion craft to the Werinn, using three SpaceX Falcon-Heavy rockets and four massive NASA SLS rockets. They would slingshot passed Venus and on toward Aragon some nine hours later. That was the plan anyway.

Harry and Abby would come back to Earth, earlier than they were scheduled to, and splash down in the same designated Pacific Ocean locale not far from Baja, California. Harry had already returned to Earth for the meeting, now he'd have to do it again. They would then occupy one of the modified Orion craft, and head to space again, with an SLS Rocket. That was the plan. Harry knew the risks, but was determined to be part of the group who went to Werinn to help them. He wouldn't be deterred. Incredibly, he'd come to like the Werinn and so had Abby. She was terrified, but she'd follow Harry to the end of the world if necessary. She trusted him and his judgement.

NASA were prepared to offer them both a million dollars to join the mission, because their sign-on would likely encourage others. NASA didn't have to do anything though. To NASA's disbelief, Harry and Abby registered first, with zero encouragement required.

Lockheed Martin already made integrated laser systems for the navy and they now had a contract with NASA to empower seven Orion craft similarly, which they did partly at their skunkworks site in Nevada and their main "white" site in Louisianna.

They were a defence-contractor and Lockheed's facility at Michoud in New Orleans was enormous, and a hive of activity. It was like its own heavily populated town, with enormous SLS rocket segments, Orion capsules and systems, and ship segments for the navy. Being built from scratch, like the Aegis combat system. Enormous warehouses were everywhere, crammed with parts of jets, planes, ships, space capsules and huge rockets. At first it looked like a crowded shemozzle, but all the thousands of people had a purpose and an agenda. Tech was everywhere you looked. If you liked the military – this place was a dream, come true.

The only "problem" with the modified Orion craft was its inability to dock. The laser turret was installed where the docking device was, to make it as simple as possible. The pins and latches and hatch itself had been removed in favour of a vacuum-proof turret that was immovable. The laser shooter, when the time came, would move to the Docking Tunnel, and would direct the movement of the craft with voice commands. Pulsed hits to a craft might destroy it, or , cause extreme metal shock and severe pain to the occupants, interior to the craft. All of the combatants were carbon and DNA based, so a similar reaction to a laser was expected.

To reach Aragon, seven giant rockets now stood in the NASA hangar, ready to slowly crawl to 39B at the Kennedy Space Center, Florida. And crawl they would, on the back of CT-2, which had two sets of huge tractor tracks and crept along at only two miles an hour.

Rockets would each carry a modified Orion craft to space to sit in a circular parking orbit around Earth. From there they would slingshot around Venus and head straight for Aragon which was now beyond Venus and the solar system, heading rapidly for Pisces.

*   *   *

Seven Orion craft headed toward Venus, to fly within one thousand kilometres of the sulphuric acid atmosphere of the planet. It seethed and churned, seemingly at arms-length from the seven craft, a planet enveloped by a runaway greenhouse atmosphere. At the surface, it was hot enough to turn a probe into a melted, bubbling puddle. Just ask the Soviets.

Harry gazed out of the fore windows of the craft and could see the lights from six other craft. Venus was huge and golden in the window. Abby gawked at it, remarking she could make out landforms beneath the outer atmosphere.

Harry tilted his head and glanced sideways at her. He knew how impenetrable the atmosphere was, and how unlikely it was that she could see anything close to the ground. The atmosphere was heavy enough and hot enough to dissolve pure lead after all. The Soviets made efforts to build vessels, which quickly melted in the acidic furnace-like conditions. And Abby reckons she can see to the ground as if it was a perfect, sunny day. He didn't feel like arguing, and didn't want to hurt her feelings, so he ignored her comments and just grunted. Soon enough, she relented anyway.

'They're probably just shadows,' Abby said. 'Anyway the upper atmosphere is where it's supposed to get interesting. Temperature is about Earth-like, right?' Harry nodded, hoping that the insanity she exposed was just fleeting. 'Techs from Earth found phosphine – a pretty good bio-signature, right?' Harry nodded again. 'Something might be floating there and respiring.' Abby looked at Harry like an Owl, rubbing at an eyelid, awed by the whole idea. The prospect of non-human life in her own solar system intrigued her, especially somewhere as caustically boiler-like, as Venus.

Abby was thinking about the last time they encountered the shift. They were rendered unconscious and pulled into it and across it by something approximating gravity, and she assumed the same would happen this time. But what if it didn't? What if nothing happened? Their plan, if you could call it that, was built around the same happening again. Being pulled into that thing was fundamental. And it was the strategy of six other craft. Otherwise, the pilots would need to do the flying which would add another layer of complexity to the incoming craft. Not one of them would agree to either soft-landing or crashing into Aragon. So, the future of the mission depended on it happening the same way. *Fuck*, Harry thought, NASA hadn't thought this plan through very well. Dragging an object in was how the object operated, Oshn said that. So, they expected the same, this time.

Orion would get close enough for that to happen – like last time, and hopefully it would be repeated seven times, until all craft had shifted to Werinn. If it was any different than that – their plan was cactus and a new one was required. Which had to be hatched on the spot. The rest of the expected mission worried her too, it seemed hastily and yes, *carelessly* hatched.

NASA seemed to pay the negatives little mind. The Werinn simply knew too much, stuff humans had spent billions of dollars on, and taken decades to unsuccessfully search for. Mankind was sick of beating its head against a brick wall. They'd far rather buy the intelligence, even if it was by arranging a tin-pot mission that was as risky as hell. The Werinn would see humanity as people that wanted to help, irrespective of the outcome of the mission. Which meant NASA intended to re-home some or all of the Werinn in the event that the Biapene were successful. Harry let his mind wander – wondering how the hell NASA would engineer *that*.

'*Focus on the mission*,' he admonished himself silently. '*Enough speculating*.' He elbowed Abby and showed her his game-face, urging her to do the same, by pointing at his face, with his fingers. She nodded and faced forward, still uncertain but she held her muscles tight. They'd been shown many times how to target and lock-on to a subject, and how to pulse-fire, but Abby was deeply unsure of their ability to deter an alien race. One whose home planet was essentially gone or at best terminally ill. That would mean they were desperate, wouldn't it?

Abby knew they were getting between a civilisation's bid for life. It could be incredibly risky. She reckoned NASAs ambitions were all wrong. It was fine to want intel and tech for the betterment of their home planet. Formulating a rescue mission that was as risky as hell, to secure benefits, was just plain wrong.

*   *   *

Harry slowly came closer to Aragon, and it was without doubt pancake-shaped and pinky-coloured the same as he remembered it, replete with metal posts and a rough, disturbed area in front of it. The other pilots knew that proximity of tech, seemed to excite the object that was buried on the asteroid. Abby saw light coming generally from the buried object. The tech on the asteroid was conscious and waited for them to cross its scope.

All the pilots knew what happened to Harry and Abby last time – they'd seen the recordings taken by their Orion, which showed the vision from its SAW cameras. So, they were waiting for the same thing to happen to them. It was how the machine rolled, apparently.

Harry and Abby edged closer to the asteroid and saw the metal bars come into view and then disappear again as the rock rotated, end over end. The rock had a light-reddish tinge to it when in the Sun's light and seemed fine-grained and layered. Where the anomaly was, it had clearly been disturbed.

There was an untidy hill near the centre of the bars, loosely packed and different from the rest. Their craft was only a kilometre from the asteroid's rear edge, about the same distance as last time, when the object took over with its magnetics that pulled them in.

If that happened again, they needed to engage their VTOL engines before they slid past the metal bars. All the pilots knew that. This was a required move and they were told as much by the Werinn.

The VTOL engines on the Orion would not alter their trajectory toward the anomaly. This action would allow a controlled descent on Werinn, because this time there were multiple craft arriving and there'd be no net to assist in landing.

Thankfully, it did happen the same way - using photons and neutrinos, Harry and Abby's craft was dragged close to the object and just before they struck it, Harry engaged their VTOL engines, which as they thought, made no difference to their trajectory. They continued their inward spiral, uninterrupted. They should have hit a hard surface, but didn't. Incredibly, they kept on moving uninterrupted.

The remaining V formation of vehicles, broke up and they all got behind the Number One craft, waiting for their turn to be dragged toward the anomaly and hopefully spat out on Werinn to VTOL safely to the ground.

Harry and Abby and their craft were instantly on Werinn, VTOL'ing to the ground, in virtually Earth-like gravity, in full, somewhat reddish light from the star that was about 3pm if they were on Earth. The other Orion craft were following them, all the pilots well-schooled in what happened last time and what was expected this time.

The star that warmed this planet was a vivid red and sat in a purple sky surrounded by a few bluish cirri clouds. Harry stared at the scene and thought how different the space-industry must be on

Werinn. On this planet - blasting through the atmosphere with rockets *was for schmucks*, he thought happily.

With a wry smile, he returned his vision to the sky, noticing how red the light was, refusing to acknowledge the bewilderment and perplexity caused by the shift - the dramatic change in contrast and brightness he was forced to adjust to, which knocked him for six last time, but this time was marginally easier to deal with.

Soon enough, there were seven Earthly ships in a line, in a place called Uskn on Werinn. Coming down, he saw a river not far away which was brim full of very blue, almost glowing, water. Surrounding the river were short, thick trees everywhere.

The main difference to Earth was the colour of the grass and vegetation, and the vividness of the water – it almost shone light blue like there was a light source beneath it. He'd already seen blue grass, but nearer to the trees, it was dark grey and black, like the foliage of the trees. How unusual, he thought? Was naturally occurring grass on this planet blue or black? Dark made sense, blue, not so much.

After the engine had fully powered down - a group of eight Werinn walked directly toward the lead craft, headed by Oshn who the humans knew spoke English fluently. Harry swallowed nervously, holding his breath, as they approached.

Oshn was at the foot of the first Orion craft and turned the handle and thumped the yoke until it clicked, then opened the side hatch with a loud clunk and a thud. All the Werinn stood on the cusp of Orion with Oshn actually inside. 'Please, come,' he said seriously, flourishing to Harry and Abby with his hand.

'We, uh...need to go with,' a muddled Abby said distractedly, pointing at Oshn and continuing the unfurling process which wasn't going so well. Her hands were slow and clumsy, her fingers were like thumbs. Harry, firstly needed to get out of his chair before they went anywhere. Both were gasping for breath and shivering violently. *Shifting* wasn't easy. The instant change in environments was a killer. Their hands and fingers wouldn't follow instructions. Fine motor skills took a while to come back.

They eventually exited the vehicle through the open hatch at mid-ships, almost falling out of their chairs and rambling spastic-like to the hatch. Both of them now stood outside the craft and fell into line to be led somewhere by a team of Werinn, including Oshn, who walked ahead and behind, with a clear destination in mind. The humans from each craft were in the middle of the group of beings looking at the torsos of non-humans.

From where Harry was, near the front of the line, he could see black trousers, covering pale, spindly legs without hair, untucked cloth covering the upper body and huge heads that extended quite a way backward. He could also smell them – a strong musky odour together with something floral. Harry reckoned they were wearing deodorant of some sort. *Of all things*, he thought, smiling drolly and rolling his eyes at no-one. Their odour could be hidden from other Werinn, but not from another species.

Abby couldn't help wonder where they were being taken...and why? Was it the mission already? They still had eight days to go. Maybe they wanted to talk strategy, she thought, or assess the weapon system. Probably both, she reckoned. Abby worried, but they'd hardly do them any serious disservice, having asked us for help. As long as they were telling the truth, she supposed.

Accept the fucking obvious, she implored herself, instead of looking for issues that her mind could dismantle and put back together the wrong way.

All of them followed the line of Werinn and eventually walked up a small red incline. They went through a wall and into an empty white room that was well lit, without having any conspicuous lighting sources. Oshn asked everyone in the room to stand close to the wall, which they all did, ending up leaning on it. Clearly, standing anywhere else was a risk.

He worked his magic on a remote control. Out of the wall came a large ovular table and twelve red chairs that seemed to be made of a hard plastic. They were all directed to them by their Werinn hosts. The Werinn were used to the tech and barely batted an eyelid when it was withdrawn from the wall.

Everyone from Earth who saw the items appear for the first time, issued a child-like "aaah". It filled the entire room, and then they sat on the chairs provided to them. It left only Oshn standing before them, panting and heaving, like a pacing colossus. Ready for action apparently. Abby didn't want to say it, but she sure thought it. Humanity was made to appear very juvenile and immature. Perhaps it was just her.

Presumably, Oshn was preparing to speak to them, because he continued to stand after everyone else had taken their seats. He stopped moving and his neck and head straightened and lengthened as he sized his audience up.

Harry sat next to Abby and it was the same for all the human pilots and co-pilots. There were seven Werinn, eight with Oshn, and they sat opposite the humans and stared straight at them. The Werinn continued to blink sideways in a display that was very off-putting. Abby brought a shaky hand to her forehead, not sure how much she could take. She glanced at Harry, who gazed back at her with a beaming expression, giving her courage in the face...of *this*.

The humans didn't know it, but life on the Werinn planet came from Biapene soon after their solar system formed. Panspermia delivered proteins and RNA to Werinn inside a meteor, and life ascended ultimately to a ferret-like animal that used to widely inhabit their planet. Over billions of years, the animal evolved into the bipedal Werinn and hence they were omnivores and also corralled several indigenous animals for food...just like humans did. On Biapene, life evolved into an intelligent reptilian civilisation, not unlike a highly evolved bipedal dinosaur. Both from the same spark of life.

'Thank you for coming, and thank you for bringing your technology to this planet,' Oshn said, making an intricate movement above his head, with his hand. Werinn for *thankyou* or similar she supposed. Abby grinned at Harry, happy that they were being welcomed to Werinn and not shown the door, like before. Amazing what *need* can do to a previously unfriendly race. And a broken relationship.

Oshn gazed at Abby and continued talking. She was still stunned that this ungainly-looking creature could speak English but understood the lessons available on the internet. It was incumbent on decoding the language in the first place which obviously occurred. The Werinn were clearly smart folk. They also received our TV signals, so Abby reckoned it sort of made sense.

'We have only met the Biapene a few times before,' Oshn said, 'and they are strikingly analogous to us, although they are a completely different species and are very different physically,' he said. *But* they are very comparable in tech, are almost the same age and have a similar affinity with polygons to feed their psyche.'

'They come from the fourth planet in our system and they were completely different in mind-set, the second-time they were here. This was after their own planet's core stopped rotating and they issued a planet-wide demand on us and threatened our entire race.'

Oshn stopped briefly and swept the humans with a piercing glare. He wanted to be certain that Mankind absorbed the gravity of his words. 'In essence,' he said, 'they declared war on us.' Oshn gasped for breath and shivered violently, from head to toe. His whole body seemed to be vibrating episodically.

'The f-first time,' he said, puffing and panting, 'the B-Biapene v-visit was planned, and they arrived to meet us because they thought the Galaxy and Universe was entirely devoid of other life. They'd found no EMAR from "others" or been witness to any techno- or bio-signatures, despite searching for a long, *long* time. Seventy of your years. They had enormous orbital telescopes and many ground-based systems, dedicated to the search. But they'd found nothing.' Oshn's eyes were glowing, because standing before him was the Biapene's answer. They were wrong.

'There was only the Werinn planet and that was in their own system. Neither the Werinn nor the Biapene could be sure that life on one planet didn't seed the other. So, whether one or the other was brand-new life was open to conjecture. It was *new* life that both planets sought. And neither planet in the system were certainties.'

'You too are in a similar situation. 'Earth's internet is full of your unsuccessful SETI searches, which interestingly, located our planet, but not the life on it. Ross128 is our star.' Oshn ran his hand over his hairless head and stared blankly at Abby. They were there – and we didn't find them. An opportunity lost, she reckoned.

'The Biapene attempted to find signatures of life and EMAR generated by "others" but had been unsuccessful and their conclusion – or at least one of them – was that their system was the only one. They took a strong fancy to our homes and buildings. Like us, the Biapene believed strongly that the pyramidal shape extended their mortal lives and amplified their personal energy. To them, as to us, it is a major source of vitality. This is more evidence that we share the same spark of life.'

'Apart from the visual, we are very similar races, and it has led to them taking a strong interest in our structures – our homes and buildings. The Biapene can live in them and draw energy and life, because of their shape. We, as Werinn, believe that this detail has led in part to their decision to take Werinn as their own.' Oshn's arms had seemingly lost all life, and were now hanging limply at his sides. He was breathless, and shook his large head.

'So, the Biapene, eight of them, came to visit us, not long ago and they were shy, nervous and flighty individuals. None of them – astronauts presumably – were comfortable dealing with space itself. Apparently, the vacuum and heights were a lot to deal with. None of them were comfortable with it, and to do a space-walk, which was sometimes required, was down to a very few. Most flatly refused to do it. Abby was stunned, and tried to equate it with Earth. She almost laughed out loud, imagining the airline industry being thus afflicted. *And* NASA and SpaceX. The global economy would be routed.

'Our view is that this mind-set will give us, and importantly you, the *strong* advantage. Your astronauts are used to space and you've said they are all trained in laser warfare, although lack actual battle experience.' Oshn nodded at Harry, hoping for confirmation, but all he got was bewilderment. Harry was scared of this assignment. He, like them all, was aware that knowing *what* to do, wasn't the problem. Experience with using the technology in anger was.

They could've sent Naval officers who were experienced with HELIOS, but they opted for astronauts, with Naval officers left to lead HELIOS training with astronauts in the Orion vessels. She imagined putting navy officers in Orion vessels, and almost laughed out loud.

Harry didn't think any of the astronauts were expected to come home. Earth cared about our welfare, but they cared about the Werinn's intel more. Harry was convinced NASA wanted intelligence from the Werinn, at nearly any cost, human, material or Werinn.

Abby wanted to back out, Harry could tell. As much as he too wanted to he was the leader and *couldn't* withdraw. He had to go through with it no matter what. He wanted desperately to protect Abby, but there was a higher calling. His employer made it for him.

Oshn looked anxious now, rubbing the back of his hairless neck. All the colour had drained from his face. He fingered an intricate necklace and grabbed it, rubbing the back of his neck with the chain. He also bit a lip if it could be called that, looking terribly worried. 'Prior to engaging the Biapene, we would like to take you around our world, so you can see what we are fighting for,' Oshn said.

'S-Sounds good to me,' Harry said, thinking *yes. Finally.* He was definitely up for seeing more of their world. The rest of them were nodding enthusiastically in agreement. They had nothing else to do, so touring the planet was fine for most of them. Others just wanted to get down to business and get the job done.

Harry was startled by the image of a huge white rounded object, not unlike a large tic-tac, that came straight at him. It emerged over the trees, making no noise, and landing silently on the black grass beside them. It had no windows, front or side, which, to Harry, was uber-strange.

He wondered if it was remote controlled? If it wasn't, how was vision actuated? Perhaps it wasn't needed. He put his mind in neutral and just let it happen. This thing was crazy. It had been in the air, but it was just a lump of metal, devoid of anything that would normally make something fly.

Harry scratched his head and gawked at the thing, now that it had landed. It looked odd for an aircraft. There were no markings or any appendages on its smooth white surface. If it was piloted, how the fuck do they see?

There were no windows anywhere. *Nothing* ruined the slipstreamed nature of its body, not writing or structure. It clearly had positive lift because it had no wings or any surfaces that were remotely aero-dynamic. It had rounded corners and was shaped like a capsule or a large tic-tac.

In fact, it *was* piloted, because a Werinn being from the craft emerged from a hatch and quickly set up a ladder for them to enter. Harry wasn't so sure about this thing because there were no aerodynamic surfaces at al l... no wings, tail or ailerons. *Nothing.* His anxiety grew.

How did this thing manage to take-off and fly? Harry had no idea, and by the muddled look on Abby's face, she had the same confused thoughts. Harry glanced at Abby and watched her fumbling with a button on her shirt. Abby grinned and took in the brightly white tic-tac. It clearly flew, so bring it on, she supposed.

All of them climbed the ladder, provided by a black active-wear clad Werinn. He had an arm out, appearing from an opening close to the nosecone of the strangely shaped craft. Presumably, there was another pilot still inside. How they saw anything was a mystery. By screen maybe, then where was the camera?

The vessel somehow took to the skies like a kite on the wind. Harry realised he could see large windows inside - down both sides of the craft. Outside, the vehicle was opaque white, but inside, it was a completely different story. The internal surface of the craft was light blue and windows like huge rips in the skin of the craft. The image to the outside was crystal clear. There was also a clear cube that let him see into the pilot's area. Harry observed the purpleness of the sky ahead of them. Incredibly, the pilots had a panoramic view outside.

'*I knew it*,' Harry roared, doing a skip on the floor of the craft. They fairly leapt into the purple sky and hit the first wisp of bluish cumulus and he could see their buildings. All of them were pyramidal and tall, the ones he'd seen nearby, the houses and sheds, were all distinctly pyramidal and quite low. He knew this reflected something distinct about them. They'd just told them about theirs and the Biapene's need for pyramids and anything polygonal. It was reflected in the Werinn and probably the Biapene general architecture

Their speed was incredible – hypersonic clearly, but there was no audible boom which Harry thought was odd. It probably indicated an advanced method of propulsion. Gravity manipulation, Harry reckoned.

The pyramidal shape extended from homes to sheds and warehouses to buildings, and every other form of dwelling and abode. It seemed anything that homed a Werinn, was polygonal. He was told this is how it had to be. But to see it close-up, was extraordinary.

Their houses were all elongated pyramids. Row upon row of them, each row separated by a red street. There were enough pyramids to house millions of them. And they extended around much of the planet, which enjoyed a climate, ocean-land differential and hydrologic cycle similar to Earth. Ross128b was a super-rare planet.

Harry and Abby focussed on the individuals on the ground as much as they could. They decided whatever was happening at ground level was very different to what happened on Earth. They weren't trying to sell anything. On Earth, people would be harassed to buy things, but not here. It seemed the crowd of Werinn were there only for transport. Some hopped into a tic-tac vehicle and it then took to the skies. Many still on the ground kept waiting, for the next vehicle perhaps. Any other reasons were a total mystery.

Harry wondered if this planet had an economy? Earthly thinking would say it had to – but looking at the creatures below, they didn't seem to be selling anything, buying anything or wanting anything, apart from transport. Perhaps in other parts of this world, it was more obvious. This planet was intriguing indeed.

From the sky, looking down at the huge crowds of Werinn, it was hard to believe, the Biapene were planning to off them all. They said whomever remained after the deadline expired, would be killed – turned to dust. The Biapene threatened to kill everything living, all biology, but they wanted to ensure they preserved the extremely prized polygonal infrastructure of the planet.

*   *   *

They were below the clouds now and still, she could only hear rushing air, but no noise from an engine…which set her thinking. The craft they were in was totally silent. The Werinn craft were like UAPs at home. Abby wondered if this planet had cracked zero-point energy, which was basically the unlimited energy of the vacuum? Energy that drove invisible virtual particles – the paddle-wheel of nature that is everywhere around them. It would be silent, just like this craft – and unlimited. Whatever it was, humanity didn't have it. Mankind was still burning fossils like savages.

Through the huge windows, Abby watched the vision of the planet change radically, the pilot was zigging and zagging all over the sky. Yet there was no momentum change. They weren't even belted into their seats and felt nothing – neither acceleration, deceleration or turning. Inertia had somehow been nulled. Abby looked around herself, and in spite of the sharp manoeuvres, she only saw stability. They were on a miraculous voyage of pure delight.

Speed was breakneck, and physics should have provided all of them with a catastrophic death-shell, yet, inside the craft, it was calm and still. Harry reckoned they could keep FTL, the manipulation of inertia was the piéce de rèsistance. *It didn't get better than that.* Earth would eat it alive if this tech was available. Clearly, amongst other things, the Werinn managed to manipulate or selectively null the Higgs field. For humans, it was magic – pure and simple.

Abby glanced at Harry, who was staring out of the window, wide-eyed, eventually moving his eyes onto her. Both locked eyes in mute testament as to what had just happened. On Earth, these manoeuvres would have killed them and turned them into soup. Their speed was incredible. The manoeuvres nothing less than astonishing.

Before they could go any further, a brilliant sac descended on the end of a rod of light in the near distance, moving very slowly, inching to the ground. They all saw it and thought the same thing. Something from space had arrived. Harry looked beyond the window and saw the object hit the ground slowly with a puff of dust.

'*What the hell?* Abby blurted. The unidentified object nearly hit their vessel. It came from somewhere behind them, fizzing past their vehicle, and hitting the ground like a slow firebolt in front of them. Whatever it was, it came from space. Inside the white craft, both eyed the landing spot curiously. The thing was sort of like a falling meteorite, but it had way too much self-control.

9

Arrival

"When something is made idiot proof, they just make better idiots." ~ *Stephen Hawking*

The "slow" lightning-strike was actually a vehicle falling through the atmosphere at high speed from space. It landed by turning in the air. Then it very slowly VTOL'd to the ground. The question they all had - was this event going to get ugly early – even before they thought it would? The vehicle stopped quite abruptly in mid-air – Abby thought it was just going to thud into the ground at high speed. But about a hundred metres off the ground, it stopped rather suddenly, pivoted and slowly descended to the ground. Even the Werinn had no idea what it was or more importantly, *who* it was.

The Werinn were almost as speechless and muddled as the humans. They were jabbering and gesticulating at each other with huge eyes – and had no answer. Certainly, no-one was expected. They only knew of one other race – the Biapene, but they themselves had promised death to the Werinn, at a future date – so it wasn't expected to be them.

The vehicle that had unexpectedly arrived from space, and was flat on the ground, was triangular and translucent, made of something that graded from perfectly clear to translucent. It quickly made itself entirely transparent and glass-like. It seemed to be a triangular craft inside a translucent sac of some kind. Which appeared to be vanishing, dissolving or evaporating.

The clear triangular craft was fully exposed now. Whatever had surrounded it, was now gone. There was movement inside the vessel, but the view was distorted by whatever it was composed of. It seemed to magnify everything. There was a lot of movement. There were dark and light arms and legs everywhere and presumably, whatever or whomever was inside was coming out.

A being from the craft was followed by another, both of them dressed in a loose golden pressure suit. They both jumped onto the ground from the bottom rung of a small ladder. They stood in front of Oshn and his friends, and all the humans.

Abby stood at the back of the group and faced the other way. Whatever was happening, she wanted no part of it. Abby had enough trouble meeting the Werinn, she didn't need another even more challenging race to deal with. By the brief look she'd had, this new species was a doozy. The forked tongue and green skin were enough to make her feel like running. '*Fuck*,' she breathed to herself, gawking at deeply carbuncled skin just before she turned away.

For the newcomers' benefit, Oshn signed vigorously above his head and had a shy smile on his face. He seemed to know the occupants well. After being spoken to, he realised that they weren't here for mischief or to create further trouble.

The new arrivals wore a mainly light blue and gold pressure suit, and had a head poking out that looked remarkably like a lizard. Carbuncled, greenish skin with eyes that blinked sideways. The tongue was deeply split and nearly always poked from the mouth. There was no tail, but its similarity to an evolved, bipedal dinosaur was undeniable.

One of the Werinn standing behind them, said *"Biapene"*, which Harry heard. Oshn greeted the visitor by joining foreheads. It was obvious they were glad to entertain these visitors. It may have had something to do with the language they shared, including a lot of sounds made by fingers striking the arm.

It was an odd picture. Why was this hideous creature being welcomed to the planet like an old friend, when he and his kind were supposed to be the number-one enemy. Confusion ruled. Harry and Abby gasped loudly when they saw it. The humans were exasperated, staring incredulously at the nonsensical scene. The Biapene were supposed to be adversaries.

Something was very wrong with this picture. They looked like best buds. Yet the Biapene were supposed to be the sworn enemy. If things didn't go to plan, they would put an end to Werinn life on the planet. They were mass murderers...weren't they?

The Biapene pilot put his arm around Oshn and walked him forward to talk in private, away from the group. This didn't look right at all. The humans were here to help fight them. To kill them. Now they were slapping each other's backs. *No...no, no,* Harry thought, snapping his head around to Abby, who gave a slow, disbelieving, head-shake. She too, thought there was something horribly wrong in all this. It just didn't make sense.

Abby was feeling ill, and her head hammered with splitting pain. The view of Oshn with his Biapene friend was too much. The humans were sequestered from Earth to kill them. What the *fuck* was going on here? It was totally and utterly illogical. They'd been told that the Biapene were the exact opposite of friends. Now the Biapene and the Werinn were hugging. Abby was sure her head would explode. This wasn't what she expected at all.

It was hard to believe that the situation had gotten worse, but maybe it had. More complicated certainly. She thought Oshn was coming back to the group, but the Biapene still had his arm around Oshn and now the Biapene was tugging at his shoulder in a display that was quite bizarre. It looked like a get together between best buds after a long separation. Oshn now went to speak to his people. This was getting stranger and more unexplainable by the second.

The Biapene were now standing behind Oshn, looking aggressive without trying to be. The main being was closely related to a reptile and was hard to look at without wincing. Harry tried to ignore him, but he was difficult to overlook.

He stood behind Oshn, flicking his forked tongue in and out of his asymmetric mouth, looking rather chuffed with himself. Satisfied certainly. Abby looked away, staring at Harry in what looked like pure agony. The pain of deep confusion and repugnance was carved in lines on her face and she scratched at her temple, trying to work this incorrigible situation out. She had to keep reminding herself that they were enemies. One had threatened to kill the other.

Abby glanced at the Biapene and very nearly had conniptions. Her heart-rate went through the roof and her legs started trembling uncontrollably. These "lizards" were wearing a light blue, in places, but mostly gold pressure-suit, gloves and shoes. There were fine fingers and an opposing thumb, but its carbuncled skin and pointy head gave it away. It was a lizard. A long, forked tongue that frequently poked from the mouth was just the start. It had eyes that were large like an owl, with very prominent pupils. Ridges of bone or hard flesh went down the centre of the head and also went the other way above the eyes to wind above the ears and disappear behind the head. The eyes were set into the bony ridge which made them look angry and aggressive from the get-go. Abby looked the other way. Collapsing to the ground is something she preferred not to do.

Oshn stood tall and thrust his chest out and was clearly preparing to talk, and appeared quite up-beat, which in itself was odd. Oshn seemed more cheerful than before, so presumably any news he received from his *"friend"* was good news.

Oshn spoke buoyantly, 'Rialten from Biapene has travelled to our planet to give us *good news*.' Harry gawked at Abby, totally bemused, but glad Oshn was happy. Harry raised his eyebrows, impatient for what was next.

'The Biapene are withdrawing all demands,' Oshn said, 'they no longer require our planet. 'They are now intending to use their shortening technology to reach a different solar system, and a different more distant planet that they are sure is habitable.'

'They do not intend to rid that planet of life, but hopefully to assimilate with it. They will throw themselves on the indigenous life's mercy and hope for understanding and empathy for their plight.'.

'*Then why the hell are we here*?' Harry heard irately from behind him, from several different human soldiers and pilots. It was an obvious question, he supposed, but it didn't obviate the fact that it was good news that was brought. The Biapene had literally changed their minds. They no longer intended to invade Werinn.

The Biapene could use their space-shortening, and effectively travel faster than light. They could reach distant systems they could previously only look at with telescopes and reach them quickly.

So, the Biapene would no longer be routing Werinn which was really good news. No battle in space...no war. It was a good result. The Werinn were saved in their entirety, without putting human lives at risk.

It was a great result for everyone, the Biapene included. Everyone would benefit.

NASA and Earth may be disappointed though, Harry thought. But maybe the friendship and sharing thing could be worked out. Afterall, we were *prepared* to help...but ultimately, didn't have to. So, any benefits we were procuring because of it, should still be coming our way. Abby thought it made sense. Harry wasn't so sure. The Werinn weren't keen on humanity because of our uber-aggression. With the Biapene pulling out of their own accord, Abby didn't think a whole lot had changed. Harry thought the opposite. In his opinion, humanity had earned zero.

Harry glanced at Abby and did a double-take, noticing that she didn't look right at all. She was opening and closing her mouth and saying nothing, smiling stiffly at others with a glazed or vacant look in her eyes and brushing the back of her hair with a hand. *Fuck*, he thought, knowing how insightful she was. She'd picked up something from Oshn that he hadn't. Abby looked like she'd seen a ghost. Harry wanted to help, which meant finding out what the hell was going on with her. Because, sure as shit, he didn't have a clue.

All these emotions by Abby were strong tell-signs that something significant, was picking at her mind. She wasn't happy with something that was said. Whatever was on her mind was a looming hurricane, Harry knew that much. And knowing her, Harry reckoned, it probably wasn't good for anyone, him included.

Harry watched Abby out of the corner of his eye for a while. Her body language remained just as bad. She was still deeply distressed by something. 'A-Are you, er...OK Abby?' Harry asked nervously, wondering seriously about her. 'You don't seem like yourself Ab, I'm concerned. I know none of this is normal, but you seem...er, different.' Harry bit his lip and watched her closely.

He had a major soft spot for Abby, so to see her so visibly upset, was disturbing him as well. He was fairly sure that it was good news that the Biapene conveyed, so why the odd emotion that he was seeing on Abby's face? It didn't make sense.

Harry kept wondering what in God's name he'd missed? Sure, as hell he'd missed something important. Abby was more perceptive than anyone he'd ever known, so something very important was off.

Abby looked at him seriously, shaking her head and walking him away a few paces. Harry could feel her heat. Abby clearly had something important to say. Suddenly, he was drop-dead terrified of what she might say, swallowing rapidly and feeling his own heat. He gawked at Abby with eyes that were massive. She went to talk and he felt his stomach tighten. He knew this was going to be big.

'Are they, uh...talking about *Earth?*' She whispered to Harry, and his eyes suddenly popped. *'Fuck,'* he yelled after digesting it. 'Earth...*shit.*' Harry felt emotional, but he was too stunned to cry. 'No, no, it can't be,' he spat, knowing full well it could be.

'Jesus Christ, holy shit,' Harry cried. 'I, uh...didn't make that connection...I didn't think he was talking about *home*, Abby. *Jesus.*' Harry loudly gasped for breath and started shivering violently. 'T-There a-are heaps of worlds to choose from that are relatively close Abby...Tau Ceti, Gliese b and c, Epic d, Proxima b and many more, a bit further out.

Although he did say it was populated.' Everything was crystallizing in a rush for Harry. He struck his fist on his forehead. 'It can't happen...no...*NO*...they won't cope. Are you sure that's where he meant?' It was taking shape in his brain now. Harry gawked straight at Abby, rubbing his eyes with his knuckles, hoping against hope that it wasn't true. But he already knew it was.

'I'm certain Harry,' Abby whispered forcefully. Ask Oshn where the planet is exactly...*ask about it,* Harry.' She was elbowing him toward Oshn to ask the question. Abby had to know for sure. She was almost positive, and if it was Earth, there would be hugely rude shocks coming in its near future. For everyone.

Even if they came as a totally benign visitor, humanity would suffer deep psychological shock just by them entering the atmosphere and setting down on the green grass of home. Humans were still afflicted with the Fermi paradox for Christ's sake. Aliens were a synonym for horror, terror and panic. If a civilisation had the temerity to just land on the planet, with no forewarning, well...it'd be massive chaos and panic, pure and simple.

'At least it explains your body language,' Harry said, grateful to have sorted that one out. He knew one gargantuan problem remained, and he had no immediate answer to it. Somehow, a giant had been awoken. And they had their eyes squarely plastered on the gorgeous blue marble that was Earth.

'Jesus Harry, forget about me, worry about Earth,' Abby blustered. 'Doesn't matter where they land...they expect to *stay. Fuck*...it'll be a shit show. What happens after? What of religions? What do we do with them? Abby was beside herself, puffing heavily and red

in the face, with sweat pimpling her forehead. Tears blinded her eyes as she tried to imagine them setting down on Earth.

One of the security agencies would surely use the vessel as target practice. They'd assume the worst...that Earth was being invaded. Abby hoped like hell the Biapene landed somewhere that would at least allow those in the ship to *survive*. Somewhere the NSA, or like agencies couldn't get to them.

Some areas of Earth were a total no-go zone, like Russia or China. Probably *anywhere* was a huge risk. *Christ*, Abby thought, wouldn't matter where it landed. It'd be akin to a horrific dream for humans, wherever it came down. Humans from any country just wouldn't understand. They'd assume the worst, that the Biapene were there to kidnap or outright kill humans. Confirmation of alien life was supposed to change the way we perceived our place in the universe, change our aspirations for space and widen our philosophical and theological beliefs. Harry doubted it would be like that at all. The Biapene were landing direct, and in one fell swoop, it'd be goodnight to the civilised structure of the Earth, *unless* it was communicated very widely and very carefully.

The Biapene wouldn't be so stupid to land in say, Africa, would they? Abby hoped not. They'd read our internet, courtesy of the Werinn and understood at least partially, the socio-political web of the world. That should have told the Biapene all they needed to know. Humanity was an insecure race. That assumed all unknown visitors were unpredictable people who had to be managed all the time, or gotten rid of. That was the human way.

The Werinn's theory was that humans as a race were violent aggressors, based on their two hundred-thousand-year history, which was well described in Mankind's internet. The Werinn believe that a civilisation is damned to repeat its history, and few could argue. And its history was one of murder and genocide.

Just landing a craft from space with zero forewarning would really test their theory. Hopefully, humanity would behave, but counting on it, would be a fool's paradise. By perusing our history, the Biapene should already know that.

Oshn had spoken at length to Rialten, and Harry found out about the planet they intended to land on. It was a planet eleven light years away that possessed an unusually large moon. And it was the third of nine planets, although the last one was a captured asteroid, he said, and lived most of its life away from the plane of the planets.

This was sadly, unambiguous evidence that the planet they sought to go to was indeed *Earth*. Abby took a sharp breath on the confirmation of destination. She knew it anyway, but thinking about it more made her blood run cold. *Good fucking luck,* Abby thought morosely, the Biapene would likely be killed by the indigenous population when they landed, and the craft destroyed.

The only way forward was to warn Earth of a pending arrival from space. At least get them prepared and in the "right" state of mind if that was possible. By "right" she meant hopefully non-murderous and viewing the episode as a scientific opportunity. Abby knew many on Earth would see the landing itself as an aggressive act...an "invasion". Warning Earth of their arrival and explaining the reasons for their landing were critical. And humanity needed to listen. Their status as refugees needed to be communicated.

Rialten left Oshn to talk to his commander. Oshn ambled over to Harry, who was standing with Abby and said, '...you are correct. It is Earth they are intending to go to.

Harry heard the words he feared and he closed his eyes tight and shook his head hard. It was the worst news possible, but *expected*, thanks to the warning provided by Abby. He imagined how humans would react, seeing the craft penetrate the atmosphere and wind its way to the ground.

He knew, many humans just wouldn't cope. And by many, he meant millions. Nor would government agencies, who would surely use the vehicle as target practice. *Fuck*, he thought. Harry could imagine the mindless terror that it would provoke. Mankind would act like toddlers and find it near impossible to share anything with anyone. This was *their* planet. Attitudes needed to change, or pandemonium would be the result.

Abby nodded to Oshn - she already knew the Biapene were coming, in fact by now, they all did. 'The Biapene propose that ten thousand of their own will travel to Earth, and initially land in Washington DC, near America's house of government.'

Oshn had his head down and looked up, 'I'm sorry Harry – but we've passed on pages of your internet, so they can learn about you and make informed decisions. It seemed a reasonable decision at the time.' Harry nodded - he already knew that.

'But now, I am not so sure.' Oshn had a strange expression on his face. His mouth was curled down and so were his long ears. It may have been a sign of remorse or regret, or maybe something completely different.

This was humanity's worst nightmare – an alien craft or crafts, setting down near the White House. What in God's name would Americans, *the world*, make of it. Abby hoped against hope that the DoD or NSA didn't shoot Sidewinders at the vessel. It would be a travesty order of magnitude worse than the planet had ever seen. Images of dead lizards ran across his mind.

Humans had to be very careful, because threatening a clearly superior race, might lead to something occurring that was very unpleasant for humans. Mankind needed to be fully briefed about *"the coming"*. If they weren't, it could get very nasty indeed.

The entire population of Earth needed to know who was coming, where and when they were coming, and why. The population needed to be flooded with details. Harry scratched his chin and looked at the creatures and the world they were on. What was on the horizon for Earth, would test the planet in a way few ever thought.

They, as in the Biapene, were intending just to land. Without any forewarning. Hoping that humans would take no defensive action against them and welcome them to Earth as refugees of a dying world. It could be disastrous. That would happen in a perfect world. But Earth was anything but perfect, especially when it came to non-humans.

The Biapene had our internet and the Werinn had helped them understand our languages. Like the Werinn, they were very smart indeed. Hopefully, the Biapene digested some pointers from the internet. If they did, they'd know we had a wide array of SAMs, and they'd understand our tenuous mind-set and general psychology. *If they didn't ... look out.*

So, it was up to Harry and Abby to provide the forewarning. To tell Earth when the Biapene were likely to arrive and why they were coming. That they *were* coming. And how they would travel through space to get here. The people of Earth would be floored.

Every aspect of life on our home planet would change. Goodbye to our isolation in the backwaters of a fertile Galaxy, hello to the laws of probability in the wider, *huge* Universe.

Whatever happened on Earth, Abby was certain it would be super-challenging. Where would the Biapene live, what would they do? Abby knew it'd be a complex shit-show which for her, there was no possibility of escape. Abby knew how it would work.

She and Harry would be front and centre, and neither could think of an immediate solution to the questions, apart from saying *NO* to the Biapene, *do not come*. Which they couldn't do. And it probably wouldn't deter them anyway. The Biapene needed a home where they didn't have to fight the environment daily for survival.

If they came to Earth no one would have a remote clue what their needs were. Their psychology and sociology were a complete unknown. As was their physiology. Basically, humans knew less than nothing about the Biapene.

The Biapene were in deep trouble, unless they were very firm with humanity about their requirements, as their need for polygonal housing and surfaces was not a human need. Unfortunately, being firm and obdurate was in contradiction to the Biapene's own general demeanour and temperament. The Biapene were a very reserved and softly spoken species. On the face of it, their disposition didn't bode well for effective communion.

The Biapene had to leave their planet, that was a given. The ozone layer on Biapene was like a crab-net and provided next to no protection to the battered Biapene. On Biapene, the amount of ionising radiation each being received was measured in Roentgens not Millirem.

*   *   *

Oshn threw his head back and took a deep rattling breath. It was punctuated with several gasps, and he continued to talk, more seriously. Harry slapped himself on the hip. He finally remembered what Rialten reminded him of. A grasshopper. A *lizard* grasshopper, he reckoned. Harry shook his head in dismay. Earth would be hit with an infestation of lizard grasshoppers. Harry was ashen white and could feel the hair stand to attention on the back of his neck. God help them all, he thought grimly. He pictured Mankind coming face-too-face with the Biapene. Appalled and reeling, were the first words he could think of.

'The AMG of Biapene, their *Amalgamation*,' Oshn explained, 'ran a planet-wide lottery and the winners and their families were joined with those that *had* to be saved, to form the garrison who would travel to a new planet and begin a new life...hopefully.'

'The decision was made,' Oshn said, 'that we exploit a new form of space travel to venture to Earth. We built new, larger starships and planned to travel out of our local system, to a new planet that they were certain offered positive habitable conditions. This planet already supported a global intelligence. So, in our view, a few more wouldn't hurt. The Biapene knew it was way more complicated than just that.

'Once on Earth, we would throw ourselves on the mercy of the indigenous inhabitants, and hope for the best.' The Biapene had read about refugees and asylum seekers in the human internet, and thought they were on strong ground, with Mankind. Asylum was regularly granted where a land was decimated by natural events or war. The Biapene believed they fitted into that category well.

The Biapene had read the human internet and overall, agreed with the Werinn. It was a risk to go to Earth. Humans were aggressive, violent, fearful and narcissistic. They were literally landing at their own risk. And it would be a large risk. The Biapene might tick all the boxes as refugees, but humans had never *ever* encountered a different intelligence. So, with human history in mind, the Biapene were nervous and very unsure about going to Earth.

Landing anywhere on Earth was a huge risk to the Biapene, with or without warning. The human population was a powder-keg, likely to go off wherever they landed. They had to choose with care. But that was a risk the Biapene were prepared to take, because they knew for certain that Earth itself would fulfil their basic needs. And reasonably sure that humans themselves would provide them with an appropriate home.

They were also fairly certain they wouldn't be exterminated like insects at a public park. When it came down to it, the Biapene realised that it'd be suck and see.

Never before had humans encountered anything biological that was off-planet. So, the Biapene expected to be something of a white whale on Earth. They also understood that humans would view them as evolved lizards.

Rialten saw his own species as pretty regular and humans as requiring some getting used to. He reckoned homo sapiens were the 'ugly' ones, with beady eyes, small heads and large ears. Such was the nature of biological architecture. It solely depended on the eye of the beholder.

Oshn continued with the reveal of the Biapene civilisation. 'They have a space telescope with a sectioned forty-foot mirror. The Biapene are familiar with all the planets and moons local to Earth, and know much about Earth itself, and its oxygen-rich atmosphere which they detected from their orbital telescope and spectrograph.'

'They received TV signals and knew of Earth's population of intelligent, technical beings. To formally contact the planet was the next step. But now they were doing even better than that – they were going there to visit...and then *stay*. The remaining Biapene population would soon be diseased and dead. They couldn't survive without a magnetosphere.'

Oshn appeared reticent and nervous, and added, 'The Biapene are a lonely race and desperately want to make contact with another species. On another planet in a *different* solar system. They knew of the planet Earth and had intercepted their EMAR but weren't convinced that they were an example of brand-new life.'

'Seeding of their planet, or the reverse, might explain that we or they are the parent. So, they wanted to look further afield, where there was no possibility that it was the same life event. This desire permeated the population and leaders, before their magnetics and ozone layer gave out. Now, they just want to perpetuate the species.'

Harry looked away from Oshn and imagined telling Jack and Pete about it, who had both returned to Gateway, and better still, telling Pat on Earth. They believed him before, after a struggle, but no *fucking* way they'd believe this. If they resisted what he'd said the first time – then they'd full on treat this situation with derision and ridicule. It sounded like delusion and invention. Pat would most definitely see it that way. If he told them that NHI's were coming to Earth to stay, as refugees, NASA through Pat would think they'd literally gone nuts.

Whatever, he silently sighed. He wouldn't put up with not being believed again, nor would he allow Abby to be another source of disbelief. NASA and all that rode her, could either take it or leave it. They'd find out for real, soon enough. They were definitely coming. Harry scratched the back of his neck and bared his teeth. That's not how he wanted it. Without warning, it would be a global shit-show.

The world simply *had* to be prepared. Otherwise, pure chaos worldwide would result.

*   *   *

Eventually, after a lot of talk, they were all led into the same huge grey warehouse, very similar, if not identical, to last time. This place was huge and they were tucked away on the side in an area blocked off from the rest by floor to ceiling with what looked like long brown sheets of thick linen.

Each of the craft looked wet and grainy again – some sort of anti-gravity pre-coating that allowed them to avoid the effect of the gravity-well entirely. The last time their ship was doused in it, Orion was surrounded by a clear cocoon. It grew into an encompassing envelope. And Orion headed for orbit without any thrust at all, like a fucking helium balloon. Up it went into the sky without being impeded by gravity, using positive lift. The Werinn were clearly smart folk. They played with gravity like it was no more complicated than Play-Doh.

Oshn thanked the humans one-by-one and formalised the fact that as circumstances had changed, the services of the humans were no longer required. The Biapene no longer represented a threat to the Werinn. Their planet wasn't eyed by them as a new home, he said. They were going further afield. To, of all places, *Earth*.

Surrounded by clear cocoons, and using their RCS, all the craft flew within the red lines of the CERN-like machine. They instantly vanished from Werinn space. Harry and Abby reappeared immediately above a pinky, pancake shaped Aragon. It was now their job to get back to Gateway, after sling-shotting around Venus. The other craft were heading back to Earth. Their job was done, without firing a shot.

10

Return

"Half the battle is just showing up."
~ *Stephen Hawking*

Jack had quite enough of the isolation and remoteness of Gateway - *again*. Despite what he thought it was gonna be, it was the same as the first time. He should have known better, to think it would improve. Both Jack and Pete had been relieved on their first stay at day forty-six, but NASA were impressed with their work, re-added them to the roster. Pete's wife was doing better on chemo. So, he sought the duty, in spite of his adverse experience the first time.

Jack thought their last time on Gateway was a bust, but their employer thought differently. Rather than resist, he and Pete acquiesced, unwilling to make waves for NASA. Jack and Pete were still like oil and water, but NASA knew better...apparently. So, they joined each other on Gateway again.

Jack had heard quite enough from Pete once again. He argued about everything, no matter how minor. Even stuff that NASA had already decided, like how much water a particular plant needs. Pete was driving Jack mad.

Their meals consisted mainly of instant noodles, and were eaten primarily in their own quarters. Generally, they would look at the Moon or read the news or watch a movie or news item, or anything on a laptop. Seeing both of them on deck at the same time was a rarity. They only saw each other when their schedules overlapped or they accidentally happened across each other. Their roster on Gateway had expired weeks ago and they once again expected more from their employer...like *following fucking contracts.*

Jack and Pete understood that the Aragon mission was important for humanity, but where was the love for them? Once again, the NASA mandate for teamwork was dead and buried. They both wanted home more fiercely than before, and once again thought NASA sucked. They'd been on Gateway for fifty days this time, heading for twice the length of their rather elastic contract.

The best they could do was grunt at each other if they happened to meet up, they hadn't spoken properly for thirty days. The crazy thing was, they both understood the need for effective teamwork when there was only two of them to execute tasks. But nothing helped. Jack and Pete thought this time, it would be different. They were wrong.

Pete felt like belting Jack, even though he hadn't spoken to him properly for so long. His feelings of rage probably stemmed from Kitty, his wife, he thought. She was very ill, but happy for him to go because it was such a good money earner. The last thing she said when he walked out the door was, '*don't be late home,*' said with a wry smile on her face, knowing what happened the first time. That's exactly what he was – late, and had been for a while.

To say Jack and Pete were glad to see Orion make its way toward Gateway was seriously understating it. They were both fucking *ecstatic* to clap eyes on it. It shouldn't be here, it was way early, but there it was, and they were elated. Harry and Abby were their ticket out of here, although they didn't expect to see either come back so quickly. Jack wondered what had gone wrong?

Harry and Abby could've spoken direct to Gateway, and for that matter direct to Earth through the laser network. Harry could've hailed Jack on the S-band, but reckoned face to face comms were required for this, and Abby agreed. Talking on the phone just wouldn't cut it. This horror demanded face-to-face.

He wanted to tell everyone who needed to know, that the Biapene were coming to Earth. What would be made of it? Would we be believed or made out to be whackos? Once Earth realised it was true, would it be the beginning of the end? Would it be a *ho-hum* moment or somewhere in between? The questions had the impact of tiny, burrowing embers inside their brains. They had no answer to any of them, so they stayed deep inside, asked but unanswered.

Harry swallowed nervously at the prospect of trying to talk with anyone about it. It sounded preposterous. Way worse than the first time. Jack and Pat would call bullshit on his story. Perhaps he was selling them short, because they *were* back way early. There had to be reasons for it. Surely, that would get them thinking.

They should know roughly how long it'd take, and they were back a lot earlier than that. Harry knew Jack would be floored when he told him the Biapene were coming to Earth FTL. Harry reckoned Jack would be hard enough to persuade, Pat would be impossible.
Jack would probably lose his lunch when he was told. *FTL* was bad enough, but destination *Earth*, that would really get him, because he would know the implications of their arrival in the first nanosecond.

Within a minute, the Orion capsule was pulled in and locked in place by twelve motorised latches. Soft-dock was now hard-dock. Harry wasn't altogether happy to be entering Gateway. More accusations of fraud or hallucination no doubt. He pictured Jack's face, lines everywhere, and his face contorted by yelling - it wasn't pretty. Jack was a tough opponent at the best of times, and this was definitely not one of those. Then there was Pat. He felt like taking Orion straight to Russia and setting down in Red Square, next to the Kremlin. Maybe he'd get a better reception there.

'*Orion 1 arrived*,' Harry toned seriously to Gateway, pressing the touch and talk, the main comms system. They entered into the now reasonably familiar, untidy confines of Gateway. It was, after many days of occupation – a single man's paradise.

Jack looked at Harry and saw his face, red with a sheen of sweat coating his forehead. Abby was the same. Looking at them both, they seemed distracted and troubled by something, not to mention hot and sweaty. Why in God's name were they back so soon?

The information Harry and Abby held would rock the planet. Both looked hot, uncomfortable and in desperate need of a shower, having clearly expended a lot of energy. The question of "what happened" filled Jack and Pete to the point of detonation, but they were both determined to wait for Harry or Abby to broach it.

Pete was concerned. Harry and Abby were just standing there, saying nothing, and looking like they'd been through hell. Pete dragged his hand through his hair repeatedly, while staring vacantly at both of them. Harry bounced his gaze from Jack to Pete and didn't know where to start, or whether he wanted to start.

There was so much to say, Harry was confused, dizzy and unprepared to talk. Because if he did, he might blurt the whole lot out. He didn't want this secret kept a secret. Nor did Abby. They both wanted everyone to know the truth.

Harry, standing in the Habitation Module, realised it was up to him to do the talking and posturing. He stared as firmly as he could at Jack and thought, *oh fuck it.* The issue had to be dealt with. The sooner the better.

'What a Goddamn trip,' Harry said breathlessly, 'We weren't needed by the Werinn – *would you believe it*, the Biapene changed their minds. Instead of invading Werinn, their plan is now to move further afield to a different solar system with a new, faster vehicle.'

Harry stopped talking and looked at the ground. He felt a bit nauseous and queasy, because he knew what was next on his list. So, he took a step backward and collected himself by breathing deeply and then exhaling from the bottom of his lungs.

'Biapene the planet, was observable from Werinn even in the daytime...similar to our Moon. And the reverse applied too. The leaders didn't want a constant reminder of what they'd done and where they'd come from. So, they called the whole thing off.' Harry finished with a quirky smile and a shrug, as if to say, *how about that?*

'The Biapene were anything but a violent race apparently, so committing genocide was ultimately rejected as a solution to their planetary woes. They decided on a far more acceptable solution, that didn't impact Werinn at all.' Harry wiped his forehead with the back of his hand. He was arrowing toward saying it, but was sweating like a stuck leg of pork, roasting over a roaring fire. He could feel it, dripping into the small of his back. He was nearly there, but he desperately needed to stop sweating.

'It was the Biapene's consideration that the vicious act they were planning would affect their society forever. So, no action was taken by the Biapene,' Harry said. 'Their new plan was made - to take ten thousand of their own to a different, distant planet by way of space-shortening. To a world that was already populated, and had atmospheric conditions that were guaranteed to be friendly to their kind of life. They didn't want to go to an unpopulated planet – because that brought with it a number of potentially nasty variables   they preferred not to have to deal with.' Harry made a brave attempt to smile which ended up faint and forced. He could hear a surging noise, ringing in his ears. Harry had tears streaming from his eyes.

Jack smiled at the outcome, and asked, 'are you sure they truly meant it, or did they just spin that story to make you leave?' Jack said, looking daggers at Harry and Abby, and wondering why Harry looked so upset?

Harry was determined not to succumb to emotion, but it was too late. He wanted to regain his cool, so he pulled every muscle tight and answered as calmly as he could. 'The story they gave me made sense, and the Werinn *certainly* believed the Biapene. I agree that xeno-psychology or xeno-sociology for us, is a total unknown, but we believed them unambiguously. It made sense. Why encourage us to leave, if they still needed help? Remember – they messaged us.' Harry wiped his brow and cheeks with a sweep of his fingers. He looked at Jack incredulously.

'Fair enough,' Jack said, 'if you both believed them, and the Werinn did too, it's job done. Do you know where they are going?

Harry turned blood-red and almost choked on hearing the question, and Jack knew that something was up, simply by Harry's petrified reaction. Raspy breathing and feverish eyes followed. Harry didn't know what to say or what to do, so he just stared at him vacantly and said nothing. Jack knew something was very wrong, and snapped his head to Pete, who looked back at him anxiously.

Having recovered some semblance of speech, Harry knew it was next on his list. He squinted at Jack and focussed, and hoped he'd accept what he was about to say. Jack's old job, was to keep Earth safe from stuff that comes at it from space.

There was no point hiding it from him, he'd find out one way or the other, and they'd need his help reporting it to NASA. Harry took a gusty breath while Jack and Pete watched him curiously, wondering what in God's name was up with him.

Harry tensed everything and just said it. 'They, as in the, er...*Biapene* are c-coming to *Earth*.' Harry quietly spoke the words. He let that sink in a bit, while flourishing with his hands to indicate that he was talking about "the planet down there". 'The Biapene plan is to settle ten thousand beings on our world.' Take *that*, he reckoned.

Jack's eyes shot up to meet his - he started to breathe like a steam train, but Harry continued anyway, talking louder, over Jack who continued to breathe loudly and make peculiar grunting sounds.

'They intend to initially land in Washington DC, North America. The Werinn have passed on most of our internet to them and taught some of them how to read and speak in English and Mandarin.' Harry exhaled from the bottom of his lungs, like he'd been holding his breath. He gazed at Jack and saw a blood red face with eyes like chicken eggs. The poor sod was coughing and hacking with eyes that were now full of tears. *Christ*, he thought morosely, I've broken Jack. He looked like he was close to a stroke. At the back of Harry's mind, he was doing cartwheels, because both of them unambiguously believed him. Score one for me, he thought.

Jack felt lightheaded and had an enormous ringing in his ears and a devastating sense of doom. Then he started spouting words as the concept of non-human arrival appeared to fully sink in.

'Fuck...shit...it can't be...it can't be...surely...it can't be?' But by the lines on his face and his deep burgundy colour, he knew it was true and REAL. *It was actually happening*. The Biapene were coming to Earth. An interstellar species. *'Where the hell are we going to put them?'* Jack's eyes were huge, his face, the colour of a beetroot, and slathered in sweat. *'Oh shit.'* he cried. *'They won't cope.'* Abby was genuinely worried that Jack might suffer a real medical emergency.

Jack was red and wet through with sweat. Pete didn't look much better, and hadn't moved from his chair, and had black circles under his eyes. According to him, "he was too old for this shit". And he might well have been right. If this was the reaction they could expect on Earth, God help the planet, Harry thought grimly.

'Who the hell is going to tell Pat and NASA about this?' Harry yelled, thinking the reaction from him wouldn't be much better. 'Can you imagine the response from JSC...from NASA sites the world over, and the rest of the Goddamn planet? It didn't bear thinking about. Harry shook his head and stared at Abby vacantly.

'Holy shiiiit.' Jack spouted and surveyed Harry grimly, throwing his hands in the air. 'The population lives in a world ruled by the Fermi paradox. Aliens, non-humans, NHI, *whatever*, are a complete anathema. Can you imagine it. *"Oh...there's a race of non-humans we've found, eleven light years away and guess what? Some of them are coming to Earth with a new FTL engine, and they're gonna stay permanently"*.

'Governments on Earth won't believe it,' Jack's voice was choked with anger and tears. 'After the Biapene land, the general population of Earth will be more mentally wobbly than those placed in care today. There will be protests, riots, demonstrations, marches in every city in every country. UFO and UAP followers will be everywhere – they will claim vindication, because if the Biapene can get here so quickly, then it's proven...*it's them. Fuck me* Harry,' Jack cried. 'They are real. UFOs are ridgy-didge and they're of Biapene, or maybe Werinn origin. *Case closed.'*

Jack closed his eyes and started humming an inane tune to himself. He couldn't believe it had come to this. He stopped thinking and opened his eyes wide. '*Christ almighty*, this is real, isn't it?' he said, staring squarely at Harry who nodded, and then let out a huge breath and smiled widely. 'It is what it is. Time, we accepted it.'

'Looting and pillaging will follow,' Harry piped, 'and murder won't be far behind.' *"The governments are hiding it"*, will be the cry. People will be everywhere – in every town, marching and demanding, breaking store-front windows and setting fire to everything. Mark my words, it'll be a shit show.'

'The human reaction will be massive, on the back of all this. They're quiet now, but give them a sniff and suddenly, it'll be across the globe and unstoppable. It'll be like holding back a tsunami with your hands. Believe me,' Harry said, 'once this has momentum, it'll be everywhere. And the opportunity provided by the Biapene is the best one in history. UFOs and UAP's will suddenly be king. Everyone will be a fucking believer worldwide.'

Harry glanced at Abby fearfully and shrugged. He had no idea who would save the planet then. The Biapene no doubt saw themselves as victims. Their planet was dying, they had to leave. But Harry knew, with humanity's tenuous mindset, it was Mankind that was the true victim. Humans simply wouldn't be able to rise to the occasion. Mankind would mean well, but would they be mature enough to deal with non-humans? The answer was probably NO.

Jack with his dark eyes and pale skin didn't look well at all, and Pete looked just as bad. Jack was shaking his head and Pete was just shaking, as they played the whole mess forward. Where would they put them all? That was the question that had them all by the balls. *Where would they house the Biapene?* Who in God's name would want them as neighbours? They couldn't put them way out on their own, either. Human options were evaporating.

The matter of where they would be put was a question of inordinate weight, that no one had an answer to. Non-humans would expect their lives to continue and their basic needs to be taken care of.

Like any refugee. It was known that the Biapene possessed a technology and a physical understanding equal to the Werinn. Significantly ahead of humans. So, with asymmetric tech and physics, the humans had much to learn.

Mankind expected that the intel of the Biapene would be shared with them. If they looked after the Biapene appropriately. Initially, the scientific community on Earth were after the dark particles, GUT, FTL tech, and teleporting live biology know-how. The rest could come later. Getting something in return for a service was called *quid pro quo* in Latin. It would be central to the human's agreement to receive the Biapene. Human beings did nothing for free, particularly when such physical wonders were up for grabs.

Harry and Abby had thought about it a lot. After copious too'ing and fro'ing, they decided it would probably be up to the UN and the USA and probably NASA to decide where the Biapene lived. They were the leaders in this sort of stuff. It was deeply space related, so NASA had to be heavily involved. It was their mission that led to it. Roscosmos and the Chinese CNSA would also be included in discussions. Everything had to be achieved the American way - by international agreement.

There were so many questions to answer. It wasn't just a matter of them arriving and then Earth reverting to business as usual. Our entire world would change. Things would never be the same. The Fermi paradox would be gone, but how would the population react? How would religions view it? The Biapene would be afforded "personhood" when they arrived and have full human rights, same as anyone else.

Acceptance of the idea that intelligent life is not unique to humans, may be difficult for some religions on Earth. It may be inconsistent with the existence of God for some of them. But again, it was what it was, Harry thought. Once they were here, he was sure they'd get used to it. It certainly wouldn't be the end of religion – there was too much money to be made. Non-humans only widened the goal-posts. Harry knew by its content and the words, that the Christian Bible wasn't just meant for humans. So, most religions would continue, because they already accounted for extra-terrestrials.

The questions had to be asked though - would there be massive rioting and looting...would the stock market's collapse and die? *Hardly*. But the deeper you delved into it, the more questions you found. One thing was certain – humanity and its infrastructure, would be tested more than it ever had been.

Confirmation of non-human intelligence was one thing. From a distant source, perhaps by EMAR, or observing a distant techno- or bio-signature. But to have it set down on the planet, bold as brass, was entirely another.

And to have it stay permanently, was something no-one on Earth had ever considered. On confirmation of non-human intelligence, many scholars believed cultural pressures would see humankind implode. Others believed the effects would be minimal. So, until it happened, no-one knew. Mankind could only guess and theorise. And their best-guess now was 'wait-and-see'.

Jack simply had to get hold of Pat - he wasn't on duty right now. Pat was busy at NEOwise at JPL, but Jack would get him. One way or the other – he would find him. He was the only one at NASA who could properly digest information like this. Jack had left urgent messages for him and would get him on the phone eventually. Jack reckoned the *knowing* would nearly kill him.

Harry knew it wouldn't be easy for Pat, he would suffer under its weight - and the very idea. Conveying or receiving dramatic, life changing, information wasn't easy for anyone. In Earth's and Pat's case in particular, because it was so bloody unexpected and the implications so all encompassing. They would impact every person on the planet and it was Pat that had to initially get his head around it.

Jack squinted at Harry and didn't feel inclined to ask him anything, but knew he had to. Naturally, all he could think about was the fucking Biapene and their impending arrival on Earth. Harry's eyes were almost hanging out of his head, but here goes, he told himself. Before he rang Pat, he knew he had to have his ducks in a row, or he would be mercilessly shot down. 'How long will it take them to get to Earth?' Jack asked uncertainly. He knew they were travelling FTL, but that didn't nail it down at all. Jack was annoyed. Everyone said FTL was the arrival time, which was a load of bollocks.

'They intend to use *"space shortening"* which is essentially warp drive,' Harry replied, 'so it will likely be thousands of times light speed – meaning it won't be long.' Harry whispered. 'They are slightly more than eleven light years away. Ordinarily, it would take them decades to get here, but with their prop, it's anything but ordinary.' Harry's voice dropped to a whisper again on the last sentence.

Jack um'd and ah'd while Harry was replying. 'Okay,thanks. So, you have no idea, *"but it won't be long"? That* really helps.' Jack gazed at him sarcastically. 'If that's how it is, *so be it*. They will arrive on Earth when they arrive. NASA will just have to suck it up...Pat too'.

The Biapene would travel by shortening space in front of them, so the C restriction limit and added mass was gracefully avoided. Their arrival time is unknown though, but arrival by warp bubble is confirmed.'

Jack gawked squarely at Harry, with arms hanging limp at his sides. 'I, um...need to telephone Pat on his personal number and you and Abby need to be ready to return to Earth. Make no mistake, NASA will want to speak to you in person. 'Pete and myself need to get ready for more bad news...our tenure up here is likely to be extended *again*.' Jack held his stomach and clutched his chest – he knew what nightmare was in front of him. And it wouldn't be good for anyone.

'We're ready Jack,' Harry said, 'our vehicle has been refuelled at ESPRIT and we're okay to go, best you focus on contacting Pat. It won't be easy, so focus on that. We are good to go.'

Jack and Pete both sighed heavily. They knew what was coming and they expected it. Jack knew they'd be here until the next rotation which JSC said, would happen as soon as they could get a rocket on 39b. In other words – *fuck knows*.

After an hour, Jack returned from the telecomm room and sat down, puffing, exhausted, sweaty, with a face infused with blood. Harry could hear him breathing in tight, angry gasps. Whatever happened on the phone had been very aerobic indeed. He'd been hit and tossed from pillar to post by Pat.

Jack panted and ranted, 'Pat said...we should've pushed back...*yes, that's right*. *"Pushed back"*. Of all fucking things.' Jack was stunned that Pat said it at all. That he even entertained the thought. He shook his head hard and hit his forehead with his fist. '*Jesus Christ - what is wrong with him.* We were somehow supposed to make the Biapene focus on killing the Werinn and *not* coming to Earth. *Can you believe that shit*?' I told Pat that we couldn't and wouldn't do that, for obvious reasons. Pat was totally off the grid. He was talking about the Biapene being encouraged by humans to kill an entire *global* civilisation of Werinn.' Jack shook his head again and seriously wondered what Pat was on.

Jack tried to calm himself, 'This guy is something else,' he said, 'NASA and Pat should know better than that.' Jack was angry and annoyed, cracking his knuckles and grinding his teeth, looking like a wreck. His hair was standing up at strange angles. Jack could feel his body tensing as he spoke about this lunatic from NASA, who questioned every word that came out of his mouth. 'He wanted their intel - he made that very clear indeed.' Jack continued to swear at the bitter pill he was forced to swallow.

Jack took a deep breath, controlling himself with great effort, and tightened his pants-belt. 'I made it clear to Pat that we weren't communicating with the Biapene at all. We were speaking only with the Werinn, as *they* were the threatened party, and humans were there to help them. Pat seemed satisfied. Eventually, after an hour of fending off his accusations, he accepted it.'

Jack ran his hand through his thinning hair. 'Well...he said he did, but I'm not so sure. After he accepted it, Pat's first concern was the people of Earth, and he asked that you and Abby come back immediately. They will send relief for me and Pete...*soon* hopefully. But they couldn't give me an exact date. NASA may have to outsource our relief to SpaceX and Dragon, which they don't want to do, but they probably don't have much choice. If they don't, we'll never get home.

*   *   *

Harry gave separation instructions to the Orion software which released hooks and latches from Gateway's I-Hab. Once mechanically boosted into free space, a short burn was followed by a larger burn which had them free of the Service Module and into the lunar corridor and eventually in the atmosphere of Earth and enjoying molecular friction, which the the craft was produced to withstand.

Three parachutes almost brought the supersonic crew module to a dead-stop above the Pacific Ocean, a jolt that was strong enough for Abby to almost bring her lunch up. Their craft floated under massive linen chutes just off the coast of Baja, California. The parachutes were gigantic - red and white striped, tight with air.

11

Earth

"The universe doesn't allow perfection.*"*
~ *Stephen Hawking*

Harry and Abby were sent to Washington with specific direct and uncompromising instructions from their employer. "*Do not* under any circumstances embarrass NASA". And they were told that several times, *ominously,* by the Administrator H. Alistair Thaddeus. They were asked, *told*, not to slander anyone, and that meant *anyone*. Be polite, and use formal language at all times. Harry glanced at Abby and laughed on the inside. All this stuff spouted by Alistair was obvious. Like Abby said later, Harry and her weren't frigging hillbillies.

NASA was aware that their employees would be talking to the media, and to members of the Whitehouse. NASA's entire budget of $27 billion might be on the line, they were told. Abby didn't care much what NASA thought, but she did care about the Biapene themselves. They'd travelled a long way to throw themselves on our doorstep. And hope for some understanding. Abby thought about their harrowing plight and was deeply moved. She doubted humans could do it. Losing their planet and billions of their people, including family and friends. Spending God knows how long on a spaceship coming to a brand-new world populated by a different species. To an uncertain welcome. What a horror, she thought. Her heart went out to them.

Abby wondered if the Biapene were any different from refugees on Earth. When their terrestrial homeland had been decimated by nature, or war, and they came knocking on a more fortunate land. They were *cosmic refugees* - no-one could deny it. The Biapene hoped Earth would allow a few of them to make a safe and secure home on Earth and be understanding of their essentials.

It's not as if you had an invite to Earth – you're travelling to a distant world and have no idea if you're wanted or not. You'd just arrive on the door-step of Earth and hope for the best. The Biapene were hoping to guarantee the survival of their species. The only thing they knew for certain was, the atmosphere was good to breathe and there's probably something to eat and drink. Everything else though, was up for grabs. The Biapene *hoped* to assimilate with humanity.

To Abby, it seemed only fair that we helped them by letting them stay. And by looking after them. She knew not all humans would share those good wishes. Many humans would wish they didn't come to Earth at all. Many humans wouldn't want to be anywhere near them. Most people on Earth wouldn't want to know them. They were a different species gut-wrenchingly, hideous.

*   *   *

The two of them had shown their I.D.'s and passed through a metal detector. They both submitted to a vigorous pat down by Secret Service officers and were ready to meet POTUS in the Oval Office.

'Has he been briefed about all this?' Abby whispered to Harry, who trimmed his beard and shaved in the cab on the way there, using the Remington PG he'd been given. Now, he was fully manscaped and ready for a meeting with the President.

Harry nodded in return, as they waited to be escorted into the POTUS lair, also known as the Oval Office.

They'd been ferried to their current seating outside the Oval Office by the Secretary of State who met them at the front door. Ted Johnston was very polite and proper, if not a tad unfriendly and mechanical. He was more like a robot than a real person. He even walked stiffly. If he spoke in beeps and dings, Abby wouldn't have been the slightest bit surprised. This guy was something else.

Although POTUS was a total buffoon, with a serious case of self-importance, his station demanded respect, even if he didn't. The four from the United Nations sat separately. They were near POTUS, in a row of chairs lined up near his Resolute desk. Harry and Abby were introduced to the UN staff by POTUS, who included the country they each represented. China, Great Britain, France, the European Federation, and Japan. POTUS represented NASA and the globe, in particular, the USA, and Canada. The President's Science-Advisor was there, sitting in a spacious chair next to POTUS and was introduced to them all. Mrs Gupta was an absolutely brilliant physicist. She watched and listened to every word the President uttered. Congress would be updated later by word and paper.

Excepting POTUS, who looked low-key, and red in the face as he normally did. The rest of them stared at him, and around at his office, terrified. None of them knew in detail what was expected of them. Their nerves were a combination of where they were, the entirely unknown, and what they knew they may have to do. All of it sent shivers of terror through their bodies.

They were here to decide where an interstellar species might live. Ten thousand of them. *No pressure*, Abby thought. She was mortified and closed her eyes and massaged a temple. Everyone else looked completely out-of-their-depth too, so, Abby took solace in that. First Contact Protocol was enacted by NASA, but that didn't come close to covering where the Biapene might stay. Obviously that scenario was never envisaged.

First Contact Protocol only quantified who would be advised and when, and who would be present at the first meeting. The rest was up to NASA and the UN. They needed to spitball answers to various questions they thought would never be asked. So, all of them were delving deeply into the unknown, POTUS included.

No human would want to be neighbours with the Biapene. That was a given. Property prices would be destroyed. All of them in the Oval Office knew there would be little demand for surrounding properties, once the Biapene moved in. They'd be unable to give them away. For free. The Biapene would be like poison to the housing market. And they couldn't put them way out in the wilderness either. Any decision was going to be full of problems. Location of the Biapene was fraught with headaches.

Protests, objections, straight-out opposition and extreme hostility, and widespread dissent to their decision was expected.

Wherever they picked would be wrong and the local government and the government itself would bitch about it as would the residents.

Harry gave them all a rundown of his interactions and knowledge of both races and what led to him and Abby encountering the creatures in the first place. The main question they all had was where they were going to go, once they arrived. Where would they live? No-one would be putting their hand up - they knew that much. They would create too many problems for the existing population. Too close, too many, too different – the list of negatives would be endless.

POTUS was determined to keep Abraham Lincoln's quote high in his mind. "All men are created equal". By "men", POTUS was using that term to describe all intelligences. So, that meant we needed to home the Biapene as we would a human.

The Biapene knew the human penchant for aggression and warfare well. And the Biapene, after they landed, would in their own gentle way, ask and eventually, if necessary, plead for pyramidal housing. They would say that it was essential for their type of life. If they didn't get it, the Biapene would eventually lose the will to live.

They would find it difficult to relay to humans, due to the Biapene's intrinsic nature, and because of the thick-headed nature of Mankind, who didn't see it as important. "It's not important to humans, so why is it important to you".

The Biapene were expected to behave like humans, even though they were an entirely different species. Most on Earth had no real idea how to treat them, apart from applying the human playbook to them. Deciding what was critical and non-critical to the Biapene was the job of the front line of humans. They were appointed by American Congress, a team that followed and added to the First Contact Protocol, as decided by NASA.

Peter Chalsman was a Senior Member of the UN Security Council and currently the UN's Rep for Great Britain. He found it difficult to believe he was in the Whitehouse, discussing *non-humans*. It wasn't long ago that such talk would finger you as a lunatic. Now, they were doing it in the Whitehouse and Congress for *fuck's sakes*. It was beyond ridiculous, but he'd seen some of the videos and was totally sold. Non-humans had seen Earth, and liked what they saw.

Earth had done a complete half-circle. The groundwork which allowed this event to be so well received was made by UAP's. There was now an agreement across America, including the CIA and DoD that non-humans were real and doing incredible things in the sky that human tech could not do. Their reason for them being here was unknown, but their interest in nuclear sites was alarming.

Acknowledgment and disclosure still hadn't happened, but there was a general global acceptance of non-humans and Mankind *not* being alone. The public realised that there was a new cold war as Russia, China and the US battled for supremacy, trying to reverse-engineer non-human technology that had crashed to the ground.

Each country wanted to be the first to zip and zap across Earth's skies. Whoever managed it first would rule the skies and the planet. They'd have huge superiority in flying ability and weaponry itself. Few doubted non-human technology could be weaponised. The world was waiting impatiently for words from POTUS. That would make the situation with non-human intelligence truly undeniable. The whole idea of UFOs, the craft and the tech, was kept quiet because the effect on the oil and gas price would be catastrophic.

Imagine a world that no longer relied on fossil fuels for energy. The UAE, other Arab states, and the middle-east generally, would vitiate overnight. Earth would quickly become unrecognisable. Oil and gas wouldn't be worth the cost of extraction. Humanity would have access to anti-gravity and zero-point energy along with many things that don't exist today. So, it's little wonder that certain governments wanted to keep the whole thing quiet. The loss of the oil and gas price on Earth would devastate economies around the globe. Seventy million people would be abruptly unemployed.

Looking around the Oval Office, Harry saw POTUS eyeballing him impatiently and watched him start speaking and running his hand through his thinning white hair. 'We can't put them near a population,' he gravelled. 'There would be huge unrest if we did. Demand and property price reductions and so on. And they'd probably be right.' POTUS eyeballed everyone in the room. Despite POTUS thinking he'd made a really salient point, everyone already knew that.

'The Biapene are an unknown quantity – no-one knows what to expect from them. But we know for a fact how the market will respond. *Negatively.'* POTUS spoke seriously and emphasised his words, almost yelling at the people that were close to him. Peter felt bilious after the outburst. He was nervous as hell, watching POTUS speak, previously restricted to seeing him on the nightly news.

By the nodding that occurred, everyone, POTUS included, agreed with the negative sentiment. It was pretty obvious stuff. Charles Nguyen, a thin wisp of a man, the rep for China who recently worked under the surly Chinese Minister for Foreign Affairs, spoke slowly and anxiously.

'I-It needs to be s-somewhere with decent weather.' That was pretty obvious too. Discussion hadn't proceeded past the bleeding obvious, with agreement all around, and nodding heads everywhere – but that was about to change, as it drilled down to the details.

Harry thought Australia, New Zealand, maybe a Pacific Island, Hawaii, Fiji perhaps, but didn't say anything. Not in the Oval Office. NASA had put the fear of God into him about talking out of turn, or just *talking*.

POTUS cleared his throat for the umpteenth time and clearly had something to say. 'I, um...agree with *all* that – [cough] what about Canada?' Pardeep Gupta nodded vigorously, 'er, my Canuck friends tell me it gets a bit cold...but basically, it's otherwise pretty good.' POTUS continued, 'Private developers have built multi-storied accommodation for the Squamish indigenous people on the outskirts of Vancouver in British Columbia. No reason it can't be repeated further north on the mainland, and even enlarged a bit. We'd have to speak to the Prime Minister of Canada, who no doubt won't be happy, and will fire back with multiple issues, but from here it's doable.' POTUS took a sip of Diet Coke and then continued drawling.

'Well, we'll have to wait on that one, but it seems, um...possible,' POTUS repeated. He had his eyes closed and did the broad math for Vancouver and smiled slowly.

'What about the potential for diseases from them? Charles said, coming dangerously close to cutting him off, although POTUS didn't seem perturbed.

'Neil Tyson was with me a day or so ago and he was very dismissive of that. Apparently, the further away something is, genetically from you, the less likely a disease is to jump to you. And there is nothing further away genetically than an off-system non-human, who has evolved from a brand-new spark of life. He reckons there is zero chance that it will be a problem. *But* there is some evidence that Covid19 and even Ebola came from space. So, who is right? Whatever the truth is, I find it hard to go against Neil.'

Harry glanced at Abby and was taken by the way her hair shone in the downlights of POTUS' office. He glanced at her speculatively, noticing that she was goggling at POTUS with huge eyes. Harry instantly wished she'd look at him like that. Things weren't progressing with Abby as he'd planned.

'Agree,' Pardeep Gupta said, quickly replying on the first bit of science in the conversation. 'I too would never go against Neil.' She said quickly. 'Any virus or bacteria from them would not have the right DNA or even RNA source-code at its core to be a problem for us.' Pardeep finished with a satisfied smile. *Take that,* she thought.

Having spoken, POTUS eyeballed everyone in the room with stony eyes. 'In any event, whatever we decide, we will need to be very careful not to say *anything* outside this room. NO media.' The folk from the UN were very excited about Vancouver. It sounded pretty good to all those present.

'We'll go with initial disinfectant, and leave it at that. Earth will not go against Neil deGrasse Tyson.' POTUS decision didn't fill them with confidence, but he'd made up his mind. He'd been installed as the General of this mission, and no-one dissented. His decision was final. POTUS had the okay of every space-industry, the UN, the G7 and Five-Eyes, to make any recommendation he saw fit.

POTUS coughed again. 'I thought I'd be fighting Dem's, not fucking aliens.' POTUS voice sank to a whisper on the last sentence, but he genuinely meant what he said. This was plain ridiculous. He was the leader of the free world, not an expert with non-humans.

POTUS had a team of specialists - all Sagan-types who could and would deal with first contact protocol. But at the end of the day, he knew it was him. He would represent the human species. By himself – *alone*. He was the tip of a very long spear.

The Biapene themselves made the hair on the back of his neck bristle. Despite his abilities in front of Congress, as Commander-in-Chief during wartime and in front of seemingly murderous Dem's...he was just a fragile human being. Born on Earth and used to Earthly issues. Incredibly, his role had widened significantly, somehow now involving non-humans from a different planet.

He knew how important these creatures were to his re-election chances. They were on everybody's mind, countrywide and, in fact, globally. If he got a good result with the Biapene his GOP re-election, was all but guaranteed. That meant the right location to home them was critical.

Since no-one else was talking, POTUS continued, looking at everyone in the room stonily. 'So, we're in agreement about Canada – I think I can sell that to the Prime Minister. He can engage the King of Canada himself. It should be a formality if James is on-board and in agreement. Which, with inducement, he will be. Trust me,' he said, like any good car salesman. POTUS knew what assets he had at his command, and what he could send Canada's way to sweeten the deal. And a sweet deal it would be. POTUS would make sure of it.

'The final thing to discuss is their location *while* the construction phase is occurring.' POTUS looked around his oval office proudly. His eyes rested on a large photo of him with the PM of Israel.

Jeff McKenzie had worked at the UN all his life even though he had a Master's Degree in astrophysics and loved anything "space" related. For the last decade, he'd represented his country of birth, Britain, with distinction, in line with the UN's founding charter.

He said to POTUS, 'it would make sense if the building and initial housing was in Canada too, but I know there is a massive shortfall of houses in British Columbia already. Any buildings and room for that many individuals has to be built from scratch. Doesn't matter whether it's use is short or long term.' Jeff pushed back his moist fringe with a swipe of his hand. He found it hard talking to the President. 'There's no way we can fit that many individuals into existing infra-structure.' Jeff sat down and looked at the floor, waiting for any questions from the group. He was a member of the eminent-dozen and would be front and centre when the Biapene arrived.

POTUS looked at Jeff and slowly shook his head and narrowed his eyes. 'I think it's best if they stay where they are, on the ship, until the long-term accommodation is ready. The buildings we will use to house them in Canada won't take long to build, if we get them all onto it. The workers will be paid by the UN and World Bank. Any expedition, I'm sure, can be paid by the USA. Otherwise, we'll be building twice...which definitely makes no sense.'

POTUS nodded his head at Jeff this time. Jeff nodded back – it made good sense to him. 'That's, um...good Jeff. He agreed with himself, which Jeff was told, he liked to do. 'Makes sense.' POTUS said, 'I'll see if the PM agrees.'

'I'm sure he won't, but the President will make him see the bigger picture,' Harry said to Abby, gazing at POTUS and realising that money and assets would be funnelled Canada's way. To the point where the PM of Canada would agree to anything. The situation with Canada was the definition of *Quid pro quo.*

POTUS was sure warfare was common amongst intelligent species, even if it didn't happen on the Werinn planet. He was fairly sure they were an exception to the rule. So, they could basically go fuck themselves. They made it out to be rare, and intimated that humanity was one of the few species that indulged in it. What a load of crap, he reckoned. Like us or lump us. It seemed, for the Werinn anyway, it was the latter.

POTUS actually didn't have a clue. With a sample size of one or two, it was impossible to draw conclusions about warfare amongst intelligent species. Still, he drew them and kept drawing. That was him. He wondered about the nature of the Biapene. Were they pacifists? Probably didn't matter – humans wouldn't really care, one way or the other. As long as they behaved themselves on Earth.

POTUS said. 'We'll go to the UN with that recommendation and see if it floats. It sounds okay to us, but who knows about the UN? If it is agreed, a Special Resolution and UNSCR will be adopted by the UN Security Council. If conditions in the ship are no good or something else goes awry, we come up with another plan. We must not be deterred. There is no one else to make the decisionn.'

With that, POTUS pressed a button on his desk, and Secretary of State, Ted Johnston appeared through the open door, and escorted them all out of the Oval Office. Next step, Harry knew, was the UN.

*   *   *

The UN General Assembly was a huge golden hall in New York that simply bespoke formality and correctness. The ceiling above them was huge and circular. It was filled with down-lights...pseudo-stars, like an effigy of the Universe itself. The great hall was indeed hallowed and had been witness to many significant global occasions. Not all of them good, but this issue seemed fitting to be decided there. It was the first visit from an extra-terrestrial society. Their location on Earth had been sent to the great hall for human sign-off.

Earth needed to decide where to locate them – where the Biapene should live out their lives. Their future was no longer on Biapene – that planet was no longer viable. It used to be a haven for evolution and life. Now, due to loss of its protective magnetics, it was a planet-wide killing-field to anything biological.

The Biapene weren't just visiting to say *'hey'* either, they were staying permanently on Earth – all ten thousand of them. Earth, to them, was a new Eden. They were the same as refugees from the Middle-East. But these beings were very different from humans. And with them, they brought the secrets of the stars. New theory, insights and intel that had eluded Mankind for centuries and cost Mankind billions of dollars in unsuccessful endeabours. The Biapene intended to swap for it. They wanted a new home.

The question had to be asked – did humanity have the intellectual capacity to look after the Biapene's needs? When the Biapene were so non-human and peculiar? The humans reckoned it'd be easy. *Not so.* The major Biapene need was entirely unfamiliar on Earth. For humans, the road to accessing Biapene intel was crooked indeed. One step the wrong way could end in disaster.

*   *   *

Harry and Abby had been invited to an Emergency Special Session of the UN General Assembly. Not as participants, but as viewers. Normally, the Assembly meets once a year in September. But this issue demanded its own special Session immediately. So, a new meeting was scheduled for the great gallery. One that looked more like a holy cathedral than a place of business.

Harry and Abby occupied a skybox high above the proceedings, and were guests only, taking no direct part in the adoption or otherwise of the resolution. Pat Ryan from NASA would do most of the leg-work. Pat was fully primed for the address.

The proceeding was due to start and Pat was ready to go. His heart was beating harder as he ascended the stairs, grabbing hold of the rail and hustling up. He had to make his way to the stage, where he would address the members and state his case in favour of Canada as the host nation. It was basically, a repeat of what he'd said to POTUS. And the reverse.

Harry looked at Abby blissfully and could tell she was ecstatic to be lying back and relaxing...with him hopefully. He could see the joy written in her eyes which were wide open. They were sitting at least five metres above the action at ground level and enjoyed the deep embroidered seats and foot-rests of the sky-box, centrally located above the glorious gallery. Abby gave Harry a crisp nod and an affectionate smile and he returned it. They were both delighted to be there, in each other's company, watching history unfurl itself.

'I feel a bit frustrated Ab. Pat's doing all the talking. I mean...that's great, it saves us doing it. But...I don't know.' Harry trailed off and stared down at his hands. He felt like he was missing out on this incredible moment by letting Pat do everything. Afterall, it was Abby and him that piloted NASAs mission to uncover it. Harry smiled bitterly and sighed heavily.

'I know Harry.' Abby replied. 'Pat is the leader...but you want to do more. I can see your frustration. You were scowling and frowning at him when he was talking. I get it, I do...but leave it to the chief. Our work is still in front of us. Just enjoy the downtime. It doesn't come very often.' Abby grabbed Harry's hand and smiled warmly at him. Harry squeezed her hand and put it in his lap. He was edgy, but with Abby here, he couldn't have been happier. Harry saw a future with Abby. She shared a lot of his own opinions and seemed happy when she was in his company. All pointers that boded well for the future. Harry smiled hugely, turning his head and taking the whole amphitheatre in.

POTUS had spoken to the PM of Canada and gotten reluctant approval for the development happening in his own backyard. At first, he didn't want a bar of it. No way became *maybe, perhaps* and then, *okay*. In reality, Canada had little choice because of clause 2.4 of the UN Charter. The PM reckoned they'd be better off in Australia or on a Pacific Island, but he eventually caved, when he realised how good it would be for Canada if they settled in his country. POTUS would give him all sorts of valuable inducements that he wasn't allowed to speak about...*ever*..

POTUS addressed the members in the UN and he was ready to put this issue to bed. He had all the knowledge he needed from Harry and Pat. This would be a slam-dunk, and a formal Resolution from the UN would put the Biapene in Canada. As far as he was concerned, it was job done.

The permanent members for Canada, the USA, France, China, Russia and Great Britain were in position. They would receive the info and decide on the most epic evidence Earth had ever heard, which would soon become legend.

POTUS' narration and speech was so impactful that the member representing France - Lorraine Beanlea, a middle-aged woman with small bi-focal glasses, was openly weeping. She held her glasses in her hand, wiping tears from the lens. She found his speech so compelling.

She was disappointed that *this* was the outcome, but still thought the whole story was amazing. To think, Earth had graduated to another level by realising for certain, that it wasn't alone. Now, motherhood statements that referred to planetary plenitude, or the size of the Universe, weren't needed. Earth knew for sure.

There was ultimately a consensus on the Biapene's location being in a brand-new multi-storey development to be built in the Vancouver, BC Canada area. After some debate there was total agreement that the development should be expedited. It was decided that the Biapene travellers should remain on their ship. If possible, until the development was ready to be occupied.

The UN only needed 2/3 of the present members to agree. But the Resolution was adopted with all members voting for it. There were no dissenters, 100% approval was obtained. It was a really good start. Of course, dissenting would require a brand-new location to be hammered out. Which no-one in the UN wanted. POTUS knew this was a rubber-stamp job.

The whole thing still depended on what conditions existed in their ships. But the UN readily agreed that this was the best plan and the least disruptive to the Biapene, who had been through hell already. Talk by the Biapene around the importance of pyramids and triangular living quarters made little impact on the humans. And indeed, was not part of the discussion. It was noted and forgotten.

Prior to entering the development in Vancouver, each Biapene would be subject to a medical clearance, as far as humanity could go with one. Their internal makeup was probably very different to humans, so the clearance was very qualitative indeed. The Biapene may be carbon-based and bipedal, but internally they probably differed from humans. That was the opinion of medical experts from a xeno backgound. They believed that organs would be similar but organisation and grouping was likely to be very different indeed.

Only around 20% of the Biapene spoke English. So, one of the 20% who was considered proficient and appropriate, would act as interpreter for the rest of them. But the whole thing would prove to be a slow process. The medical clearance would be a difficult Q and A session that would take too long and produce questionable results.

The Biapene were known to be a reptile of some sort and they wondered if they should engage the services of a herpetologist.or a vet but it didn't seem right, and the quandary remained unanswered. The medical doctors made it known they were less than enthusiastic to work on them. If any died, which was likely, human attendees didn't want to be responsible, or have it on their record. The whole medical thing was turning into a massive arse-covering debacle.

Professors, astrobiologists and even xeno-archaeologists had picked apart xeno-care and determined that medical help for the

Biapene would be far too qualitative because the Biapene were probably so different to humans.

Any Biapene who failed the first eyes-on "test" would be subject to further analysis and possibly treatment, which was going to be tough because their unknown physiology. Thirteen established American doctors had volunteered to work with them. They had access to PET scanners, MRI, CT, Gallium scanners, and Ultrasound.

They would use them all. It was designed to make an intolerable situation, more bearable. At least they'd be able to see what they were doing, even though they probably wouldn't understand the finer details. The Biapene reaction to human drugs would remain a mystery, until they could test them over a decent period of time. Serious problems were expected.

*   *   *

Although it was decided the Biapene would go to Canada, but the pyramidal component that was so important on their planet and enshrined in their law had, unfortunately, been totally ignored on Earth and buried in the chaotic rush to house them.

Mankind desperately needed to get the Biapene off the streets. Humans knew that getting hold of their intel depended on keeping them happy. But to-date it was a haphazard path they were on. Those humans who watched their actions closely, feared the worst. The conditions and living environment planned for Earth differed greatly from those on Biapene. So the question was, could the Biapene cope with their Earthly abode and remain satisfied? Most thought they wouldn't be able to cope.

Harry and Abby watched part two of the official proceedings from their elevated position in the UN. Harry looked at Abby, who was sitting next to him and wondered about her fairly sudden disinterest? *He knew he wasn't invisible.* Abby looked at him like he wasn't there most times. Her eyes looked around him and through him. Harry had felt like he was making progress, but now, he wasn't sure. He stared wordlessly at her, while his heart pounded, but she hardly seemed to know he existed. She'd shown some interest, but right now, it was a bust. Thankfully, he had something up his sleeve, that *might* tilt the tables in his direction.

Harry's ex-girlfriend from years ago knew Abby from a girlfriend, who was still good friends with her. So, indirectly, Harry knew a bit more about Abby than she thought. That might help him, he reckoned. Given his lack of current progress, his intent was to make full use of this intel and try to align his life goals with hers.

Harry liked Abby, and was getting more and more desperate to have her like him. She was a work-colleague, he knew that, but he really liked her so decided to carefully use the intel he had gleaned.

It should seem purely natural, he knew that too, but he reckoned he needed help to push him over the line. If it worked, she'd never know any different, he hoped. Everything he'd tried so far had been for nothing. Abby still looked at him like he wasn't there most times. He didn't like it. He wanted to be front and centre in Abby's life.

Harry was ready to talk to Abby and try it out. Turning to her deliberately, he looked directly at Abby. He made full eye contact, and said cheerfully, 'I really want to travel you know … perhaps after I get sick of NASA.' Harry smiled ebulliently. The proceedings with the UN had concluded, so he didn't think Abby would mind him talking about something personal. 'Iceland would be nice…mountaineering up Mt. Keilir, maybe explore an ice-cave or two, snowmobile or just trek somewhere … anywhere in Iceland would be great. Y'know, see a glacier or an iceberg. Then of course there's night-time, enjoying a brandy or a scotch at the bar or in a room with a roaring log fire.' Harry smiled at Abby like a Chesire cat. He knew he had her.

Abby turned fully in her seat and smiled widely at Harry. *'Holy shit,'* she said happily. *'Really Harry?'* Abby purred, licking her lips. 'Iceland … Reykjavik, is a place I've always wanted to go. Since being a little girl … *Amazing.'* Her face brightened with the suggestion. She smiled warmly at Harry. 'The midnight sun, the glaciers…the trekking. And you too?' She asked, peering up at him, and twitching her nose.

'Yup.' Harry nodded effusively, feeling bad to use the information that had been leaked to him, but it wasn't far from what he liked anyway. He enjoyed trekking for trekking's sake. Throw exploration and discovery into it, and he was sold. Especially if he could do it with Abby. The whole thing excited him beyond belief. Clearly, Abby was rapt too. She liked the idea of Iceland with Harry. Hallelujah, he thought to himself. It seemed to have had an impact.

Abby remembered reading about Iceland in her younger years, under the bed-covers, watching and reading the glorious pages with a penlight. She had a travel brochure on trekking and skiing in Iceland. Abby remembered her love for the sites around Reykjavik and the instructors who wore black Activewear that was tight in just the right places. She loved those pages the most and remembered her adolescent feelings for the photos in her favourite tourist magazine, which was well-read and dog-eared. Abby felt like crying, when she thought how unlikely it was to have her ancient history intersect with her current NASA role which included Harry.

Abby wiped the tears away and gazed at Harry without blinking – she couldn't believe that this man, with whom she'd shared so much, also shared such a similar, simpler personal aspiration. She felt smitten and looked at him full in the eye for a moment, sizing him up. Harry now had both arms on the ledge in front of him and laid his head on his arms.

Abby looked at him in a brand-new light. Well, *fuck me,* who would have ever known, she thought to herself, still gazing yearningly at Harry. She wondered what other similarities lay bubbling beneath? She'd never thought of Harry like that but now that she was, a feeling of warmth imbued her loins. She continued staring at him and couldn't stop smiling euphorically.

On the Orion, she was way too busy to think of anything like romance, but now, things had changed, and slowed down a bit. Harry had shown her a different side to his life that just happened to be in tune with hers. How intriguing, she thought, still grinning.

'*Here we are.*' Harry yelled excitedly. They were being put up by NASA – together – at the Capital Hilton – not far from the Whitehouse. In separate rooms of course. Essentially, they'd be the ears and eyes of NASA. Together with Pat, who was there as an official from NASA HQ – Houston, Texas. It sounded easy, but NASA expected a detailed report daily from Harry and a video meeting every three days. NASA remained a challenging employer for both of them.

Harry felt the call of nature, so he went into the Capital Hilton. He was elated to see Abby's head turn and follow him as he walked, Harry saw it out of the corner of his eye. He wasn't invisible, after all. Abby gazed at Harry and thought how good he looked. She also felt some pride, watching him - *he* was her partner in space. And it might even go further than that, who knew?

No-one knew when the Biapene were arriving, but Harry and Abby needed to be ready, which suited both of them fine, the environment was way better than Houston and they continued on full pay. And maybe best of all, they were driven to the District of Columbia by a driver from NASA, through Baltimore and Philly.

Abby looked forward to spending more time with Harry, who'd shown a side to her that she found categorically alluring. She gazed at Harry and the view beyond, with beaming cheeks. The future looked pretty good. Not only was he a NASA astronaut, but he was a closet trekker in Iceland apparently. Earth and them were about to host their first interstellar visitor. Abby anxiously and optimistically looked forward to it, stoked with how things were going right now.

*   *   *

The Biapene would soon land on Earth's doorstep. And Earth had no choice but to look after them like legitimate refugees. Afterall, their home planet was decimated.

No options held water at all. Let them loose on society or tell them that we won't provide lodgings? Shoo them away like flies at a footy game? ... *I don't think so.* If they wanted to stay, it was probably in humanity's interest to assist them to do it. They weren't leaving their own planet for no reason. The Biapene were genuine refugees.

But try explaining Earth's decision to the general population. Earth was damned if they did and damned if they didn't. It didn't matter what the agencies and governments of Earth did, it would be *wrong.* The fact that we would essentially offer the Biapene money and agree to provide for them wouldn't go down well with a lot of Earth's lower-income population...because we didn't do it for them. Envy and resentment would surely rear their ugly heads.

They would object to the selective treatment of the Biapene and think it grossly unfair. What about humans that screamed out for better care...or more money, or less tax. Times were tough for many households and hearing that the Biapene would be "looked after", was difficult. Even if they were from another planet.

It led to questions no-one on Earth knew how to properly answer. The bottom-line was, and there was no getting away from it - many humans were poorly treated even though there was "enough" to go around. Unfortunately, some governments were horrendously corrupt keeping everything and giving its people very little.

Why look after non-humans when so many humans on Earth live in poverty? That was the general tenor of signs carried by thousands in almost every country. They were rubbing shoulders with UFO-believers who carried placards like "we told you so" and "full disclosure now" that referred to the Biapene and Werinn as the main source of Earthly UFOs. They were keen to hear from the American President. He knew, apparently, as did some in the CIA, DoD, Congress and the Pentagon.

With the Biapene's ability to travel FTL, and their understanding of anti-gravity and quantum-energy, the response was expected. *They* were the reason for the discs and the tic-tacs and the kidnappings and the surgically precise excision of cattle organs. It was the Biapene that did it, and maybe the Werinn. They were some of the *non-humans* in vessels that zipped and zapped all over Earth's sky, being labelled a "national-security" risk and a danger to aviation.

The Speaker, in American Congress, had spoken about non-human craft in our skies who were so curious and concerned, about Mankind's technology. Many wondered if they were Biapene or maybe Werinn, from the Ross128 system. They seemed to tick all the boxes.

Nearly every large town or city in every country had people parading down a main street and interrupting traffic. They weren't happy with the Biapene's arm-chair ride they were receiving from governments. Their own people, *humans,* weren't treated nearly so well. The main question was "why"? What made them so different?

Millions of humans slept outside globally. Evictions from houses and businesses happened daily, inflation hit most households hard, cost of living was increasing worldwide. Everything cost more – food, energy and retail. Debt levels were out of control, bankruptcies surged, millions died from disease, malnutrition or starvation in Africa and Asia. Corrupt governments cried poor, while individuals from the same government were rich beyond reason. It wasn't fair, was the cry. There were so many problems on Earth, yet the creatures from Ross were housed and catered to free of charge, like they were royalty.

Of course, humans needed to house them, because we were civilised. The Biapene were legitimate refugees. But it didn't mean we should ignore our own. That was why so many people didn't like it – *help us too.* This was the demand on social media in every country.

Mankind generally realised the Biapene couldn't be left to fend for themselves once they landed. They needed to be segregated from humans and fed, at least initially, and probably long-term. Most humans realised that too, but the opportunity it provided to protest, demonstrate and object was too good to pass on. China led the world in protests and demonstrations, followed closely by the US, Russia, Asia and Europe. Africa had its own problems, but in some places like Nigeria, it was as bad as the rest of the world. So was Australia.

In China, every town had enough people protesting against their own treatment and standard of living. They compared themselves to the Biapene, who seemingly got money for nothing while the Chinese were on the streets illegally, from Yining in the north to Guangzhou in the south, and from Kashi in the east to Beijing in the west. There were two million people in Chinese prisons, and the number was growing rapidly.

The government and their "police force", which included many from the paramilitary, dragged protestors away, but they were replaced by others. The Chinese people were very serious. There were too many people on the streets for the government or anyone to deal with. And the numbers in China were increasing.

Once again, the Chinese media made no mention of the marches, but the country's domestic output was suffering, because those normally on a farm or in an office, were on the streets. And the President didn't like it and had never seen anything like it. He thought the entire world had gone mad, and that wasn't far from the truth.

The same was happening in Russia, from Moscow to Magadan in Siberia, the people were protesting, and in places, revolting and looting. Crime was everywhere. Windows were smashed and goods stolen *en-masse*. The war in Ukraine had stopped as a result of the Biapene – there was no-one left in the respective armies to fight the war. Most of the Russians were in Moscow or Saint Petersburgh, protesting with everyone else.

The US was the same, from Washington State to Florida. People were on the streets, rioting, protesting and generally causing unrest. Fear dominated the streets around normally quiet suburbs. Violence monopolised the city-streets of major capitals and towns. No-one went out after dark, anywhere in the world. If you did, you were quickly confronted by groups with killing and chaos in mind.

Many people thought that the Biapene and Werinn were already here, and had been for a long time. Some of their vessels had crashed, and were now sitting with the US at Lockheed Martin, Almaz-Antey in Russia, or Chengdu in China, just waiting to be reverse engineered and understood.

In many places worldwide, there were no emergency services, even in first-world counties. They were either stretched to breaking point or simply closed due to mistreatment of officers. "Mistreatment" meant luring officers to a location for the purposes of murder. No-one wanted to be a paramedic now - Heart-attack, stroke or anything serious...*good luck*. Require life-saving help? ...*call later.* Self-help was the only "service" available.

Few could properly fathom why the non-humans got a better deal than humans. A good proportion of people accepted it, and grasped the concept behind their favourable treatment, but they were completely drowned out by those who opposed it. The governments, NASA and the UN's position on the non-humans was a no-brainer.

Governments kept repeating their stance, but it had little impact. They bought a lot of time on every source of legacy and social media, saying they had no choice, and staunchly defended their actions as "humanitarian". They were coming to us cap-in-hand from a dying planet. Still, despite being legitimate refugees, the protests and the unrest continued, across the world.

Images of "aliens" were plastered everywhere, Twitter, Facebook, Youtube and every other form of social media – they adorned all Mass and Digital Media. Newspapers were almost front to back with stories, new and old, about non-humans. Images of non-humans were on stoby poles, store-fronts and every flat surface worldwide. They were coming...to stay. Earth was about to change radically, what humans thought would never happen...*did.*

*   *   *

There were many folks who believed UFO's or UAP's were really Biapene or Werinn vessels. Problem was, the Biapene and Werinn had said they'd never been to Earth before. Harry and Pat didn't buy it. 'They've been to Earth before, trust me,' Harry said.

'W-What do you mean?' Abby looked at Harry, knowing something important was probably coming. He did a lot of talking and listening to the Werinn, without her. So, he knew stuff she didn't, direct from the horse's mouth.

With wide eyes, Harry said, 'The Werinn told me that in fact they did come to Earth in trans-medium vessels, and even lost a few craft here, after avoidance measures were required, but didn't work so well. Apparently, our nuclear bombs screw with their propulsion and anti-gravity. The Werinn came to Earth several times, before finally downloading our internet and deciding that they didn't want to meet us in person. Human beings weren't for them. It was possibly the Werinn at Roswell in New Mexico. They were the source, for at least some of the UFO's, stretching back to the 1800's and maybe back further than

193

that. The Biapene have been venturing to Earth for more than two thousand years.' Harry took a breath and sat back.

Abby drew in a hissing breath and felt herself suffocating. *'W-What?'* She blustered. Broken thoughts mainly around the Giza pyramids, hit her hypothalamus like meteors. *'Fuck me,'* she whispered to herself. This stuff was almost too much for her.

'Yeah, it's amazing alright. The Werinn were drawn to our planet by its colour and the gasses they detected. Soon, the Biapene became super-curious about humanity and its growing technology.'

'So, it's actually true,' Abby whispered huskily, holding her chest with a trembling hand, struggling with the idea of the Werinn or the Biapene being aboard some of the UAPs on Earth. 'Weather balloons and swamp gas, indeed,' she snapped bitterly.

Harry was gazing at Abby vacantly, taking raspy breaths with bulging eyes. He wiped sweat off his forehead with a swipe of his hand, thinking about something that still played on his mind.

'The Biapene and Werinn thing reminds me of a camping trip with my old man, when I was really young, back in the 1980's. We were in the Tucson Mountain area in Arizona. He was collecting mineral specimens from the dump of the old Yuma mine, and he dragged me along to help. We camped near the old mine and after a glorious sunset we saw it.' Harry had that vacant-scared look again.

'My old man had a set of binoculars that he tried to use.' Harry smiled wryly at the image of his father tied up royally in the strap he had strung around his neck. He remembered seeing absolutely nothing through the dirty lenses. The binoculars were so dirty they were a complete waste of time, yet his dad was so proud of them. Harry stared at Abby without blinking, clearly thinking of his dear old dad, until he shook his head to right himself.

'Triangular and like a set of wings, it moved through the clouds and all over the sky. It was orange and then there were three of them. Moving so quickly...they zig-zagged all over the sky and looked and moved very differently to an ordinary plane. We were petrified that they might land close to us, so we packed up the car and high-tailed it back to a Best Western in Tucson. The next day, we drove back home to Houston in Texas to headlines that four states had seen the damn things.' Harry stared at Abby knowingly and whispered huskily, 'that thing was probably from Werinn or Biapene.'

*   *   *

Harry gazed at Abby who was sitting next to him in the back of the taxi that headed toward their hotel in DC. She smiled at him with glowing cheeks. It was all he could do to hold back from kissing her. Abby looked and smelt amazing. Dressed in a white skirt and pink jumper, he had more than just work on his mind. They'd shared the greatest moments in Earth's history, touching non-human tech for the first time and seeing a populated exo-planet. All that would pale in significance if Abby could get to Iceland, and take it further with Harry.

Harry and Abby were coming close to their hotel in DC. Their lodgings were very different from their homes near Houston. These rooms were huge, lavish, and beautiful, even from the outside. The houses they rented in the Bay area were average at best.

Now that the Sun had set and night encroached – the hotel was lit up by thousands of globes lit their way to the entrance. The driver brought the vehicle almost to the hotel's front doors. Their luggage was loaded onto a golden carriage and taken toward the elevator by a uniformed employee who had blonde, straggly hair and wore his hat backwards. He said, 'Hello,' to them with a huge grin and very blue eyes and grabbed their gear with one arm.

Harry and Abby got a room each, that was gorgeous and side by side with a park view which they were very happy with. Having adjacent rooms made Abby's heart beat a little quicker.

Since Harry had mentioned Iceland, Abby couldn't stop thinking about the future with Harry. She had to keep reminding herself that she was on duty. The mere sight of Harry made her flush and feel warm. Abby could tell that her reaction to Harry's presence had changed. She could feel it, deep within, every time he was close.

The rooms, TV's and beds were enormous and there was a light and cupboard on both sides. But the best part was that the rooms were made up and cleaned every day, and there was room service at any time of the day or night, a service that was brand new to them both. Harry loved room service and ordered Arancini balls at 3AM with a glass of red wine...*and the best part was ... NASA would pay for it.* With Abby's recent behaviour, her warmth toward him, and room service, Harry felt like he was in paradise. He wasn't used to this much attention. So far, his plan was working beautifully.

Their work wasn't difficult. It was even enjoyable. Essentially, they were NASA's agents here – to relay information, immediately before and after the Biapene landed, which they were expected to be all over. Pat from NASA HQ was there as well. They would drive to the landing location as soon as they knew where it was. There was a NASA driver on standby, two rooms down from them at the Capitol Hilton. A few special knocks on his door were supposed be enough to get things rolling. It was the driver's responsibility to monitor all media and be totally aware of location details when it happened. That was his number one and only job.

NASA would know the Biapene were here anyway, with all the space hardware that was looking out for Earth – Pan Starrs telescope in Hawaii should see it first. They were on standby to do exactly that. It was either ground based and pointing into space, or in orbit of the planet or the Sun. All of them, including Hubble and JWST, were on high alert, waiting for them to come into range.

NASA had eight space-based telescopes and priority access to ninety-four platforms globally. Every one of them, it was hoped, would pick up the vessel. The impact of its propulsion on the visual was unknown, and it was expected to be difficult to detect. The Biapene and their craft were in a warp-bubble.

Once NASA confirmed the Biapene were in fact here, they would have a dramatic presence in Columbia. Until then, Harry, Abby and Pat would continue to do the job for them. When the Biapene's landing had been confirmed, NASA would then dispatch a team of Associate Administrators and Directors in two vehicles.

Everything Earth had was on high alert – Earth itself, the ISS, Gateway, JWST, Hubble, SpaceX, and every NASA person and facility around the globe, from Hawaii to Spain. They were all waiting. All they needed was the Biapene.

12

Biapene

"The Universe doesn't allow perfection."
~ Stephen Hawking

Abby gave Harry a ream of paper on Mt Hekla and even more on the Svínafellsjökull glacier and Reykjavik in a big cardboard box that was full to the top with paper, to the point where Harry now regretted his decision to say it to her. She was going way over the top. Harry got what he deserved though, he supposed. He showed an interest and a curiosity, but he underestimated her enthusiasm severely. Because it went way beyond simple enthusiasm. Harry gave a little, but Abby gave a heap in return. Harry's interest in Iceland was measured in centimetres, but Abby's was measured in metres. Her "enthusiasm" was a mania.

She was obsessed with the north. Fanatically gripped by what Iceland had to offer. Somehow it had her tied up in knots and she wouldn't be right ever again, until she travelled to the icy land. She saw it as a magical fairyland which it wasn't. It was simply a rather cold destination on Earth, not far from Greenland.

Abby darted her eyes over the room and clenched her jaw. Her eyes were fiery and focussed, every time she spoke about the beloved location, that she was sure Harry shared. Abby was beyond happy that Harry revered the place too. Now, she apparently had someone to share it all with.

Fuck, Harry thought. This was turning into a nightmare. What had he done? He'd roped himself into it too. *Voluntarily.* He saw it as it really was – a land far enough north that bathed in almost year-round snowfall and fuck-all Sun, for most of the year. Abby though, thought it was way more than that.

Instead of a country, it was a land of mystical enchantment. *Unicorns and fairies.* And Harry had now latched himself to Abby's wagon. *Fuck me,* he thought, shaking his head. What on Earth had he done? He'd wilfully joined with a mad-woman.

Abby was ecstatic – watching Harry's every move, which he noticed, and liked. His desire to somehow look after Abby hadn't changed but this stuff with Iceland didn't help. All he'd managed to do with his actions was feed the addiction, bring it to the surface. It was already a strong desire, but now, with him onboard, it was a stone-cold fixation.

It was his own fault and he had to run with it to the end. Every chance she had, she talked about trekking in or near Svínafellsjökull. Abby talked and talked...then talked a bit more about Iceland. It was fine to be smitten with a place, but this was getting ridiculous, and Harry knew it all stemmed from his own stupid wrong doing. Which had snowballed in front of him like a nuclear mushroom cloud.

Now he'd just have to suck it up. His relationship with Abby was definitely on the improve, so he'd focus on that. But Harry was concerned that Abby was giving the Biapene's arrival no mind ever. All she talked about was mountaineering and hiking in Iceland.

It was called severe pre-occupation, and he knew it. His own fuck-up. It was like Groundhog Day, except Abby was getting worse. She desperately needed to go to Iceland, to get it out of her system.

He knew he was obsessed too – with her. Harry tried to think only about the Biapene, but he struggled, especially in the depths of night. He could still *smell her.* The Iceland narrative, as intense as it was, hadn't affected that. Harry thought it would, but *nuh-uh,* he was still as infatuated with Abby, as he was before it all started. Her mere presence set his pulse racing.

That night, after dining in-house and consuming several glasses of rosé, Abby, after finishing her meal and paying for it on NASA's tab, grabbed Harry by the collar and took him straight to her room, and to her bed. All the pressure and gravity of the last days were released as she got what they both wanted. The timing was good, because next day, *all hell broke loose.*

They were eating breakfast together downstairs, in the all-day dining room, staring at each other without blinking. The day Earth thought would never come...was now front and centre above them. The Biapene craft descended from the sky and the whole world was spellbound. Starting with Washington DC.

Harry didn't want to leave his eggs and toast. Eventually, he put his shoes back on and dragged himself away from the table and the enticing smell of hot bacon. He knew this *had* to take priority. But it was hard to break the heaviness all the same. Harry loved bacon.

Abby followed Harry closely out of the restaurant to stand on the concrete sidewalk. Other people had arrived and many just stopped where they were, and looked straight up, following the gaze of others. In a few seconds, nearby shops and other buildings emptied of people, and they all ended up standing with Harry and Abby in a crush, looking up at the bright blue sky.

The horde on the pavement swelled almost instantly. The crowd inclined their necks and looked up as one. The crowd was pointing at "something" in the sky and making collective '*ooh*' sounds that took over the whole area. Some people in the all-day restaurant, and in the kitchen of the hotel, ran outside near them, to do the same thing. They bustled past Harry and Abby. People elbowed them as they struggled by and added to the mass of humanity. People stood at less than arm's length all around them. It was a massive, seething ocean of humanity, that all clambered for a better view. All were there to share a common purpose. Every person on the footpath wanted to see what was coming at DC, from the sky.

People were on the streets for as far as the eye could see, up Constitution Avenue - buildings and shops were empty. The eyes, pointing hands and fingers of the street-people, told the story. There was something up in the sky that *wasn't* human aviation. It had them all wondering...*was this it? So quickly?* Most knew how the Biapene planet was eleven light years away for Christ's sakes. FTL was one thing, but this was insane. This would even beat *the Enterprise.*

Wherever Abby looked, eyes were wide, stares were incredulous and mouths were open. Most rightly supposed that it was *them.* It had been forecast for weeks by the government, so most people knew what was likely coming at them from up there.

The only thing that wasn't known was exactly when the Biapene would arrive. Incredibly, it was *now* apparently. The people of Earth had been bombarded with information about the Biapene. Earth had been initially advised of the arrival of the non-humans by a very serious and sombre President who told them why they were coming. And roughly when, where...and how. The President took pains to state that the Biapene were very different to humans physically. But they were very friendly indeed.

At cloud level, the crowd of people on the streets could see three black objects, that were descending slowly and fairly much straight down, each at slightly different altitudes. They were clearly spinning and looked exactly like saucer-UFOs of yesteryear, to which, Harry shook his head and smiled wryly at Abby.

'*Triangular,*' Harry mused, as he continued smiling and gawking straight up. Harry could hear nothing from the ships and likened them to NASA craft generally, and jets in particular, both of which were deafening. But these vessels were moving left and right, but generally descending toward them, making no noise at all. All they could hear were crowd noises. The contrast with Earthly vessels was dramatic and intriguing. They clearly used very different propulsion.

The three craft moved slowly through the atmosphere, and were triangular in plan, but looked like a set of wings when viewed from behind. Harry grunted knowingly at the different shapes these craft presented - depending on which aspect you took to look at them.

The entire DC area had an unimpeded view of the descent of these odd black vehicles, that zigged and zagged, and moved toward them, largely unimpeded by Earth's gravity. Clearly, these craft had capabilities that Earth craft didn't come close to. Harry wasn't surprised with the odd, movements of the craft. NHI craft did the same in Earth's biosphere. Their movement and speed weren't bridled by either gravity or inertia. They were called UFOs or UAPs, but they were very real indeed.

Harry and Abby's phones rang at the same time. Harry got rid of the call but Abby took time to answer it, receiving a sneer from Harry. The call was from NASA in Houston. They advised that multiple craft had breached the Karman line. *Der,* Abby thought, looking squarely at the new arrivals. She was polite but got him off the phone quickly. They were here, for Christ's sake. *Er...we know.*

Pan Starrs telescope from Hawaii saw the vessels doing something very unusual indeed, which they'd already notified NASA about, and their first words were that "it was impossible". There were three craft which was a surprise, but more significantly, none of them showed evidence of heating by friction when they entered Earth's atmosphere. Didn't matter what light you looked at them in, visible, ultra-violet or infra-red. There was no glow at all - no compression and no heating whatsoever. It was odd indeed.

Unexplainable and baffling, by Earth standards. It was the first time this had ever been observed. By its very nature, anything coming back from space, or *coming* from space and hitting the molecules of the atmosphere are heated to red hot. As everyone on Earth would attest to – there was no getting around it. NASA and other space industries had obviated the heating with thick heat shields to protect incoming craft. These craft needed none of that.

They entered Earth's atmosphere easier than a hot knife through butter. *Nothing* appeared hot. No-one had an explanation, apart from making motherhood statements about the Biapene's space-industry and that it was better developed than Earth's. NASA watched with curiosity and envy. To them, to Earth generally, it didn't make any sense. It was a technology unknown on Earth.

Harry and Abby looked up from the foyer of the Capital Hilton and first noticed how incredibly blue the sky was. It was a hot and calm day in DC with only a few clouds in the sky. Perfect for a landing, any landing, from space. There was definitely no rain, and the wind was virtually nil. At ground level people were everywhere.

No-one wanted to miss the incredible moment that had been relentlessly advertised by the government. "The Biapene were coming", they'd said, over and over. *Yeah, we know,* was most people's response. The population was sick of being told. Just bring it on, most said. Get it over with.

The landing of the Biapene would herald the moment when Mankind formally graduated to a new level, punctuated by the broken Fermi paradox. Everyone truly involved knew that this day would be immortalised, to live in history forever. Many wanted to be part of it. Some of the population were just shit-scared.

The baseball game stopped over the road, along with most of the traffic on Park Street and 6th Street. Cars had come to a halt on roads, and people exited cars while still on the road. All of them looked up. The streets around the Whitehouse became a car-park.

Wherever you looked, everyone was standing still and gawking skyward. The baseballers were immobile. Staring skyward at three large, dark objects in the air descending toward them. Most of the people ended up running toward the tree-line, but some didn't know where to go, and ended up running in panicked circles. If it wasn't so serious, it'd be hilarious.

The NASA driver finally found them and ran up to Harry and Abby on the pavement, puffing and heaving, and weaving through the crowd. The poor bugger could hardly speak. 'I, uh...finally... found you.' He exhaled with agitation and was bent over from exhaustion. 'I checked your rooms with the Night Manager and found them empty.' He drew in a breath raggedly, lifted his cap and ran his hand through his hair. 'I followed the trail to *here*.' He pointed to the craft in the air.

'No problems Rahid, job done,' Harry said, patting him on the shoulder. Harry pointed at the three craft in the air, but needn't have bothered. The entire crowd was transfixed by the objects that were gradually getting larger and more detailed above them. These things were expected, but their appearance in the sky of Earth still shocked. Especially the fact that there were three of them and each was so bloody big. Earth expected one vessel but got three. They looked like three massive black mirror balls shaped into triangles.

Abby gazed upward and her wide eyes shone with excitement, to finally see these things in the skies of home. She brought a shaky hand to her forehead as she watched them come in to land, totally silent, a moment she'd dreamt about almost every night since she'd heard about the news. She was excited, emotional and terrified by the extraordinary sight, to finally see it, in Washington of all places.

This part of Earth was so iconic. The internet, no doubt, held a lot of sway for the Biapene, she reckoned. Even though the Werinn didn't want to friend Earth because of it. The information it held about humanity was repellent to the Werinn and then the Biapene. But the latter relied on the good favour of humanity. So, they were quiet about it. They didn't judge humans for that very reason. Because they knew the backlash they would receive.

Three identical black tetrahedrons with a raised portion near the front, presumably for the pilots, were getting slowly larger and more detailed in the sky. These things were now huge above them and had four lights that were clearly visible and dazzling.

One was on three of the extremities and one light was in the middle near a long and thick antenna. Harry felt sure the lights were involved with propulsion, somehow. But any guesses, were exactly that. Harry wondered if these objects were similar to the one that crashed near Roswell in New Mexico, or the ones that reside with aerospace companies.

Plausible deniability is the name of the game, so, the US government hands all like objects to its defence-partners. Other countries do the same. These Biapene craft though *couldn't* be hidden from sight. The public had to be invested, or something unpleasant would likely occur.

*   *   *

It was interesting that there were no windows anywhere on the craft, not even for the pilots, which brought navigation into serious question. Harry imagined trying to dock in a window-less craft. He remembered the tic-tac that had no windows on the outside, but inside, it had huge portals to view with. Why should these craft be any different? Have tech...use tech.

All the vessels reflected sunlight like flat mirrors. It hurt the eyes of anyone who looked directly at them. The vessels themselves were pitch black in colour and were made of something metallic that glinted like glass in the sunlight. All the vehicles were extremely vitreous. The humans nearby, held hands to their faces, to shield the light reflected by the craft.

Hopefully, Harry thought, they'd learn everything about the vessels and about the beings inside – propulsion, components, psyche and evolution. *The lot*. He was driven by what the Biapene knew. Because he knew they knew things Mankind desperately wanted to understand. The dark particles, visceral theories and cosmic tech beckoned - stuff humans had dreamt about and not captured for centuries.

Many people didn't share Harry's level of intrigue with the ships. Some ran screaming bloody murder, before they'd even landed. Perhaps they had no idea about the visiting Biapene and hadn't seen any of the announcements. If you lived under a rock – it'd be a hell of a shock. Seeing them descend from the sky and land. They probably thought humanity was being invaded

People previously living on the streets took refuge anywhere it was offered – in shops, or hotels or anything with a door and a roof.

They were asked *not* to come in – but they barged in anyway. Thousands of them. Into safety, they thought. Away from the sky-things.

The baseballers, the crowd, and people walking dogs had wisely vacated the park. They left and found refuge elsewhere, giving room to the descending vehicles, which settled noiselessly to the grass. Their silent method of propulsion was unknown. The only thing people took notice of, was their utter quiet and their massive contrast to Earth-based technology.

Their descent to the ground was as quiet as a moonbeam, the three of them coming slowly toward the ground and landing. A translucent heart-shaped cocoon that surrounded each vehicle vanished as soon after they landed.

Clearly, humany's space-industry could learn a lot from the Biapene themselves. That was part of the reason Earth wanted to keep the Biapene happy and satisfied. Their intelligence, physics and cosmic theory were critical to their relationship with Mankind.

A sizable industry had grown on Youtube and in the legacy media, guessing ways of rapid travel by the Biapene. Astonishingly, they'd gotten here in slightly more than a week, much quicker than light. *Eleven light years.* Ideas varied from Alcubierre Drive to wormholes to breaking physics itself.

Guessing at travel methods dominated social media, some uproariously funny, some deadly serious, and everywhere in between. Everyone wanted to know how they got here quicker than light.

$E=MC^2$ was smashed by the Biapene which had humanity floored. Einstein was our greatest physicist, but his work had been side-stepped like it was nothing more than a nursery-rhyme. And many wondered how in God's name they did it?

*   *   *

An enormous crowd crushed forward in DC, destination triangles. People ran from the pavement and out of buildings, shops and hotels and sprinted toward the vehicles like gnats chasing a worm. Crowds were being shooed back by hundreds of NYPD and DC Police. They tried to hurriedly fix police tape and hammer in stakes at the same time. Surrounded by a surging ocean of humanity, who showed no fear of the non-human triangles. They came at the Police-line in a deluge.

Thousands of people clambered and scrambled for proximity. The police were forced to taser several people. Some refused to follow directions and got dangerously close to the triangles inside the barrier. The zapped humans were taken away in paddy wagons as examples to others. *Do so at your own peril*, the Police screamed.

Humans knew the Biapene wanted to stay on Earth, so few of them appeared frightened of the ships. Most humans reckoned if you wanted to stay put somewhere, you'd be on your best behaviour. Only problem with that thinking was, that was *human* behaviour. These weren't humans, or even close. They were *reptilian*.

Eventually, the NYPD and DC Police succeeded with the stakes and the tape that managed to keep most of the crowd behind it. The entire mass of humanity kept behind the tape and three shining craft sitting by themselves on the grass.

No-one knew if these craft were dangerous to the touch, or even proximity. The Police tape was marked at a spot where the best guess of safety was. There was a cop with a Geiger-counter and a thumb in the air. Evidence that all was okay, apparently. There was a strong suggestion that advanced energy systems issue ionising radiation which is dangerous to humans in high doses. People were burnt near the RAF base at Woodbridge, very near Rendlesham Forest in England. Also, at many other global sites, where humans were exposed to interstellar craft, AKA some UFOs or UAPs.

The Police had gotten the entire crowd behind the Do Not Enter tape, after chasing down a few interlopers. The Police and NASA had done tests and were pretty sure the vessels weren't lethal to the touch, or proximity, but they weren't taking any chances.

Any of the crowd who slipped under or over the Police tape were quickly tackled to the ground and hauled away in NYPD paddy wagons. There were at least twenty of them parked end-to-end on 6th Street, a message to all. Infringe and these vehicles are for you.

The American DoD weren't far away. They arrived en masse to ensure all the craft behaved themselves and did what Earth assumed they'd do.

The DoD ringed the Whitehouse and had filed across the Memorial Bridge in a line of armaments that stretched a kilometre, stopping on L St NW, near, but out of sight of the ships. So, they were close to the triangles, but couldn't be seen. They were there "just in case" but most in the know didn't expect trouble, because the Biapene were here to stay.

The DoD had eleven KF-51 Panther Abrams tanks, all of them equipped with surface to air missiles and auto-canons. They also had a hundred fully armed troops in armoured personnel carriers that were connected to Pat by walky-talky – *just in case*. They believed they were ready for anything. They had no idea what the Biapene were capable of. But assumed that they represented a threat, simply because they were non-human and had no home to return to.

They could get more assistance in need from the Bolling base which was nearby and on standby to assist. It was expected that all would be friendly though, according to the intel. This was backup only. And hopefully it would remain as a backup and wouldn't be needed. Because God help Earth if they were needed.

The Biapene had weaponised their technology, and unlike the Werinn, they could wipe the planet clean of all animal life if they wished. Without using nukes. And they could do it quickly from audial weapons on the vessels. Upsetting the Biapene was a path to global destruction. Humans didn't know it, but the Biapene looked at death very differently to humans. Biapene couldn't be held hostage because dying was welcomed. If the cause was right, the Biapene would take the required action and welcome death. If their death was brought on by taking affirmative action, so be it. That was all hard-wired into the Biapene brain.

Pat had the Walky dangling from a strap around his waist. He was always on the lookout for risk and uncertainty, which were synonyms for this whole damn event, he reckoned. The NYPD and DC Police said they had it all covered. But he doubted they had anything covered and didn't understand what they were dealing with. Their primary focus was to watch and worry about the state of the crowd. Anything to do with the Biapene was someone else's job.

There were lines of cars and vans and people everywhere. On the streets, footpaths, and in the parks, and on top of gardens. So it was a potential chain-reaction if something got going. Panic would spread among the crowd like wildfire. The NYPD and DC Police watched everything and everyone closely to ensure nothing started.

There was no movement or noise from the craft or the crowd. Everything was quiet - steam rose off each vessel like mist. The craft did nothing and the Sun continued to blast off their surface like a mirror. The cop with the Geiger-counter was still there, and still had his thumb in the air.

No one could believe they got here so quickly. It seemed impossible. Everyone was taught from grade school that nothing travels faster than light. Albert said so. *Relativity* said so. Even to travel at light speed itself was impossible. It would need more energy than there was in the Universe. Yet they were here. *Eleven light years in just over a week.* The Biapene were so advanced that they'd found a way around it. Wars had a lot to answer for.

What they were made of? Well, that had the same effect - it left the crowd of people mesmerized. The crafts were extremely shiny and black and, to the people, they looked like black mirrors, not unlike a supercar. These craft got to Earth from Ross in about eight fucking days which floored everyone. Eight weeks, *eight months,* would be unbelievably quick. But eight days?

It called for something more exotic than Harry could think of right now. He reckoned it had to involve space-folding of some type. Whatever it was, the tech was brand-new to humans. That was a massive understatement. He also knew at those speeds, even the humble hydrogen atom would be a craft killer. Did moving in a warp-bubble protect the craft from that? Harry had no idea and relegated it to the other million or so queries in the basket titled *WTF.*

The discovery and characterisation of dark matter and dark energy by the Biapene, unlocked several gargantuan benefits. They came in the form of negative-mass and anti-gravity and new elements to boot. These propelled their space-industry to extraordinary heights, they thought they'd never reach. And their discovery did so quickly.

NASA and Earth generally, hoped it would be the same for Earth. Once the Biapene came good on "the quid pro quo". Earth was sure that if they looked after the Biapene, their intel would be gifted to humanity in a gesture of thank you. Mankind had lofty aspirations that were genuine objectives, that only they knew about. Earth needed the Biapene booty like a drug addict craving the next fix.

The Biapene space industry jumped forward overnight after dark matter was found. By its interaction with the Higgs field, gravity could be manipulated and nulled on demand. Vessels could float to orbit, or use gravity differential as an unlimited propellant, and when dark energy was found, FTL travel was made possible by space-shortening. A space-warp-bubble became instantly realisable. The Biapene were *cock-a-hoop* and applied the new knowledge to their space industry. Now the Biapene had warp drive.

NASA and America's aerospace and defence partners couldn't wait to inspect the vehicles, to glean as much as they could about how these craft got here so damn quickly. Rapid travel through the cosmos had Earth generally, and its research stymied.

Warp Drive had always been an unrealisable dream, but NASA and the other space industries admitted they needed something similar so they could go as far as they wanted to in reasonable amounts of time. Humans understood the folly of trying to "speak" to the pilots of the Biapene ship. They would have to rely on cooperative reverse engineering by NASA's defense partners and the Biapene.

The humans would bring in certain Biapene together with engineers from Lockheed Martin and Northrop Grumman and physicists from Harvard, Princeton and MIT universities and the private sector, to really nut it out. Hopefully, they could understand it

Taking one of the ships to an already established reverse-engineering hub at a Lockwood's skunkworks was a must. They already had a few craft that buzzed Earth skies, of non-human origin, but their attempts to back-engineer them were unsuccessful. They hoped for more with this craft, because this time, they'd have a non-human to assist. Someone that hopefully understood it already.

It was very likely that the propulsion of these vessels used off-Earth technologies, and brand-new particles, which would make it way harder to comprehend. This made the cooperation, teaching and assistance of the Biapene an imperative. Opportunities like this were one in a billion and it was beyond critical that humans took full advantage of it.

It was probably Mankind's one and only chance to understand things that were currently beyond them. It would likely save Mankind billions of dollars and decades, if not centuries of experimentation.

Otherwise, Mankind would always be in the Biapene's shadow. Finding the dark particles and formulating theory that explains quantum gravity was tough, and possibly beyond humans altogether. So, the Biapene's intel was very, *very* important. In essence it would be akin to stumbling over the holy grail.

Pat from NASA, Houston, was in DC, with the Eminent Dozen who were the frontline group selected to meet the Biapene. The Chairman of the Joint Chiefs and Head of the DoD were back with their troops as were eight other Generals in the DoD. The Eminent Dozen themselves were all "Carl Sagan types" – astrophysicists who had a deep and lifelong interest in space and all its potentials.

They were people who *deserved* to be there at this quite astonishing juncture in time. Many said humans were likely to intercept EMAR from an intelligent civilisation in the next decade or so. None who made that claim expected it to be direct contact. None on Earth would have dared to make such an outlandish prediction...yet, somehow it had happened.

It was ridiculous and crazy, insane and ludicrous, yet it was reality. The potentials of the Universe were almost limitless, because it was so damn big and it had been realised on little old Earth. This backwater of a very ordinary Galaxy that was especially fertile. That galactic richness had descended on a blue world that harboured a carbon-based intelligence. It was now ready to say "hello" to a totally different version of intelligent life.

Quite abruptly, the three craft from Biapene started to vibrate and pulse at regular intervals, as though readying to take off again. All three craft pulsated rapidly, almost in unison, and inched upward like helium- balloons you were struggling to keep grounded.

The three craft were about six feet off the ground, when landing gear appeared from the base of each craft. They just popped out on each craft and they settled onto them. The craft's full weight was taken by the gear. Then all three craft were still again. A very brief period of animation had the crowd buzzing, salivating for more.

Normally, on Earth anyway, landing gear would descend *before* the craft lands. But with these, it seemed, it was the opposite. The three craft now rested on silver legs about two metres long that appeared to have flat, rectangular plates on the bottom, for the ship to rest on without movement. There was no suggestion of wheels.

Behind Pat and the Dozen was a huge circle of police-tape, grass, and bent posts. Holding back thousands of Washingtonians and others, patrolled by hundreds of NYPD and DC Police who were pushing people back and yelling at them to cease and desist. The Police were flourishing tasers. The crowd was growing in size and density, pushing against the Police Tape until it was tight all the way around. Groaning and ready to snap.

Everyone had been repeatedly told that the Biapene meant us no harm and wanted to stay permanently on Earth. This message had been hammered into the population by endless messages on every type of media - legacy and social. One of the DC Police held a megaphone and repeated the message over and over to the crowd.. The crowd was told the Biapene would soon leave by bus to Canada. And they meant *no* harm to humans. The Biapene were tame.

After an hour of silence from the three vehicles, Pat slowly moved toward the first craft, like it was alive and hair sensitive, getting closer than anyone had. From a distance they were silent, but close up, he could hear the one in front of him exuding a low humming sound that was just audible.

Pat had no idea why it would be doing *anything*. It should be entirely off, he thought, but it could be an ancillary device, like air-conditioning, he supposed. It didn't sound like that though - the entire vessel was vibrating and pulsing. The lights on its underside were turning off and on, in some sort of pattern that meant nothing to him.

Whatever, Pat thought to himself. Behind him, something unusual came into existence. A lightning strike or something, had hit the grass, that left every hair on his body standing erect. Even his beret was blown off. He whirled around and there standing tall, was a Biapene in all its glory, looking straight at him. The creature was flicking its tongue in and out of its small mouth.

Pat jumped and then reared back. Clearly, this thing must have teleported there, and that's what the beam of light was. One second there was no-one, no ladder, no open hatch, then...*him*. Pat gawked at the lizard, dazed and confused.

He heard the crowd go "*ooooh*", then he heard high-pitched screaming, that, together with the sight of the lizard, made the hair on his body stand on-end again. Pat stared at the creature quizzically, full in the eye, and was horrified by its tongue. His eyes were fixed on the split red muscle that seemed to be constantly in motion.

Taking a whistling breath, the creature looked like it wanted to speak. It was readying. *Fuck*, Pat thought, glancing hopelessly at the Eminent Dozen. This is *the* moment, he supposed. Pat knew he needed to watch him and try to glean something from his body language, because sure as hell, what came out of his mouth would be double-dutch. His similarity to a bipedal dinosaur was both upsetting and unmistakeable.

'I am Rialten,' the Biapene said, in pretty good English. He, she or it, pointed toward the craft, in a very human movement. 'We have your internet and have decoded several of your languages from the Martian satellite. The Werinn passed your internet on to us when we decided to come here.' Rialten looked relieved to be here.

Pat was super-stunned and looked at Rialten with glassy eyes and ringing ears. He found it hard to believe, although he knew the Werinn did the same. Pat shook his head and kept looking at him. 'W-Wha?' He mumbled. To hear this creature, which looked prehistoric to Pat, speak in English was a bombshell shock to everyone who could hear him. There were a lot of wide-eyes, open mouths and confused looks near him.

Pat and most others thought he'd talk like spoken hieroglyphics or beeps and squeaks or hand movements. Something totally unfamiliar, and entirely foreign, but *incredibly*, it wasn't like that. They were the same as the Werinn. They could actually understand him. Pat gasped and his mouth fell open. Even though fatigue had settled in pockets under his eyes, they fully opened and stared at Rialten without uttering a word. The lizard, incredibly, was speaking English.

The creature had fingers and legs, sort of like a human, but the head area was much bigger. It looked like a lizard, although it stood upright on two scaly legs, like we did. It had a forked tongue that frequently stuck out of its mouth, skin was greenish with lumpy scales, and large stony eyes built into a long bony structure that punctuated the entire head area. Pat couldn't see any teeth inside the small lipless mouth, but assumed they were there...somewhere.

The Biapene looked angry and aggressive from the get-go. All up, they definitely weren't attractive to human eyes...more like depictions of intelligent dinosaurs. Most humans, on seeing them, would scream *monster*. Yet, they possessed many physical secrets that Mankind could only dream of. It was a good lesson for every homo sapien. The Universe was a big place, not meant just for us.

The Eminent Dozen moved in on Rialten like rats to a corpse. They wanted to converse with this incredible creature who amazingly spoke a human language so well. They crushed in to meet him. They never thought they'd be presented with such an incredible, ridiculously unheralded opportunity...*but here it was*. A living, breathing answer to the Fermi paradox. Rialten was now ringed by twelve humans and he did his best to answer all their questions.

He spoke to them all confidently and assuredly. Peter Hood, one of the dozen - took control and pushed them all back a bit, enough to allow Rialten breathing room, which he appreciated, raising a paw in Peter's direction.

Rialten felt anything but confident though – surrounded closely by twelve humans that all wanted a piece of him. His hearts were beating out of unison and he was dizzy as a result. Rialten was woozy and unsteady on his feet, but he held fast and refused to succumb to it. He stood tall and tried his best to ignore it, but it was difficult. Rialten was certain he was swaying. He planted his feet and held his thighs tight to keep himself straight. Humans were a very superficial race and this was an example. If pain or discomfort wasn't displayed externally, they had no idea how you were feeling. Rialten walked back a couple of steps to get his balance. Then came forward and spoke as strongly as he could, ignoring his own distress.

'Our planet and our population have been decimated by radiation from our star. Because our planet's angular rotation and magnetosphere have vanished,' he said. *'That's* why we are here. Rialten breathed in shallow, quick gasps, looking directly at Pat, who grimaced in empathy. Pat reckoned he was breathing hard, like a backyard lizard with his tongue doing a lot of work. Pat felt the emotional panic reaction tickle his skin. He reviled spiders and snakes, and his visceral reaction was almost the same.

Having drawn breath to fuel his voice, Rialten continued. 'You are a very fortunate race. You have a planet and magnetosphere that is healthy and shields your population from danger. Lethal levels of radiation from our star and from space itself, bathe our planet 24/7. Unless we retreat underground, which a few have, the population of Biapene receives way too much radiation. Enough is received on the surface to cause widespread genetic changes to individuals, which is demonstrable as serious disease.' His voice contained a touch of hysteria as he spoke about his homeland.

'Staying underground is not sustainable.' He exhaled brokenly with agitation. It was clear that he had suffered extreme hardship during the voyage to Earth and before it. 'We left most of the population behind, to face the radiation.' Rialten's eyes narrowed and the dry scaly skin on his face became moist and the blotches deepened in colour.

'We didn't even know there was a problem until a disease resembling Earthlings' cancer started afflicting the planet's population in a runaway epidemic.' Rialten said in a flat voice. 'Cancer was occurring like a pandemic and it was everywhere, and then we knew for certain something horrid was happening.

We discovered the core of our planet had stopped rotating when the planet itself came to a halt – rotation of the core and the planet itself was just a memory. One doesn't invoke the other, but I guess we should have known. The magnetosphere vanished and the ozone layer became nitrous oxide, and we didn't know, until cancer started running rampant.' Rialten's tone was bleak and he was obviously heartbroken by those that were left behind to die in agony. No doubt, some of those were relatives and friends.

'The population went out in the daytime as they normally did and effectively, got cancer, or a lot of them did. Now, with no magnetosphere at all, the planet is completely open to space and our flare star. It is a literal killing field, if, like most, you are on the planet's surface.' Rialten's voice broke and he coughed quietly to himself and looked down. 'It is a very sad state of affairs on my home planet. Hospitals are closed and Doctors are all overrun. It'd be a lot worse now.' Rialten was grieving badly for the people left behind.

'How long did it take to get here?' George LaComb from the Dozen asked, knowing they had to travel about eleven light years through space to get here. It would say a lot about their technology. He knew they got here stunningly fast and FTL. He was almost frothing at the mouth as he thought about their incredible capabilities.

'Took us eight days,' Rialten said matter-of-factly.

They were all astrophysicists in the group and were all dumbfounded and totally floored. George saw blinding fireworks explode behind his eyes. The answer was always going to be crazy, but it was even more batty and ridiculous than they thought.

'...*eight...d-days*?' George whimpered hoarsely. '*Holy fuck*,' that's...truly *a-amazing,*' he said, 'eleven light years in eight days. And you've avoided relativistic effects...*truly fucking incredible*, utterly mindblowing,'

'*Ridiculous, i-insane*,' Jeff McKenna piped in, red in the face and pimpled with sweat, knowing what it meant. They got here a whole lot quicker than light, which to him was impossible. To Jeff, it meant breaking physics. Nothing on Earth could even come close to it. He couldn't get past it, Einstein said it was impossible. But apparently not. In truth, the Biapene had deftly sidestepped $E=Mc_2$.

That meant the Biapene ships were carrying some very exotic hardware indeed...*or* they came from somewhere a whole lot closer. But that didn't make sense, after what they'd heard. Harry told them exactly where the Biapene came from – *he'd fucking been there.*

This was like a drug induced hallucination. '*Eleven light years in eight days,*' Jeff repeated slowly and incredulously, with a face coloured like blood. The rest of the dozen were whispering "eight days". They were all baffled and thunderstruck. They'd heard the absurd and the illogical, but it was true. They'd been taught since their early years in physics that nothing moves faster than light. High technology, it seemed, had found a way around the mass issues.

'We would be happy to show you our craft,' Rialten piped. He saw Jeff's eyes, huge and round, and his face dotted with sweat. He couldn't believe any of what he'd heard. Foundations of human philosophy were creaking, crumbling in front of him, like day-old cake.

NASA were always trying to come up with solutions to the ridiculous distances they needed to span in space - and in one fell swoop Earth came into contact with the tech of the Biapene. They themselves can cover insane distances with the snap of their fingers.

Teleporting and FTL, these things, were centuries beyond Mankind, but not so the Biapene. So, NASA rightly, wanted their secrets. NASA wanted it all, like ravenous predators, they wanted the lot, even the bone marrow.

NASA and the science-community generally, were banging their heads on a brick wall, and so far, had only gotten to a few percentage points of the speed of light. Nuclear rockets, fusion, even anti-matter wasn't going to do the job. Jeff could see the future, lit up with fire-works. "Do the Biapene's bidding", keep them happy and *maybe* they'll share their secrets. Jeff reckoned that had to be the way forward for Earth and Mankind. Because, it seemed, we couldn't do it for ourselves.

NASA and Earth needed the tech of the Biapene. Without it, humans weren't going anywhere. Non-human craft in the skies showed us what was possible. With non-human abilities, like the Biapene had, humans could zip and zap all over the skies and in space at tremendous speeds. Inertia and gravity would no longer be a problem. Mankind could turn on a dime and float to orbit.

Rockets would become yesterday's technology, like the steam engine. *Obsolete.* Everything would change - houses, buildings, roads, transport, energy. Wings and other aero-dynamic surfaces would no longer be needed to fly in the atmosphere – positive lift could afflict the most cubic of objects and it would still fly like a bird.

Electricity as it is today would be like public phone boxes and floppy disks. Energy from the so-called Zero Point and Planck Space would run everything. Earth would exploit the energy of the vacuum, rendering every other source of energy redundant. So, it was beyond critical to mine the Biapene while humanity had the chance.

*   *   *

Jeff heard they might have folded space, but how they did it, was a total mystery. The best he could come up with was to assume the dark particles helped them create truly masterful tech that allowed free movement, whether in air, water or space.

'We didn't travel faster than light directly.' Rialten said, seeing Jeff's furrowed brow and general sweaty discomfort. 'We circularised a patch of space that was shortened in Earth's direction and lengthened behind our vessel – we didn't travel faster than light, our patch of space did. Our craft just happened to be in that patch.'

Jeff had no voice to speak to the group. When the query was raised, and then answered by Rialten, he immediately grabbed his neck and started massaging, realising he couldn't breathe through it. He took a whistling wheeze, and almost collapsed to the ground, trying to get his head around what Rialten had said. He dragged in a hissing breath as he struggled to absorb the answer. He grabbed his water glass.

Jeff drank deeply and Rialten continued after making sure Jeff was okay 'You are free to view our propulsion if you choose.' Jeff managed to slow his breathing and wipe his forehead with a swipe of his hand. He knew this could be the greatest moment of his life.

Jeff imagined what might happen. This was where the impossible was handed to humanity, gift-wrapped. There was no "standing on shoulders of giants" here, like Einstein and Newton, it was straight-up gifting of technology. Jeff envisioned huge loops of metal and silvery capsules everywhere...but he was confused by the mere shape of the Biapene vessels. It didn't make sense, from his very limited viewpoint.

Humans had devised modes of "space-shortening" craft previously, and they always boasted prominent toroidal rings. The Biapene craft had none of that. They were just simple triangles. Just regulation space vehicles. Jeff was so intrigued - he was ready to bust. What humans considered as critical to their design was just plain wrong, according to craft that accomplished the task successfully.

'We will er, take a l-look...in time,' Jeff nervously stuttered. He reckoned the human engineers from Northrop's and Lockheed's would have no idea what they were looking at, even though they'd seen some pretty exotic stuff. The Biapene propulsion probably used dark matter and negative mass - both were unknowns on Earth.

If in fact it was brand-new technology, no-one would have a clue what they were looking at. He strongly believed that aerospace companies and defence partners of the US had received non-human vessels from the feds. Their attempts to reverse engineer them would be beneficial here, and this time, they'd have the help of the makers.

Jeff was certain that this machine only worked because it used particles and forces humans were yet to discover. Replicating it to a workable model wasn't going to happen, based on what we currently knew. The Biapene possessed brand new technologies. They didn't exist on Earth and wouldn't, even if it was gifted to humanity.

The Biapene would have to tell us how to find the dark particles before anything else. Everything would take time. US aerospace companies and defence contractors, would need major Biapene help, if this tech was to crystallise in the short-term.

Jeff gazed, irritated and impatient at Rialten, crossing and uncrossing his arms. He must be joking, surely? 'We can look, but trust me Rialten, we will not know what we're looking at, either the components or the overall machine.' Jeff said. 'You can explain it to us to your heart's content, but the individual components are unknown on Earth, so while we might understand what it does, we'll have no idea, how to put it all together because some of the ingredients are *missing*.'

Jeff threw his arms in the air and shook his head. He reckoned Rialten should have known that anyway. Jeff accepted that the Biapene had superior technology, but the least Rialten could do, was acknowledge there was more involved than just mere looking.

Everywhere Jeff looked and everything he could think of, ended in a big fat negative. Reverse-engineering was one thing, but truly mastering the how and whys of its operation, was way more important. Jeff could feel his own heat, he felt hopeless and desperate – and he hadn't even seen the propulsion yet, just fantasised about it. And the Biapene reckon we can build it, just by looking. *Yeah right*, he thought.

'Sourcing and capturing the particle components – forget about it.' Jeff boomed. 'Earth hasn't discovered it, so there is no analogous technology. In short, it will mean little just by looking. With a lot of help from yourselves, we will *slowly* come to understand it, then we can, under supervision, put our deductive reasoning to the test.' Jeff was biting his lip and looking down at his shoes. He honestly didn't think they'd ever be able to do it, with or without help. Jeff reckoned humanity "folding space" was in the same basket as traversing wormholes. Very unlikely to happen.

Rialten looked at Jeff, poked his tongue out and smiled sympathetically. 'We will get to your dark matter and dark energy...and how to find it, do not worry. You only have to house us properly and it is all yours...*everything* we know. And once it's done, and you find it, the rest, like building it, will be relatively straight forward.' Rialten said, smiling and sticking out his forked tongue. Jeff was stunned, taking a quick intake of breath - being educated in astrophysics by a lizard was astonishing, but in line with the probabilities of this grand Universe.

'Thank you Rialten, I'll get a few from Lockheed to start the ball rolling on the building part. They're the ones who manufactured a lot of our craft, so I guess their input will be required.'

The Dozen were still buzzing around Rialten like gudgeons to a worm, and were still hanging on his every word. They were thanking God that the day had come. All of them were dazed by the majestic being that stood before them, from Ross128 b. A brand-new reptilian intelligence. For them, he was the Fermi paradox personified.

Possessing advanced technology and looking like *him* didn't make sense, or sit well with most humans. But it was worse than that. It seemed, based on what was said, that the whole idea of them having an advanced technology was completely absurd and downright wrong. It was akin to a dog designing the next iPhone.

Humans were a narrow-minded lot. Advanced intelligence had nothing to do with physical appearance. But few on Earth realised it. It only demanded an oppositional thumb and fingers, and dexterity and probably stereoscopic vision. Then you needed a large and advanced brain to control it. Then *anything* was possible. The sky was the limit. The physicality of the Biapene suddenly made reasonable sense.

*   *   *

The fact that Rialten spoke the Queen's English was great, but really tough to reconcile. It seemed wrong and weird, but Pat understood how and why he spoke it. *Internet*, he thought, which made sense. Pat had always wondered how it would go if someone that wasn't human got hold of our internet. Now, it had come to fruition. And Pat reckoned the outcome sucked. The internet not only had a host of language courses, but it nicely gives a history of humanity, *no holds barred.* So, whatever non-human manages to read it, they'd get an unabridged history of Mankind, from day one. For humanity, this may prove to be very bad indeed.

Our reputation as a species was very important, and if you read the internet, wars seemed to occur all the time on Earth. The overall takeaway was that humanity was an extremely aggressive, imperialistic, warlike species. If you didn't get that, you weren't being honest with yourself. History *is* history.

John Pastro, an Emeritus professor from Harvard University was one of the Eminent Dozen. And he also found Rialten hideous, which he assumed and hoped, he'd eventually overcome. Because he simply had to, realising how much could be learned from them. He goggled at Rialten like he was about to deliver a miracle. Which he found odd, because Rialten looked so primitive and prehistoric.

John looked at Rialten sheepishly, 'Can we, um...see your ship now...briefly of course,' he blurted, hoping he hadn't overstepped the mark, seeing Jeff next to him and whispering, *'f-fuck...this is hard'*. Jeff nodded back at him and saw his red face and bug-eyes and realised that this was only John's second exposure to the Biapene. He found, just talking to them, difficult.

JP was scared stiff being in their presence. The green scaly skin that varied in colour and the dark eyes had him by the balls. For John, Rialten may as well have been a garden-variety lizard standing up. John was stunned that this creature had a technology to die for. JP watched his every move with huge owl-eyes. Jeff reckoned if it wasn't so historic and weighty, it'd be comical. The poor guy was disturbed and intrigued by every move the creature made.

JP's eyes darted nervously back and forth from Rialten to the others and his hands were shaking like a cheap washing-machine. The man was a nervous wreck. Pat took John by the shoulder and sat him down for a rest. The guy was chomping at the bit to see more of their tech, but first, he needed a good rest or he would faint and collapse to the ground in front of them.

s'Yes, um...indeed, you can look at our ship,' Rialten replied, looking and sounding a bit unsure, doing something in his waist pocket. It seemed as though he was pressing something, but he couldn't really tell. Jeff saw a flash of a whiteness in his pocket. He wondered if it was something as banal as a remote control.

A silver entrance to the ship descended to the ground. Now, the first Biapene craft was joined to Earth with an appendage that looked disturbingly like a curled silver tongue. It emerged and descended from an open hatch in the ship. Now they had a way in. Pat wondered where the entry was, now he knew.

The twelve were directed toward the tongue. Walking underneath the lustrous black craft, John realised the exterior was composed of minute triangles, only visible from close-up, and was mirror-smooth. The group entering the craft was headed by Jeff, with John right behind him. Moving underneath it, John thought it was interesting that there was no obvious propulsion on the extremity, but he now knew why. These objects surfed on a bubble of space, so there was no need for propulsion on the craft, just a lot of negative mass. The Biapene did the fine navigation with gravity, he reckoned.

It was noteworthy that all prospective "drives" contemplated by Earth had huge rings around the craft to act as "negative-mass generators". What was so interesting was that these craft had none of that. They were just three-sided polygons. Very plain vehicles, unusually so. Propulsion through space was enacted by the warp-bubble itself, shortening space in the direction of Earth.

The entry to the first ship looked like a silver slippery-dip, and even worse, it looked a little wet. It was steep and there was no sign of any steps, or anything to make traction better. Jeff looked at it, sighed heavily, and said, '*oh what the hell…*' and tried to walk up it, desperately hoping he didn't make a fool of himself. Which looking at it, was in the cards. He also realised that hundreds of Biapene had used it. And their boots and shoes appeared to be nothing special. So, away he went.

Surprisingly, it was quite adherent to walk on. All of them saw Jeff's steadiness on the surface and followed quickly behind, seeing the boots penetrated the tongue which gave good traction indeed. They all noticed the growing odour as they ascended the "tongue" toward the spaceship proper and knew what the odour probably was.

Jeff got to the top of the tongue which apparently was level one and nearly keeled over from the stench. It hit him like a sledge-hammer. This place stunk. Jeff was wearing a hardhat with an inbuilt light that came into its own in what was a very dim interior. He also needed a tight peg for his nose.

He knew this was the first time a human had been inside non-human tech. Jeff's eyes bulged as he looked around at the dimness, and his breathing became raspy and rough. He was terrified. This place smelt like an uncleaned roadhouse toilet. Clearly, sanitation was a problem for this craft. This level was wall-to-wall with creatures, and the Biapene didn't give it close to a high enough priority.

Facing him, were lines and lines and lines of creatures, lit up by the bulb in his helmet – the Biapene presumably – standing upright, row after row of ugly mannequins. They were upright because there was no room to sit or lie down. There were literally thousands of them, all stuffed in. Elbow room from one creature to another was nil. No doubt level two was the same.

This level was an open room and stunk to high heaven - unwashed non-human biology. It was *worse* than the smell of the pig-shed at a local festival. JP held his nose and waved his other hand maniacally, glancing at Jeff, who wrinkled his nose and swallowed rapidly, with a look of utter disgust on his face.

Amazing what the Biapene would do to avoid a terminally-sick world. There were thousands of arms, bodies and legs everywhere. Some large beings were holding smaller ones and very small ones – babies presumably. Jeff's light illuminated the first few rows of individuals, but there was plenty behind them, still shrouded in the shadows of darkness. Jeff wondered if they even knew the craft had landed...or for that matter, taken off.

Some looked lifeless with closed eyes – there wasn't even enough room to fall over. They were literally stuffed in, *worse* than a Japanese supertrain. Jeff found the scene heart-breaking. The remnants of a doomed world, billions left behind, to die in agony.

A few little ones ran between legs and around fully-grown Biapene who were either totally disinterested, or openly annoyed. The little ones were making high-pitched howling sounds as they ran and hid with tongues out permanently. Some of the adults made hissing sounds when they were annoyed by children. The beings that were lit by the headlamp were a massive, seething ocean of Biapene.

It was a scene of incredibly smelly congestion – like you'd expect during the 1700's, emigration on wooden ships on Earth. Thank God it was a relatively quick trip through space thanks to its propulsion. Otherwise, the lot of them would have died. He assumed they didn't eat during their voyage...but what about fluid? Incredibly, there was no evidence that they did that either. The focus was squarely on getting to their destination as quickly as possible. It looked as though they left at the last minute and just stuffed 'em in. God help them if any were sick with a transferable disease. It would have gone through the vessel like a nuclear chain-reaction.

This is definitely not what he expected of a non-human race. Pat thought there'd be plenty aboard, but reckoned there would have at least been some discreet rooms and hatches. But there was none of that, the level they were on was one giant room.

The Biapene were literally hanging from the ceiling, not in compartments at all. No wonder it stunk of biology. Clearly, the general philosophy was to get them in, worry about everything else later on. The more individuals they saved...the better, apparently. It seemed that keeping them happy and healthy was ignored.

Jeff dry reached and then vomited, he tried not to, he tried to keep it down, but it came anyway. The stench and the vision were just too much, together with the mortifying thought that *billions* of them were left behind. The whole lot was overwhelming. Pat and John would follow close behind – so far, this ship was horrific and disgusting. The epitome of a rapidly organised trip for as many Biapene souls as possible. Only the most basic and unavoidable biological needs were catered for. It seemed that food and water were a bridge too far.

Going up to the next level was the same silver tongue...of adherent and penetrable metal, also without steps. Pat could tell it was the same up there, he could smell the potency already.

'I already know what's waiting for us up there,' Pat said, repulsed, from behind his hand, which was clamped firmly over his nose. Jeff and John nodded, and Rialten just moved on, determined to get this over with. Pat was on the second level, and he pointed the light on his helmet straight ahead. This was the same as the first level, one huge room. A jam-packed, squirming ocean of desperate, smelly creatures.

Pat was keen to get off the craft and as far away from it as possible, all the rest of the humans too. They'd seen enough and smelt way too much. The Biapene themselves couldn't stay on the craft any longer. Conditions were too cramped and were dangerously unsanitary, which would probably turn lethal soon enough.

The entire ship had an atmosphere that was retchingly foul. And there were young Biapene aboard that needed to be removed and saved from this horror. Sorry POTUS. That would be their strong recommendation. This place would be a death sentence if the Biapene were to be kept here much longer. None of the craft could act as a holding area for the Biapene, while their permanent lodgings were being built.

If these were human craft, there would be seats and buckles and probably rooms everywhere, to keep people from flying all around the vessel. Once outside the atmosphere, they'd all be weightless and subject to momentum shifts. Pat had images of the ISS in his head, with astronauts floating everywhere. But the Biapene in these vessels, apparently, had no such problems. If they did, they would have been scattered everywhere on both levels.

It appeared that they had no problem with either weightlessness or momentum. These individuals stood up, pressed together, for the entire trip. For humans we'd require every individual to be strapped tightly into a seat. None of the Biapene showed transit injuries. That could only mean one thing. And it was stunning.

It meant that weightlessness and inertia during their journey could never have been a problem. Clearly, the Biapene knew a thing or two, that humans didn't. All the humans wondered where the source of gravity was?

The statement by POTUS that the Biapene stay on the craft could not happen. In a more perfect world, it was a great idea. But the general congestion and filthy conditions demanded that they get the Biapene off the three craft at the earliest time. There were too many of them, and the structure of the ship was all wrong to hold them. And the ship stunk and was fetid. The sooner they got out of there – the better for everyone.

The humans made their way to the tongue and descended to the ground, glad to be on the grass, outside, free of the potent and quite horrific stench. John stumbled a few steps forward, happy to be in cleaner air, coughing, struggling for breath through a half-closed throat. The putrid atmosphere within the craft was hard to get rid of.

Jeff was busy talking to Rialten and he was getting emotional or angry, if his rushed hand movements were any guide. Things had suddenly gotten way more complicated. They would need a half-way house for this mob, prior to their long-term Vancouver lodgings, which were currently being expedited.

With the vessels out-of-the-question as a half-way house, a new site for the Biapene had to be formulated quickly. Pat desperately wanted to keep the Biapene healthy, which involved getting them off the ships, whether they liked it or not. The vessels were a death-trap. He had to consider their well-being, both physical and mental, because sure as hell, these craft were no Hilton Hotel. Disease and pestilence were everywhere they looked.

God knows how many Biapene had collapsed and died on their way here and been carried over to the airlock by their own and spaced. But one thing he did know, was that the dead probably died where they stood, and probably stayed there. There wasn't enough room to fall to the floor. Horribly, they probably died standing up. It was a cramped hell in there. In terms of not bathing and sweating fiercely - eight days was a long time indeed.

Jeff looked straight at Pat and said under his breath, 'assuming the Biapene are right about the new, stronger particle collider in China,' Jeff said. 'If they are...what do we do?' He whispered in a squawk of protest. 'We can't let Earth become another Biapene. Our magnetosphere is critical to life. We'd have to stop CERN *and* China. *Fuck – good luck with that*. Jeff's voice was sharp with sarcasm. In other words – it was impossible.

Jeff shook his head and continued. 'All I can say Pat, is that, based on what Rialten has told me, I am really worried. What was once conspiracy and troublemaking, is now very fucking real.' Jeff sighed dejectedly and continued in a monotone voice, knowing they were all in a very leaky boat indeed. Without a magnetosphere, he knew Earth's entire population was at severe risk.

'The LHC is okay apparently, but this new facility in China is too powerful for Earth.' Jeff clenched his jaw and they looked at each other uneasily. They were both really worried, because if it was true, it was goodbye to humanity. If the Biapene believed it – should humans do the same? It was a quandary of Earth-shaking possibility. The Biapene claimed the planned Chinese collider and its lattice-magnets were too powerful for Earth. They are seven times as powerful as the LHC, and would degrade the Earth's magnetosphere, as the colliders did on Biapene. They claim the same would happen on Earth.

That was the question. Based on the Biapene's standing with technology, mathematics and physics, the answer had to be yes. But humans still questioned their judgement. Even if they were right, no-one on Earth could likely stop it from happening. Pat believed no-one could stop CERN *or* China. Both were unstoppable forces on Earth.

Jeff um'd and ah'd about what he'd said but knew they had no hope of stopping them. He knew it'd be like making a banana milkshake without the bananas. Both realised they didn't have a prayer of stopping either. Signing a petition or protesting simply wouldn't do the job. They would need an Order from The International Court in the Hague – an arm of the UN, that covered the globe.

It really didn't matter what they managed to extract from the Biapene, they didn't have a hope with the Hague. If they did manage the impossible, and get an order, Beijing's solicitors would fight it until hell froze over. If they ever got an order which was highly unlikely...*executing* it, might be the most difficult, expensive and convoluted process of all. In other words, *FUCK IT*, no-one had pockets deep enough to fund it. Not on the basis of qualitative evidence anyway.

Best they forget about legal action. They would contact CERN and make their demands known. It was all they could reasonably do. Anything else would be a bust and they well knew it. All Earth could hope for, was that the Biapene were wrong. The electro-batteries, used to tighten trajectories of particles were a thousand times as powerful as the LHC. The energy of the longer circuit in Beijing were like nothing the world had ever seen. So, the claim made sense.

It had a clear congruence with the problems on Biapene. A world that closed all its colliders after angular momentum of the planet and its core were lost. There was no empirical evidence, but the Biapene believed we were going down the same road. Inviting Armageddon. And the Biapene had a better grip on physics than Mankind. So, their opinion should matter.

*   *   *

Jeff could see a fleet of large, glinting vehicles – a long line of large, heavily articulated Greyhound buses with black tinted windows coming up 14th street and mounting the curb to drive across the grass to a point very near the vessels. The taped off area was being pulled apart to give them access to the vessels.

Hundreds of NYPD, DC Police and some CIA and DIA operatives descended on the buses to regulate the transport. The Biapene were travelling from Columbia to Vancouver in Canada to short-term accommodation in compartmented warehouses. They would remain there until their permanent buildings were ready, in about six months' time. Until then, that would be their home.

The first thing the Biapene uttered when the humans started a conversation about accommodation, was their need for polygonal rooms or housing. Triangular faces and polygonal shapes were of extreme importance to their species, they said.

For general wellness, vitality and life. This shape was critical, the Biapene said seriously. The information was carefully conveyed to humans by an Elder. There were two on each ship, but Dagkan, pronounced *Dargkan* was rebuffed. Not rebuffed by saying "no", but it was assumed by the managing humans, that the Biapene were only conveying a preference that didn't have a lot of significance. Because it wasn't important to humans, it was considered to be a preference that could be done without. Humans couldn't have been further from the truth. The golden ratio, unlike Mankind, was critical to the Biapene. Without it, their species wasn't viable.

Dagkan, and in fact, all of the Biapene, were a softly spoken and gentle race, so equating their tone or volume with importance was a mistake. Xeno-psychology varies greatly from species to species, and humans were yet to realise it. Everything for them was based on the human-world - another big mistake. The humans knew no other intelligences, so their outlook was narrow indeed.

Polygons were critical to the Biapene's survival, but so too were the humans and their planet. To keep in their good graces and maintain a good relationship was key. Forceful behaviour wasn't a Biapene trait.

If humans knew anything about the Biapene mind, it wouldn't be a problem. But humans didn't. The Biapene were a diametrically different race. So, making demands was not part of their general psyche or behaviour. They were mild and benign, and this could easily be taken for consenting.

All US government buildings including repairs, and new roads constructing, were suspended until the Biapene development in Canada was complete. All US manpower was re-directed to the new development in Vancouver, as POTUS had promised to the UN, to NASA, and to the world.

*   *   *

Dsun was one of the Biapene transported to Earth in the general population of the three craft. He was horrified by the happenings back home, as were most of the population. Few could believe how bad it had become – and so quickly.

What had been a gorgeous and rare planet, home to their young, and the entire population of Biapene, nurturing and promoting evolution of their species over billions of years, was now a killing field, a wasteland of disease, radiation and dead or dying biology. What used to be vibrancy, magnificence and opulence was now just dead. It was a travesty, he reckoned, thinking back to the once upon a time stunningly, wonderful good times. Dsun swallowed rapidly and massaged the top of his hairless head.

In their future, those left behind on Biapene had ionising radiation, disease, suffering and death to look forward to. No-one could stay inside forever. The absolute necessity for calories and hydration would kill the population. It was either expose yourself, or live underground with few facilities, which only a limited number of Biapene decided to do. There were several networks of caves in the north of the planet, that were populated with several thousand Biapene. The lack of facilities scared most off, especially those with families. Most of the remaining population took the decision to live "normally" above ground...come what may. Their fate was sealed by their rather unstable star.

Dsun received a copy of some of the human internet in several envelopes handed to him. To say the humans were a craven, warlike race was an understatement Initially, he didn't think it changed much, but after speaking to others, including Elders, his mind was changed. It did matter. *Once vicious – always vicious.* It was part of the human makeup. Part of the human psyche that it would never, ever lose.

Dsun could see his family's future, written in the nature of human history, and he wasn't hopeful at all. Humans had decimated all previous races they'd encountered for the first time. Why would the Biapene be any different? Because they came from space - he didn't think so? As far as he was concerned, the Biapene future on Earth was bleak indeed.

Dsun was sure that with their history, humans would quickly rise up against them. He'd seen how Mankind treated other minority and first nation races and lower animals. He, and the entire travelling party, were horrified by what was waiting for them.

He wouldn't be surprised if there was warfare and battles between the two species in the near-future. If humans were going to house them in prismatic buildings and rectangular housing, there'd quickly be distress, fatigue and death among their own population. He knew the Biapene couldn't survive like that for long.

And he also knew that communicating their needs to humans was woefully ineffective. He knew it was a combination of the Biapene's reticence, the Biapene grip on English and the listening skills and bias of humans. Dsun acknowledged that polygons weren't vitally important to any life-form on Earth. Polygons therefore took on the status of preference or option. To the Biapene, it was vital.

Now that they were on Earth - Dsun felt like he had no choice. It had to be done. The future for his people looked grimmer than grim. He wouldn't subject his family to the vagaries of the human race. He could see the future, he'd read the internet, and it looked bleak. As he saw it, the Biapene on Earth had little hope. All he could see in their future was pain, suffering and death.

Dsun used to be a pharmacist on his home planet, so, he knew exactly what he was doing. He did all the tough and delicate work prior to leaving the planet and boarding the vessel. Why he did it, was a whole other question related to where he found himself and the probability he and his family would be subject to Mankind's ire.

He fundamentally disagreed with shifting planets to Earth, although he understood the reason why. He chose to be part of it only because of his family. Earth was the wrong choice. Dsun was now convinced, it would end in disaster, a feeling entrenched by his brief discussions with humans and information on the human's internet.

He took with him option B, which he'd decided to use. Dsun's path was clear in his mind. He'd decided that there was no future in this venture to Earth, as there was no future on Biapene.

He'd started with dry potassium nitrate and added sulfuric acid, heated and filtered it. And he had a ceramic bottle full of concentrated nitric acid. It was brought aboard in his coat pocket and easily passed the meagre checks prior to departure. Dsun started sweating and felt mega-hot and tingled every time he thought about it. What he was concocting had the acidity to denude flesh and bone in microseconds. It was like a bomb in his pocket.

It was *time* to do this, and he knew it. His sweaty palms were impeding his ability to hold anything with surety. There was no future for him or his family, or his people on this planet, as he saw it. The indigenous intelligence they'd decided to join were a warring, selfish, aggressive lot that would soon get tired of hosting the Biapene. Our entire ten thousand would eventually suffer enormously at the humans' hands. He could see it emblazoned in the human's history.

Already, their most basic need, the need for triangular living spaces was being sneered at by the astronauts who visited Werinn, and by the humans here on Earth. No doubt, that attitude pervaded Earth. No-one would give a damn about his family's needs, and the Biapene generally. Despite telling Mankind what we needed for long-term sustainability.

The Biapene got prismatic buildings and rectangular rooms. In other words, they got none of what was so important. The Biapene's needs were overlooked or disregarded as a whim. The fact that it was essential to their living requirements didn't seem to matter. He knew the humans wanted certain intel from the Biapene, but he for one was certain that they didn't deserve it. But he wasn't the decision-maker.

Sweating freely now, Dsun was concerned about the closeness of everybody. There was no room to do anything privately. Especially what he had planned and wanted to do. Individuals in front of him and to the side were pressing. They were all elbow to elbow. He could feign feeling ill, and maybe pretend to faint, but that would only attract attention, and get him hauled off to the side by the sentinels. That definitely wouldn't do. Dsun wanted to keep it all away from his young son, who was very curious.

Everyone was so close, he decided to just do it. Dsun pulled the ceramic flask from his pocket and laid it down at his feet, just behind the adult right in front of him. No-one was any the wiser, so far. They all knew they had landed and nearly everyone looked at the pilot's door for directions, keen to vacate the craft.

It was very quiet on the ship, while individuals waited to exit, which had Dsun on edge. He made clinking noises, but tried to hide them by moving his body. The person nearest him looked suspicious but made no attempt to intervene, and was more concerned with his partner, than him. He probably assumed he was playing with his young-one, which couldn't have been further from the truth.

Dsun could smell the people close to him and the ship generally. It smelt tangy, sweet and similar to rotten onions. Unpleasant and similar to the confronting odour in and around the soup kitchen for the unhoused, he had visited back on Biapene.

From his loose pants pocket he pulled out a vial of glycerine. Enough was added to cover the top of the nitric acid. Dsun carefully picked up the ceramic flask and replaced the cap and carefully put the vial of glycerine back in his pocket. He looked gently at his wife and child, and violently shook the flask of nitro-glycerine. Which was pre-made with a small amount of cadmium, to render it super-strong.

*   *   *

All the humans and the Biapene who were inside the Police-tape were blown off their feet by the explosion. The crowd in a full circle, felt the pressure wave from the sudden, violent release of energy, that rearranged hair and blew hats and scarves off. Every one of them knew that something apocalyptic had happened.

The Triangles that sat either side of the detonation were hit by pieces of the exploded wreck but sustained no visible damage. It seemed that damage to the exterior was protected by a very resilient surface alloy indeed, to fend off micro-meteors. From the inside though, it appeared as though the craft was way more fragile.

Pat and Jeff were almost hit by a fiery, smoking remnant of the craft, that whistled above their heads and landed, doing smoking cartwheels on the grass behind them. The triangular ship was no more, and the other two vehicles were blown back a metre or so. They were now separated by thirty or so metres with a black wreck and bloodied body parts strewn all over the grass. Repulsive devastation.

Pat took a few steps backward and with bulging eyes and a pounding heart, observed what was a dreadful scene around him. There was red blood everywhere, dripping from severed limbs and broken Biapene bodies. Despite the disgust and revulsion, he was stunned that these creatures actually had *red blood* like humans.

He looked closer and almost vomited from the overwhelming stench of wet coins. Their haemoglobin was iron-rich just like ours, he thought. Pat knew that some animals like crustaceans, carried hemocyanin and their blood was blue as a result of the copper. That's how he thought non-humans would be. A banal observation, he knew. But right now, that's all his brain could manage.

The scene was bloody and horrendous. Dsun had used enough high-grade explosive to totally destroy the ship from the inside out and kill most of the Biapene onboard.

The remnants of the craft and the pieces of the Biapene creatures were now distributed all over the oval as horrible and blackened bloody bits and pieces. Everywhere it seemed, were bloody parts of the creatures that travelled to Earth in the middle Triangle. If any Biapene survived, it was too early to tell - way too smoky. There were even body parts in the trees adjacent to the park. Pat nearly brought up his lunch at the sight. There was a Biapene head up in a tree. Enough to make the most hardened human run.

Emergency Services were on their way. Pat could hear sirens wailing over the crowd, that had just got to its feet and returned to the Police tape, following the blast. The crowd was assured by megaphone that all was now in order. The entire scene was a smoke-filled battlefield, nothing was observable through the grey smoke – the ships, the creatures or the Police.

The crowd had thinned quite a bit. Many had run to their cars and left the scene, following the explosion, convinced that a "war of the worlds" scenario was unfolding. Those that remained were watching the scene a little more closely. The assurances by megaphone helped.

The physiology of the Biapene was very different from humans, beginning with dual heats. The cardiovascular system was on the right side of the body. The liver, it seemed, did the work of the kidneys too. Different planets...different life. The Biapene might have been distinctly different from humans, but their bodies still worked.

At least they were carbon-based and respired in a similar atmosphere, he supposed. Pat was sure there were some pretty bizarre intelligences out there, that would bear no resemblance to humans. They would terrify homo sapiens – literally make their hair stand on end.

Surgeons would rather work on a Biapene than something that evolved from a slug or an octopus. At least they'd have some idea, versus no clue at all. Better some than none, Pat mused, looking at the grounds, which resembled a bloody battlefield, *after* the battle.\

*   *   *

Ultimately, twenty Biapene survived the blast, but three required amputations and had to suffer the indignity of human carers in the short term. It was their job to teach volunteers from the Biapene population how to do it. Incredibly, they had no carers on their planet, it was done by AI.

Prescribing the Biapene painkillers was an interesting exercise. Opium-based drugs and Morphine were fine, but simple Paracetamol was a potent poison and it killed three Biapene before humans caught on. The Biapene knew of it, but obviously called it something different.

Doonia, one of the remaining Biapene on the first craft, heard the double-thud explosion and feared the worst, demanding to see someone in charge. He was told to "pipe-down" by the NYPD several times, but he kept asking and repeating it, assuming they'd have to relent sooner or later. Eventually, it happened – they were sick and tired of him. He was taken to see Pat, who was the most senior human they could find.

Doonia was red in the face, and looked at Pat apologetically and felt ashamed that he had so obviously annoyed the humans, something they were warned never to do.

'My name is Doonia, and it seems that one of our craft is, uh...*gone*.' He cast his large eyes sideways and winced and said

something emphatically in a strange foreign language. He was fluent in six human languages, but it was none of those. It was probably a curse word in his native language, the humans really had no idea.
Doonia breathed in quick, shallow gasps. 'Are they all dead?' Doonia asked brokenly, yelping quietly, in anticipation of bad news. Pat shrugged, because he wasn't sure. 'It doesn't look good,' Pat replied.

Doonia lowered his voice. 'I can help,' he said. 'I am one of the designers of the craft. How they managed to detonate an explosive is a great mystery.' His rather long, flat head was totally devoid of hair and he had a marked divot right in the middle, which he rubbed with two pendulous fingers.

'My name is Pat,' he said in return 'and there are about twenty of your people in hospital in various states, but I am afraid all are severely injured and we believe are close to death.' Pat paused to make sure it made sense to him, which it appeared to do, by the maudlin look on his non-human face, and proceeded.

'The rest unfortunately, because they were so close to each other, are dead and have been taken away. Those in hospital who recover, will eventually re-join everyone else in Canada when they are well enough to do so.'

Doonia looked morosely at Pat and nodded his thanks. Then he looked straight into Pat's eyes and swallowed hard. 'What I'm about to say is potentially catastrophic to your planet, and it is why we needed a new planet in the first place. Our concern is that it may happen to you.' Doonia's eyes suddenly became round and owl-like and WHITE, covered by some sort of pale membrane.

He'd gone from gruesome to truly, drop-dead hideous…like a feeding shark or a demon. Then he was suddenly back to normal. The membrane had gone from his eyes. Pat exhaled with distress. This was the last thing Pat needed.

'Sorry about that,' Doonia said. 'It happens when we are really worked up. It is basically a panic membrane. We are all born with it. Some of us have it removed, but clearly…I haven't. We have little control over it.'

'It's fine,' Pat said. 'No problem.' *Fuck*, he screamed to himself. Pat thought the sight of Doonia's "panic membrane" was something that'd stay with him for the rest of his life. He was sickened and terrified by the image and his heartbeat was only just returning to normal. He desperately needed to get used to them as a species, but this episode did the exact opposite. Pat was sure he was about to be attacked.

'The really concerning part,' Doonia started loudly,' is the effect of your collider on the magnetosphere of Earth.' Pat had heard it all before, but Doonia was determined, so Pat let him go. 'When your LHC collider was increased in power early in the century, a crack in Earth's magnetosphere appeared and stayed open to ionising radiation of the Sun for fourteen of your hours.' Doonia's voice had taken on a new note that concerned everyone. He seemed to be almost pleading with them. He had taken on hair-raising parallels with a Praying Mantis. Whatever he was saying, he really meant.

'That's an awfully long time for Earth to be exposed to the solar wind,' Doonia said with feeling. 'Of note, is the fact that the collider started up with *increased* power when the crack occurred. And now CERN is planning a new collider in China that's not only three times longer, but *seven times* as powerful as the LHC. Doonia's voice begged them.

Surely, this gives humanity huge pause.' Doonia looked at Pat like a parent about to scold a child. The Biapene had discussed the issue and had huge concerns for Earth and its magnetosphere.

The Biapene had developed the know-how to travel FTL. They had discovered, characterised and quantified dark matter and dark energy and slotted them into an expansive list of Standard Particles that we didn't have. They were no dummies, or conspiracy nuts. They had a better grip on the Universe than us. So, it was very difficult not to accept their opinion, empirical or not.

Doonia thought he was making no progress at all with the humans. He could see there was a distinct *ho hum* element, *heard it all before*, attached to the human reaction. He could see it in their eyes and plastered all over their faces. Doonia decided to change his approach completely. He would go from pessimism and negativity to the positive, even though it was slated for later.

Er...okay, we can show you how to make carbon-plastic cement which can be mixed like ordinary concrete, not unlike that on the Werinn world. They said that you liked it, so we took notice. You liked its ability to absorb atmospheric carbon-dioxide and fix discarded plastic, both of which are a problem here on Earth.'

Pat nodded vigorously. 'You got that right,' he said. 'Its affecting our climate now...so anything that helps would be gratefully accepted. Nothing we've come up with has helped much.'

'In that case Pat, you need to listen to me carefully, because this will be a game-changer. 'The stuff has stronger tensile strength than normal concrete,' Doonia said, 'is red in colour and uses micro-processed plastic that absorbs carbon dioxide when it cures. If used in your USA alone, for new buildings and upgraded roads, it will absorb all your excess carbon in the atmosphere, six giga-tonnes of carbon-dioxide, and remove all your waste plastic – forever.'

'The carbon is drawn from the atmosphere and fixed in the concrete.' Doonia had his shoulders back with a knowing grin on his face. He knew *they'd*, like it. Doonia realised the planet was currently fighting climate change and losing. This would tip the scales in Earth's favour. It'd cure Earth's climate-change problem for sure.

'*Holy fuck,*' Pat piped, '...that is absolutely stunning. So, climate change and disposing of used plastic smoked just like that. *Incredible.* Surely, it's not possible...to be that easy, but it seems like it is. We could also give it to other countries...really take down carbon and do away with waste plastic...we still burn coal, so it'll help with that, even though greener alternatives are slowly gaining headway, and some countries still use plastics.'

'*Anyway,*' Pat breathed, 'that's a great way to kerb climate-change and get rid of used plastics, assuming we are able to copy your tech.' Pat stared hopefully at Doonia, holding his breath, hoping like hell that it didn't involve a technology they didn't have.

'It's quite easy,' Doonia said, 'The binding substance is drawn from a plant you don't have, according to your internet. We have brought some seeds with us, and thankfully it is not on the ship that exploded. You will have to rear it, but there is no reason it wouldn't grow here. Polymers are drawn from the mature plant and mixed with the rest as a binding agent, like your cement. That would be your new asphalt and concrete. The amount of each component needs to be exact, but we can assist with that. I have samples with me.' Doonia gently placed the seed-box on the ground. 'They need to be planted and grown to maturity in an area that receives plenty of rainfall, and by removing seeds, additional plants can be grown until fields full of plants are grown to maturity to support a brand-new industry. One that removes atmospheric carbon during curing.

Pat's whole face spread into a smile. He knew people on Earth would love the idea – it was so easy.

*   *   *

It was time, and Pat knew it. Time to grab the history of Earth by the scruff of the neck and give it a hell of a shake. Pat, Jeff, John and nine techs made their way awkwardly up the silver tongue, to get their first decent look at the interior of a Biapene craft, now that it was empty of creatures. There were now no beings onboard, apart from the humans who were accompanied by Doonia, to inspect the engine that propelled the craft.

The first thing they noticed once they entered was being engulfed by heavy darkness...and the solitude. It was just them. Pat felt a chill run through his whole body although it wasn't cold. He tried to stretch his eyes as wide as possible but all he could see was an impenetrable black coal mine. Pat switched his cap-light on and it cut a bright swathe ahead of him. There was unsettling darkness on either side and a piercing arrow of light in the middle. It illuminated free floor space and the feeble outline of something door-like in the distance. This was where they stuffed all the Biapene in. Now it was cleaned of all blood, feces and the like. All that remained was oppressive darkness and tons of free space. Pat thought of the Tardis – he was sure this thing was bigger on the inside than the outside.

The technology that allowed the craft to shorten space and in effect enable FTL flight, was at the rear of the craft on Level One. Four of the nine techs onboard were from NASA and Lockheed Martin. They were part of the team that initially engineered the Orion craft. Two were from BAE Systems, and three were from Boeing. All of them, doubted that the Biapene technology would make much sense to them. Because it was based on stuff that was brand-new to humans. New technology that likely used several unknown substances. So, look and learn was probably all they could hope to do. The trio from Lockheed's were schooled in non-human tech from several craft that were all-domain, *trans-medium* – air, space and water. They were in possession of these craft courtesy of the federal government. To hopefully, reverse-engineer them. To see what made them tick – and enable their stunning abilities.

They'd received them from the US government so that their arms-length, plausible deniability came into force. As a defense-contractor, their code of silence was embedded into everyone who worked there.

One of the UAP's in their possession was from Roswell in New Mexico. From a UFO crash in 1947. To date, they'd been unsuccessful in getting anything positive from it. Even though it probably zipped and zapped all over the sky when it was going. And possessed anti-gravity and inertia-sponging and the ability to fly FTL. They didn't expect anything different here. Maybe, with the intel from the Biapene, and new technologies and particles, that might change.

Inside, the craft was eerily empty and anthracite dark, and still had that horrible sweet-bitter stink of stale biology, but it wasn't as sharp because the creatures had gone. The single floor they were on was mainly empty of rooms or compartments...or anything to divide it from being free space.

These craft were clearly nutted together at the last minute – and priority was given to stuffing the most bodies in. Any room dividers were removed or not built. And the propulsion was the same. It was designed to get them from Biapene to Earth as quickly as possible. The whole place, thus far, seemed crude and unrefined – although the propulsion system was clearly next level.

Pat imagined humans being forced to find another planet – if Earth became a similar killing-field. Humans wouldn'y put up with similar conditions. Humans were way too precious to cope with that shit, he reckoned. But if it was a choice between life or death, perhaps not. Maybe this was the best they could do at short notice.

Pat also knew the Biapene had gravity for their entire voyage to avoid floating all around the vehicle. Pat compared it to the ISS where humans floated everywhere and suppressed a gurgle of laughter. Humans had a lot to learn from the Biapene, They had a handle on space-tech that we could barely dream about. Gravity was something they seemed to know about intimately, having access to anti-gravity and gravity itself, probably as an infinite propulsion.

No doubt they knew what the force-carrier for gravity was. The Higgs field was a known quantity too, they were familiar with it in a way that humanity wasn't. Pat wondered if their "inertia-sponging" was achieved through a manipulation of the Higgs field.

The Biapene beings were sent standing up, to fit the most bodies in. It was a relatively quick voyage, so it seemed appropriate – but eight days and nights standing up would test anyone. Pat imagined – or tried to – standing up for eight days and nights in a row. While going to a new world where the majority of your species is left behind to die and your reception on Earth is a total unknown. It'd be a nightmare of unimaginable proportions. Having your family with you added an extra layer of horror to it.

It put the Biapene that made it here in a new light. Each one of them that arrived on this planet had experienced their own personal hell. They deserved the veneration of humans. Pat knew the Biapene magnetosphere was no more, and their planet and the remaining population was being ravished by radiation. But he doubted he himself would choose to leave a planet no matter what the circumstance.

But now, the vessel was empty of beings and had been cleaned cosmetically by humans. All the creatures had gotten out and into the busses as quickly as they could. They'd had quite enough of this vessel for obvious reasons. They got into another vehicle of Earthly origin this time, that stayed on the planet.

Pat looked up and said to Doonia, 'where to now?' He was keen to see what made this extraordinary ship tick. And so too were the techs from Lockheed's, Boeing and BAE who stood ready to move, with huge eyes, holding their breath. They expected a treasure-trove of tech that would dazzle them. Doonia pointed to a hatch that was open. By his stride, and eyes, that's where they were headed.

The machine that controlled movement of the vessel wasn't far away. Pat's heartbeat increased and throbbed in his ears. He knew he was about to come face-to-face with omnipotence, that which Earth has always dreamed of. Essentially, warp drive.

There were few hatches, because there were almost no rooms. Apart from the control and pilots' room ahead of the group. They were approaching one of the rooms and the hatch was half open, looking rather dark and ominous. Inside were the drives of the ship that were obscured by coal-mine darkness.

'Through here?' Pat said, flourishing tentatively toward the dark void and open hatch, hearing his heart pounding in his ears. This is where Doonia had pointed.

Pat was told quietly by the cleaners that there was a small silver box near the main tech of the craft. They went to pains to say that they were scared of it and didn't touch it. They cleaned around it, without disturbing it or moving it, or even *touching* it. Maybe it was a bomb, they said? Pat's intrigue level rose a bit, but he had bigger fish to fry. So, for the moment, he forgot about it.

Pat hadn't forgotten where he was though. *A Goddamn alien ship* – built entirely by non-humans. It was dim and there were now only a few people aboard, most of them human and not responsible in any part for building it. The craft was one big fat unknown, from top to bottom. It wasn't a human creation, so anything was possible. He didn't expect anything dangerous – but one craft had already exploded anomalously, which added to the tension and pressure and scare-factor he was feeling.

Judging by Jeff's wide eyes and raspy breathing, he was feeling his own brand of terror at the dark and foreboding surrounds. Exploring a dark ship brought with it a number of unknowns and phantasms that sprung out of the darkness. Add to that, it was of non-human origin, and you had something that was terrifying.

Without the creatures' chatter, it was silent, dark and open, which brought its own version of horror along with it. The human mind was fertile, and the very nature of this huge, open non-human room, planted many seeds that weren't welcome.

The open hatch ahead held the propulsive guts of the vessel and the compartment that held it was darker than the rest of the ship, or maybe it just looked like that from here. Doonia said that this held the FTL drive, so onward they went into the dark void, ignoring the apparitions that seemed to dart from every dark corner. The room they were entering was as black as oil.

It was like entering a coal mine - on either side of Jeff's light beam it was impenetrable and syrupy. The darkness seemed to crush from all sides. Pat aimed the light upward from time to time, to make sure there was nothing coming at him from above.

The room they were slowly moving through was critical to the ship. It held the FTL drive and even though Pete Jenkins from Lockheed assisted with formulating the Orion craft, he was sure this would be something completely unfamiliar.

Pete thought *WTF*, and walked freely forward, expecting anything, waiting for his mind to be blown. Pete tried not to think of the most recent non-human craft they'd received from the Federal government. They'd tried to reverse-engineer them, but they'd gotten nowhere. They were permanently hounded because the US was competing with China and Russia, but we had nothing useful to offer them. It was clear that they used particles which Earth and humans hadn't discovered. Attempting to find a work-around yielded nothing, despite trying for decades.

Everyone at NASA agreed, Mankind had a long, *long* way to go before Earth developed anything like the Biapene had. Finding the missing link between quantum physics and the macro world would help immeasurably, they were all sure. And so would discovering and characterising dark matter and dark energy...*95% of the Universe.*

The Biapene had somehow perfected both the gravity model and FTL travel. They'd developed tech and discovered things about the Universe, humans ached for. Comparing technology head-to-head, humans lost out badly, even though they were roughly the same age. The question of why, can be asked...the Biapene say warfare is the reason, but it can't really be answered to Mankind's satisfaction.

Hopefully, all the missing human intel could be filled in by the Biapene. The humans hoped that they positioned themselves in the right way so the flow of intel was free-willed. The humans put their trust in quid pro quo. The humans would supply a service and be "paid" in intellectual property by the Biapene.

Mankind needed people from Lockheed Martin, Boeing and BAE to truly nut out the Biapene tech, look at it, reverse engineer it, take it apart and evaluate its components, then put it back together again, engage skunkworks, when necessary, and get familiar with it.

Pat was sure it wouldn't help because there were parts of physics we just didn't know about. There were critical missing-links. Still, it wouldn't hurt for human techs to look at it...even if they didn't truly get it. They possessed a lot of experience in reverse-engineering non-human craft. Hopefully, it'd help.

The NASA guy moved through the door opening, following Pat and Jeff and Doonia from Biapene. They all walked slowly into the dark void which soon got a lot darker. Everyone was wearing a hardhat with a light at the front to help shine a decent light on the contents within. Looking at something unfamiliar was hard enough, assessing it in dimness was nigh on impossible, and they all realised that. Their own pumping hearts were all they could hear. All they could see were beams of white light cutting like lasers through absolute darkness.

Pat shone his hardhat-light straight ahead. Inside the room was another hatch that was shut, but to one side of the hatch was a large, clearly uber-complex machine. He was stunned by all the tech which fell into view – there was silvery metal everywhere - pipes, cylinders, tubes, chambers and wires. It was sort of what he expected, but the complexity was stunning. Wires and cables from the machine went into the floor in a huge cluster.

Pat felt his legs tremble and start shivering when he realised what he was gawking at. 'This is it,' he said, trance-like. *Holy fuck in a frogsuit*, he shouted to no-one and everyone, and heard its echo come back a couple of times. Now, Pat was blocked by the others, who gawked at the tech, realising what it did, but not knowing what did what.

This was one complicated machine, and it reminded Pat of the Large Hadron Collider, which he'd visited some years ago. Complexity and density of tech were his lasting impressions. It was the same here, he thought. This thing had eight huge pipes that led into it and on them were fins, as though they travelled through the air, which they most definitely didn't. Apart from maybe the LHC or a fusion reactor, it resembled nothing they'd ever seen.

And the Biapene lizards built this thing from scratch. Pat struggled to believe what was in front of him. It was something that had eluded humanity forever. Built by lizards. Essentially, it was warp-drive. Pat was floored by these incredible creatures, that looked so primeval.

Between the huge pipes were rows of metal that presumably rotated when the propulsion was fired up. Never before had Pat looked at something and been so completely muddled and bewildered. This was akin to his first look at the guts of the LHC. All of it was a total mystery and gave him an unsettling feeling of stupor and confusion that he didn't like. Even though he was a very intelligent man and had a PhD in Physics and had published many papers on science, this intricate machine made him feel stupid.

Pat knew broadly how space-shortening worked, but none of the tech he was looking at made any sense. He supposed that's how it rolled with brand new technology that you obviously didn't comprehend. The Biapene had kicked this one way out of the park. A morass of wires went straight into the floor and probably wound down to feed more tech and eventually wound its way up to the antenna.
Pat was in awe – all the humans were. This piece of complex hardware in front of them, shrouded in darkness, sent this craft hurtling forward at thousands of times the speed of light. *Warp drive.*

Every hair on Pat's body was standing to attention as he gazed at its complexity and realised what it could achieve. He clenched his teeth and felt jealousy hit him hard. Pat wondered what NASA would have achieved?

John Rheems from Lockheed was on his haunches rubbing his chin with one hand and pointing with the other, intrigued and captivated by this machine, to the point of conniptions. Then he was frowning, scowling, looking closely, then further away, turning his head to the side, realising its familiarity. He didn't have a clue how it worked, but conceded it looked familiar. He'd seen this tech before.

Eventually, he shrugged and stood up. This thing was very similar – maybe identical – to some of the non-human "UFOs" in their possession, that they were still working on, to reverse-engineer. He realised he was missing something very important. It would take months, maybe decades to copy the tech. And a small requirement – humanity needed to find and characterise dark matter and dark energy and learn to manipulate it.

This method of space travel involved stretching the fabric of space-time in a wave, which caused space ahead of an object to contract while spacetime behind it expands. Humanity desperately needed the Biapene's help with this and other tech, and intel that we didn't have. *Before* we accomplished a thing. And that went for the other reverse-engineering too.

An object inside the wave would be able to ride the region, known as a "warp bubble" of flat space without the imposition of time dilation. That was the theory, but the tech in front of them bore no similarity to any of that, as far as Pat was concerned anyway.

The techs they brought with them were walking away from the machine and shaking their heads. Both groups were dejected. The guy from Lockheed laughingly said, 'I'm gonna need an instruction manual with this.' Pete didn't say it, but the ship looked very similar to some of the 'flying saucers' that the feds had handed to Lockwood for reverse-engineering. The feds were currently ensconced in a cold war with China and Russia. The first to unravel the secret tech of non-humans would be awarded "king of the world" status. This pushed Pete, John and the team at Lockwood on. They reckoned an autocrat in charge of this technology would be horrendous. This was a cold 'war' the US *had* to win.

Humans would need a lot of help from the Biapene. Or they would spend years, or possibly decades reverse-engineering it. Pat saw the metal box the cleaners had talked about, secreted underneath the machine. It seemed to be made of a shining silver metal – probably aluminium, but possibly anything suitably bright. It had no handles or lock on it. Having bent down to retrieve it, Pat found the box to be unusually light.

The contents sounded like seashells when he shook it. From a security standpoint, he knew he was doing the wrong thing by shaking it, but he doubted the Biapene would harm Mankind. Doonia's eyes were glowing in expectation. He obviously knew what was inside.

Pat jimmied the top off the box and found seven or eight crudely octahedral reddish translucent minerals.

'Diamonds,' Doonia said. 'On your internet, red diamonds are very rare on Earth. These are fairly common on Biapene and were brought as a gift to your world. Prnhuin was supposed to present them, but he was an Elder in the exploded vehicle. He is unfortunately deceased.' Doonia spoke in a monotone and looked down at his empty hands. 'They are yours Pat – do with them what you will.' Seemingly, he'd totally lost interest in them. There were other things that demanded his attention.

Pat gazed with soft eyes. 'I know someone who needs a diamond. The rest are yours Doonia – give them to Earth or NASA or whomever. It ain't my purview to distribute Biapene gifts such as these. Pat grabbed one diamond and pocketed it. Doonia replaced the lid on the remaining specimens and put the box in his backpack.

Pat looked at the machine in front of him and couldn't, for the life of him, work out how it managed to achieve all that it did. What made space soft and malleable...what made it contract and expand? He knew it worked, because they got here so damn quickly. But how they managed to do it remained a total and maddening mystery. No doubt, dark energy was involved, but how and where? He felt like kicking the machine, but realised the futility.

Pat wanted to check out the room behind the door – because it looked very out of place and in a way, special. It was the only room on the entire ship, apart from the pilots and the propulsion. The hatch was shut on this room, which was also unusual. The Biapene had to stand outside, squashed together, but the hatch to this room stayed firmly closed. An intriguing quandary, Pat thought.

Doonia had implored him not to worry about it, and seemed to be pretty worked up. Which heightened Pat's interest in this strange little room. It was on a craft essentially uncompartmentalized.

Doonia was now standing in front of the hatch as though guarding it. Pat was told that it was locked and there was no key available. So, he pushed Doonia to one side and gave the hatch a hip and shoulder, but to no avail. It held fast. Jeff saw what he was trying to do, and being a lot taller and thicker-set than Pat, his hip and shoulder busted the hatch wide open. Inside was a small, largely empty and dim room with a few skeletons off to one side.

The skeletons had cracked and in places broken and displaced human like skulls with ribs on each side of a prominent backbone. Pat knew they were human, because Harry had told him about the human versus Biapene physiology, which Harry learned direct from Doonia. The Biapene themselves only had nine ribs each side of the backbone and a very different, bigger skull. These had twelve ribs.

What the hell?' Pat spat, knowing something was up, bending down to inspect the first skeleton. He stood up, narrowed his eyes and squinted at Doonia, who shrugged back at him. The inference was clear. 'How did they get here?' Pat demanded.

'No idea,' Doonia replied frankly. 'This is the first time I've seen them.' Doonia was flushed in the face and realised he was being accused. By someone of the same species as the skeletons.

Pat looked him up and down suspiciously. 'So, you don't know how they ended up on the vessel? I'll tell you something then.' Pat said aggressively, glancing at the skeletons and gazing at Doonia with an angry, downturned mouth. 'This craft has been to Earth before and taken humans and ended up killing them.' He used his hands to point toward the skeletons. 'Not you, maybe, but some of your, er...species ...*maybe* a long time ago.' Pat turned his head, bared his teeth and shook his head at such *reprehensible* behaviour, knowing that indeed the Biapene were responsible for some of the reports of triangular UFO's. A fact that could be qualitatively attested to, by John and Pete from Lockwood. All humans were aware of the accusations. Why or how else could they have yellowed human bones in their craft?

'I will ask about it.' Doonia said, with sad eyes. He was as shocked and disappointed as Pat. He knew they were there, but had no idea how or why?

'You do that.' Pat returned, looking wryly at Doonia and nodding, knowing it was too late for anything meaningful to happen. This issue was all done and dusted. He also knew that it wasn't likely to be Doonia that any ire should be directed toward.

Pat knew that FTL travel wasn't new technology as the Biapene said. What a load of crap, he thought. The Biapene had probably used it to get to Earth for hundreds, maybe thousands of years. They just didn't want us to know. Pat wondered about Roswell in New Mexico? He gazed at Doonia with new eyes. Maybe the reports and drawings of lizard-like aliens, both ancient and recent, had some credence, he reckoned, nodding his head to himself.

13

Pyramids

"Intelligence is the ability to adapt to change."
~ Stephen Hawking

Harry and Abby were still in in the Capital Hilton. And had been since the visitors landed. Still updating NASA by text and video every day. There had been a huge crowd of people surrounding the remaining two craft for days. Hanging over the top of the Police-tape, the crowd was initially fifteen, in places thirty people deep. But as time had marched on, many had had their fill, and it was now substantially thinner.

Harry watched Abby's every move, smiling hugely. He wore a permanent grin, walking and following Abby with a light, bouncing step. He had it bad. Harry's desire to look after Abby had intensified to the point where sleep was just a memory.

People kept arriving at the scene by car, bus, train or foot - it seemed everyone wanted to see the craft and where the Biapene landed. There were hawkers now, looking for an opportunity to sell to the crowd. The hawkers were pushing or cycling or driving their stands around the perimeter of people, pushing for a sale. They sold everything from hotdogs, sausages, chocolates or sandwiches to watches or alien-emblazoned clothing, trinkets or posters. All of them were inscribed with "Biapene" somewhere. 'Aliens sell', was the clear mantra of the hawkers. And they were trying hard to sell the lot.

The crowd hadn't seen the occupants of the vehicles, only a few glimpses as they boarded the bus – obscured by hundreds of NYPD and DC Police in long lines. The first sight of them by Lance Brannigan was typical of a human laying his eyes on a non-human for the first time. He was a Sargent with the DC Police in Arlington and he was nothing short of mortified, when he first clapped eyes on them.

Lance saw a face that was deep green and hauntingly carbuncled with large black eyes that blinked the opposite way to humans. The creature looked straight at him and stuck its forked tongue out and hooted an "animal" sound in his direction.

Lance felt instantly weak and almost collapsed to the ground. He dropped the large towel he was holding, and had a painful tingling in his chest, which extended up his left arm. Lance focussed on the ground for the rest of the exercise and refused to look up until they had all entered the buses. He was petrified and never wanted to go through it again, certain he came within a whisker of a heart-attack. He had suffered from occasional restless legs for years now, and both of his calves twitched for days following, leaving him bed ridden. His GP put it down to his unfortunate non-human encounter which had hit him hard. The outlook for Joe Public was grim indeed. But NASA and governments generally weren't concerned. They had bigger fish to fry.

Harry and Abby watched the extraordinary scene from the balcony of their room. They were both sitting, drinking coffee and gazing at each other and thinking on the crazy goings-on with the triangles, not far away. They were pretty sure they had the best view of anybody. Abby pushed into Harry to get closer to him, and get a better view of the park. Harry gazed at Abby without blinking and Abby came closer and nuzzled Harry's neck. Both had it bad.

The planet's legacy media providers were lined up end-to-end on 14th and 17th street and E street NW. On many channels, it was twenty-four-hour coverage. Their vans were mobile newsrooms and they were lined up end to end. Everything that happened, no matter how small, was reported to the public.

Most countries in the world took it and televised it live to a stunned public. Users of Instagram, TikTok and Twitter saw their apps crash. Social posts were straining the systems, and new photos, videos and texts were over five hundred million per day. Humans were using technology like never before. Communication brought relief from shock. A problem shared is a problem halved, apparently.

Harry and Abby were now a fully-fledged item and had been together, and enjoying each other for the past ten days and nights. They were still in Washington to be NASA's eyes and ears. Harry spoke to them each day and gave a detailed rundown of daily events, including video, which Abby forwarded to HQ in Houston daily. Harry used his phone to take notes and detail events. Despite the fact that a horde from NASA HQ were here. Harry and Abby continued their reporting, and would continue, until they were told not to. They were still being paid at a higher rate, so Harry didn't want to rock the boat at Houston.

Both were entirely smitten with each other. Abby especially, looked forward to their future together. They made plans to venture to Iceland as soon as they could get holidays from NASA. Both couldn't wait to get there. Harry had firm, future plans, but it also depended on his bank balance. Iceland was a long way away, so airfares were pricey. As were the woolly outfits and trekking equipment. Abby just wanted to step foot there, she didn't care about inanities like money and equipment. Harry was just keen to spend more time with Abby, whether in Iceland, or not. His plan had worked perfectly.

They had each booked leave for two weeks in about two months' time and as yet, NASA hadn't said no. Delta Airlines had offered him a discount on European travel, so Harry intended to book flights with them. He'd book accommodation too, and hoped and prayed that Abby didn't find out about his inside information.

Truth was, he enjoyed trekking and he'd go anywhere, if it was with Abby. So, the utility of the info was probably moot. But he'd keep it a secret anyway. In Harry's opinion, she wasn't the sort of person to take that stuff in her stride.

Both Harry and Abby had wrenched their eyes off each other, and were watching Pat below, as he emerged from one of the craft with several others, when the only remaining occupied Triangle started drifting into the air. It floated upward into the cloudy sky. Pat and the entirety of those on the ground watched it do things that seemed wrong. It wasn't a balloon - it was a multi-tonne vessel, without wings or aero-dynamic surfaces, yet somehow it had positive lift. With no noise at all, it rose into the air, from a standing start.

It was known by many humans, that the Biapene had access to anti-gravity, so it wasn't a total surprise. Humanity was used to seeing helium balloons float away on the breeze, but not massive, heavy, vessels. It looked counterintuitive, to see massive objects acting like that. It was like seeing a Naval Destroyer suddenly start noiselessly lifting above the ocean.

Still, get used to the new world, Harry thought. The large vessel in front of him pitched into the sky, without any observable thrust or noise. Humanity would expect rocket power to actuate it. But there was nothing. Still, it lifted. Abby stood up from her chair and took off her sunglasses. She looked at the craft through her binoculars, not believing it was actually moving up.

Abby gawked at everyone near the craft and scanned the distant crowd who collectively issued a *"WOOOW"*. Everyone tilted their heads and stared at the retreating craft. It was like a magic show. Abby watched the heads of the crowd angle back as they saw the ship slowly rise higher and higher with positive lift, like a balloon on the wind. It continued heading skyward without the slightest suggestion of power.

Once the Triangle got to about two thousand feet, it engaged some form of propulsion, presumably chemical RCS or OMS, but equally likely, gravitational drive, and away it went like a shot, maintaining the same altitude, which would keep it away from commercial aircraft. It literally flashed away. From behind, Pat reckoned it resembled a "wedge" or a "set of wings", quickly losing all form among the clouds. Pat had to admit it looked like a classic UFO. Soon, it went beyond the horizon and the sky was clear.

The Biapene had read parts of Earth's internet. They focussed on what interested them most. First it was the nature of humanity, and its penchant for warfare. Then it was triangles, pyramids and polygons generally.

Humanity generally said, *"huh?"*. Such was the nature of xeno-psychology and non-human neuro-biology. Understanding the Biapene need for polygons required deep emotional thinking and respect for the nuts and bolts of an interstellar species. Mankind needed to realise that the Biapene might differ from humans in the most basic areas. Humans failed these criteria. The Biapene were wrongly treated as analogous to humans.

Biapene buildings were almost all pyramidal or triangular Most were a derivation of isosceles. Home dwellings were the same. Most were tetrahedrons or pyramids, and the wiring of the Biapene brain required them. The need for the morphology was akin to metabolising nutrients – it provided energy and strength. To humans, they weren't worth anything.

There was one part of Earth, the Biapene *had* to see...to touch and to feel. It was in Egypt. They'd read about it in the pages of the internet and it held them spellbound and speechless. All of them felt the adrenaline and the pull from something truly alluring on Earth. And incredibly, they were built a long, *long* time ago and they knew a bit about them, from the *old texts* on Biapene, and with the internet.

The Biapene gawked at the mighty pyramids of Giza, over and over and over. The squealing, hooting and shrieking was only the beginning. Trembling, jabbering, chanting and collapsing, followed for many of their kind, to the point where human managers banned ordinary Biapene folk from reading any pages of the internet. It was too much for too many, and fainting *on mass,* was something humans couldn't allow.

*   *   *

The Triangle was on its way to north Africa, across the Atlantic Ocean. Harry watched the vessel disappear from sight. A set of wings getting smaller and then losing all definition and vanishing entirely. It moved quickly and low over the ocean from its landing site not far from the Whitehouse.

The pilot pushed forward on a lever that was black and circular with a large hole in it. His hairless hand was entirely wrapped around it and through it. His long, thin index finger activated something that ripped out of the two rear corners of the craft silently. This vehicle was nimbler than anything owned by Earth's military and a lot faster. And incredibly, it was hypersonic and displaced *inertia*.

The vehicle was hurtling forward, under no pull from Earth's gravity. The Pilot saw the ocean briefly, a blurred light green blue, but moving hypersonic, it didn't last long and then a landmass came. He knew exactly where he was.

Before they got over the continent though, eight triangular vessels flashed straight up to their height, from the ocean, exiting without a splash and with an indistinct *'glulp'*. Bshn – the primary pilot, sensed the craft were below him, and communicated with them. Bshn didn't realise there were any craft from Biapene on Earth, but there was, and they were now with him.

These craft were sent to Earth by the Biapene rulers some time ago, to gather as much info on human tech and weaponry that the software on the craft could hold. The smaller craft were informed that now, there was no planet to return to because of the failed magnetosphere. So, they ultimately agreed to join the larger craft. There was no-one left on the planet that would be interested in the info about Earth.

The Biapene had a special relationship with water, that humans didn't have. Concentrated electrolysis reduced the viscosity and broke the hydrogen bonds in water and allowed their craft to enter or exit bodies of water without splashing. The Biapene could accelerate beneath it to incredible speeds, that humans couldn't touch. Craft on Biapene regularly break the sound barrier in water, underwater vehicles flashing around at 3-4 kilometres a second.

Now, in their wake, were eight black triangles all similar but smaller than the main craft. The black triangles all departed the ocean with no splash and no noise. They each had lights in the middle and on each corner of the craft, like the larger craft, lights that not only assisted with illumination, but were intimately involved in gravitational propulsion.

From the air, Africa was dominated by yellowy-orange sand dunes and moving black dots amid the sand. Occasionally, there was a town, looking like a collection of boxes, strewn together, surrounded by kilometre after kilometre of curving sand dunes and desert. Below them now was sandy desert and from hypersonic, their speed was now only Mach 1.

They flew into Libyan airspace and on to Egypt, with Cairo and the Suez Canal in the distance. Even from several thousand metres in the air, the pyramids of Giza looked amazing and very distinctive. The Biapene, were deeply aroused and excited by the pyramid's proximity. Bshn was stunned, they appeared *exactly* as they did in the old *texts*. They hadn't changed a zack.

Tourists and residents alike, *everyone* on the ground, including most of Cairo and boats in the Suez Canal watched the triangular vessel. It came in to land on the hot sand of Cairo, only fifty metres from grand Cheops itself. It was the mightiest of pyramids. The landing vessel lifted only a puff of sand. Most humans knew of the triangles and the newcomers, but they were supposed to be in America? None knew of their fondness for polygons.

Within five minutes of landing, more than three-thousand Biapene were all around the great structure: on it, up it, and around it. They didn't have a fear of humans, although the reverse didn't apply, when they saw a horde of Biapene pour out of the craft. All the Biapene came down the silver tongue and onto the sand of the Sahara, on their way to the great pyramid. And they could feel the energy pouring off the great structures, and all of them immediately knew why the ancient Biapene helped build them.

All on Biapene had read about the pyramids and realised they were of great antiquity. The weight of the blocks and the precision with which they were cut and placed together was a testament to the ancient Biapene. They used anti-gravity to great effect. Humans knew it was special, and so did the Biapene. Now, the pyramids of Giza had non-humans all over them again. On top, around and on.

Bshn himself was stunned that it wasn't documented. He knew humans suspected, but they should have *known*. Humans just didn't have the technology, according to the internet. The big pyramid was nearly five thousand years old – built with huge blocks of granite and limestone and tools that could barely cut wood. Seriously, it was a *no-brainer.* The Egyptians had a lot of help. To build structures that were beneficial to both races.

The blocks were as precise as human tech *TODAY* could muster. Renrnor was the highest-ranked elder on the craft and he was floored at humanity's idiocy. He knew the oldest craft Biapene had sent here was six thousand Earth-years ago. The pyramids were mostly the work of the Biapene ancients. *Period.*

There was a huge, rather diverse ring of humanity around the vessel. It comprised tourists, residents, Bedouins and locals on camels, stretching around Cheops pyramid, petering out behind the pyramid itself. It was five deep and more everywhere else. The crowd was bustling and lively and chanting. Everyone wanted to see what was happening. The Biapene returned to the craft and reluctantly, left Cheops behind. Too many locals meant trouble.

14

The Golden Ratio

"The thing about smart people is that they seem like crazy people to dumb people."
~ Stephen Hawking

Watching the Biapene and listening to them, humans realised their folly. But the problem was, the Vancouver development was half finished. It was built along the lines created for the indigenous Squamish race in Vancouver, which at the time, seemed appropriate.

Never was it truer – what is good for one is not necessarily good for another. Their buildings were prismatic and worse, the rooms were rectangular or cubic. They were fine for the Squamish, but not so for the Biapene. They wouldn't do at all. And the humans finally realised their mistake after it was too late. They could rectify the problem, but it would be expensive and take even more time.

The only correct thing to do was to demolish the buildings at the cost of the consortium. The Hazmat report and permits had been obtained by the developer and now the boys from Fleck would come in and get rid of the sub-structure, sending most to recycling and the rest to waste. It would cost the Consortium a small fortune, but all costs would be underwritten and paid for by the UN and World Bank.

Being the focus for many hundreds of men, the new pyramidal structures were almost complete. They were enormous isosceles triangles, thin at the top and wide at the base and there were eight of them. Three Elder Biapene perused the plans before they were built and they gave the okay – the humans realising that they should have done so in the first place.

The ratio of the slant height of the triangles relative to half the base dimension equalled 1.618 in the rooms on the ground floor. This was termed "Bedusa" in the Biapene language and the Golden Ratio in English. The Biapene Elders ensured that each apartment and the overall structure included "Bedusa". It was part of architectural and general law on Biapene and Werinn.

They moved the short distance from Blueridge to Northlands by Vancouver Charter Bus Company and happily entered their new and final accommodation. After a lot of to-ing and fro-ing, and having endured torturous non-polygonal rooms, they were finally in suitable houses. And from them, the Biapene drew energy and strength and pain was zeroed. For humans, it appeared job done.

To humans, it was ridiculous and inconsequential. But to the Biapene, it was life or death.

15

Quid Pro Quo

"If it must be done, it's best done bravely"
Stephen Hawking

Minaj, Glalsk and other Elders from all the vessels were close friends and shared a combined nine hundred and twenty-two Earth years in age. They realised that there was a big problem with communication between the Biapene and the humans, both in language, and how it was understood.

Even though humans had finally agreed to house them in polygonal rooms with triangular walls, they didn't truly know why. It was brand-new to humans as something essential for life. Nothing biological on Earth had such a need. So, familiarising with it or understanding it, was difficult. For the Biapene it was simple – it was life or death.

Acquiring the Biapene's intel and technology was contingent on Mankind building polygonal living spaces for them, and appreciating why they needed it. Hence the humans needed formal direction and clarification from the Biapene Elders. And Mankind needed to document it and send it to every human on Earth that had anything to do with the Biapene. It was a critical learning experience for Mankind.

The Biapene intellectual property was at the crux of this entire episode. Also, it would hopefully stop the flood of complaints and the frequent grumbling from the Biapene. To be forceful and demanding, wasn't any Biapene's nature, and not in their genetics. To get any action, these creatures had to start dying hand over fist to make humans ask questions, and truly listen to the response.

It would have been a whole lot easier just to listen to the Biapene in the first place, rather than fobbing them off. Or expecting them to just be thankful that something, *anything* was being built for them.

Humans didn't truly comprehend how invigorating and centring the triangular structure was to the average Biapene. For humans, it was nutrients, food and sleep that gave them energy and vitality. The Biapene were very different indeed. Food and nutrients were important, but the impact of triangular rooms was doubly critical to their race. Without them, they withered and died. And were unable to reproduce, first becoming tired and depressed, then suicidal.

Pat was told by Oshn and Glalsk, that the secrets of the Universe were held in Biapene hands. The "dark" particles, FTL, quantum gravity and teleportation of living biology, would be available to humanity *if* they did the right thing. Which meant housing them all in appropriate polygonal buildings. So their species could live a long and pain-free life - and reproduce.

The three of them, Glalsk, Minaj, and Prelfk, wearing long sleeves, long pants, large boots and a full burka made their way by NASA vehicle to the west-end of Vancouver. To Library Square on W Georgia Street. NASA had rented a boardroom for a formal meeting. To allow the Biapene to fully inform their "keepers" on the importance of polygonal rooms to the Biapene race. Information that formed law on their world.

Because, to date, huge mistakes had been made which cost time, money and a lot of Biapene health and lives. Given what the Biapene offered to humanity, it beggared belief to see how they were treated. The G7, 5-Eyes, and POTUS himself were horrified when they found out about the reconstruction of the Biapine housing project.

'*You must be fucking joking,*' POTUS screamed into the phone, when he got wind of the problem. If they need polygonal rooms, that's what they get. *Jesus,* it can't be that hard, can it?' POTUS was spitting all over his phone and didn't expect a reply from Ted Johnston, the Secretary of State, on the other end. This wasn't that sort of phone call. 'Just get it done Ted...whatever they want, *for whatever reason*, they get it. There is a lot riding on this.' With that, POTUS disconnected the call and threw the phone at the white wall. In a bluster of cursing and profanity, he dropped himself into his padded chair next to old Resolute. '*Fuckers,*' he yelled to no-one.

POTUS, as leader of the Consortium, had told the human managers to *just work it out* and *do whatever is necessary, without limit,* because the Biapene were a very valuable resource. The humans regretted their behaviour, because there was so much to be learned from the Biapene. A formal meeting with the Biapene was the humans first step in rectification.

The room was numbered "916" and it not only had a huge table and many chairs, it boasted an electronic whiteboard and a mic connected to an amplifier. This meeting was to show the Biapene, their concerns were being listened too and digested by humans. The meeting was demanded by all G7 nations, Five Eyes, and POTUS himself. The feedback from the Biapene was negative indeed. Pat was contacted by Ted Johnston of the Whitehouse who told him what they wanted and when. It was an angry, irritated demand, and Pat didn't need to be told twice. What POTUS and G7 wanted, they got.

The Biapene's technical intel was critical to Earth and it was Pat's and the Consortium's job to get it. Just the search for dark matter yearned for a solution and had cost the world a fortune to search for it. The G7 leaders and POTUS listened to a presentation on the issue by Lockheed Martin and were blown away. The world had spent a hundred billion dollars on the hunt for dark matter alone, enough money to make the French PM wobbly on his feet. Luckily, Macron was sitting down when it was revealed. He had no idea it was that much - in fact, no one did. It hit them all like a baseball bat.

It reinforced, to the whole audience, that the Biapene's comfort and satisfaction was paramount. The G7, POTUS, space industries worldwide, the UN and even the US Congress had demanded swift action or the Biapene would refuse to play ball. Essentially, they would disavow what was owed to Mankind. *Quid pro quo* would disintegrate. The Biapene would essentially show the middle finger to humanity and few would blame them.

Around the large oak table sat Pat, Jeff, Harry and Abby, and four from the DoD, and the humans knew exactly what they had to do.

On the other side of the expansive table were the three large Elders from Biapene. It looked like a Mexican standoff as both sides of the table looked suspiciously and heatedly at the other.

Glalsk was a huge Biapene and he stared at Pat with a hostile glare and at the same time was painting the roof of his mouth with his long slitted tongue.

Pat broke the uncomfortable silence. He stood noisily and directed himself toward the three Biapene, refusing to be put-off by their massive and belligerent appearance. They glared at their human counterparts with erect tongues, open mouths and large wide eyes. The green, scaly skin visible under their burkas glinted under the down-lights of room 916. Abby felt a shiver run up her spine.

'G-Gentlemen,' Pat said uncertainly, 'you understand English and are fluent with it, so I will use it, unless there are any issues, which you must inform me of.' The three of them nodded, and removed their burkas at the same time. For the first time they were undisguised. Abby held her muscles tight, to avoid a negative facial reaction. Their reptilian nature was obvious to all.

'Glalsk – your turn. You know what we're here for,' Pat said tentatively. 'We are keen to learn about the significance of triangular shapes to your species. We understand that you have been trying to impress their import since you arrived...in the main *unsuccessfully*, and for that, we apologise emphatically.' Glalsk flicked his tongue in and out, then slowly got to his feet.

'Acquainting with new concepts isn't easy for humans,' Glalsk said imperially. 'The shape of a room does not significantly affect a human's sleep pattern or state-of-mind as far as we know – that is backed up by your internet.'

'Before you go further, Glalsk,' Pat blurted, sounding like he'd been holding his breath. 'Know that we wish to maintain your race in appropriate lodgings in return for the physics you inferred would be, ours.' Pat realised his entire future depended on him getting it.

Pat remembered the last phone call from POTUS, and the value that he and the rest of humanity, placed on the intel of the Biapene. He said it'd cost us another hundred billion and take the best part of a century to achieve. There was some tech that POTUS doubted we'd *ever* develop. That must have been the opinion of his science advisor, because sure as hell, he wouldn't know.

That made treatment of the Biapene, even more critical. Essentially, the Biapene were Mankind's *ticket*. Pat realised that any reference to 'we or us' was actually a reference to *him*. Pat was responsible. If there was a problem with obtaining it, he would be crucified, no-one else. He'd spoken to POTUS and knew it, and while he wasn't happy about it, Pat applied common sense and was content. He was indeed the tip of the spear.

Glalsk gestured to the other Biapene by using both hands above his head, folding his fingers into a vague star-shape and they did the same back to him.

Then he said to the humans with emphasis, *'We live inside triangles.* The only reason we live long and fruitful lives is the energy produced by pyramids and triangular faces. Without that we become listless, lethargic and eventually, lose the will of life. Females lose the ability to become pregnant. Our psyche demands pyramids.' Glalsk held his palms up and out and went totally quiet. He made strong eye contact with everyone and continued. His voice was softer, accent-free and highly intelligent. Glalsk wanted to make sure he was heard clearly.

'All houses and buildings on Biapene are produced to ensure that the ratio of the slant height to half the base dimension, using identical units, equals 1.618.' Glalsk stopped again to make sure they were all with him. He needed to be sure that all the humans understood what he was saying. This opportunity was critical to their people, and he knew it. The humans had organised the meeting because they were concerned about human understanding of their needs. Pat simply had to make it work.

Glalsk guzzled the water provided by inserting the top of the glass in his mouth and angling his head backward, alarming all humans, and once finished, he continued as though nothing was up.

'Quite simply, Glalsk said, 'our psychology demands polygons. We are very different from humans, who have no such need. So, it is not surprising that you have found it difficult to understand.' Glalsk drew a sharp breath, and sat down before quickly standing and continuing to talk.

'But, now that you know formally, hopefully we can turn that page and get on with co-existing properly.' Glalsk smiled generously and signed in a complex fashion above his head, using both hands. Then he grabbed Pat's right arm and shook his hand firmly. He did the same with Jeff, Harry and Abby. The big Biapene truly believed what he'd said and hoped humanity would take the words to heart.

Pat gawked at all three of them, a furrow cutting between his brows. Now was as good as time as any, he supposed. Because this probably wasn't a great way to end such a cooperative meeting. But he wanted a response, so he drove straight ahead.

The mission, as directed by POTUS, the G7 and Five-Eyes had been achieved admirably. What Pat was intending to say now might ruin all that. He thought about it and knew he needed to bring it up with this audience. It was all he could think about. *Fuck it,* he eventually decided. It was too good of an opportunity to let slide.

He coughed loudly, clearing his throat, saying to them all, but mainly looking at Glalsk, asking a very pointed question indeed. *'Why were their human skeletons in your craft?'* His voice rang out in the room, loud and harsh. It sounded like an accusation. *Shit*, he thought to himself, after he replayed the sound of his own voice. It was heavy with accusation.

Glalsk glanced at the others, off-put by Pat's frankness and suddenness. 'Er…yes,' he said uncertainly. 'You weren't supposed to see those, but there is a good explanation, and it involves the Werinn whom I believe…you have met. It's probably not right to talk about them in their absence, but equally, we won't take the fall for them.'

Pat scowled at Glalsk and raised his eyebrows, massaging one temple. He wanted a response NOW. The whole issue was bothering him and it got in the way of doing what POTUS demanded.

Glalsk swallowed heavily, then spoke, 'the skeletons were given to us by the Werinn, when they supplied us with pages of your internet. We didn't ask for them, but we got them anyway. It was the Werinn who collected the humans for research. We would not do such a thing. With his head down, he looked at Pat remorsefully.

'Remember, they also possess space-shortening technology and they previously went to Earth to do their work on your planet, research that wasn't known to all on Werinn. Millions on Earth watched your Apollo vehicles take off, but not so on Werinn. Their Union sent their triangular vessels to Earth in secret, and few on Werinn and most in their space services, knew nothing of the trip.

'These craft travelled to Earth several times and spent time there each journey and noted the escalating technology on Earth.' Glalsk looked at Pat with stony eyes. 'They even lost some craft and individuals there, which I believe you have.' Pat shrugged and glanced at Jeff who did the same thing back to him. Glalsk was referring to the aerospace companies, who were in possession of several UFOs, handed over by the US government. The behaviour of the Chinese and Russian governments was unknown because they were communist-based and "closed". But they were expected to be similar. In other words, they also held UFOs and non-humans.

Pat had a pinched mouth and sour expression and looked angrily at Glalsk. '*Research indeed,*' he said angrily, realising that his anger and annoyance shouldn't be directed toward the Biapene. 'The Werinn told Harry and Abby that they stopped their ventures to Earth once they'd read our internet. That they turned around and returned to their planet. They didn't state they'd already been there.' Pat was opening and closing his mouth without uttering any sound, and swallowing rapidly. Pat wondered what the real story was. This whole thing smelt of something very off.

Glalsk was recorded on CC-video and everything he said was included in a detailed paper that was forwarded to a huge addressee list including POTUS and every country leader and space services company on the planet, including NASA, SpaceX, Blue Origin, ESA, JAXA, CSA and Roscosmos. No-one that needed it, missed out.

Pat prepared a paper from Glalsk's words and sent it along with the video. The paper described an essential psychological need of the Biapene and possibly other species. It was made clear that mental demands can be so strong that they become physical needs. That are required to simply survive.

Humans needed to do a better job of listening to new species. Because their living requirements may seem obtuse. But in reality, might be very important to its simple ability to survive.

16

Disclosure

"Not only does God play dice, but…he sometimes throws them where they cannot be seen."
~ Stephen Hawking

The Press Secretary for the US told the media that POTUS would arrive in the James S Brady room at 2PM to make a major announcement that was "globally important". The 49 seats in the room were quickly reserved by the media. There were guesses, inferences, speculations and predictions – but none of them were right. In fact, none were even close. This was a world-shaking announcement about something that had been hidden for eighty-years.

POTUS arrived, with the Secretary of Defence, and the big-wigs from the CIA and the Joint Chiefs by his side. The Biapene had told him direct that it was the Werinn at Roswell in New Mexico. And at Rendlesham Forest in England and the Biapene in Varginha, Brazil. And numerous other sites, including the Ural Mountains in Russia and near nuclear and secret military sites all over the world.

POTUS had always believed in the reality of UFOs as being an off-planet intelligence. Because he had seen one. He was near Fort Worth at night with his father and together, they saw three lights in the sky that did things no ordinary aircraft could do. The lights displayed the "five observables" and zipped and zapped all over the sky, formed a triangle, before seemingly landing somewhere in the distance.

POTUS was then a congressman and he and his father winged it in their Chevy. After the event, POTUS was thunderstruck and realised that UFOs, replete with extra-terrestrials, were ridgy-didge. When he first started in the Whitehouse, one of the first things he did was ask a friend in the East Wing what America knew about UFOs. His friend had worked in the upper echelons of the CIA and said he'd get back to him. That he'd do some digging.

He not only didn't get back to him, he disappeared entirely. POTUS meant to follow him up – but the pressure of work from his first term had so far stopped him. He'd rung him internally and was told he no longer worked there. The President realised there was something malevolent going on, by simply trying to access information on UFOs and UAPs.

POTUS received the information from the Biapene first-hand, so it was his to do anything with. And he knew exactly what to do with it. He couldn't wait to share it with his people. The CIA, DoD and the Joint Chiefs scrabbled and fumbled, advising him emphatically and repeatedly, against it, citing Defense Policy and Article 1, Section 8 of the American Constitution. '*Don't do it,*' was the passionate advice. "You won't live to regret it", they warned. There were even more ominous warnings, but he refused to back down. The inaction had gone on too long. Still, the robust advice, took on the tone of a life-ending *warning.*

'*Public interest disclosure,*' POTUS fired back, on more than one occasion. He was determined that the official denials would end, and he wouldn't be put off by officials citing bullshit laws. The CIA and the DoD wanted to meet, but so far, he'd managed to avoid them. He knew what happened to JFK when he marched toward disclosure, so he knew extreme care had to be front and centre.

But the public deserved to know – there was so much disinformation on the topic – he'd had enough. *Arr fuck em*, he reckoned, referring to the CIA, DoD and Pentagon.

POTUS stood tall behind the podium and read from the teleprompter, and made the pronouncement to a room full of wide and teary eyes. Among the players in seated residence were the NY Times, CBS, MSNBC, FOX, CNN and NBC. Reporters were standing five-deep near the walls. The information they all heard would fill the media for weeks, in all its guises. Everyone the world over, wanted to hear the details of the President's talk.

Tomorrow, POTUS would address the American public by fronting TV stations, NBC, CBS, FOX and ABC. He would tell them exactly what the Biapene had told him. So, a huge slice of the American public would know the truth. And it would be picked up by the media globally from Russia to China to Fiji. He'd already broken into TV programming once to advise the American people of the Biapene coming to Earth. Now he'd do it again, to advise the truth about non-humans. Earth was a draw-card, not only to the Biapene, but to many species of non-humans. The Americans counted eight different species so far. And that list included the Werinn, and of course, the Biapene. Now we knew Roswell and many other sites were real. The Universe was full to bursting with life, POTUS finished on, with a slow, steady smile.

He would take no questions from the media, so any accusation of a coverup would not be his to answer. He knew parts of the Pentagon and the CIA, amongst others, had a lot to answer for. POTUS was also aware that President Eisenhower had met with Elders from Werinn at the Edwards Airforce Base in New Mexico early in 1954. But he kept that little pearl to himself.

Thankfully, the Biapene were still prepared to work with humans, despite the errors and oversights they'd made. They agreed to provide humans with all the intel they possessed, because humans were working hard, though inefficiently, to house them the way they desired.

Several Biapene would move permanently to California's Silicon Valley – to NASA-Ames, to new triangular buildings to be built near the main Research Centre. Many of the science community, from CERN, Lockheed Martin and like aerospace companies.

Physicists from Stanford and Carnegie-Mellon universities and others, would visit and stay. And the details for the missing theories would be hammered out. They would have global access to everything and everyone, as the highest priority For anything that got particularly difficult. Anything or *anyone* from anywhere in the world, could be called for and the bills paid by the UN, the World Bank or NASA. Money wasn't a problem for this project.

It was stated well by Patrick J Livingstone from the Hague who was also working with the Biapene. That humans needed to be far more cognizant of non-human needs. The words of "others" needed to be taken far more seriously and literally. The Biapene were ignored or overlooked because the shape of rooms wasn't significant to Mankind. Sometimes that's how it has to roll, he said. "Species were different from humanity - from the ground-floor to the spire. Even if a species talks in a whisper all the time, their words are as important as someone who yells.

Humans always thought their history was first-rate. The art, the sculptures, architecture, the Olympics, technology, music, Leonardo Da Vinci, Michelangelo, Albert Einstein – the list of accomplishments by humans was simply amazing. But somehow, they were all overshadowed by Mankind's general nature. So many wars for economic and territorial gain and Nationalism left humanity labelled as a murderous. Vicious, cruel, violent, aggressive, brutal, or ruthless. These were all descriptions by third parties from other worlds who had perused the human internet. We were not to be touched or even alerted to a presence. Humans were profoundly dangerous.

So said the Werinn and the Biapene, anyway. The only two interstellar species Earth knew of.

The Biapene weren't stupid though. They didn't come to Earth and *demand* pyramidal housing. They were refugees after all. But they did expect humanity to listen to their essential needs, because they had much to offer, based on the content of the human internet. Quid Pro Quo was how the Biapene expected it to work.

*   *   *

Abby and Harry had gotten leave from NASA and flew to Reykjavik for an Iceland holiday – finally, they got time in the icy paradise. When the wheels of the Boeing 777 hit the cold tarmac of the runway, Abby felt like she'd touched heaven. She put her head back and breathed deeply, finishing with a gusty sigh and a small high-pitched yelp. Beside her was her boyfriend, and beyond the aircraft's window was a glorious panorama. Her youthful dreams were materializing before her eyes.

They had kayaked on the Jokulsarlon Glacier Lagoon and were now standing in one of Vatnajokull's giant ice-caves. The glacier surrounding them was the largest in Europe. The ice-cave was nothing

262

short of stunning. On the ground were rocks and running water, but above their heads, the ice glowed in shades of blue Abby never knew existed, and in places was light-blue and crystal clear. Abby felt like she'd entered a magic show as she gazed at this absolutely dazzling example of nature. Everywhere she looked, the ceiling glowed phosphorescent blue.

She could feel tears dropping from her eyes and then freezing and falling to the ground and disappearing in the flowing water. Abby found it hard to believe she was finally here – in Iceland, standing in a crystal ice-cave with her boyfriend Harry, who looked at her hungrily. This was truly paradise. She was cold but the warmth of his stare pushed her on.

Harry was fidgeting in his pocket and pulled out a small black case. Despite wearing crampons on his shoes and holding an ice-pick, Harry got down on one knee and tapped Abby on the back. She turned to him and surprised, she said, '*fuck,*' which reverberated in the cave. 'What the hell Harry?'

He struggled closer to her, and with glowing cheeks, he said, 'I love you Abby, and what better place?' Harry looked around, then back at her. 'This place is amazing, stunning, wonderful...just like you.' Harry gave Abby a yearning look, and without blinking, said, 'will you marry me – it's cold down here so a quick answer would be nice.'

'*Yes, yes...of course Harry,* she said with enthusiasm. They hugged and kissed under a glorious blue ceiling, lit by a magnificent Sun.

Harry opened the case and exposed a shiny ring. 'What better use for a gem from Biapene.' Abby narrowed her eyes and extended her finger happily, and the ring slid perfectly into place.

Three stones were cut from the raw octahedron that Harry received from Pat. He gave it to Harry and said, 'you know what to do with it.' Two were ten carat monsters and one was 3.5 carats, perfect for a super-impressive wedding ring. Abby's ring was set in pure gold and the stone was a brilliant-cut red diamond from another planet, created in a distant solar system, home to Ross128b.

The ring and the other two stones were worth almost a billion dollars and befitted a couple who'd broken the Fermi paradox and put their lives on the line to the benefit of their home planet.

Harry and Abby walked hand in hand, deeper into the cave. Their explorations in Iceland had only just begun. There was much more to follow.

NASA and Earth generally were very happy with the outcome. They would receive Biapene's intelligence – and get the answer to the "glorious-four", characterising and confirming dark matter and dark energy, FTL propulsion and details of the Grand Unifying Theory. Currently Earth had a theory of macro gravity – which was essentially Einstein's theory of relativity, and quantum mechanics.

Neither of those spoke to each other and no-one one on Earth could work it out. It was Einstein's great regret. The Biapene would bequeath Earth this GUT, which humans had sought for centuries. Combine that with the solution to climate change and teleportation, and you had an absolute standout winner. All Earth had to do to get these keys to the Universe was to keep the Biapene happy on Earth. Lodging them in polygonal rooms, and understanding why it was essential, was a critical first step.

So, Mankind now had the key and was slowly turning it, which would ultimately unlock and reveal an Aladdin's Cave. It would contain astrophysical bounty that had cost humans billions of dollars and decades of time to search.

In one fell swoop humanity procured it all from the Biapene. Now, there was nowhere that was out-of-bounds. The Universe had indeed become Mankind's oyster.

THE END

ABOUT THE AUTHOR:

Scott Bywater lives in Adelaide near the southern coast of Australia with his wife Mary and two kids, Josh and Alysha. Scott has an Honours Degree in Geomorphology from Flinders University, and an obsession with anything astrophysical. While at University, he published three mineralogical papers in the Mineralogical Record out of Tucson, Arizona. To help facilitate writing on the subject he taught himself the finer details of quantum field theory, General Relativity, and in particular, String Theory and anthropic cosmology. Scott believes that anyone who has looked up at the night sky and wondered why, or contemplated some of the deeper reasons for their existence, will derive much pleasure from this book.